FIVE MONTHS
ON THE NEW YORK TIMES
BEST SELLER LIST!

The Most Publicized . . .

♥

The Most Controversial . . .

♥

The Most Headlined Novel of the Year!

the EXHIBITIONIST

the EXHIBITIONIST

a novel by

henry sutton

A FAWCETT CREST BOOK
Fawcett Publications, Inc., Greenwich, Conn.
Member of American Book Publishers Council, Inc.

THIS BOOK CONTAINS THE COMPLETE TEXT OF THE ORIGINAL HARDCOVER EDITION

All of the characters in this book are fictitious, and any resemblance to actual persons, living or dead, is purely coincidental.

A Fawcett Crest Book reprinted by arrangement with Bernard Geis Associates.

Library of Congress Catalog Card Number: 67-13097

Printing History
Bernard Geis Associates edition published October 30, 1967
First printing, September 1967
Second printing, October 1967
Third printing, November 1967

First Fawcett Crest printing, October 1968

Published by Fawcett World Library
67 West 44th Street, New York, N.Y. 10036
Printed in the United States of America

to **WILLIAM COFFIN** and **ROBERT JOY,**

mes semblables, mes frères

ABOUT THE AUTHOR

Henry Sutton, whose real name is David Slavitt, was born in White Plains, New York, in 1935. He was graduated from Phillips Academy in Andover, Massachusetts, and from Yale University and then went on to receive his master's degree from Columbia University. Mr. Slavitt is the author of a forthcoming play, The Cardinal Sin, which will be produced on Broadway, and he has just completed a new novel entitled The Voyeur.

PROLOGUE

It wasn't any lack of human feeling. There were peo-ple in the town who said it was that, but it wasn't. In fact it was a kind of declaration that, yes, by God, he was human. Human beings are not animals and ought not to behave like animals, and because Sam Houseman believed this he controlled himself. The screams from the back room wrenched his heart, but he would not close the store. He would not indulge himself. The store remained open, and he stood behind the counter and sold bags of feed and harness straps and horse liniment, just as he did any other day. Or, no, he was busier, for people from the town came in to buy, just to see him standing there, working, waiting on customers, while his wife screamed out in the back.

The veterinarian's horse and buggy were out in front. The veterinarian was delivering the baby. There was a doctor in town, but he was a drunk, and Sam had refused to let him come near Ellen. Better a sober vet than a drunken doctor. But people came to see Sam, and they saw the vet's buggy, and they got that wrong, too. They thought he was just being cheap, hoarding the money that he called his capital. But he didn't give a damn what they thought. His whole lifetime in that town had been one long lesson in the art of ignoring what people thought. Or, to put it another way, and more positively, the confidence to believe in himself and what he thought. And to impose himself upon the town. It had taken years and cost him countless bloody noses and blackened eyes, but he had given as many as he got, and he had triumphed at last. From the day he'd beaten Jake Kern in the woods in back of the schoolhouse, nobody had ever called him a bastard again. Not to his face, at least. And what they called him behind his back was not his business, but theirs. He had learned to draw that kind of fine line.

Ellen screamed again. Sam did not even pause in the measuring out of a ten-foot length of chain for Frank Spenlow, but only clenched his teeth more tightly. There was nothing he could do anyway. Doc Gaines, the vet, was back there. And Sam's mother. And Ellen was a healthy woman. So he measured out the chain, and got the chain cutters, and cut off the ten-foot length. Spenlow paid him. He made change. Spenlow left. And even then with the store momentarily empty, he did not relax or give in to the impulse to go back and see if everything was all right. He did not give in to impulses. He didn't believe in them. Control, control.

In the back room Ellen lay on the bed, waiting for the next contraction. Doc Gaines sat sprawled in a chair in a corner of the room, the stub of an unlit cigar in his mouth, swinging his pocket watch by its chain. Beside the bed on a little stool Mother Houseman sat and held Ellen's hand. Every few minutes, as a new contraction seized her, Ellen would clench Mother Houseman's hand so tightly that it hurt, and they actually shared the pain of labor. As the pain subsided, Mother Houseman said, "Good." She believed in pain.

Mother Houseman. It was not Mrs. She had never been a Mrs. As bare and comfortless as the room was, she suspected it for its luxury. The presence of a doctor—even of veterinary medicine—and of another woman to give comfort and to hold onto was not anything she had enjoyed when she had given birth thirty years before. And a husband in the next room. Poor Sam had come into the world as casually as any of the lambs on the ranch. And he had been called Samuel after Samuel Tilden, whom the newspapers had said was the new president. And then even poor Mr. Tilden, sucked in, somehow, by the run of bad luck they had been having, was robbed of the Presidency; but Mother Houseman had refused to change the name. She had nothing against Mr. Hayes, but what kind of name was Rutherford?

So it was Samuel for Mr. Tilden, and Houseman, their own name, hers and her father's. Sam's father's name, his last name, she never even knew. He was an advance man for a traveling show, a carnival-cum-medicine show, and he appeared one day in town with posters and tickets and cigars for the men and paper fans for the ladies. And it was just by coincidence that her father, Amos, had brought her down with him that time. He went to town only seldom, and most of the time he left her up in the hills on the ranch. But this time he'd suggested himself that maybe she'd like to come with him. Afterward, after it was all over, they never talked about it, but she'd always supposed that her father had decided it was about time to think of marrying her off and that the way to do that was to let her be seen a little. So they'd ridden down to town, and that was how she met the good-looking fellow with the paper fans. He'd given her one and had been about to turn away, but then he changed his mind and inquired as to whether he might be privileged to buy her a lemonade. Amos was busy talking wool prices and said, "Surely," and went back to his discussion. After all, where could they go to? What could happen? It was just a little town, a couple of streets, and a few yards of wooden walks and hitching posts. Amos had looked at the fellow, who said his name was Jason something-or-other, and he'd seemed all right. So Amos had said, "Surely," and gone back to the talk about wool. And half an hour later he'd started to worry, and half an hour after that he'd gone out to look for them.

Martha had known there was something funny about the lemonade and had tried to drink as slowly as she could, but it was so nice to listen to him talk, so pleasant to watch the way he looked at her, the way he flicked his eyes all over her, that she had allowed herself to finish the first glass and to accept a second. No, not merely allowed herself to do so, but wanted to do so, wanted after a while to run off with him, even got impatient waiting for him to get up and take her away. But he just sat there across from her in the booth in the hotel saloon, waiting for just the right moment, for her impatience to build to its highest pitch, and then, finally, and very quietly, he suggested that maybe she'd like to go for a ride. And she said yes.

He had a little buggy, and he drove her out of town, and the heat was like another glass of lemonade and worked on her the way whatever it was in the lemonade had worked. She was flushed and giddy, and even the motion of the buggy was odd, soothing and exciting at the same time. And then he drove off the road and into a clearing and made love to her.

She knew what it was all about. After all, she was seventeen and had grown up with the sheep and knew that it was all perfectly natural. But what she didn't know was how very nice it was, and how quiet and dreamy it was afterward when the sun beat down on them and the cicadas rasped and a bird called out from somewhere up in a nearby tree. They lay there awhile, resting and listening to the bird and feeling the warmth of the sun, and then he got up and asked her if she wanted to stay with him. And of course she did. It was either that or walking back to town. She knew that he couldn't drive her back. Her father would kill him. He'd probably beat her some, too. So she climbed into the buggy and went with him.

It was four days before Amos caught up with them. They got all the way to Spoon Gap, and through Spoon Gap, and they rounded a bend, and there her father was, standing in the middle of the road with a shotgun pointed at them.

"All right," he said. "That's enough lemonade."

"You're not going to shoot that gun," Jason said. "She's up here right beside me."

"Get down, Martha," Amos said. It was quiet, even conversational, as if he were neither demanding nor imploring, but merely suggesting, only because she might somehow be more comfortable down on the ground, beside the buggy.

"All right, now," Amos said. "What have you got to say for yourself?"

"Not a thing," Jason said. It was not what Amos had expected, not the pleading or the whining, or the promise of marriage. Now that Martha was down from the buggy seat, he had gone brave, in the wrong way and at the wrong time.

"Nothing?"

"Nothing."

"All right, then," Amos said. "Get down."

"No."

Amos raised the shotgun, aimed it at Jason,

seemed to be about to shoot, and then stopped. "Come on," he said. "There's no sense in scaring hell out of the horse."

Jason got down from the buggy.

"Turn around."

"What for?"

"Because I say so."

"No, wait. Look, I'll marry her."

"You might, but you'd run out on her."

"No. I'll stay. I'll marry her and I'll stay."

"I don't think she'd have you."

"Sure she would. Wouldn't you, honey?"

She heard him, and she was thinking about it, trying to make up her mind, trying to think clearly out there in the glare of the sunlight, and not just look at the dull sheen of the gun metal or the shapes of clouds off on the horizon. She was thinking about it when he tried to prod her and said, "Come on, Margaret, let's get married."

"My name isn't Margaret," she said, "it's Martha."

"Turn around," Amos said.

He turned around. Amos picked up a rock about the size of a man's head and went up behind Jason. Then, suddenly, with all his strength he cocked his arm and smashed Jason's head with it. He fell, and maybe was just knocked out, or maybe already dead. But Amos picked him up and put him in the buggy, and Martha got into the wagon, and he drove back to Spoon Gap, not the town but the gap itself, and where the ravine is steepest, he stopped, picked Jason up, and threw him over and down. Then, without saying a word, he got back up into the buggy and drove home.

Some weeks later she told her father that she thought she was pregnant.

" 'Tisn't surprising," he said, absolutely flat.

She delivered the following spring, with her father

helping her just the way he helped his ewes in lambing, gentle and efficient. "What do you want to call him?" he asked. She decided on Samuel, for Mr. Tilden.

"Samuel what?"

"Houseman, I guess."

"I guess," he said, and he went outside, whether in grief or joy or merely fatigue she never knew.

Or cared to know. It did not do to inquire too closely into each other's thoughts and feelings. In the solitude of the ranch, isolated up in the foothills of the mountains and spreading out over its thousands of barren acres, the essential thing was easy enough to see: the sheer work of survival. She did the cooking and the cleaning, and he looked after the sheep and tended the garden, and it was a tight-lipped existence. For days the only human speech was the babbling of little Sam, crooning to himself in his crib, but even he was a quiet child. He talked late and never very much. And he was still silent, she thought, standing out there in the store, clamping his jaws together, and waiting.

Ellen's grip on her hand tightened again, and she cried out. Then, as the pain passed, she smiled in an apologetic way and said that she was sorry to be such a baby.

"No, you go on and holler," Mother Houseman said, and thought to herself, but did not say, And thank God that you can holler. By rights she knew that she ought to be in the other room, holding Sam's hand. What pain he bore, what grief he knew, she could only guess at. His whole life had been that way. He had learned the lesson of silence at the ranch and had learned it again in town when he had come down out of the hills to school. The little snide remarks, the open taunts, the baiting he had endured. It was only when one or another of his schoolfellows had called him a bastard to his face and in front of his classmates that he had fought. And won, too, because the life on the ranch had been arduous enough to toughen him up. Now the worst that anybody called him was "Silent Sam," which he didn't mind, or didn't let on that he minded. God only knew what he really thought.

What a stranger he was, even to his own mother. That reserve of his was like an oddly shaped box that contained something, but what it was she had no idea. She had waited, year after year, for him to reveal himself, or, more precisely, for him to reveal something of his father in himself. But there was nothing. He was as silent and as gray as the mountain boulders. Or as Amos. She had hoped that the grandfather and the grandson might unbend to each other, but their dealings with each other had all the solemnity and deliberation of the dealings of bankers. It had struck her, once, that little Sam's reserve might be a kind of emulation of his grandfather's manner and an expression, therefore, of affection or even love. But it was so perfectly maintained that she couldn't tell. And, of course, neither of them ever said anything.

When they did speak, they addressed each other formally, as "Grandfather" and "Grandson," being very careful not to blur the definition of the relationship. Or, on rare occasions, as on a birthday when Amos gave Sam a jackknife, they would relax the merest hairbreadth, so that Sam would say, "Thank you, sir," and Amos would answer, "You're welcome, boy." But never son. Never in all those years.

The pains were coming faster now, and Martha told Doc Gaines that she thought maybe something was happening.

"About time," Doc Gaines said, and he put his cigar butt down and picked himself up out of his chair.

It was another half hour before the baby got itself

born. Doc Gaines held it up, gave it a spank, and it started to cry, great lusty cries. Martha waited a moment, saw that the baby was all right and that Ellen was all right, and then went out to tell Sam. Not that he shouldn't have been able to hear the crying. But he hadn't come in.

"It's a boy," she told him.

He didn't say anything. He stood there, holding onto the counter so that his knuckles and fingernails were white, and just nodded. Martha heard the crying of the newborn baby and thought, Yes, go ahead, go ahead and yell. Scream. Cry.

Sam let go of the counter and drew a deep breath. Then he went in, silently. Oh, the silence. She wondered what would have happened if she hadn't got down from the buggy that day.

"We'll call him Amos," she heard Sam say. "For my grandfather."

"All right, Sam," Ellen said.

"Amos Meredith Houseman," Sam said, putting Ellen's maiden name as a middle name, perhaps as a way of thanking her.

"Amos Meredith Houseman," Ellen said.

And in the front room, leaning on the metal-topped counter, Martha felt tears welling up in her eyes. She wished the youngster well.

CHAPTER

ONE

♥ "It is a crime . . ." she prompted.

"It is a crime to fence with life—I tell you,/There comes one moment, once—and . . ."

He couldn't remember. It was difficult enough to memorize all those lines, to get the words to follow in their proper order, one after another, to remember the cues, and to say the rather florid speeches when he was standing still, but to move around, to remember where he was supposed to be standing, to follow the blocking that she had worked out and still to get the speeches right, that was even more difficult. And yet he had managed that. But he knew she wasn't satisfied. She wasn't satisfied with the movements, which she thought were too wooden and mechanical. And she wasn't satisfied with the speeches either. Oh, he'd got them down, and he could say them and get all the words right, but they, too, sounded wooden and mechanical. She didn't think that he had the feeling of them, the sense of them, that he understood the force and passion of the Rostand play.

And so, in the dining room of her house in Spoon Gap, with the chairs and the table all pulled over to one wall, they were dancing. He, Amos Houseman, was dancing with Mrs. Thatcher, the teacher of English and Dramatics at the Spoon Gap High School. And it wasn't just an easy two-step, but a tango, with all the elaborate flourishes and turns, and while they did the tango, she made him say the lines, feeding him the cues, and prompting him when he blanked—which he did rather frequently. Demosthenes had practiced his speeches on the beach, filling his mouth with pebbles and declaiming to the waves, but this, Amos thought, was even tougher. It was crazy, absolutely crazy, but if this was what Mrs. Thatcher wanted, then this was what he would have to do. He had agreed at the beginning to undertake all the work that would be involved, and she had warned him that it would be arduous and difficult. And he had said he would do it. But he had not imagined it would be anything like this, so strange and so personal.

"And God help those . . ." she prompted.

"And God help those/Who pass that moment by! Uh . . ."

"Not 'Uh!' Better absolute silence than 'Uh!' You are courting a beautiful woman. You love her to distraction. And for her sake, and for the sake of your love, and for your own sake, too, and that of your pride, you are elegant and stylish, and underneath that style and elegance your heart is absolutely pulverized. And you are wretched because of your ugliness and your huge nose. And so you tell her, with all the eloquence at your command, the things that you feel. But you don't say 'Uh!' "

"I'm sorry."

"Don't be sorry," she said. "But do try to think of

what the words mean and what Cyrano means by them."

For her, it was agonizing. She doubted her decision, her choice of this rather gangly, quite awkward, and yet surprisingly handsome boy for the lead in what she knew would be her last senior play. It had been a choice of desperation. She had wanted to do *Cyrano* and had decided, after her trip to Denver and the doctors, that this would be the year. It was this year or never. And in Amos Houseman, she had thought she had found a passable Cyrano. A possible Cyrano. He had a kind of grace, when no one was watching him, an ease, a rangy swing when he walked, and a kind of independence and confidence when he stood still. But to draw those qualities she had seen in him, or had thought she had seen, out of him and onto the stage, to get him to project what he had inside him, that was proving to be more difficult than she had expected. And that was her job—to teach her students, or if it came to that, this one boy, to take the disciplines of art seriously. For the art itself. And this was her last chance to do it. The doctors had diagnosed that numbness in her fingertips and the dead tiredness she sometimes felt in her calves as Parkinson's disease, and they had described to her its sure and inexorable progress.

So it was truer than young Amos knew, and truer, even, than Rostand had known. "There comes one moment, once—and God help those/Who pass that moment by . . ."

That was what she had thought when she had picked Amos to play the lead in her last production. She had told herself that this time, this last time, she would take herself and her job seriously, take the boy seriously, and try, with every resource at her command, to teach him and to inspire him, and to infect him with the theater. He had never been in any of her plays, but that was because of his father's suspicion of the stage, and in fact, his dislike for it. But she had gone to Sam Houseman, and had begged him, as a dying woman, a widow, childless, to let her have the boy for this one production. She had asked it for the sake of the school, for her own sake, for the sake of Christian charity. He had not beeen able to refuse.

But now the problem was more difficult, for it was the problem of Amos Houseman's stiffness. It was not just the part, or the stagecraft that she had to teach him, but the art of wearing his own body. He looked, now, as if he had rented his torso from Jack's Formal Rentals and was afraid of it and uncomfortable in it. And to remedy this lack of ease, she had brought him home with her to tango.

"You're still reading the line as if you were reading a line. Think of it as something you'd tell a girl you loved. You have been in love, haven't you?"

"No, Mrs. Thatcher."

"Well, not a great love, but a small infatuation. I mean, you have kissed girls, haven't you?"

"Oh, yes," he said. He was embarrassed, but that was something. It was something to work with, or to work against.

"And more than kissed, too, haven't you?"

"No, Mrs. Thatcher."

It was a risk, a great risk. And she tried to calculate the odds. She knew they were long enough. She reckoned not only on the boy's shyness and the restraint—and even constraint—of his upbringing, but on her own age. She was thirty-nine, and, while she had once been attractive, there were now lines on her face of worry and of weather. Still, she was tall, slender, had a figure that was at the very least adequate. And there was a fineness of line, especially around the neck and chin, which she had retained. And he was young, which was in her favor, young and full of health and vigor, which no amount of parental strictness and repression could kill. She would bank on that, not because it was prudent or safe, but because it was necessary for her purpose and because she would prefer to try and to fail than to go down to defeat and mediocrity without having ventured everything for the career and the life she had chosen.

She changed the record, putting on something slower than the tangos she had been playing, and she invited Amos to continue dancing with her. They danced a few steps, and, in order to get his mind on something besides the dancing, she had him start the speech again.

It is a crime to fence with life—I tell you,
There comes one moment, once—and God help those
Who pass that moment by!—when Beauty stands
Looking into the soul with grave, sweet eyes
That sicken at pretty words!

"But think of the bitterness in it, the passionate bitterness with which he expresses contempt for the 'pretty words' he has been using in the hope of blinding her to his un-pretty face. It's a cry of torment! Open up!"

"Gee, Mrs. Thatcher, I try to, but it's . . . Well, it's embarrassing."

"All right, let it be embarrassing, but not paralyzing. To be self-aware is what you want, but not self-conscious. Kiss me!"

"What?"

"Kiss me." The abruptness, the peremptoriness of the command were in her favor. She had to take him by surprise. At least at the beginning.

He hesitated, looked away, looked back at her, and then with the most touching kind of awkwardness, slowly, hesitatingly, carefully, as if he were afraid of breaking something, he kissed her. And then again more surely, and then a third time with some beginning of authenticity and even pleasure.

"Now read the line!" she told him. " 'It is a crime . . .' "

He began again. His voice was thick with emotion now, and if it was not the reading that she would settle for in the end, it was, at least, a reading, a real reading with some meaning and actuality behind it. It was still crude, but it was a start.

She told him that he was improving and that it was beginning to sound as though he were saying the words to a girl rather than to an audience, and, even as he was thinking of her praise and recalling the reading of the line and the feeling that had gone into it, she moved his hand around her body, from where he had been holding her, and brought it to her breast.

Then she sent him home, praising him for his progress and saying that they had done enough for that evening.

It would not be until the next evening that she could find out how her desperate venture had turned out. And when Amos appeared at the appointed hour and read the lines again, he read them better than ever before. And she suggested that they try the exercise of reading the lines while dancing, and only then found out that it was all right, that it was fine, that it was all she had hoped for. He held her close and danced with confident sexuality. He did not kiss her, but he was not oblivious to what had happened the night before, nor trying to ignore it. She kissed him rather lightly, almost flirtingly, but it was as if she had depressed the plunger of a detonator. His eagerness was explosive. He clutched at her, kissed her, held her, virtually devoured her. They fell upon the couch, and with a furious haste they made love. He was clumsy of course, but the kind of raw, innocent passion he had in him was beyond technique or art. He entered her and plunged and reared and bucked like a wild animal. And then he lay exhausted upon her, his head on her breast, while she stroked his hair. She let him rest for a while, and then, as if it were only a way to pass the time, started to cue him, and had him say some of his lines. This time there was that *profondeur* that she had missed, the trace of sadness, the acknowledgment of human fragility that no virginal boy could have been expected to project or even to imagine.

It had been a crazy idea, she knew, but it was working. It did what she wanted it to do, and it got out of him what she had hoped to be able to draw out. Again and again they made love, and then, often on the still rumpled bed, naked, she had him declaim the speeches. The bed, she told him, was very like a stage, about the same height as a stage, and after all, they were both places for passion.

When the time came for the three performances of *Cyrano,* her efforts proved themselves. He was splendid, and through him the rest of the cast seemed better, too. The whole production had the weight and suppleness of flesh to support the flights of fancy and poetry. It was her triumph and his. It was also her swan song.

A week after the last performance she invited him to go out riding with her, and he accepted, thinking that they would make love again. They rode out, on horseback, into the spring woods. The air was clear and warm. It was the kind of beautiful day which happens only in the foothills of mountains, their grandeur and stern majesty not forgotten but put aside for the moment, as if they were in a mood of rare indulgence. They dismounted and lay down in the tall grass, but it was not to make love that she had brought him out into the foothills. It was to say good-bye.

"We shall never see each other again," she told him.

"Never?"

"No," she said. "I shall be going away. And you shall be too."

"Just to college."

"Even so . . ." she began. She stopped, and then, after having thought and considered for a moment, asked him, "Do you want to go?"

"To college? Sure. I guess so."

"You could . . ." she began, but she stopped.

"I could what?"

"No, I've meddled enough in your life."

"I could what?" he insisted.

She plucked a blade of new grass and carefully wound it around her finger as she told him that he had been good, not just in a high school way, but really good. And she asked him if he didn't want to try his luck in the theater. If it didn't go well, he could always go back and go to college. To the mining school that his father had chosen for him. Whether the suggestion was the result of her love for him or for the effort and attention she had invested in him, he never knew. And it didn't even make much difference, because he had his own reasons. There was gratitude to her, and love. And there was his own respect for what they had built together. And there was his father, Sam, from whose dreadful shadow he so much wanted to emerge.

"Where would I go?"

She told him about the Pasadena Playhouse, where an old friend of hers was on the board.

He thought about it for a moment and then smiled and admitted, "I guess I might give it a try."

She kissed him and ran from him, and he chased her and caught her. But after he undressed her and was taking off his own dungarees she ran from him again, and he chased her once more. They were like two wonderful wood creatures, a nymph and a faun, playing at hide-and-seek, and she nearly let him catch her and then fled again, jumping into the still icy water of the lake. He jumped in afterward and caught her and tried to make love with her in the lake. But it was too cold. The water was achingly cold, and he couldn't. He held her, and her small breasts were like flowers of great delicacy. And she clung to him as a vine to a tree, with strong tendrils.

They went home that day without having made love.

And he remembered that day even longer than he remembered the other times when they had made love. Because of his failure? Or because of the delicacy of Mrs. Thatcher—Lila—who would not press him too far or too hard to do what she wanted him to do, or to go on with the beginning they had made.

He wrote to the Pasadena Playhouse, and she wrote to her friend, and he was accepted as an apprentice. Sam was livid with rage. All of the years of punctilious correctness of his life were being thrown away just like that, by his only son, and he was furious. That burden of bastardy that Sam had carried, balancing it like a weight on his head, felt heavier than ever, for his son's departure for the theater seemed to him a reversion to the shady, shabby world from which that stranger had appeared to beget him and die. All the years of strictness and careful rectitude, all the beatings and scoldings impersonally administered to Amos in the old privy, all the lectures were for nothing. Amos left, and Sam did not speak to him. He didn't even say "Go to hell!" let alone "Good-bye."

Amos got to Pasadena. He changed his name. Amos was too biblical and stuffy. He just dropped it and used his middle name, Meredith Houseman. Five weeks after he got there, he got the news that his father had died, had popped a blood vessel in his head and died. Just like that.

Meredith considered this, and realized how he would never have had the nerve to come out to California if his father had died during that three-day rage. If Sam had died then . . . Well, it didn't bear thinking about. But it had been a near thing.

He walked aimlessly, throwing himself into the activity of walking, feeling the fatigue come and then abate as he swung into the true rhythm of his lanky stride. Not only the fatigue, but all awareness, all conscious thought submerged itself in the pacing. Even the awareness of time. When he did think to check his watch, he discovered that he had been wandering around for an hour and a half. He grabbed a cab, went back to the hospital, and burst in. The elevator man told him that he'd had a baby girl. Dr. Cooper had already left. Elaine said, "You son of a bitch, where were you?" and turned away from him. He sat with her for a while, but he realized that she was sleeping again. He went out and asked the floor nurse if he could see his daughter. She directed him down the hall to the nursery, where another nurse, in a mask, held up a tiny, wrinkled little creature with black hair. His daughter. Tears came to his eyes. He wiped them away. He nodded his thanks to the nurse and went back to Elaine's room. The floor nurse told him that Elaine would sleep for several hours and suggested that he might as well go and get some sleep himself.

"I suppose I might as well," he said. He would explain to Elaine tomorrow. He only wished he could explain to that red, wrinkled little girl.

"Shall I call them or not?" Tish Curtiss asked her husband.

"No," Clint said.

"Why not?"

"It sounds perfectly dreadful. Even thinking about it makes me sick. Look, I hardly know the guy."

"After all the time you spend with him at rehearsals?"

"Yes."

"Well, I don't believe you," she said. "But even if I did, it wouldn't make much difference. He doesn't know anybody in town, and he's probably lonely, and it's just a decent thing to do at a time like this."

"Poor, lonely Meredith Houseman. What are you, crazy?"

"No. I don't think so. As a matter of fact, I think you are. Here the guy's wife has had a baby, and the most natural thing in the world is for people who know him to have a little party for him."

"Good. Let people who know him have as many parties as they want. You don't know him. And neither do I."

"But you're his director!"

"Don't say it like that. It makes it sound as if he owned me."

"All right, he's your star."

What Clint Curtiss was concerned about was not the party, of course, but the play. Or, more precisely, the production. The play was a straightforward little comedy, a perfectly conventional but rather attractive bit of fluff. But the production, one of Arthur Bronston's brainstorms, was bizarre. Bronston had taken Curtiss, one of the young directors of the Provincetown Players, and combined him with Meredith Houseman, the latest concoction of the Hollywood studios, and put them together with all of the rapt curiosity of a small boy playing with a chemistry set.

"With your talent and his looks," he'd said, "we'll do very well."

"But what about his talent?" Clint had asked.

Bronston had bit off the end of a cigar, spat it into the wastebasket.

"I think he's got some. Maybe a lot. Anyway, I like the way he walks."

"In his last movie he was on a horse most of the time."

"Very funny," Bronston had said, and then he leaned forward across his huge desk and pointing with his cigar as if it were a pistol, asked Clint whether he wanted the assignment. "This is Broadway. You want it or don't you? All this shit about all the new talent around, not getting a chance . . . Well, I'm giving you your chance. And as far as Houseman is concerned, don't be such a snot. I want him because my wife likes him. Saw his pictures three times. All three of them. She says there isn't a woman in America wouldn't like to get it from him. You understand me? That's not just Hollywood publicity. That's cock. And that's theater. A deal?"

"A deal," he had said. And now four months later they were working together, he and Houseman. And each suspected that the other considered him some kind of freak. Oh, they'd been friendly enough, but friendly in the way diplomats are, without any real intimacy or real warmth. Which was all right. They were, after all, only working together on a play. And they were working pretty well, which was why Clint was reluctant to upset things or to risk what they had going already for the possibility of more.

"Well?" Tish asked.

"Look, I don't even know whether Elaine's had the baby yet. Maybe it'll be stillborn. Or a monster with one eye on a stalk in the middle of its forehead. Or Siamese twins—"

The phone rang. It was Meredith.

"It's a girl!" Clint repeated to Tish. "Six pounds two ounces. Everybody's fine."

"Great," she said, and then whispered, "*invite him!*"

"Tonight?" he asked, covering the mouthpiece of the phone.

"Tomorrow night," she said.

"Look, Meredith, why don't you come on over here tomorrow night. We're having a few people over and—"

Houseman didn't even wait for him to finish the sentence. Clint nodded to Tish that, yes, Houseman would come. "Oh, about seven-thirty," he said into the phone. "Hey, congratulations from both of us. What are you calling her? . . . Great! . . . Yes," he said. "No, forget it for tomorrow. We wouldn't get anything done, anyway. Get some sleep."

"What was that all about?" Tish asked.

"He's calling her Merry. Meredith, actually, but Merry. In spite of what happened today in Europe."

"Good for him."

"Now tell me what the real reason is."

"I did."

"The real, *real* reason."

Laetitia got up, crossed the living room, and poured herself another dollop of brandy. She held it up to her nose, swirling the amber liquid around in the snifter for a moment, and then said, "You remember what Bronston told you about him?"

"What?"

"About every woman in America . . . having the hots for him?"

"Yes?"

"Well, it makes for a great party doesn't it?"

"Now? My God, Elaine's just . . ."

"Exactly. And there won't be a woman there who doesn't know that. I mean we're celebrating it, aren't we?"

"Yes, but what does that mean?"

"Don't be dense."

"For Christ sake! What?"

"It means, love, that he's presumably horny as hell. And it should be a marvelous party. Absolutely marvelous."

Jocelyn Strong circled one of the prints on the contact sheet, leaned back in Ralph's black-leather-and-chromium chair, and held his sterling-handled magnifying glass up to her eye. The magnifying glass had been her present to him, for his birthday. She had thought of having it gold-plated, to make it vermeil, but had decided against it. The present had been enough the way it was, and more than enough. Jocelyn prided herself on the fine calculation she was capable of applying to matters of this sort. Her liaison with Ralph was no squashy schoolgirl crush. The vermeil would have been more than he was worth, and more than their hasty trysts were worth. It was practically a business relationship anyway.

It was odd, though, the way the glass reversed everything. The whole room was upside down. She moved it away from her eye to see the whole room blur and then focus again. Which was what had happened to her. Everything was in focus, but inverted. The job, her career, Ralph—it was all crystal clear, but different.

Now that she had decided to break it off with him, she had decided that she almost liked him. Genial, a little inept, but goodhearted, and fairly straight about himself and the world, he was not such a bad fellow. But it did not do to be sentimental about him. Here she was, in his chair, at his desk, doing his job while he had a nap in the infirmary. She put a piece of copy paper into his typewriter, set up the head for the caption, and figured out the number of characters that it would require. She doodled for a moment, fiddling with words and word order, and then came up with a solution that satisfied her. It was not unlike the stupid pleasure of doing a crossword puzzle. One was pleased to have it come out and to have it fit.

What she had planned for, the simple, even simple-minded promotion through Ralph's good offices, was irrelevant now. The attack on Poland had changed all that. It was easy enough to see now that there was going to be a war. Certainly there would be an economic boom. Probably both. But either way for a girl in the news-magazine game it meant all kinds of opportunities that could never come along in peacetime. All those men going off to fight or going off to cover the fighting would leave all those beautifully vacant desks behind them. Still, Ralph had been relevant, as a way of getting to one of those desks. But the offer from *Pulse,* which had come through two days ago, had made the whole affair irrelevant. A total loss. She could have done just as well without it. Not that she regretted it. Ralph had not been at all bad. And it would have been insane to bank on a war, to rely on Hitler more than on herself. Still, she would be leaving, and it was important to her to establish that she had been using Ralph and that he had not been using her. To establish it to him as well as to herself, so that there could be no confusion, and no embarrassment.

It was a problem. Or it had been until Tish had called. Now it was all so easy. What better way could there be to end it with Ralph than by beginning with someone else? And who better to begin with than Meredith Houseman? That would be a clear enough declaration of independence. He would be at the party, Tish had said. And that was all she needed to know. The fact that he was the glamorous new thing on Broadway, or would be in a month, hardly detracted from her enthusiastic anticipation. Ralph could go back to his wife in White Plains and think about her and Houseman.

She leaned forward in her chair, looked again at the print she had circled, and called for a copy boy. She attached the caption to the contact sheet and put them both in the Out box. Then she took a sheet of memo paper and wrote a note to Ralph: "Can't make it tonight. I have to visit my cousin in Queens. J." She put the note in an envelope, wrote his name on it, sealed it, and stuck it in his typewriter, with the cables from the overseas bureaus and the mimeographed stories that were already starting to accumulate for the early form.

She picked up the phone and made an appointment with her hairdresser. She felt quite pleased with herself and with the note. The idea of her having a cousin in Queens! It was absurd enough to be delicious.

There were flowers all over the room. The studio had

sent an enormous arrangement, as had Arthur Bronston, the producer of *Honey, Do,* and, of course, Meredith had brought a great display of glads. In her new silk bed jacket Elaine lay in bed, looking at all the flowers and trying to guess how much they all must have cost. She was pleased with them, but uncomfortable, too. She didn't know any of the people who had sent them. Oh, she had met them and said how-do-you-do and had smiled as prettily as she could in acknowledgment when they had complimented Meredith's talent and success. But they weren't her friends. They hardly had any. They moved around so. It was nothing at all like what she had imagined, back in Tallulah, Louisiana, when she had married Meredith.

Oh, it had seemed fine. It had seemed like every girl's dream come true. She had pinched herself to make sure she was awake and not just dreaming. And now two years later she was still pinching herself, trying to wake not from a nightmare, but from the dreamlike unreality, the frustrating insubstantiality of their life together.

Elaine had come from Tallulah to Hollywood in the conventional way, having won a contest for a screen test. She had been a cheerleader and baton twirler at Tallulah High School and had gone down to Tulane, where she had begun her freshman year. And then the contest man had given her the silver cup, and her picture had been in the *Picayune*, and she had gone to Hollywood with about forty-five earfuls of good advice, very little of which was necessary. Elaine had known her assets and her liabilities. Her looks were on the plus side—now. She was temporarily beautiful, with very fair skin and a slender body that emphasized the size of her breasts. Her hair was so light as to appear bleached, but it wasn't. She was shrewd enough to recognize that she was a fading type and therefore shrewder than most of the hopeful girls and boys who turn westward (ho!) for Hollywood and success.

Like a clever lawyer, she saw her best chance in a good settlement, and it had been upon Meredith that she settled. His looks, his talent, his charm seemed to her to have the best chance of any at the Pasadena Playhouse, where she had gone to do her scouting, because that was where the serious ones were.

And then, as if in a story, all the sensible reasons paled in the glare of what was, really, wonderfully, love. And all they had to do was go back to Tallulah and get married in the First Baptist Church with her mama and her stepfather and live happily ever after.

Well, they had not been unhappy. She had not thought they were unhappy. But there had been no test of their marriage, no strain yet, nor pressure. And now with the baby born she felt terribly blue and empty—not only of the baby but of everything. Here she was, in a strange room, with flowers from strangers, and Meredith busy with the play and having all the fun. The damned flowers weren't for her at all, or the baby, but for him. All except his, anyway.

She tried to remember the article she had read in *Reader's Digest* about postpartum depression. The point was to look at the bright side of things. She had a nice flat belly again and she could drink without getting sick or worrying about the baby being born with a craving for alcohol.

It was partly for this reason—that they brought with them the opportunity for a drink and some fun—that she brightened considerably when Jaggers came into the room, with Clint Curtiss just behind him.

Sam Jaggers, Meredith's agent in New York, presented a sterling silver toothbrush from Jensen's. "Everybody has a silver spoon these days, but a silver toothbrush is useful," Jaggers said, presenting the absurd object to Elaine.

"Do you use silver polish with it or toothpaste?" Meredith asked.

He had been sitting by the window, with the script of

the play, going over the new line changes. It was like having a life-size statue of him in the room. But now, when the others dropped in he put the script down and said witty things.

"Well, all I've got to say," said Clint, "is that it serves you right. All matinee idols ought to have daughters. To put the fear of God in 'em. Right?"

"Right," Jaggers said.

They bantered back and forth. Elaine had no complaint to make. They were very nice. Especially Clint, who sat down next to her bed and paid court to her the way Southern gentlemen did in novels. Jaggers and Meredith were by the window, joking, or discussing business, or both. But she felt as if she were a part of things again, or at least that she was around where things were happening. But then the nurse came in to say that it was time for Merry's feeding.

"Do I have to?" Elaine asked. "I mean couldn't you give her the bottle this one time? I'd hate to send all these people away."

"Oh, that's all right," Jaggers said. "We can go out into the hall for a while."

"Oh, do stay," Elaine tried again, but it was hopeless.

They were all too considerate, and Meredith was insistent. They went away.

The nurse brought Merry in, in the little bassinet with the gauze cover over it, and Elaine gave the baby the bottle the nurse had prepared.

She was pleased when Meredith came back. It was nice of him to come in and keep her company, especially nice considering that he had left his friends out in the waiting room.

But no, it wasn't just to keep her company.

"What the hell was all that about?" he asked.

"I was bored," she said. "I didn't want them to leave. I was having a good time, and—"

"The hell with the good time. The baby is more

important. They didn't mind. This is a hospital, not a hotel. They know that."

"Well, I know it, and I'm trying to forget it. It's just so lonely in here so much of the time. And it's nice to have friends around, even for a little while."

"Jesus Christ," he said. "I wish I understood you. They're not important. She is!" He pointed at the infant in her arms.

"I know. Well, here she is."

"And that's where she should be, too."

"Don't be angry," Elaine said.

"I'm not."

"Promise?"

"Yes," he said.

But then he got up and went back out to Sam Jaggers and Clint, to keep them company. She was so angry she could have spat.

It didn't make her feel any better, either, when they came back, hung around for a few minutes, and then Jaggers and Clint left. Meredith stayed behind to sit with her and read his script. But before they left Clint said, "We'll see you tonight, then?"

"Right!"

"What was that about?" Elaine asked after the two visitors had gone.

Meredith told her about the invitation.

"And you're going?"

"Yes, I'm going."

"Wonderful. Have a good time."

"Look, I have to go. It's business."

"I didn't say a thing," she said.

"It's what you're thinking."

"Well, I can't help that, can I?"

He didn't answer. He just sat there in the chair and turned the mimeographed pages.

Ice tinkled in the glasses, and the liquid sound of

laughter and the babble of good conversation swirled like two currents meeting to form bubbles and eddies. Carlotta Rohan's beautiful gray eyes seemed to take in the whole room at once, as she entered, blossoming into the Curtiss' living room like a pale white flower on a long stalk. Clint was surprised to see her, but absolutely delighted. He kissed her on the cheek and introduced her to the people she didn't know. He got her a drink, a plate of hors d'oeuvres, fussed over her, and clearly took every possible joy in her being there. It was so good that she had come. It was, he thought, so good of Tish to have thought of asking her. In just the right way, to just the right kind of evening. For perhaps the fifth time he beamed and said, "Oh, Carlotta, it's so wonderful to see you."

She smiled gracefully, appreciating the fervor of Clint's greeting, and the delicacy, too, that had reduced him to such inarticulate protestation. And she thanked him for everything that he felt but wasn't able to say.

Carlotta was the widow of Mark Rohan, who had been Clint's closest friend at the Yale Drama School. Together they had come to New York to breathe a little life into what they considered the moribund contemporary theater, and their friendship had continued and grown even stronger, which was an unusual thing in a world where the blight of competitive envy and jealousy touched all but the rarest hearts. They had rejoiced for each other in each accomplishment, each success, and had learned from each other, too. And suddenly, Carlotta had called Clint one night to say that Mark had been killed in an automobile crash, and Mark junior, too. Carlotta had left right after the funeral for the Caribbean, but the memory of her husband and her son had pursued her, even in those islands of bays and beaches that seem to have no past, no memory, nothing but the freshness of the present moment. She had suffered a mild nervous collapse and had been hospitalized for a time. And all of this, she understood, made

Clint uneasy. One is hardly comfortable with human mortality, human fragility, or any of the things which her very presence must suggest. But she was not merely a symbolic personage, and she could tell that Clint was glad to see her. And she was glad again to observe the gestures, to hear the inflections of the voices, to float along on the surface of the talk of friends. It was just like the old days.

In the lobby downstairs Meredith Houseman looked at himself in the mirror. It was in part a reflex action, the result of all those years, those awful years, of selling himself, meeting producers, impressing directors, reading for parts, doing film tests, going to parties where he might be seen by someone important. It wasn't like that anymore. He didn't have to sell himself in that old way. But in a new way, now, he still had to. He had to conform to what he'd managed to sell. Oh, he'd be on, all right. With all those little-theater people that Clint knew, he'd be on—the big bad actor with all the money and publicity from Hollywood. It'd be more or less charming, depending on how civilized they were, but that would be the tone. He shot his cuffs, adjusted the knot of his tie, and touched the call button of the elevator. He waited for the car to descend, opened the door, and was about to push the button for Clint's floor when beyond the slowly closing elevator door he heard a female voice. "Hold it, please."

He pushed the "Door Open" button, and the door slid back.

"Thank you," she said, breathless from trotting across the lobby. "You're Meredith Houseman, aren't you?"

"Yes," he said.

"I'm Jocelyn Strong. I suppose I should have waited for Clint or Tish to introduce us. But it's awkward, isn't it, having to turn to someone you just rode up in an elevator with and shift, right then, to fellow guest?"

He didn't know quite what to say, but he smiled at

her, that old reliable sincere smile, and said, "How do you do? Glad to know you."

"The pleasure is mine," she said, but the way she said it, looking at him with wide, dark eyes that seemed to burn out of her pale face, made it more than a formal rejoinder. When the elevator stopped, she turned and got out ahead of him, and he realized that he hadn't even noticed whether she was attractive. She was, somehow, so striking that attractiveness of the conventional kind didn't even enter into it. He wondered who the hell she was. Maybe, he thought, the evening wouldn't be so bad after all.

As it happened, the evening worked out splendidly. The erotic puppetry that Tish had idly imagined was in abundant evidence. One could hardly weave through the living room to the kitchen to get ice cubes without feeling the strings of the puppeteer jerking and manipulating the figures that seemed to sit or stand or walk or talk quite independently—which was exactly the point. There was a kind of satisfaction in watching it, a triumph over Clint, who merely directed his people on stages.

Meredith was only vaguely aware of what was happening. He was accustomed to the attention of women. It was part of his stock in trade. It had always been part of his life, and it did not occur to him to question it. Essentially a narcissist, he found the admiration of women agreeable and even reasonable. They shared his own opinions after all. Even the discussion, which Tish initiated, seemed to him not at all odd.

"Your adoring public will adore you all the more, now that you've proved your manhood," Tish said. "It's like those dear savages Margaret Mead writes about. They despise virgins. The way to be alluring, there, is to bring forth a bastard. It proves that one is fertile."

"But surely those were women bringing forth bastards," Jocelyn corrected.

"I know that, darling. I was going beyond her, actually."

And so they flirted about the subject of whether Meredith seemed to be more or less alluring now that he was a father. He sipped a brandy and listened, as if they were talking about some public figure, not himself. And he noticed Carlotta, a little off to one side, who was also listening or half listening, and considered her beautifully serene profile, luminous with the lamp behind her, as in portraits of saints of the *seicento*. She had that same clarity of feature, the precision of brow and cheekbone, and the paleness that allowed the delicacy of her bone structure to show through at their admirable best.

"I should think it would be a burden on your daughter," she said, possibly because she was aware of his gaze upon her. "Daughters are always in love with their fathers, and then they outgrow their fathers. I should think it would be difficult to outgrow you."

"Not so difficult," he said. "When you really know me, as presumably my daughter will, I'm not so much."

"I wonder," Jocelyn said.

For Tish it was absolutely delicious.

And for Meredith, too.

He had been, for the two years of his marriage to Elaine, a faithful husband. Work in Hollywood had kept him busy. And those few opportunities that had presented themselves had seemed to him too tawdry and stupid to pursue. Ambitious starlets and bored stars. But these women were not at all like that. Or, no, it wasn't the women themselves so much as it was his own state of mind. The silly but still annoying quarrel he had had with Elaine was more to the point. And in an odd way the baby, which was a sign of the stability of their marriage, allowed him to consider some discreet wandering, in much the same way as undoubting faith may sometimes allow a believer to consider the possibility of sin. It is only the doubter who is compelled to spend all his time in fasting and prayer. Besides, all he was doing was *thinking* about it. That was allowed, wasn't it? As the old joke went, he was married but not yet dead.

But the thinking was more complicated and therefore more dangerous than Meredith supposed. For one thing, he did not reckon on the thinking of the others. He was not surprised, but only pleased and reassured, when, out in the kitchen where he had gone to refill a bowl of potato chips for Tish, Carlotta apologized.

"Whatever for?" he asked.

"I don't often make personal remarks of that sort. It was quite presumptuous of me."

"What?" he asked blankly, staring at her lovely gray eyes, and then, with effort, remembering that she had said something about Merry's relationship to him and what the problems or dangers of that might be. "Oh, that. Don't give it a thought. It was a lot less personal than most of the remarks, wasn't it?"

He smiled as if they were sharing between them some rich private joke.

"But they all know you terribly well," she said. "Don't they?"

"No. Except for Clint and Tish, they're all new to me."

"Goodness," she said, and carried it off, too. There was a mildness about her that gave even this mild exclamation a kind of force. "How extraordinary!"

"Happens to me all the time," he said.

"What a burden for you."

It was then that she told him about her husband and her child and how they were killed in the automobile accident, presuming further on him, not because everyone did or not just because of that, but also because she felt that she could and had not been able before to speak of these things so easily. And he listened to her, attending to the telling more than to the thing told, because of her remarkable way of holding her chin high and the poignant fragility of her slender neck.

So it was Carlotta whom he was thinking about, but it was Jocelyn whom Tish meant when she congratulated him on his triumph. They were all in the living room, but he was over near the phonograph, going through the albums of Eddie Duchin records to find one that he wanted. Tish had come over to him, ostensibly to help him find what he wanted.

"Jocelyn?"

"Oh, yes," she said, *sotto voce*. "She's been seducing herself all evening for you. You must notice these things. They're terribly amusing."

"Terribly," he said, rather wryly.

It was not unreasonable for him to investigate and try to determine if what Tish had said was at all true, and Meredith found that Jocelyn was not impossibly remote. He was not sure how much to discount for her New York career girl sophistication and the slight brassiness that can be a part of that role, but at the very least she maintained the pretense of flirtatiousness—which was all he was interested in. Wasn't it? Yes.

But he did not think seriously about Jocelyn, because he was aware, from time to time, of Carlotta's cool, almost ghostly gray eyes upon him from across the room. They watched as he and Jocelyn tried to shock each other and failed. Or was it just that?

"I remember when I was a kid," he said, "somebody once told me that it was kid stuff to *talk* about sex and much more fun to do it. It made a hell of an impression on me. It was the cleverest remark I'd ever heard. But it was wrong, you know. It's fun to talk about, too."

"They needn't be mutually exclusive," she said, looking down for some reason at her hands. Without thinking about it he looked down, too, and noted that they were immaculately manicured and that her fingers were long, tapered, and ringless.

"I suppose not," he said.

"Good," she said and turned away. It was a curious moment indeed. But he had no intention of following it up.

He sat down next to Tish and joined in the conversation that she and Clint were having with some other people about Brecht, and forgot about it.

Much later in the evening, when people started to leave, he offered to get Carlotta a cab. She declined, pointing to his fresh drink and suggesting that "The Armenians are starving. You'd be wasting perfectly good brandy. I'll be all right."

He let her go, sat down again, and finished his drink, feeling very good indeed. He had had a good time and had been a good boy. A nice, delicate line. Jocelyn had left, and now Carlotta, and here he was alone and a little drunk and more than a little tired.

He said good night and left himself.

As he got out of the elevator and started across the lobby, thinking of nothing at all but getting some sleep, he heard a cough. He looked around, and from out of the alcove where the mailboxes were, Jocelyn appeared.

"Neat?" she asked.

"What do you mean?"

"Oh, come on now. You can relax. She's gone," Jocelyn said.

"Who's gone?"

"Carlotta, of course. Surely you must have noticed. She was trying to outwait us. Just to make things difficult. And after we'd arranged things so nicely."

"Arranged what?"

"Now what do you suppose?" she asked.

"Oh, did we?"

"That was my impression," she said. "But if you've forgotten, then I'll forget it, too."

He laughed, and she did, too. The laughter broke the tension for a moment.

"I'm sorry, its just that . . . well, I've never been seduced before."

"Haven't you? I don't believe you."

"Have I?" he asked. "Yes, I guess I have."

"All right, then," she said, as if there were just no point at all to any hesitation. "Let's go, shall we?"

It was the degree of bluntness that carried it off. She was so far beyond the reaches of what he thought to be ordinary behavior that he had no idea of how to answer her. Of course that was precisely the point—that no answer was possible. There was nothing for him to do but to follow her out to the street. He was about to hail a cab, but she whistled a shrill, piercing whistle and took care of that, too. She did, however, give him her address and allow him to give it to the driver.

They went through the park to the East Side. She let him pay for the cab, but then took over again, opening the door and getting out of the car herself, pushing the elevator button and opening the door of her apartment. He had hardly had a chance to look around and was at the point of suggesting that maybe they might have a drink when she kissed him, and as he adjusted to the kiss and was beginning to enjoy it, warming to it and to her, she disengaged from the embrace and went off to the bedroom.

"Fix drinks, will you?" she ordered. "Bring them on in here."

It was weird. It was as if he were on a conveyor belt in one of those old silent movies, except that instead of a buzzsaw, there was a bed at the end of the belt. He wasn't sure that he liked it, but neither was he willing to admit that he didn't like it, or that he might be frightened of it or could be defeated by it. It was like a challenge that she had thrown at him. Almost with a kind of grimness, he went to the bar to fix . . . What? What did she want? Or did it matter? He didn't think it made any difference and decided on brandy, which was what he had been drinking at the party. Brandy and soda. It took him a moment to get the ice cubes and to find a bottle opener to open the soda bottle. He poured the drinks and then took a sip of his before going off in the direction of the bedroom.

She was already naked, lying on the bed.

"Here I am, tiger," she said.

"Here you are," he said, handing her one of the glasses.

He took a slug of his brandy and then took his jacket off.

"That's right," she said. "Take it off. Take it off!"

The way she said it, she might have been at a burlesque show, watching some stripper. He went with it, though, playing the game her way, unbuttoning his shirt slowly, making a big thing out of each little button, and then taking the shirt just off the shoulder. She whistled, lower than the cab-catching whistle, but with the same thrilling vulgarity.

"It gets me right here," she said. He looked. She was stroking her pubic hair.

He stopped the strip act, now, and just got out of his clothing as fast as he could. But even to that she had a taunting quip. "That's right, you big horny bastard. Move it a little."

It could have been absolutely chilling and deadening, but it wasn't. He was very much excited by the whole bizarre mood she had established, that peculiar mood of blatant sexuality which, at the same time, mocked itself, or him, or maybe herself. It was as definite as it could be, and yet uncertain, like an expanse of polar glacier that is deep and wide and riddled by treacherous crevasses. One had to pick one's way carefully.

As he took off his shorts, she saw that he was aroused, and whistled again. Was she acknowledging his victory, his success, his manliness? Or was she still merely goading him on? It was all very fast and there was no time for reflection, but he had a momentary glimmering of the thought that, somehow, it was all very sad, that she was as vulnerable and weak as she pretended to be strong and aggressive. He took another sip of brandy, not to stall, or certainly not to stall her, but to think, to try to pursue that inkling he'd had.

She would not permit it. He had not yet put the glass back on the night table when she pulled him down onto the bed. He had all he could do not to spill the brandy. By the time he'd got the glass more or less balanced, she was on top of him, kissing him, and holding his head in her hands.

She stayed on top of him, riding him, using him, triumphing over him, exacting from him some kind of retribution for all the deficiencies she felt as a woman, obliterating by this unwomanly performance of a womanly act all the frailty and weakness she supposed herself to have, hated herself for having, and yet was saddled with. Well, she would saddle him. She would ride him, Meredith Houseman, the very ideal of maleness, the actor, the movie star, the big beef-cake boy. Her head was thrown back so that from beneath her he could see only the sharp angle of her chin, the clenched jaw jutting out over the bounce and sway of her breasts, until, suddenly, with a great shudder, she collapsed upon him to feel her triumph as he collapsed within her.

Beneath her, it was all so clear, so hugely clear, that he could with effort manage to think about the most remote and insignificant edges of it, the chance associations, the relations between it and other things, but not about the thing itself. He thought for instance of a curious passivity that was a part of his career, in which, for all the nonsense of the big billing and the designation "actor" he was the creature of a writer and a director, passively receiving and carrying out their orders. Stand on this chalk line. Move from here to there on that speech. Think this way. Talk that way. Gesture now and now and now. In an idle way, he wondered whether Lila Thatcher had realized how much she had started and how the paths they had made together in the woods outside Spoon Gap would be beaten down and widened into a trail, a rough road, a superhighway of experience.

For all of its complication, the reverie took only a fraction of a minute. Jocelyn brought him back.

"Well, okay," she said. Her voice was soft now. She was still on top of him, but as she lowered her face to kiss his brow and his eyelids and his lips, she was gentle and tender. She lay down beside him. He lit a cigarette for them to share, but she didn't want any of it. She just lay there, occasionally stroking his arm. Then she fell asleep.

He got out of bed, dressed, and looked down at her. He had no idea what to make of her, what to think about her. Or about himself. He wasn't even certain if he had liked it. Oh, well, it wasn't important. It was, as Cole Porter had put it, just one of those things. They had used each other. They would not, in all probability, ever cross each other's paths again.

He left the bedroom, turning out the lights as he did so. In the foyer, he checked his appearance, adjusted his tie, and then left the apartment. He latched the door so that it would lock when he closed it.

CHAPTER TWO

♥ The play was all right, the reviewers had said, trivial but pleasant. Meredith Houseman, however, was a hit. The play, he thought, was better than the critics had thought, but he wasn't going to argue with them. If he thought about it at all, he thought that Jaggers had been preternaturally shrewd in picking *Honey, Do* as a vehicle that would be just right to show off his client's abilities. It was like picking a horse for a star of a Western. You didn't want the horse to be too big, so that the star would look like a kid on this huge animal. But it had to be big enough so that the man on its back would have stature and could fill up the frame.

Meredith lit a cigarette and relaxed. He had taken off his makeup, showered, and was finished for the night. He felt like a businessman after a good day. There was nobody around, no reporters, no well-wishers from the theater world. It was a perfectly routine evening, and he delighted in its ordinariness.

After the excitement of the New Haven tryout and that last week before the opening, and after the big splash of the first couple of weeks of the run, it was nice to come to the theater, do a job, smoke a cigarette like this, and then go home to Elaine and Merry. He could start to spend a little more time with them now, he thought.

He stubbed out the cigarette, put on his sports jacket, and left the theater. He grabbed a cab. They were easy to find, now, after the big rush when the theaters up and down the street had emptied. That half hour made all the difference. He gave the cabbie his address, and leaned back to enjoy his feeling of slight fatigue. It was the feeling of work well done. A good, solid feeling. It had been a hectic month, tough on him and tougher on Elaine. But it had been worth it. And he promised that he would make it up to her now. He promised that as much to himself as to her. And that made him feel good too.

He paid the cabbie, got out, nodded in answer to the doorman's salute, and went inside. He took the elevator up to his floor, and, as the door was opening, wondered whose baby was crying. Who else had a baby? And why should they let it cry like that? It didn't even cross his mind as a reasonable possibility that it could be his child. After all, there were three adults in there to take care of her—the nurse and the maid, and, of course, there was Elaine. So it just couldn't be Merry, yowling like that in high, piercing squawls. But when he opened his door, the crying was louder. And when he called out, "Hello? I'm back!" and nobody answered, he thought, *My God, it* is *Merry*, and ran down the hall to the nursery.

There she was, in the crib, fists clenched, face red, and yelling with such force that each inhalation of breath racked her tiny body. "Elaine!" he called out. "Miss Swain! Margaret!" He remembered that it was Miss Swain's evening off, but where the hell was Margaret? Where was Elaine? What kind of nonsense was this, leaving a baby alone this way? He picked his daughter up to comfort her. She was filthy. He put her down on the Bathinette, took off her kimono and diaper, and carefully wiped her clean with the cotton balls in the jar and the baby oil. Then he took a diaper from the big pile below the Bathinette, folded it, put it down on the top of the Bathinette, put Merry on it, and pinned her into it. All the time, while he was doing these things, he kept talking, as much to himself as to her, for he had never changed a baby before, and was not sure of what he had learned from watching. "There there, it's all right," he kept saying. "Daddy's here and everything's fine. It's all right. Daddy's here and everything's all right. It's all right."

But Merry didn't think so. She continued to cry, even though she was now clean and dry. What else could be the matter with her? Maybe she was hungry. He went out to the kitchen to get a bottle. "I'll be right back," he told Merry, feeling a little foolish. But he knew he would feel even more foolish out in the kitchen. How the hell do you make a bottle? He hadn't the vaguest idea.

It was odd, he thought, that the kitchen light was on, but then, as he entered the room, he saw Margaret lying on the floor. Evidently she had been getting Merry's bottle when she fell, for there was a pool of milk, and fragments of the broken bottle were scattered all over the floor. Meredith knelt down to see what was the matter with her. Or, actually, to try to find out if she was alive or dead. He had no idea what could have happened to her. Had there been a burglar? Had someone attacked her? Her face was cut, and she had been bleeding, but the bleeding had stopped now and there was only the dried blood on her cheek. And around her mouth there was some kind of foam. He felt her wrist but couldn't find a pulse. But she was warm. He felt his own wrist and found where his pulse was, and then tried her wrist again. It was there, slower than his, he thought, but steady enough and strong enough. But what the hell did he know about it? The woman needed a doctor. He ran back to Merry's room to make sure that she was all right. She wasn't. She was crying, still. But he couldn't stop to give her a bottle. That would take half an hour, at least. But she was in her crib and seemed safe enough for the moment. He ran back through the hall to the foyer, stopped to unlatch the door, and then went out into the hall, where he rang for the elevator. He waited impatiently for the whir and hum and muffled clank of chains and cables to stop, and for the elevator to open.

"Yes sir?" the elevator man said.

"Is there a doctor in the building?"

"Yes, there is. Dr. Roseblau. Franz Roseblau."

"Get him, would you? It's an emergency!"

"Yes sir," the elevator man said, and he closed the door.

Meredith ran back to the kitchen. There was nothing he could do for Margaret. He was afraid of moving her, and, actually, a little bit disgusted by that foam around her mouth. He wondered what the foam meant. Rabies? It seemed unlikely. But Merry was still crying. He went to the refrigerator, found that there were more bottles of formula, and took one out. He got a saucepan, filled it with water and put the pan and the bottle on the stove to warm. He wondered when Miss Swain was supposed to come back. And where was that doctor? And where in the hell was Elaine?

He tried the bottle on his wrist as he had seen Miss Swain do before, and it seemed neither hot nor cold. He guessed that that would be all right. He took it into Merry's room, picked her up, sat down in the wooden chair that Miss Swain used and gave Merry the bottle. Most gratifyingly the cries stopped, and the tiny girl subsided into blissful sucking. He watched her suck and watched the redness of her face dissolve back to beautiful baby pink. He opened her fingers and stuck his index finger into her hand, which closed on it. All her fingers clenched his finger, and he studied the incredible tininess of the fingers and fingernails. In her hand, his finger was as thick as a tree trunk.

He heard the door open.

"Hello?" a man's voice called. It was the doctor.

"I can't come out now," he called to the doctor. "But look in the kitchen."

"Hello?" a woman's voice called. It was Elaine.

"I'm in here!" Meredith called back. "In Merry's room."

Elaine came into the nursery.

"I don't understand it," she said. "It took me the longest time to get the elevator to come down for me."

"Where the hell have you been?" Meredith asked her.

"Over at Jane's," she said, and giggled.

She had been drinking. It wasn't just the drinking or the giggle or the memory of Merry's yowling and crying, but all those things together that made Meredith get up from the chair, put Merry carefully into the crib, and then, when she was settled, turn to Elaine and smack her across the face.

Then he went out to the kitchen to talk to the doctor and find out what the hell had happened to Margaret.

It was painfully bright, like the sun itself, and almost painful to look at directly, when Jaggers stopped rocking back and forth on the upholstered desk chair, leaned forward, shook his head, and said, "I'm sorry, Meredith. But there's no way around it. She has to have custody. You could try to fight it, of course, but it wouldn't do any good. You'd lose. Unless you can prove that she's a prostitute or a dope addict or, preferably, both, she gets custody. All you'd get would be an awful lot of terrible publicity that wouldn't do you any good, or her, or, in the long run, Merry, either. People remember these things. You're well known, you know, and in ten years, in twenty years, you'll be better known. And people remember this kind of thing. It's a hell of a burden to put on the girl, isn't it?"

It was indeed. Jaggers' words cut like knives, but the sharpest of all of them was "burden." It was the last thing in the world that he'd wanted to be to his daughter. He'd known what it was, himself, to carry a father's troubles around on one's shoulders. And his father had known it, too. And all he'd wanted, the one thing he'd wanted more than anything else in the world was to be a good father, a friend, a companion, an understanding, reliable, supportive father to this small child he'd helped to bring into the world. It was a damned shame.

He had explained to Sam Jaggers the way that evening had been, how he had come home to find Margaret on the floor with that foam all over her mouth. It had been a *grand mal* seizure, an epileptic fit, but he hadn't known that. And how he had had to change and feed Merry, and the rage he'd felt. And the slap? It had not been a slap at Elaine so much as at everything that had happened, and at her having let it happen. But there was unsoundness in that, there had to be. One slap could not rupture so much in any ordinary marriage. It was like a sudden strain on what appears to be sound timber that has been riddled with post-powder beetles, boring, boring. He had left the house and gone back to his dressing room to sleep there. And then the following day he'd called her and had apologized to Elaine, and she had accepted his apology, and everything should have been fine and would have been if he had not before saying good-bye referred one more time to her having been drunk. And she had argued about that, and he had argued back, and he had just decided not to make an issue of it when she hung up on him. So he'd spent a second night and a third in his dressing room. And then had moved to a hotel.

He did not tell Jaggers about how he had tried to

call Carlotta. But she had been out of town. So he'd called Jocelyn Strong, not out of desire for her so much as for a way to get back at Elaine. And it had worked out that way, too, because the columnists had picked it up and run their sniggering little item about how "The star of *Honey, Do* is doing a bit part in the old Who Was that Lady? routine." And Elaine had seen it, and had picked up the telephone, exactly as Meredith had expected. But she hadn't called him. She'd called a lawyer.

About Elaine he felt reasonably calm. There was a certain regret, of course, as one might expect about any such failure, but his tranquillity about the break with Elaine rather surprised him. It was as if he had understood their marriage only now that it was breaking up. He liked Elaine, still liked her, and he wished her well. But he realized that he had chosen her, and that they had chosen each other, for the most fortuitous and trivial of reasons. Each had found in the other some sympathetic strain, some recognizable and therefore congenial characteristic, that had enabled them to become friendly amost instantly, lovers instantly thereafter, and husband and wife within a week. The only trouble had been that this shared trait upon which they had based so much and gambled everything was a need for strength, a submissiveness, a dependence. And each had somehow assumed that the other was strong, reliable, dominant, and each had been disappointed.

Well, those were the risks of the game. But what seemed unfair and wrong to Meredith was that he and Elaine had not been the only losers. There was little Merry, who had made no mistake or miscalculation, and who was now cast out into the world by judicial whimsy and entrusted into Elaine's, not his, keeping.

"But think of your own life," Jaggers said, rocking back and forth. "Think of it as a judge would think of it, in a family court. You're an actor, which is bad. You travel around the world, shuttling back and forth between New York and Los Angeles. You haven't any fixed residence, really. Not that there is anything necessarily wrong with any of this, but there can be. There often is. And the public—and judges are a part of your public—tends to resent your glamorous life, and therefore is hardly likely to give you the benefit of the doubt. No, there's no sense in fighting it, because there's no hope of winning."

"But what can I do? I can't wave good-bye to a three-month-old baby, and forget about it."

"By no means," said Jaggers. "What you can do, indeed what you must do, is to wave good-bye and not forget about it. Wish her well and keep track of her. And I shall keep track of her, and we shall see what happens."

Denver James crept along the roof of the moving boxcar. There was nothing especially difficult about it, except that he had to move quickly to get to the end of the car, climb down the ladder, and jump right after the train passed the cactus that was the marker. For forty yards after that cactus plant, the ground had been prepared, dug up, padded with sponge rubber, and then covered with a thin layer of dirt. He had to time the jump so that he'd hit the sponge rubber, and he had to fall away from the train and land with his face away from the camera. No single piece of the action was especially difficult, or even especially dangerous. If he missed the prepared patch, he'd have a hell of a landing, and maybe bust a leg, but he wouldn't miss. No, the hard part was getting it all right, and timed right, and landing at the right angle, with his face the right way. For fifteen hundred bucks. About two minutes' work, not counting the time for waiting around, and for makeup and diddling around with wardrobe so that he would look like the pretty-boy star up there on the screen.

The wind was a son of a bitch. It wasn't dangerous or anything like that, wouldn't affect the jump, but could ruin the shot by blowing his hat off, which would make the whole bit funny, and he'd have to do it again. So holding himself so that the wind was blowing his hat against his head, and watching for the cactus up ahead, he got down from the boxcar roof and climbed down the ladder. He crouched to spring, and then, when the cactus whipped by, he pushed free of the train in a strong, graceful leap. He hit hard, rolled a couple of times, and came to a stop.

"Cut," the director yelled, off in the distance. The assistant director made a throat-cutting gesture, and the cameraman stopped the camera.

Denver James lay on the ground. It was real ground, for he had rolled off the sponge rubber. He lay there, trying to inhale. He had hit very hard, and had knocked the breath out of himself. He hoped it was only that, but mainly he concentrated on taking little shallow breaths that wouldn't hurt so much.

"You all right?" the assistant director asked, as he knelt down. He had come running up to Denver as soon as he had seen that the stunt man was slow in getting up.

"Don't know."

"Jesus Christ!" the assistant director said. He tried the ground with a foot. "The sponge is over there."

"Hit the sponge. Rolled."

"Jesus Christ!" the assistant director said again. "Hang on, I'll get the doctor. Where is he, anyway? He's supposed to be right here."

He went to get the doctor. Denver tried breathing a little more deeply. It wasn't quite so bad. He couldn't take a really deep breath yet, but he could fill his lungs about a third full without pain. He guessed he was OK. In a systematic way, much as a pilot running through his preflight checklist, he checked his extremities.

Arms, legs, hands, feet. Yes, he guessed he was all right.

The doctor came running up.

"Well, now, let's have a look," he said, all hearty and palsy. "Sorry I wasn't here," he added. "I waited and waited for them to shoot this damned scene, and I just couldn't wait any more. I was off in the crapper."

"That's OK," said Denver. "I guess maybe I'll live. I think I just knocked my wind out a little."

"Well, let's see now," the doctor said, and he felt around the ribs, poked and palpated, and every now and then asked, "That hurt?" and waited for Denver's "Nope."

By the time the doctor was through with his on-the-spot examination, Denver felt well enough to get up, and the doctor let him. They went off to the studio infirmary for a couple of X rays, just to be sure.

It took a while before they got the X rays developed, and Denver felt fine by the time the technician came out of the darkroom to tell him that he was fine. "Thanks," he said. "I figured." And saluting with one finger touching his forehead, he left, feeling better all the time, to go to the paymaster's office and pick up his three grand. Two stunts, at fifteen hundred per. A good week. And off to Mehico! Fun and games until the dough ran out, that was the reward for having lived through the job. And another job would be the penalty for all the fun and games. It was a vicious circle, but vice, as some barroom poet had said, is nice. Denver thought so, anyway. It was expensive, a little, but what the screw! With this game he could afford it. Some of the other stunt men, he figured, were just crazy. He thought, for instance, of Jay Abbott, with his wife and his daughters and his life-insurance premiums, worried all the time that the next time might be his last time, and somebody else would be beating his time with his wife before he was cold in the ground. Jay Rabbit was more like it. Nervous? Jeee-sus!

It took nearly an hour to drive from Culver City north to Beverly Hills, but it was still only three or so when he got there. They could leave that evening, maybe. Or early in the morning. He didn't care. He didn't care about anything.

Elaine welcomed him with an enthusiastic kiss as soon as the front door was closed behind him.

"It went all right?" she asked anxiously.

"I'm here, ain't I?"

"Yes, you're here."

"Then it went all right," he said, thinking that women do ask the most damn-fool questions sometimes. He went into the living room to the liquor cabinet and fixed himself a drink. He wasn't exactly living with Elaine, but he was there enough to know where the booze was, and to feel free to build himself a drink when he felt like it. It was an all right house. He was comfortable there. Of course, it was a warning, too. All these houses were warnings, because all these houses were owned by women who had thrown their husbands off, or had been thrown off by their husbands. It didn't matter which. Denver James had learned early on that there was nothing in the world like a Hollywood divorcée. Hot to trot, and yet sensible about things like marriage. What woman who wasn't a complete fool would throw over the kind of alimony that these dames got to get married to a stunt man who might wind up dead in a week? No, there was none of that shit. Loose as a goose and nice and easy. Some guy had once put it pretty well when he'd said, "Go Dutch, kiss French, and screw American!" Who the hell was it? He couldn't remember. But the important thing was that he had remembered the advice. They could carve it on his goddam headstone if they wanted.

"Did you eat?" Elaine asked. "Are you hungry?"

"No, I didn't. But I'm not hungry. Not right yet. I'd just as soon wash up first."

"Sure," she said.

He finished his drink, poured himself another, and went upstairs to the bathroom. He left the door open, and she followed him in. He stripped, and turned on the shower, adjusting the temperature of the water to the hottest that he could stand. He saw that she was looking at him, as if she were a hungry kid and he were the world's biggest banana split, and wondered for a moment whether he ought to jump her now. But, no, it'd be rushing things. And wasting water. All that nice hot water running down the drain, while she talked about going or not going, played with it, played with him, thought . . . The hell with it. He knew enough not to trust a woman's thinking. Feeling was what counted. Feeling. You want a favor, you ask a man before, but a woman after. Anybody knows that much. So he decided to wait until after, and got into the shower, where the hot water could run down his body and soothe the bruises he'd taken out on the back lot, jumping from the train. She stood outside, holding his drink, and every now and then he'd stick his head out and she'd give him a sip.

"Great! Thanks," he said. This was, without a doubt, the way to live. For as long as it lasted. But the hell with that. There were certified public accountants and registered pharmacists and shoe salesmen—a whole world of little men in brown suits and brown mustaches, who lived little brown lives—and you read about them all the time, getting hit by runaway cement mixers, and falling down in their little bathtubs and breaking their little necks. And with the war coming—and everyone knew it was coming now—there just weren't any odds any more.

He came out of the shower, and dried himself, and then turned around for Elaine to dry his back. Then he turned around to let her dry his front a little more thoroughly, and, when she started to slow up a little, he pulled her to him and kissed her. They went off together to her bedroom, a great big room, with a fireplace in it. He watched her as she shot the bolt on the bedroom door and pulled her dress over her head. She wasn't wearing anything under the dress, which was nice and efficient. He figured that with this kind of preparation, they were halfway to Mexico already. Sure, she'd have to leave the kid for a while, but it was either that or leave him for good. Or, actually, watch him leave her, because leave he would, first thing in the ayem, down to Tijuana and points south.

The racing of his mind slowed and then stopped as the play of his hands over her body became more and more absorbing. He was taking it slow, waiting so that she would beg for him to get into her, and come like a goddam moose, and the languor of their embraces was like a cloud that he floated on. She was one nice piece. And soon enough she was begging him, and in a nice, slow, easy way, he rolled over, onto her, and into her, smooth as a pickpocket's hand into a mark's pocket, when they heard the front door slam.

"Who's that?" he asked.

"It's just Clara, bringing Merry back from a walk. It's all right. The door's bolted."

"Good," he said, and he continued with his lovemaking. But it wasn't all right, it wasn't right at all, because the little brat had seen a squirrel on her walk, and she was all excited about it and just couldn't wait to tell Mommy, and up the stairs she came, clumpclump clumpclump, clumpety-clump, and up to the door of Mommy's bedroom to knock and bang and stand outside the door whining that she wanted to come in and tell Mommy about the squirrel.

Ordinarily he wouldn't have cared, but this wasn't just any screw, but an important screw, a persuading screw, and if he didn't persuade her with this one, then he wouldn't persuade her at all, and would have to go to Mexico alone, and would knock around the Tijuana cribs again, and get rolled, or get into a fight in some bar and get thrown in jail, and have to bribe his way out, and however it happened, he'd be broke in two weeks, and back jumping off trains in three.

"She'll go away," Elaine said, but it was a hope more than a prediction. "Not now, Merry," she called out, but hearing her mother's voice, the kid became only more insistent, and whined louder that she wanted to come in.

"I'm sorry," Elaine said.

He was sorry, too. Sorry, and damned sore, and more sore than sorry. He disengaged himself from Elaine and her embrace, got up and walked across the room to the door.

"No!" Elaine cried out. But he wasn't paying any attention.

He opened the door, and roared at the little girl, "Didn't you hear what your mother just said? Not now! Come back later. Beat it!" He would have gone on, for the little girl had not moved, but was standing there, staring at him, frightened by his shouting and yet curious about his nakedness, and that thing that jutted out from the hair, there, between his legs. But he heard a gasp from the staircase, and he looked up to see Clara standing there, staring at him, easily as curious as the kid.

"What the hell's the matter with you?" he shouted at Clara. "Why don't you take care of her? That's what you get paid for, isn't it? Goddam whining and banging about the door . . . What are you staring at? Me?"

"Y-y-y-yes," she said.

"If you did your job and took care of the girl, I wouldn't be here. If she busts in here with stories about some squirrel, then don't look so damned shocked if I come out here with my squirrel. Ah, shit. Look, take her away, will you? Go play with her. You can play with yourself on your own time."

He slammed the door. Presumably Clara, who was a student, part time, at UCLA, hustled little Merry off somewhere, because there was no further disturbance from the hall outside the bedroom door. Elaine lay on the bed, too shocked to speak. Or too frightened. He took some satisfaction in realizing that she was too fearful of losing him to reproach him for the awful thing he had just done. He got back in bed with her. But it was impossible to recreate the mood that the interruption had broken. Neither of them was really interested in continuing, but he had convinced himself that only by screwing Elaine could he get her to go with him, and he got back into bed, and finally, back into her. But it was no good. He couldn't make her come, in either sense of the word.

"Shit!" he said, sitting on the edge of the bed and smoking a cigarette. "You want to come with me to Mexico. I want you to come with me. Why not?"

"Because of Merry," she said.

"What about the girl? Why can't she take care of her?"

"She goes to classes. She . . . I just can't leave her with Clara. I hardly know Clara. And she's only a kid herself."

"Shit," Denver said again. Well, he would leave in the morning, he thought.

But he didn't. He and Elaine got dressed and went downstairs to the kitchen so that he could have something to eat. He hadn't had any lunch, and it was half past four. And into the kitchen Clara came marching with all the defiance she could muster, to quit on the spot. Which really tore it, Denver thought. But he was wrong. Forgetting entirely about Mexico, Elaine sat down and wrung her hands, wondering what she was going to do, because she couldn't take care of Merry by herself, couldn't stand to be cooped up that way, never going out, never seeing anybody, never doing anything. She had to have someone. And he suggested that what she needed was a vacation from Merry, not with any idea in the world that she would listen to him. But she did. And agreed, and wanted to know how she could manage it.

"Give her back to her father," he suggested.

"No, I can't."

"Don't be a sentimental slob."

"I'm not. I need the money. Most of what I live on is the child support that he pays me."

"Well, then, put her into a school for a while."

"A school? You're kidding. She's only three years old. She's just out of diapers, for God's sake!"

"That's all right. They've got schools for three-year-olds."

She thought about it for a minute. Then she said, "You mean orphanages."

"Well, sure, some of the kids there are orphans, but not all. And you wouldn't be leaving her there forever. Just for a week or two. And she'd be better off there than if you left her with Clara. You said so yourself, before Clara did her little bit for the cause."

She thought about it, and then decided that maybe she'd go, the next day, to look at one of those schools, and he changed his mind, and decided that it was a shoo-in, and that she was going to come with him. So he'd hang around another day.

They made a few calls the following morning, got the names of a couple of places, and drove out to see them. They left Merry at the first place, the Crestview School for Girls, and then, as soon as they'd stopped at the house for some of Elaine's things, were off to Mexico.

According to the agreement, Meredith had the right to visit his daughter every Wednesday afternoon from one o'clock until four, and every other weekend, from nine o'clock on Saturday until six o'clock on Sunday afternoon. He did not often come on Wednesdays, because Merry's nap interfered with his visit, and also because he was usually busy shooting, and he could not ask the studio to let him have Wednesday afternoons off. A shooting day, then, cost anywhere between ten and thirty thousand dollars, and a visit to a child who was probably going to be sleeping anyway just wasn't worth half a shooting day. But two days after Elaine and Denver had left for Mexico, Meredith was working on a picture that was shooting out in the Mojave Desert, just over the hills from Los Angeles, and in the most improbable way—though, indeed, it happens now and then, even out in the desert—it started to rain. There were hurried consultations between cameraman, director, producer, assistant director, associate producer, and wrangler, and a decision was made—to call the studio. There a decision was made, and they said whoever heard of rain in the desert but the hell with it, break for the day. And at twenty of eleven, on a Wednesday, Meredith found himself quite free. He got into his car and drove back to Los Angeles, but somewhere up in the mountains, on the way back to the great sprawling city, he decided that after all, even for just an hour or so, he might stop by and see Merry. He had the car and could take her for a ride, buy her a sandwich and get her home in time for her nap, almost. Ah, the hell with the nap, he thought. It'd be fun to see Merry, and he was going to do that.

He turned off Wilshire Boulevard, drove the five blocks to the next turn, made the turn, and then pulled up at the curb. He went to the front door, rang the bell, waited . . . and waited. He rang again. He knocked. He couldn't figure it out. Where would she be, on a Wednesday? Was Merry sick? Was Elaine sick? Had something happened? He went around to the back of the house, not for any particular reason, but just to look. And he found a note that Elaine had left for the milkman: "No milk until further notice." He was puzzled, but not really worried. Maybe she had gone away for a couple of days. It was annoying, because she should have let him know. He had a right to see Merry on Wednesdays. But, being as reasonable as he could about it, he decided that she couldn't possibly expect him. She knew that he was shooting, and that would mean that she had just assumed he wouldn't come. And if he wasn't coming to see Merry, then what she did was her business. Idly, he wondered where they were. It didn't even occur to him that Merry might not be with Elaine.

He came back that night, just to drive by the house. There were no lights on. So she was away. He wondered whether to make a fuss about it, but decided that it wasn't important. He'd let it go.

He called on Thursday but got no answer. He called again on Saturday, and still there was no answer. And on Monday, when he tried to call and couldn't get anyone at the house, he began to worry. He called Arthur Wemmick, Jaggers' partner in Los Angeles, and explained what had happened. Wemmick said that he'd look into it and get back to him as soon as he could. Meredith didn't hear from Wemmick until late Tuesday afternoon, and he was annoyed that the man had taken so long, but his annoyance left him instantly, partly because he realized that Wemmick must have been on the phone almost constantly during the entire interval, but mainly because his annoyance had given way to grief and rage at the news that Wemmick had for him—that Elaine was somewhere in Mexico and his daughter was in an orphanage in Santa Monica. He got the address and drove out there, right away.

The Crestview School was neither on a crest nor in view of one, nor was it even a school, really. It did not look as bad as Meredith had feared it would. There were no high Dickensian walls, no cavernous public rooms through which small waifs in starched gray uniforms marched in long, somber lines. It was, in fact, a converted mansion, run by two reasonably presentable spinster sisters and a staff the size of which Meredith could not begin to guess. Miss Sears—the elder one,

Miss Evelyn Sears—explained to him that Meredith was having her supper just then. He wasn't sure that he liked her calling Merry "Meredith," which seemed a little chilly, somehow. But he explained, patiently and cheerfully, that he hadn't known where his daughter was, and that he'd just found out half an hour ago, and that he wanted very much to see her.

"I can understand that," Miss Sears said. "But these children have a schedule, you know, and we find that it upsets them to have abrupt deviations of this kind—"

"I'm sure that's true, but I'm not an abrupt deviation. I'm her father! And I want to see her. Please," he added, figuring that there was no point in being more antagonistic than necessary, but adding immediately that if it became necessary, he was ready to punch this woman right in the mouth.

She said she would get the child. He thanked her.

What struck him most, when she brought Merry into the office, was the little girl's quiet, almost withdrawn quality. He had to coax her to sit on his lap, and only after a few minutes did she react—and then by crying on his shoulder. He explained to her that he would have to leave her there that night, but that he'd be back in the morning to get her, and that they would eat up all the peanut-butter-and-jelly sandwiches in the world together. And she smiled at him, and gave him a kiss. And he thanked Miss Sears again, and left.

He called Wemmick. Wemmick explained that Elaine was within her rights, and that if she had gone off somewhere for a vacation, she could have left the child there. "She should have notified you, of course, and it would have saved you a lot of worry—"

"Look, Arthur, it isn't me and my worry. It's that kid. That sad little girl. My daughter. It's her worry that I'm angry about and I want to do something about it."

"We can write a letter and complain," Wemmick said.

"You mean I can't get her out of there?"

"No, you can't."

"But that's crazy. It's wrong."

"I'm sorry."

So he called Sam Jaggers long distance, and woke him up in the middle of the night in New York. He apologized about the lateness of the hour, and the stupid time gap between the coasts, but explained that it was about Merry, and then explained where Merry was and what Arthur had just told him.

"I'm sorry, Meredith," Sam said. "But Arthur is right. There's nothing you can do. You're right, too, and it is lousy, but there it is. She's put Merry into this institution, and she has the right to do that, just as she would have the right to send her away to camp, or to boarding school or to college. All you've got is visitation rights."

"But she's three years old! She's only three!"

"Are they mistreating her at the school?"

"Of course they are!"

"I mean beating her, starving her, anything like that?"

"No!"

"Then we're helpless. But, Meredith . . ."

"Yes?"

"I'm sick about it, too."

"Thanks, Sam. Thanks."

He hung up the telephone and wept.

Win a few, lose a few, the saying goes, and the saying, Denver thought, was about right. Well, he'd lost this one, and no question about that. Denver carried Elaine to the car, propped her against it while he opened the door, and put her inside. He closed the door, then went around and got in on the other side, and, from the driver's seat, arranged her so that she wouldn't fall on him while he drove over the ruts and potholes of the Mexicali streets. He patted her cheek, trying once more to bring her around. But nothing. He gave her a good slap that left a red mark on her face. Still nothing. She was out cold. He'd never seen anything like it before.

Oh, sure, he'd seen women pass out from drinking too much. He'd seen Elaine pass out from drinking too much. Twice in Tijuana, and once on the road from Tijuana to Mexicali, and once after that in Mexicali itself. But this time took the cake. They'd been sitting in the cheap little nightclub, slugging back the tequila and watching the strippers. She'd been drinking like a fish. Well, for that matter, she'd been drinking like a fish the whole time they'd been in Mexico together. With a vengeance. As if she'd been trying to drown herself. Which, he thought, was maybe what she was trying to do. Maybe he never should have made her come with him, never should have suggested that she put her kid away for a while, never should . . . But what the hell! She was a grown-up. She knew what she was doing. You can't make someone do what they don't want to do, anyway. Some hypnotist had told him that once, and it was even more true with people who weren't hypnotized. But she had been hitting that bottle. And he'd been just as pleased. Wild on the bottle, wild in the bed, they said, and she had been, yes, she had been that. But this evening she'd been out to break the world's record. World's champion boozer. Which was OK with him. Only she wanted to be the world's champion screw, too. Which also was OK with him. Fine with him. But the rules she made up for the championship were ridiculous. He couldn't figure it. She was great in the sack, and should have known that she was great in the sack. But just because he'd looked admiringly at the stripper, the young one who could throw her tits around so fast, she'd got all upset. Well, even that was all right. You can't argue with a drunk—not that she was *a* drunk, but she was drunk then. As a skunk. Anyway, she'd got all huffy about the stripper, who was, she'd said, too skinny and just padding around up there, and not putting herself into it.

"They never do," he explained.

"Then they *ought* to."

"What do you know about it? You ever been a stripper?"

"No, but I'm a woman."

"That's different."

"The hell it is! That's the whole point."

"No, this is just pretend. And she pretends good."

"I could do better."

"Sure."

"You don't believe me?"

"Sure, I believe you."

"You don't, either. But I'll show you. . . ."

Just then the stripper finished her strip, flipped her G-string, flashed the wooly-wooly, and disappeared behind the curtain. There was a weak round of applause from the four or five occupied tables. And suddenly Elaine had got up and was climbing up on the stage.

"Hey, Elaine! Are you crazy? Get down from there. Come on, honey. It's time for us to go," he'd called, but the leader of the four-piece combo had figured that, if only for laughs, it might be kind of funny to give her a few bars, and they started playing, and she started dancing. And there was a big hand from the tables, bigger than the one for the stripper who'd just finished, and a couple of shouts of "Sit down, you," so he figured he'd sit down. It wasn't worth brawling about.

It was a funny kind of strip. Regular clothes aren't designed for that kind of thing, anyway, and she was drunk, so that she shuffled around, out of time with the music mostly, and pathetic, but still good-looking enough so that it was, by God, fascinating to watch. And it was convincing, because of its awkwardness. She got out of her dress the way a woman gets out of a dress, fumbling a little, and getting the zipper open, finally, and pulling the damned thing up over her head. And she got out of her slip, too. And there she was, dancing around in her shoes and stockings and her garter belt and panties and her bra. And she had a time trying to get the bra unhooked in the back, and the tables were cheering and clapping, and finally she got the bra off, and waved it around and tried to bounce her tits the way the stripper had, and of course couldn't, and there were a couple of laughs. And the laughs killed her, and all of a sudden she stopped, and right there in the middle of the stage, stood there, hiccuped, and then barfed all over herself. Loud cheers and whistles from the tables, and nothing for Denver to do but to get up there and pick her up, and take her off in back of the stage to clean her up a little, and put her dress on. It was a little disgusting, and a lot embarrassing. That was when he carried her out to the car, propped her up and drove her back to the hotel, thinking about it as carefully as he could, and decided that maybe the whole damned thing had been a mistake, and he'd be better off in Mexico by himself.

He carried her up to the room, and put her on the bed. He took her dress off again, and the rest of her clothes, and tried to wake her, but he couldn't. The hell with it, he thought. He went into the bathroom, and took a shower to get the smell of the vomit off him. And when he came out, he tried one last time to wake her, thinking that maybe she deserved a good-bye screw. But she didn't rouse. But he did, thinking that he deserved a good-bye screw. He deserved something for getting her back to the hotel room. Jesus, if he'd left her there, every tomcat in Mexicali would have jazzed her back out in the alley behind the club. He slapped her face again, not hard, but a slap. She didn't move. He pinched a tit. Nothing. Then he stopped playing with her, and started playing with himself. Booze and sex, huh? Drown in degradation, huh? Well, he'd give her a little degradation. Excited now by the idea and by its novelty—because this was something he'd never done before—he stroked himself vigorously and finally ejaculated on her chest. Curiously he watched the rivulet of his semen as it ran down between her breasts. Be the sex champion of the world, he thought. He left her fifty bucks to get home with, and he left her for good.

CHAPTER

THREE

♥ Spontaneous, direct, ingenuous—call it what you will, but there is an innocent simplicity which people like to attribute to children, and do, whether it is true or not. Surely, no one likes to assume that a child, a little child, is calculating, or is even capable of calculating, using other children and grown-ups, too, the way a bridge player uses cards, counting points, figuring tricks, sloughing, finessing, cross-ruffing. Particularly, no one likes to think that a little girl could be that way.

But she was that way, knew she was that way, and knew, too, that she was pretty, and that her prettiness, her golden ringlets, her bright blue eyes, her pert nose were all taken by grown-ups to be sure signs of her innocence, and she used that, too, the way a bridge player uses a void. In a peculiar way it was innocent, and she was playing, as other children play with dolls or blocks, but she played the games she had been taught, and those games involved the people with whom she lived. She was, after all, the stepchild, and she had had to learn how to compete for attention, for affection, with her half-brother when he was born. Even before that, she had discovered how far she could impose upon the limited patience of her stepfather, in what ways she could appeal to him, to what degree she could rely on him. It was like a game. But it was not a game, not at all. There was nothing that could have been more serious to her than her efforts to insinuate herself into the family, to establish herself, and to keep herself there and out of the school where she had spent so many bleak years. School? Orphanage! But whatever its rightful name, she was determined not to go back, not to let herself be sent back, as she had been so many times before.

So she learned how to play, how to live, how to play at living. And the line between the two was difficult, sometimes, to draw. She had begun by using her brother, almost shamelessly. And it was amazing that neither her mother nor her stepfather saw through the transparent stratagem. Of what interest, really, is a newborn child? Mainly, infants sleep. Or eat. Or dirty their pants, or drool. Or sometimes belch. It's not much of a range. But Merry learned very quickly that by singing to her baby brother she earned the affection of her stepfather, and even the admiration of her mother. She would sit, for long, boring minutes, while her mother fed Lyon, in order to earn the dubious pleasure of being allowed to hold him afterward, and pat his back, ever so gently, until he burped. She didn't care at all about the burp, or about the brother, but she did care about the smiles of approval and the pieces of candy she got for going through her little routine.

But then, as Lyon grew up, she found that she really did like him, and even loved him, because he was someone to talk to, company of a kind. And then, he was someone to talk with, to play with—even when no one was watching who would make the inevitable remark about how well they got on together, to evoke the inevitable grin from Elaine. And the piece of candy from Harry Novotny, Elaine's husband, Merry's stepfather.

Those pieces of candy were sweeter than their manufacturer ever knew. They were tangible signs of achievement, rewards for a trick well played. Out in back of the house, in the cages, she had seen her stepfather give the animals pieces of sugar, or small dog biscuits, or cheese, or bits of meat, in just the same way, and even if he didn't see the similarity, she did. It was all as clear as it could be to Merry. Perhaps, had she been a little more sophisticated, she might have come to the point of asking herself the one, awful question: who was the trainer, and who was the animal?

In a way, she envied the animals. Their position at least was clear. Their lives were not pleasant, were in fact quite miserable, and she had learned to protect herself from their misery and to insulate herself from it by withholding any emotion whatever from them. Cats, mice, rabbits, dogs, lions—there were two lions—and monkeys might seem a child's paradise, but for Merry there was nothing out in the cages and pens in back but the tools of her father's trade, of no more interest or appeal than the meat in a butcher's refrigerator holds for the butcher's child. Harry Novotny's meat was alive, but that was the only difference, and small difference it made.

He had told her, of course, and had been unmistakably clear about it, but she had not been able to believe it, as a novice card player will simply not be able to believe his partner's opening bid of five diamonds. "All this business about loving the animals," he had said, "is all hooey. For the press agents. For the public. Loving the animals, you could lose your shirt. I beat the animals. I beat them good." He told how he trained the cat to walk a tightrope, jump over the six mice that came out from the other end of the tightrope, and not bother the mice. He was talking to Elaine at the time, but Merry was there, and Merry was listening. "The cat learned to walk the rope. That was easy. I put the cat up on a pole and put its feed on another pole, and the only way to get to the food was to start out and cross on the rope. One cat wouldn't do it. Starved to death. The second cat learned how to walk a tightrope. Then I started with the mice. Always the cat ate the mice. I must have gone through a hundred mice. And I beat the cat! Boy, my arm was sore from beating that cat. And still it kept on eating the mice. Cats do that, you know. But finally I figured it out. I stuffed the cat's throat with gauze. It couldn't swallow anything. It could hardly breathe. But it could breathe a little. And it just jumped over the mouse. Then two, then three. It was a damn good trick. But it didn't have an ending. So you know what I did?"

"What?" Elaine had asked.

"I made the mice go into little boxes, and then they parachuted out of the boxes to the ground, and the band played some patriotic songs. The mice that came out with the parachutes weren't the same mice that went in the boxes. They were double boxes. But what the hell, all mice look the same, right?"

"How did you teach the mice to parachute?" Elaine asked.

"Teach? The boxes opened from the bottom, and they fell out. And the parachutes opened. Sometimes they didn't open, but what the hell, they were only mice. And most of the time they opened. Then it was a good trick. I made a living from that trick for three, four years. All over Europe."

Novotny was a short, swarthy man, who proclaimed himself to be the best animal trainer in the world. He probably was, too, and in Hollywood he had found a market for his special talents—in fact, the best of all possible markets. He had not fled Europe, but had merely found himself in the United States, traveling with a circus, when the war broke out. He had gone to Hollywood, had started out small, but had, in the eight years of his American residence, built up a very good business. He owned a house, a nice house out in the valley, with a barn behind it, and the pens and all the cages for the animals. He also owned Elaine, and two children. One he had begotten himself. The other had come with Elaine, already nicely weaned and toilet trained and able to talk by the time he had married the mother. And to get an animal already trained was to save an awful lot of work and bother. So he was pleased.

For her part, Elaine was pleased, too. Harry was a strong man, a good man to lean on, and yet, perhaps because of the very ridiculousness of his trade, a man who was not at all threatening or challenging to her. Occasionally there had been quarrels, and once or twice Harry had even beaten her, but always the beatings had been measured, and for her own good. He had come home to find her drunk one night, and had beaten her exactly as he had beaten a recalcitrant mule earlier that day, and with the same experienced hand that left no permanent injury, that inflicted pain without actually causing damage. She never got that drunk again.

But off in the bedroom, Merry had heard her stepfather pummeling her mother, and had made the connection, which was no more difficult or remote than that between the pieces of candy he gave her and the tidbits he gave his beasts and birds. And in a way she, too, was reassured by the apparently logical order of the world that Harry Novotny created.

So it could not have been said, in all fairness, that Merry was a calculating little girl. She was, rather, a little girl who had been taught, been trained actually, to calculate. She did it very well, as if her survival depended upon it. Indeed she thought it did. But proficiency of that kind demands a medium of expression, and it was perhaps for that reason alone that she walked out onto the airfield one April afternoon, tagging close behind the plump lady with the purse in one hand and the packages tucked under the other arm, climbed up the ramp, and boarded the plane for New York. Nobody asked for a ticket, because little girls don't need tickets if they are riding with an adult. And nobody questioned her because her hair was neatly brushed and she was wearing a pretty red dress, patent-leather shoes, and a light-blue coat, and obviously, she belonged to someone. Her heart was beating and her breath was shallow, and she half expected that the people in the plane would be able to hear her heartbeats, they were so loud, but nobody said anything, and she buckled her seat belt when everyone else did, and still, as the door of the plane slammed shut, and as the engines sputtered, whined, and caught, nobody said anything, asked her anything, or even came to look at her ticket, and then the plane started to taxi to the end of the runway, and the stewardess buckled herself into her seat back near the door, and Merry knew that she would get away with it. She had considered bringing Lyon along with her, but had decided not to. She had wanted to, but she was afraid that something terrible would happen, that perhaps the plane would crash, or that she would be punished, beaten like one of the animals, and she didn't want anything to happen to Lyon. So she had promised herself that she would bring something back for him somehow. She had eighty-five cents with her. She could buy him a set of souvenir views of New York.

The engines roared, and then the plane started forward, gaining speed, faster and faster, and Merry was sure that it would never get off the ground, that something was wrong, that the plane would just keep on going, on the ground, until it crashed into something after the end of the runway. She started to cry. The woman next to her leaned over and patted her arm.

Merry held her hand, and squeezed it very tightly. The plane was suddenly airborne.

"Are you all alone on the plane?" the woman asked.

Merry thought for a minute. There was nothing they could do to her now. They surely wouldn't turn around and land again to put her off. And besides, she was obviously alone. So she said, yes, she was.

"And you're going all the way to New York, all by yourself?"

"My daddy's meeting me there," she said. That was not strictly true. What she had planned was to go and visit her father. She would meet him. That was why she had chosen New York over Mexico City or Kansas City or St. Louis, which were all posted on the different departure gates at the airport. She had thought that New York would be fun, and she could meet her father there and have an ice cream soda with him before she went back home. And, besides, that was the farthest away of any place she could have gone. Which made it safer. She had observed that if you do something a little bit bad, you're likely to get a spanking—for breaking a glass, or for spilling ink on the floor—but if you do something really terrible, like opening the car door while the car is moving, all you get is a scolding, and tears, and hugs. So New York, because it was farthest away, was in a way the safest place.

The woman next to her said that she was very brave, and a very big, grown-up girl, despite which she helped her with the tray for the lunch they served, and got a pillow for her and a blanket, and helped her arrange herself so that she could take a nap, and then helped her with supper, too, and even asked the stewardess for an extra glass of milk. Merry was as good as she could be, both out of gratitude to the nice lady and because she knew that the stewardess, seeing the two of them, naturally assumed that they must be together. And that assumption was her ticket.

Merry did not know what time it was when the

stewardess woke her. She had been napping, and the blanket was covering her, but the stewardess was checking on seat belts, because they were going to land. Merry thanked her, and the lady in the seat beside hers helped her to buckle her seat belt. The plane dropped; she could feel it dropping because her ears felt funny, as if she were going down in an elevator. And then it landed, and the engines suddenly got louder, and she was sure that there was something wrong, and she held the lady's hand. But there was nothing wrong, and the plane stopped. Merry smiled a smile of triumph and relief, feeling good because she had made it, had really done it, but then the stewardess announced that they were in Chicago. Her heart sank.

Immediately Merry began thinking. What should she do? Anything? Nothing? The safest course, she decided, was just to sit where she was. Yes, that was it. Just hit there, next to the lady beside her, and pretend to doze, until the plane took off again. Or, maybe, go to the bathroom, and then come back to her seat just before the plane started. Well, she could do that if she had to. But certainly if she could get away with just sitting there, that would be the best thing to do. And she had just decided on that, when the woman undid her seat belt, wished her a good trip, and got up to go, to leave the plane, to get off at Chicago. . . . It was awful! She waited a minute, pretended to be fiddling with her seat belt, and then opened it and followed the woman off the plane. This plane was dead. The stewardess assumed that she was with that woman. She had, therefore, to get off the plane when that woman did. Or have another ticket. So off. It would not be difficult, she thought, to start over again, and get another plane for New York. She had come this far, she thought, and she could go the rest of the way, too.

And would have, too, if the stewardess had not been so helpful, had not called out to the nicely diminishing, beautifully receding back of the kindly woman, "Wait a moment! Ma'am? Your little girl!"

"Mine?" the woman said, turning around. "She's not mine!"

Merry ran for it. And the stewardess ran down the steps after her. And from the gate to the airport, two men in uniforms came out and started chasing her. She could see it was no good running, so she stopped. She just stood there, waiting for them, until they came up and grabbed her. And then it was boring, boring, boring, as they took her to the office inside, and asked her questions, and asked the woman questions, and tried to sort it all out to find out who she was. She didn't care. All she had was eighty-five cents in her pocket, and they could have that if they wanted.

The trouble was that nobody believed her. It was kind of funny, actually, because she could understand perfectly well why they didn't believe her. There she was, a stowaway, or whatever you call it for airplanes, who had come from Los Angeles to Chicago, and they asked her who she was, and, naturally, she told them: "Meredith Houseman." She might as well have said she was John Wayne or Gary Cooper or Henry Fonda. Of course they didn't believe her. The woman who had been next to her in the plane remembered that she had said something about her father meeting her in New York.

"I was lying," Merry said.

"Well, it's very bad to lie," said the ground hostess, who was trying to help. "You understand that, don't you?"

"Yes," Merry said, lying. She didn't understand that at all. What had been bad was to go on the plane. The lying was merely a necessary part of the other thing.

"Well, then," said the hostess, who was being so sweet and reasonable that Merry wondered how she could stand herself, "why don't you 'fess up and tell us your real name!"

"Meredith Houseman. People call me Merry," she said for the umpteenth time. But she toyed with the idea of making up another name for them. They deserved it, with that " 'Fess up" business. "I'm Meredith Houseman's daughter."

The hostess shrugged, looked at the man behind the desk, who was some sort of big deal, and he shrugged, too.

"Do you want us to call him up?" the hostess asked.

"Yes," she said. She really didn't. It wasn't what she wanted at all. She wanted them to put her on a plane to New York and let her call him from there. Then it would be a surprise and fun. It wasn't any fun if they called him up and told him that they'd caught his daughter in Chicago. It'd spoil everything. But, on the other hand, she didn't want to sit there in that dumb office for another hour, and hear them badger her with questions.

"What's his telephone number, Merry? Do you know?"

"No," she said.

"You don't know your father's telephone number?"

"No."

They looked at each other again. Obviously they didn't believe her. Oh, they believed that she didn't know the telephone number, all right, but they didn't believe who she was. It was ridiculous.

The man behind the desk called information in New York. It was an unlisted number. Of course. So he called Celebrity Service, which is a service that keeps track of everybody who is anybody, for magazines and newspapers and airlines and anybody else that needs to know where celebrities are, and how to reach them. They gave the man Sam Jaggers' number. The man called Jaggers and apologized for bothering him, and explained that there was a little girl there who claimed to be Meredith Houseman's daughter.

"About nine," the man said, answering a question

that Jaggers had put to him. "Blond, blue eyes, pretty . . ." he said, and then he listened. "All right, just a moment," he said into the phone. "Tell me," he asked Merry, "when is your birthday?"

"September first," she said.

"What's your brother's name?"

"Lyon," she said.

"Yes, sir," he said into the phone. "Yes, of course. No, not a word. Yes. She'll be on the next plane. She should get to New York in a couple of hours. Yes. You're quite welcome. Glad to be of help."

He hung up the telephone and asked Merry if she wanted anything to eat. She said could she have a glass of milk, and the hostess ran out to get it for her. Ran. It was pretty funny. And she was going to get to New York, after all.

Meredith was surprised to find that Sam seemed to agree with him. Or perhaps agree was too strong a word. He did not quite know himself what he thought, what he wanted, what he was going to do. But Sam seemed to be leaning toward caution, and to be reluctant to advise anything sudden. . . . But what the hell, that was Sam all over. Lawyers are notoriously cautious, Meredith thought, and agents are often cautious, and Sam Jaggers was both. But he was more than that. He was a friend as well. And as he sat there on the couch, looking a little silly holding the fragile demitasse on his knee, Meredith listened carefully, attentively, confidently, to Sam Jaggers. Measuring out his periods with slow nods of his great, leonine head, Sam explained his reasons for advising Meredith to go slowly with this business.

"She's not running away," he said. "Or at least I don't think she is. There isn't any reason for her to be running away, at any rate. She really is being well taken care of. This Novotny character seems to be all right. He does pretty well. And Elaine seems to be all right, too. She's settled down with him, it seems. And there is a child they have, a little boy. Lyon, his name is. And he and Merry seem to be getting very good care."

"How do you know that?"

"Because I've made it my business to know that."

"You're pretty thorough."

"I've done what I could."

"But why would she do a thing like this? Why get on a plane at all, if not to run away? Why come to see me, if not to run away? And why run away if everything is all right, and she's being well taken care of?"

"Kids do funny things sometimes."

"I guess so," Meredith said. "Well, we'll see."

"Sure," Sam said. "You'll get a chance to see her, anyway. And to find out for yourself."

"And will it make any difference?" Carlotta asked. She had been silent, waiting and listening, all the time they had been talking. "Do you really think that it will make any difference how she seems? The thing is for you to decide what you want to do. What we want to do. And do it. But this looking at the child, and trying to tell from her what you ought to do, what we ought to do . . . It's perfectly awful. It's like having a dress sent home to see whether you like it or not, and then sending it back if you don't like it enough. It's like getting a painting on approval. But with a child? With your own child?"

"It isn't like that," Meredith said. "Really, dear, it isn't."

"I hope not," she said. But she thought it was, and he knew it. And he knew, too, that she had already decided what she wanted to do, and that was to keep Merry, to use the fact that Merry had climbed on a plane as a club and with it to threaten or beat Elaine into giving her up. And he knew why, too. But he said nothing. And Jaggers peered over the tops of his spectacles and said nothing. And Carlotta said that they'd better get ready to go out to the airport, and got up and took Sam's demitasse.

"No need to rush," Sam said. "The limousine is downstairs."

"Thanks," Meredith said. "I forgot all about it."

"You asked me. It's there."

"Good. She'll get a kick out of it."

"I suppose so," Jaggers said, "but I should think it'd be you that she'd get the kick out of."

"I'm the ice cream," Meredith said. "The car is the cherry on top."

"OK, OK."

"Ready," Carlotta said, coming back from the bedroom, where she'd run a comb through her hair. "Let's go!"

They went down the elevator in silence, and in silence walked through the lobby and out to the waiting limousine. Each was busy with his own thoughts, and not only busy with them but trapped by them, for none could quite bear to tell the other two what the arrival of the little girl at the airport meant to him, or why it meant what it did.

Meredith helped Carlotta into the car, then got in himself, and Sam got in after him and closed the door. It was Sam who told the driver, "Idlewild. American, please." The car pulled away from the curb and into the traffic.

Sam Jaggers was worried by the neatness of it. For the little girl to appear now, to interrupt everything at a critical moment in the negotiations, was exactly what he would have wanted. It was a damnably intricate problem, this contract business. He didn't want Meredith to sign. Certainly he didn't want him to sign for more than a year, which could be two, maybe three pictures. It was a wild, strange new business, and Meredith, he thought, ought to hold back. Individual deals for individual pictures, with the studios fighting each other to survive, and all of them together fighting television—that was the way to do it. No more of this long-term slave-labor stuff. It made Sam's blood boil to see Meredith get fifty thousand dollars for a picture, and have the studio turn around and lend him to another studio for five hundred thousand, making a fantastic profit for doing nothing, nothing at all, nothing but owning Meredith. It made Sam angry to think of that without even pausing to dwell on the forty-five thousand dollars that was his 10 percent of the four hundred and fifty thousand. It was the principle of the thing. How many pictures does a man have in him to make, how long can he ride on his youth and his looks, and how can those fat bastards take all that money away from him? Well, there was a new day dawning, maybe right then, downtown, at the talks on the new contract that Meredith had flown to New York for. But Merry, coming this way . . . How would she affect things?

In a way, Sam hoped that Meredith would keep her, or would let Carlotta talk him into keeping her. It would all be so simple that way. Meredith would not want to go to Africa, that way, but would want to stay home with his daughter, either in New York or in Los Angeles, and make a home for her. And if he didn't go to Africa, then he couldn't do the movie about the life of Cecil Rhodes, which would mean that he wouldn't sign the contract, which was exactly what Sam wanted. And yet, and yet . . . he just didn't like it. It was messy and disorderly and unbusinesslike, even for such an unbusinesslike business as his. The intrusion of a nine-year-old girl shouldn't affect things. It did but it shouldn't. And because it did, he promised himself he'd be very careful, very careful indeed, not to interfere, not to seem even to approve or disapprove, but to let Meredith decide for himself, with Carlotta, of course, but for himself. That terrible responsibility of friendship was the worst part of representing these people, he thought. The worst part and the best.

If Sam was silent because he did not want to influence Meredith's decision, Carlotta was just as silent, but for an entirely different reason. She wanted the child. She wanted the child so much she was afraid that anything she said would be excessive, extreme, and might somehow put Meredith off. It was, after all, his child. And it was a delicate situation, in that she wanted him to want the child, but not to feel so guilty about having left her with the mother that it would be difficult for him to welcome her, to accept her, to fold her into their family like the egg whites into a soufflé. She wanted it to be that complete and that gentle.

She knew that she could force it, if she wanted to. And she did want to, or at least a part of her did very much want to. But to bring up all that old unpleasantness now would be so unfair to the little girl, would be such a burden for her to have to carry. And not only for the child, but for Carlotta, too, and for Meredith. And the thing was that if things went right, Merry would be the substitute, would be their child, would in fact very nearly erase what had happened during the war.

Meredith had been in New York, on leave for a couple of weeks. He had called her up, and they had had dinner together. Oh, a splendid dinner, with two kinds of wine, and juicy, thick steaks, and hothouse strawberries the size of lemons, all very extravagant and very expensive, and she had remarked, quite innocently, about the cost of it all on a sergeant's pay. And then he had explained about his part in the war effort, and she thought she understood why he seemed so different from what she had remembered. He was not an ordinary sergeant, he had explained, but a movie star, still on contract, and still on salary. Half-salary, but still, that was a lot of money. The whole thing was crooked as hell, and altogether lousy. He had enlisted because the studio told him to enlist. It was part of a promotion for the last film he'd made. And the deal was that he got into Special Services—the studio arranged that—and went around touring the country, selling war bonds.

"It sounds pretty good."

"It's rotten. Of course it's pretty good. It's the softest job in the Army, probably. And I hate it. And I keep thinking that if I had any guts, I'd apply for a transfer, and go into the Rangers or the Paratroopers. The studio'd be furious, of course. But I'd be doing something useful."

"What you're doing is useful. Anybody can be a paratrooper. Not anyone can go around selling bonds."

"Then I wish I were just anyone. I really do. This movie star thing is bad enough in peacetime, but then at least there are the movies. You act. You get up in the morning and go to the studio, and it's a job, and you can feel like anybody else, because you're doing a job. But this is crazy. I'm a movie star with no movies. It's like being a king in exile, or a former heavyweight champion—something large and ridiculous."

Over the brandy and coffee, he admitted that he only thought about requesting the transfer, but knew he wouldn't do it. And that he only remembered the peacetime life of a movie actor as being useful and sensible, but he knew it wasn't. And then he told her the story of that evening of the party, and how he had decided not to accept Jocelyn's invitation, and how she had been waiting for him down in the lobby.

"That kind of thing happens to actors, but it happens to bankers and dentists and schoolteachers, too," she said.

But then he told her about how he had broken up with Elaine, and the way the papers had picked up his presence in a restaurant with Jocelyn, and had run it to amuse their readers. And then he told her how the call to Jocelyn had been his second call. "I called you first. I—I'd been living in that damned dressing room, and I was lonely, and all I wanted, really, was someone to talk with."

"All?"

"Mainly. Honestly!"

"I'm not sure that's very flattering."

"It should be. It was meant to be. I called you because I still had hope that somehow things could go on the way they were. And I could imagine spending a perfectly innocent evening with you, just talking, just enjoying your company, just being with you. And that wouldn't have broken up anything. But you weren't there, and suddenly I thought, *To hell with it, to hell with it all.* And I called her. And it hit the fan. As I suppose I knew it would. As I probably intended for it to do."

"I see," she said.

"And—and that's why I called you this evening. To be with you. To enjoy your company. To relax."

"Just sit around and talk?"

"Yes," he said. "If that's the way it is, then that's fine. I mean, there doesn't have to be anything else—if you're involved with someone. Or even if you'd just rather not get involved with me right now."

"Right now?"

"I mean, with the war and everything. Who knows? I could fall off a platform somewhere and sprain an ankle. But you know what I mean."

"I know. But . . ." She lowered her eyes and, with her fingernail, traced small squares on the tablecloth. "What if I'm not involved with someone else, and if I'd just as soon . . ."

"Marvelous," he said, and with his hand he covered hers, and stopped her from her nervous tracing of squares.

"It's so simple," she said, smiling, confident again, and happy. "It's just like in the movies."

"Funny," he said, "but that's why they have me selling those damned bonds. People only seem to believe things if they've seen them in movies. Not only this, now, but even in the war. In battles. Time after time they've had soldiers come back from real battles, and say that it was just like in the movies. So they use me, instead of a real soldier, and somehow I'm more real than he is. It's odd, isn't it? But everything is upside down and inside out, that way, these days. Did you see the headwaiter as we came in? He was unhappy because the first thing he saw was my uniform, and I'm only a sergeant. And he looked very unhappy. But then he noticed my face, and saw that I was Meredith Houseman, and I'd been turned into a full colonel at least, judging from the way his expression changed."

They talked, pleasantly, happily, cheerfully, during another round of brandies, and then they went back to Carlotta's apartment. Meredith wandered around the living room, looking at her books, especially all the art books in the oversize shelves on either side of the fireplace. She made some more coffee, and watched him from the kitchen doorway as he looked around the room, not snooping so much as enjoying, getting to know her through her books, her lamps, her paintings and drawings, and letting her get to know him. She liked the way he looked, the way he fit in so handsomely with the room, seemed comfortable in it, and part of it. She liked the way he stopped to study and admire the little Degas drawing—which was small and not at all imposing, but quite the best thing in the room, and important to her because Mark had bought it for her for their first anniversary.

"It's a beautiful room," he said, when he became aware that she was looking at him.

"Thank you."

"And you're a beautiful woman," he said.

"Thank you," she said again.

And then he kissed her, and it was suddenly not so simple after all, but complicated and wonderful and even frightening, because it had been so long, so very long, and her body felt odd and strange and awkward. She was worried that she would be gawky and graceless, and that she had forgotten what to do and how to do it. Could you forget? Was it like riding a bicycle, or could you forget how to do that? But with great gentleness he was holding her and kissing her, and then, slowly, deliberately, he undid the buttons in the back of her black dress.

She stepped out of the dress and led the way into the bedroom, still feeling timid and graceless and bashful, as if she had never been married, never borne a child, never made love. She kicked off her shoes and rolled her stockings down, wishing that she could do it better, elegantly, or at least with the wonderful directness of that girl in the drawing of Manet. Or was it Monet? Anyway, that drawing. Then she took off her underthings, but left on her sapphire-and-diamond earrings, hoping to borrow some of their glitter, their elegance. Meredith, however, sensed her nervousness, or seemed to, for he was very tender, gentle with her as if he were making love to a young girl, kissing her and stroking her and fondling her as if they had all the time in the world, as if they were idly amusing each other from the rich depths of satiety. But he was eager, eager as hell. She could tell that from looking at him. And when, finally, he went into her, it was really as if she were a virgin again, because she was so out of practice, or maybe it was just that he was so damned big. Or not, actually, that big. Not damned big, but wonderfully big, for very soon the old ease came back, and she remembered how it was, how marvelous it was, and loved it, loved it, and said, over and over, in a faint voice, "Oh, I love it, I love it, oh, I love it, yes, I love it."

She changed, in a few moments, from demure virgin to abandoned courtesan, and, after her long abstinence, found herself shooting up with incredibile rapidity to wild heights of excitement. "Oh, God, yes, oh, good

God, yes," she said, as she came, but he had not yet come, was not yet even near it, and he kept thrusting away in her, in a great, rhythmic battery upon her, which surprised her, even shocked her in that she found herself responding to him again, and coming again, almost immediately, and yet a third time, when she felt the hot gush of his seed in her.

They lay back exhausted, and she put her head on his chest, and snuggled against him, and felt good. But then she heard a hiss, an odd sputtering from the kitchen.

"The coffee!" she said. "It's boiling over. The little percolator does that."

"I'll get it," he offered.

"No, you lie there. I'll get it," she said, and she got up and padded into the kitchen for the coffee.

It was a gorgeous, wonderful evening. They sat on the bed and drank coffee, and made love again, and then had cheese and crackers and talked, and they decided to go away for a while, for the rest of Meredith's furlough. The following morning they went down to Grand Central Station and caught a train for Cape Cod. They rented a cottage on the bay side of Wellfleet, a funny gray, shingle cottage with a great fireplace in the living room, and an enormous picture window that looked out over the bay. And they climbed on the dunes and made love, and ate lobster and made love, and swam and made love, and drank Tom Collinses in the afternoon and made love, and sat around by the fire in the fireplace in the evenings and made love, in the rocking chair, with Meredith sitting in the rocking chair, and her sitting on Meredith's lap, with him rocking back and forth in the chair while he was in her.

But the furlough came to an end, and they had to go back to New York, and then Meredith had to go on to Chicago to join his unit and sell more bonds.

"I'll call you when I get back," he said.

"Yes," she said.

"I've never had such a wonderful time in my life," he said.

"Nor I."

"And I—I love you."

"Yes," she said, and she kissed him. "Yes, yes, yes."

He broke from her embrace and left. And she understood that he could no more stand the idea of parting from her than she could stand the parting from him. And she understood, too, that he would come back, and they would get married, that it would be all right, that they had found each other. It was perfect.

Or not quite perfect. A couple of weeks later she found out she was pregnant. The damned dried-out rubber of her damned old diaphragm, which she had not used or thought about for all those years, which had lain in the back of the linen closet on the top shelf in its round plastic case, had betrayed her. Her very abstinence over all those years had betrayed her. The thing had not held, the rubber had cracked somewhere, and with it the round perfection of their idyllic week had cracked, her dreams had cracked, their life together had cracked.

But she had not permitted that to happen. She had refused to call Meredith, to tell him, to force him to marry her. It was too awful to think about under any circumstances, but with an actor, and especially a movie actor, it was just impossible. It was too common. Every tramp and whore in Hollywood tried it, and more of them were successful at it than not. And Carlotta could not bring herself to do anything that even resembled that kind of meanness. She thought, for a while, of having the baby anyway, but that seemed just as bad, or even worse. No, she had to choose between the baby and the man, and she chose the man. She went down to Washington, D.C., where there was an eminent abortionist then practicing, taking care of most of the women on the Eastern seaboard, and she had her abortion. It was a nice, clean abortion, with anesthetic and everything, or at least a local. She could hear the scraping of the curette as she lay on the obstetrical table with her feet spread high in the metal stirrups, but she couldn't feel anything, or only occasionally. Twinges. And one sharp pain. "Sorry," the doctor said, and went right on. It seemed to be all right. On her way to the station for the train back to New York, she saw a billboard with a large sign announcing a bond rally for that night, featuring, among other speakers and performers, Meredith Houseman. She didn't know whether to laugh or cry. She decided, after a couple of drinks in the bar car of the Pennsylvania Railroad club car, that it was probably funny. It was the only thing that she regretted not being able to tell Meredith about.

But it was less funny than it first had seemed. The abortion was not all right, after all. There was an infection that developed, and she went to see her regular gynecologist in New York, who rushed her to the hospital and performed a hysterectomy, taking out everything. In Doctors Hospital, where Merry was born the night before she had met Meredith. She would never, never, never need a diaphragm again.

She had resigned herself to childlessness. She had accepted it, and hardly even thought about it any more. She had told Meredith that she had had an abortion, and a hysterectomy, but she had never told him of his involvement. He, too, accepted their childlessness. But now that little girl, his little girl, was dropping out of the sky, as if the crazy, whimsical world were finally making up to her, in its offhand way, for the death of Mark, Jr., and for the death of that other child that had never even been born, and had never had a name. It was their chance. It was her chance. She said nothing. It was too important, she wanted it too much to say anything, to put it in words. Silently, her lips tight together, she concentrated on the child and on him, in a kind of prayer.

The car pulled up in front of the American Airlines terminal, and the chauffeur ran around and opened the door. Sam, Meredith, and Carlotta climbed out and walked briskly to the information desk.

"Mr. Carlsen's office, please," Sam said.

"Down that corridor, room 112," the hostess replied.

They approached the door. Meredith knew that his mind had been wandering, dragging its heels by seizing upon unlikely and unimportant things, in order not to think about Merry. He was frightened. What if he couldn't stand her? What if he loved her instantly? Either way it could be terrible. How had he let his life get messed up this way? He remembered the moments of high resolve for Merry's future that he had felt when he had seen her through the window of the nursery in the hospital a little while after she was born.

Sam knocked on the door.

"Come in."

They went in.

"Mr. Carlsen?"

"Ah, yes. Mr. Jaggers, of course. And you're Mr. Houseman and . . . is this Mrs. Houseman?"

"Yes," Meredith said.

"The plane is in the landing pattern now, and ought to be on the ground in ten minutes or so. Sit down, won't you? Would you like a drink, or some coffee?"

"No, nothing, thank you."

"Well, I'll leave you alone, then. I'll go down to the plane and meet the youngster, and I'll bring her right here. Will that be all right?"

"Yes, that'll be fine," Sam said.

"Yes, thank you," Meredith said.

Mr. Carlsen disappeared. They sat down in identical chairs—modern, upholstered in blue, matching the rug, the walls, the uniforms. . . . And they waited.

"You arranged it very well," Meredith told Sam.

"They did it. I just told them what we wanted."

"They did it well."

"Yes," Sam said.

"You think I ought to do an endorsement for them? An ad?"

"Maybe. We'll see. Let's think about it."

"OK," Meredith said. "Always cautious, aren't you?"

"Yes."

"Carlotta, what are you thinking?"

"About Merry," she said.

"Of course about Merry. But what else?" he all but snapped.

"Nothing else."

"Oh," he said, chastened.

Ten minutes? It seemed as if hours had passed before Mr. Carlsen came back, but then, suddenly, there he was, with Merry at his side. Meredith looked at her, and she looked at him, and neither spoke for a moment.

"Well, Merry," he said. "It's good to see you."

He had not spoken because he was entirely absorbed in the fantastic resemblance. It wasn't any ordinary thing of her taking after him. She *was* him—had his nose, his eyes, his forehead, his chin. All the features were smaller, of course, and subtly softer, but there they were, and they looked as good on her as they did on him, which was to say very good indeed. It was weird to look at her and see himself, see what he would have been had he been a girl. Then, when he spoke, it was mainly to break the silence, a kind of apology for staring. And yet the amazement was still there, audible to one who was listening for it.

Merry, of course, was listening as carefully as she could. She noted the intensity of his stare, the slight upturning of the lips—in pleasure at seeing her? amusement at her exploit? or was it his habitual expression?—and the slightly throaty voice in which he said, "It's good to see you." Did he have a cold? Or was that real excitement?

Well, nothing ventured, nothing lost. She might try.

And he did look a lot like her, which gave her perhaps just the slightest surge of confidence—enough, anyway, to hazard it. She ran to him, arms wide, and said, "Oh, Daddy!" And it worked, it worked. He opened his arms, and folded her in them, and picked her up, and swung her about the room and kissed her. And when he put her down, Merry could see that the woman with him—her stepmother?—was crying. She had hit the jackpot. It was a whole bag of Novotny's candy.

They hurried out to the car. Merry wanted to sit on one of the jump seats, because she had never been in a limousine before. They asked her about her trip, of course, and she told them, even venturing the truth. She told them how she had heard at a birthday party about plane trips from a friend of hers. Well, not really a friend, but one of the people she saw at birthday parties. Being Meredith Houseman's daughter, she got invited to some good parties, with magicians and clowns, and pony rides and everything. But one of the boys at Harry Sabinson's party had told her about how he had flown from New York to Los Angeles alone. He had a ticket, of course, but nobody ever asked him for it because he was only nine, and they just assumed that he was the son of the man next to him in the plane. He had kept the ticket until Los Angeles and then given it to the stewardess as he got off. And wasn't she surprised! And everybody said that he'd been a jerk, and he should have kept the ticket and should have turned it in for a refund. And he said that that wasn't honest, but what he meant was that he was sorry he hadn't thought of it himself, and so of course he had to say it wasn't honest, as if he had thought of it but decided not to do it. And Merry had been thinking about that for weeks, wondering whether she could just go down to the airport and fly somewhere. And the only place she could think of to fly to was New York, because, after all, she did have a father there whom she hadn't seen for years.

It was funny, and they laughed. No scolding, no

shouting, no whipping. It was all right. Merry relaxed a little. She had the feeling that everything would be all right. They drove back to Manhattan, and to the apartment. Sam came up with them, and waited in the living room while Carlotta and Meredith put Merry to bed. They gave her one of his pajama tops to use as a nightgown, kissed her good night, and tucked her in.

Then Meredith called Elaine again. He had called before when he had heard from Sam that Merry was in Chicago.

"Hello? Yes?" Elaine said.

"Elaine? Meredith. She's here," he said. "She's fine."

"Oh, thank God."

"Yes," he said. "Look," he said, "how about letting her stay here for a while? I haven't seen the child for a long time."

"That's not my fault, is it?"

"No, I suppose not. It's not important, anyway, whose fault it is."

He had tried. He had gone to see her from time to time, when he was in California, and when he could get free for an afternoon, but it wasn't a regular thing, and each time he saw her it upset her, and her being upset upset him. So he had stopped. He sent birthday presents, of course, and Christmas presents, and picture postcards from time to time from odd places, but he had not seen her for nearly three years.

"Well, how long then?"

"A couple of months?"

"No," she said. "No."

"Oh, come on, Elaine, she's my child, too!"

"Come off it! You haven't been interested in her all this time. Suddenly she's important?"

"I'm concerned about her. And I feel guilty, too. But mostly I'm worried. Her running away this way hardly inspires confidence."

"I don't need your confidence. Or want it."

"A month, then?"

"No. Why should I?"

"Look, I have rights, too. I have the right to see her for two weeks a year."

"In July!"

"Be reasonable!"

"For you? Hah!"

He covered the mouthpiece. "Sam," he said, "I can't get anywhere with her. What should I do?"

"Let me," Sam said.

Meredith handed him the phone.

"Hello, Mrs. Novotny? This is Samuel Jaggers. Do you remember me?"

"Yes."

"I was along this evening when Mr. Houseman picked up Merry at the airport, and it was a very moving scene, very moving indeed. They really were quite happy to see each other."

"I don't care about whether Meredith is happy!"

"But she's your daughter!"

"Not Merry! Meredith."

"I beg your pardon. I wonder whether I may speak frankly with you?"

"Why not?"

"Would you consider transferring custody of the child to Mr. Houseman? For a remuneration, I mean."

"Remuneration?"

"Money."

"How much?"

"What would you think fair, Mrs. Novotny?" he asked. Meanwhile, he took a gold pencil from his inside jacket pocket and wrote "$50,000" on the top sheet of the little scratch pad next to the telephone, with a question mark after it. He showed it to Meredith. Meredith nodded yes.

"Just a minute," Elaine said.

Sam covered the mouthpiece of the phone again. "She's discussing it with Novotny," he whispered.

"What sort of figure did you have in mind?" Elaine asked, after her little conference with her husband.

"Twenty-five thousand?" Jaggers suggested.

"Make it twice that," Elaine said, after another pause and, almost certainly, another conference.

"Very well. Fifty it is. Mr. Wemmick, my Los Angeles associate, will call on you in the morning with the appropriate papers and a check. Good night, Mrs. Novotny."

"Incredible!" Carlotta said when Sam had hung up.

"Isn't it?" Sam said. "But now you have to tell me what you want to do. I can have Wemmick go out and get her signature on the papers, and then turn around, take the papers into court, and have them award you custody on the ground that she was willing to sell the child. Or you can pay it."

"Pay it," Meredith said. "I'd rather."

"All right."

"It's bad enough as it is."

"What is?" Carlotta asked.

"My being able to buy the child that way. Fifty thousand dollars is a lot of money to Elaine, and to that animal trainer of hers. But to me it's two or three weeks' work."

"Before taxes," Jaggers said.

"Even so. But you know what I mean."

"Yes," Carlotta said. "Still, I'm glad you did it. I wanted it. Very much."

"I know. I did, too."

"Well, then. Good. It's done," Sam said.

"Thanks, Sam. Thanks . . . I just don't know what to say."

"You don't have to say a thing," he said. "I was glad to be able to help."

Sam left. Meredith and Carlotta went into the guest bedroom—Merry's bedroom now—to look at her again. She heard them coming, got back into bed, and pretended to sleep. They never suspected that she had been listening at the door all the time.

Merry liked the apartment. She did not know, of course, that it was Carlotta's old apartment, and that Meredith and Carlotta kept it only as a *pied-à-terre,* because, with rent control, it cost less than what they would have spent at the Plaza or the Sherry Netherland or the St. Regis in the course of a year. But they were hardly ever there. Nevertheless, for Merry it seemed to be home. And for the first few days it was heaven. There was Central Park right nearby, across Fifth Avenue, and there was F.A.O. Schwartz to go to with Carlotta for toys, and Best's for clothes, and Rumpelmayer's for sodas, after an inspection of the animals in the Central Park zoo. She didn't seriously expect that life would continue this way forever, but on the other hand, she had no idea what to expect, what to imagine. Her father went downtown every morning, and talked, when he came home, about conferences and contracts, and what Sam Jaggers said and what Mr. Kitman said and what Mr. Siegel said and what he had said. And she assumed, not unreasonably, that that was what he did. And made movies, sometimes. But he never seemed to talk about that.

But then, suddenly, he did talk about that. And he was going to make a movie. He seemed very pleased, and he had been very excited when he came home, so she was pleased, too. And he sat down on the edge of her bed and explained to her that he was an actor and that he made movies, and she said, "Yes, I know, Daddy."

"And I have to go where the movies are, where they're getting made. You understand that, don't you?"

"Yes," she said, because nothing could be clearer, and obviously they were all going somewhere, now, to make a movie.

"Well, I have to go to Africa now, to make a movie."

"Yes, Daddy?" He was being slow about it, to stretch it out, the way you hold back on the best thing at meals, sometimes, so that when everything else is gone you have just plain, pure corn on the cob or whatever else it is that you especially like.

"And I'm afraid we're going to have to leave you here," he said.

"All alone?"

He laughed and explained that, no, she would be put in a school, a very good school, a nice one that she'd like. And that he'd be back in eight months or so, and they'd see each other after that. She cried. She told him she wanted to go with him. She begged, even, but he said that the milk wasn't pasteurized.

"I won't drink any milk. I promise. I won't touch it. I don't even like milk that much."

"No, dear, I'm sorry. Africa is just no place for a little girl. Really it isn't. I wish it were. I wish you could come."

And so, after another month, she went into the Stokely School. Another orphanage. Back where she'd started.

CHAPTER FOUR

♥ The cards slapped down on the table. Eight, nine, ten, and one face up. The six of spades.

"Double," Carlotta said.

"Well, I still have a chance, then," Meredith said.

They were playing gin rummy, three games at once, keeping score in boxes. The game was called Hollywood, and, as Meredith said, it was the only trace of Hollywood in the entire production.

He was exaggerating, but not unreasonably. It was hot, hot, hot. And the air was full of the dust of the dried cow dung that the Masai tribesmen used to build their huts. And for fuel, too. No matter how frequently Meredith and Carlotta bathed, there were always the gritty flecks of cow-dung dust floating in the air, settling in their hair, lodging in their clothes. It was awful.

They were less uncomfortable than a great many of the crew members, of course. They had a trailer and an air-conditioner. Inside, it was not so bad. But out in the glare of the sun and the heat of the lights, the flies and the cow dung competed with each other as to which could be the greater nuisance. And the Masai warriors outdid them both. It took so long to get them to do anything. Dennis Frazer translated the director's requests into Swahili, and Richard Mobutu translated from Swahili into the Masai dialect, and then the headman repeated the orders, and invariably they got garbled somewhere along the way. Or were ignored. The wristwatches, for instance. Either the Masai for "No wristwatches" was very like the Masai for "Everybody wear wristwatches," or the warriors just didn't give a damn. But there they were, up on the screen in rushes, the savage tribesmen greeting Cecil Rhodes, and all the goddam savage tribesmen were wearing wristwatches! And the most painful part of it, the funniest part, the best and worst part, was that almost none of the watches told time. They had all rusted out long ago. But the Masai wore them as tokens of civilization.

"We deserve it," Frazer said. "We made them what they are today." Frazer was Sir James Frazer's grandnephew, who vaguely disapproved of the production of which he was a part, and who specifically disapproved of himself.

"I'm glad to hear that," Gerald Lester, the director, answered. "I shouldn't like to think that we'd been gratuitously cursed. We'll shoot it over."

Which meant at least another week in the cow dung and the heat, waiting for the rushes to come back from civilization, and another $50,000 or so tacked onto the costs, which were already beyond the budget and all belief. And Meredith sat in his trailer, playing Hollywood with Carlotta, and losing.

As it turned out, that day's shooting, too, was ruined. There were no wristwatches on any of the Masai—Frazer and Mobutu had seen to that, inspecting them all before the shooting of the retake began—but one of the warriors dropped his loincloth and didn't say anything about it. Maybe he didn't want to get thrown off the film and lose the dollar a day that the company was paying. Or maybe it was a practical joke, a kind of revenge for not being allowed to wear his watch. But in the rushes that came back the next week there were howls of laughter and dismay as, just to Meredith's left and a little behind him, the naked warrior stood with the longest goddamned dong that anyone in the screening room had ever seen.

"Why don't you leave it in? No one will ever believe it, anyway," Frazer suggested.

"Sure," Lester said. "I would, but that damn thing will set American race relations back twenty years. There'll be a wave of lynchings all over the South. All over the world!"

"Again tomorrow, then?" Frazer asked.

"Of course," Lester said. "It's a hell of a business, isn't it?"

"That's for sure," Meredith said. And he went back to the trailer to tell Carlotta.

But for all the craziness of the making of movies, the business of movies is crazier still. It is the manipulation by hundreds of people of millions of dollars in an attempt to please and amuse and entertain an audience of tens of millions, and the most improbable and remote causes produce, perhaps because of the peculiar refraction, sudden, powerful, intimate results. It is like the rays of the sun converging through a lens upon a blade of grass: suddenly the blade of grass chars, smolders, and burns. The lenses of the movie business are like that, and Meredith was in front of a movie lens.

There he was in Africa impersonating Cecil Rhodes and pretending to hack an empire out of the jungle. Ten thousand miles away Milton Berle, impersonating a human being, yelled "Makeup!" got hit in the face with an outsize powder puff, and carved an empire out of another jungle. Television had hit. That curiosity of the 1939 World's Fair, stored on the shelves during the war, had emerged suddenly as a way of life. All over America people were buying television sets, sitting down after dinner to watch Uncle Miltie or Ed Sullivan or old movies—anything at all, because it was right there in their living rooms, and it was free. In Hollywood and in New York the movie executives huddled, chewed their cigars, chewed their fingernails. Their world had fallen apart. Contracts were dropped as the studios cut back on production, pulled in their horns, hoping to ride out the storm. The starlets were the first to be let go. Fox dropped Marilyn Monroe, a bit player and an available date for visiting executives from the East. Joseph Mankiewicz had to plead with Darryl Zanuck to re-hire her so that he could use her in *All About Eve*. She was one of the few to hang on at the bottom.

At the top it was the same song, but louder and more elaborately orchestrated. The studios cut their contract players loose, cut the payroll, cut the overhead. It seemed to be a sensible, economic move. But the effect of that economy was to inflate the sums that actors could command, send the bidding sky-high, and make those actors whom the studios had already established rich beyond the wildest imaginings. Sam Jaggers had committed Meredith to a two-year contract, which was a shorter term than usual. He had been cautious. And lucky. Meredith made four pictures in those two years and then was dropped. His contract was dropped, but he was taken up. His face was familiar; his name was known; he was an attraction, a box-office attraction, something the people in their living rooms would go out to see, put on their shoes and hire a baby-sitter and pay admission to see. The first picture he made after his contract had expired brought him more money than the four pictures he had made under the contract. The second picture brought him twice as much. By the third he was no longer an actor on salary, but a production company, co-producing and sharing the profits. And it was all perfectly reasonable, in its way. After all, what the producer did was to sign Meredith and then take Meredith's signature to the Bank of America, where his commitment to do the picture could be used as collateral to raise two million dollars. Control of that kind of collateral deserved co-production credit and co-production profits.

It also turned Meredith into an exile. A million dollars after taxes in the United States is a little more than a hundred thousand dollars. In Switzerland it is nine hundred thousand dollars. In Monaco it is a million dollars, because there are no taxes. Meredith became a Swiss corporation, with offices in a villa on the Lake of Geneva a little above Montreux. And he had to stay out of the States for three years or pay taxes on all the money he'd earned during all that time.

So he stayed away. Merry came to visit them in the summers, which were as important to him as to her. They were one of the few ties that still held him to the recognizable world. No matter how rich he was and no matter what country he happened to be living in there was something reassuringly familiar and comfortable about the idea of a summer with his wife and daughter, swimming, playing tennis, horseback riding, loafing. He could afford to take it easy and devote his summers to himself and his family. He had reached that enviable pinnacle where he worked only if he wanted to, only if he felt like working. Never again, for the rest of his life, would he have to do anything—not, anyway, for money. There was a trust fund for Merry, another for Carlotta, and they each had shares in the production company which was the corporate form of himself. They were all millionaires.

There he was, on the screen, big as life. In the

close-ups he was bigger than life. Pith helmet on his head and trusty native bearers at his side, he greeted the savage warriors with rubber balls, bouncing them high into the air. And the innocent savages scrambled for the rubber balls, and Cecil Rhodes had triumphed once again. Merry laughed. It was a funny scene. Not all that funny, not worth seeing a fourth or fifth time, but funny enough. He was not attending to the picture, really, but to Merry, sitting beside him in the screening room he had had built in the west wing of the villa. What he enjoyed was her enjoyment. The pictures he could hardly stand. He came out of these home screenings feeling invariably depressed. They were such a flimsy excuse for all the money, for all the fame, for all the success that had come to him in such oppressive abundance. It was almost as if the luxury with which the world rewarded him for his parts in these really indifferent movies was a kind of sarcastic comment, so exaggerated as to be meaningless. Not that he was a puritanical soul who equated meaningfulness with virtue. It was just that his success was beyond belief—belief in it, in the movies, in himself. And so he clung to Carlotta and Merry and for Merry's sake endured another showing of *Rhodes*.

When it was over, Philippe raised the houselights slowly. It had been ridiculous to put a rheostat in a home screening room, but there it was, along with the motorized curtain and the motorized draw draperies that covered the wall of windows. But Merry liked it, and she applauded, which was ridiculous, too, but sweet.

"Thank you, Philippe," Meredith said.

"Monsieur," Philippe said from the projection booth. He came out to open the door for them.

"All right, off to bed now," Meredith said.

"You'll tuck me in?" Merry asked.

"Sure."

She was already in her pajamas and bathrobe. They

walked through the hall to the living room, where Merry kissed Carlotta good night, and then they went upstairs to Merry's bedroom. He tucked her in, kissed her good night, and went downstairs again to Carlotta.

"More coffee?" she asked.

"Yes, thanks."

She poured a fresh cup from the silver coffeepot on the tray before her, put in the cream and sugar, and handed it to him.

"Thanks," he said again. "Well?"

"Well?"

"I don't know," he said. "I just don't know. It's all so mixed up. I just don't know what to do."

"The thing is to do what's best for her," Carlotta said, as if it were simple.

"Of course. But she wants so much to stay here with us. And how do I know what's best? I mean sending her back to school seems to be the right thing, but only because it's exactly what I don't want to do and what she doesn't want, either. It's the old business about any food that tastes terrible must be healthy as hell. And it just doesn't work. Or at least it doesn't always work."

"But you remember what you told me yourself at the beginning of the summer."

"Yes, I remember," he said. He took a sip of the coffee and put it down. He didn't want coffee anyway. Or a drink, or a cigarette, or anything but to keep Merry with him. But she was right. He had rejoiced at the beginning of the summer when Merry had appeared at the Geneva airport, a pudgy little girl, suddenly awkward and shy, and looking less like him than she ever had before. He'd been depressed at first by the way in which her childish beauty had blurred and faded, but then Carlotta had assured him that it was perfectly normal and that in a couple of years she would be more beautiful than ever. And that had depressed him even more, because of the awful glimpse it had given him into his deepest thoughts about his own life. One of the things he had wanted most in life was a feeling of closeness with his children, and here he had a child, a bright, attractive child, and he could not get close to her but had to protect her from himself and his life for her own good. She was rich, but she didn't know that and couldn't know it. The tinselly glamour of a movie star's life was something he tried to keep away from her in the same way that he tried to keep impure water or unpasteurized milk or hazardous machinery away from her. They had put her into that school, originally, to keep from her the burdens of his work, the continual moving around, the vague, gypsy-like life of an actor. But now they were keeping her there to protect her from the fruits of his work, the indolence, the rootlessness, the continual self-indulgence of it. He wanted her to know what work was, to know what a routine was, and to have some order and sense in her existence, and he knew that she wouldn't find it with them. He had said all that at the beginning of the summer in long talks with Carlotta after Merry had gone to bed, tearing each painful admission out of himself and hoping that Carlotta would find some reason to disagree with him, to show him that he was wrong, was mistaken, had somehow overlooked something, and that he was talking foolishness. But no, she had agreed. Sadly, sympathetically, and as understandingly as she could, she had agreed with him. And it had been settled. But that had been at the beginning of the summer. Now at the end of it, after the good times they had had together on the lake, riding on the back roads that went up into the mountains, which began to look a little like the Montana mountains after you got away from the neat little farms and vineyards, now he wasn't so sure.

"But she wants to stay," he said again. "She wants so much to stay. And isn't it just possible that by sending her away again we're hurting her more?"

"It's possible," Carlotta said.

"Well?"

"Well, where will you be—where will we be this fall?"

"I don't know," he said. "Right here."

"What about Venice for the festival? What about New York for the opening of *Two Brave Men?* What about skiing at Cortina d'Ampezzo? Are you going to pass it all up this year?"

"We can take her along."

"With a tutor?"

"Sure, why not."

"Because it'd ruin her, and you know it. She's got to have some kind of sense to her life. We love her, but love isn't enough. It just isn't."

"Do you? Do you love her?"

"Yes. You know I do."

"Then how can you talk this way? How can you send her back so lightly?"

"It isn't lightly. You know it isn't."

"I'm sorry," he said. He had gone too far. He sat there silently, regretting that he had put himself into the wrong, not so much for the wrong itself as for its effect on the argument, as if it were an encounter of adversaries and not a mutual discussion between husband and wife. No, no, that wasn't the way to think of it at all. He would begin again. Start fresh. Think.

And then he made a suggestion out of nowhere, surprising even himself. "Why don't we adopt a child? It'd be good for Merry, but it'd be good for us, too. We can certainly afford it, and it'd give us something at the center of our lives . . . I don't know why we never thought of it before."

"No."

"Why not?"

"Just no. Isn't that enough?"

"No," he said. "It isn't."

"I don't want to," she said.

"But why not?" he asked. "Just because you had an

abortion once, does that mean that our lives have to be ruined by it? What has it got to do with us, anyway?"

"It has to do with us," she said.

"How? You had some fling with some son of a bitch, and we've got to pay for it? I don't see it. Look, I'm sorry about the abortion, and I'm sorry about the hysterectomy. But can't you understand that that's past, that it's part of the past and that we don't have anything to do with that? I don't."

"Yes," she said. "You do."

"I?"

"You were that son of a bitch."

"What? But why? For God's sake, why?"

She told him when it had happened and how it had happened, which was as close as she could come to why it had happened, close enough, anyway, so that he could understand a little and could accept the weight of it, like rocks on his chest. He could hardly breathe.

"Oh, my God!"

"And so you see," she said, as if continuing a perfectly reasonable, perfectly ordinary conversation, "I really was glad when Merry came and we got her, and I do love her and think of her as our child. I do love her, I do."

"Yes," he said. "I know that. I know that now."

"And all I want is what's best for her."

"All right," he said. "All right."

"It's awful, isn't it?"

"Yes," he said. "But what shall I tell her? She'll be so unhappy about it."

"Tell her—tell her that we discussed it and that I thought it would be better for you."

"But she'll hate you for that."

"She'll get over it. The important thing is that she shouldn't hate you. Not now. It's very important for a pubescent girl to have a good relationship with her father."

"You sound like you've been reading books on the subject."

"I have."

"You're wonderful," he said, and he managed a smile. But it was difficult, because the weight of those boulders was still pressing down on his chest. He felt as though his lungs would burst, as though his heart would break.

Or, no, it was not that bad. It was not that total, for somewhere the fabric of his grief had snagged on something. Something that Carlotta had said. What was it? Oh, yes.

"What do you mean, 'pubescent'?" he asked.

"Arriving at puberty," Carlotta said. "She menstruated last week."

"She did? Did you . . ."

"I explained it all to her, and we had a long talk. She was very calm about it and more interested in a curious intellectual way than anything else. She's a bright youngster, you know."

"Yes," Meredith said. "She is."

"She did say one funny thing."

"Oh?"

"Well, I explained to her about intercourse, and she listened very gravely to the whole thing. And then she asked quite seriously, 'But why would anybody want to do *that?*' And I couldn't think of any good reason."

Meredith laughed. "Why would anyone want to do that, indeed?" he repeated. "Come on," he suggested, "let's go for a walk by the lake."

The next morning after breakfast Meredith told Merry that he and Carlotta had talked it over and had decided that, really, the best thing for Merry was for her to go back to school in the States.

"You and she decided?" Merry asked.

"Yes."

"Or just she?"

"Both of us," he said.

"But she was the one who thought I should go back, wasn't she?"

"I agreed with her."

"But she was the one."

Meredith thought for a moment. It was such a lousy thing to do, to put the blame on Carlotta that way. And yet he remembered what she had said about the importance of his relationship with Merry. And it was true, after all. "Yes," he said.

"I thought so," she said.

There were no tears, no outbursts, nor even sulks, but Merry was rather aloof and distant for the few days that remained of her visit. She was perfectly polite, answered when she was spoken to, and seemed normal, but still not quite normal. It was as if she were not almost thirteen years old at all, but much older. Carlotta said that it would be better if she did cry, if she did have a tantrum to let it out, somehow. But she didn't. Nothing.

It was Carlotta, herself, who was on the verge of tears. Her own child, her little boy, her son, had been killed. The other child, hers and Meredith's, she had murdered because of her pride. It had seemed, at the time, the right thing to do. But later, it had all gone wrong. And now, the young girl she thought of as her daughter, the girl whom she loved as a daughter, felt rejected, was not able to understand that what Carlotta had done had been done for her sake and not for any other reason than love. She remembered how, at the airport, Merry had not kissed her good-bye. No one could have noticed. Any observer would have supposed that it was only inadvertence and the confusion of a departure. But Carlotta had felt it, and felt it still. There were tears, always, waiting to well up in her eyes at the least cause. For no cause at all. It was like the depression she had gone through after the death. After both deaths. And what made it all the worse was that she relied now entirely upon Meredith. There was no other purpose, or cause, or excuse for her existence. And he had seemed broody and withdrawn ever since she had confided in him, and told him the one thing she had promised herself she would never tell. He seemed gloomy now and depressed. Perhaps, she thought, he only seemed so to her because she was depressed. She hoped so.

"Rosenberg! MacArthur! Kefauver! Truman! I tell you we gotta have gash."

"Well, we had Ethel Rosenberg, too."

"Great! I can just imagine cub scouts all over America jerking off to a picture of Ethel Rosenberg."

"Cub scouts don't jerk off. It's boy scouts."

"You were a slow boy, that's all."

"How about a cover on boy scouts?"

"Terrific! That's the best idea since somebody thought up a cover on athlete's foot! Was that you?"

"How about a cover on syphilis?"

"Syphilitic boy scouts? There's an expose!"

"Gash, I tell you. Gash. At least syphilitic girl scouts."

"Same thing. Where the hell do you think the boy scouts get it?"

"From other boy scouts."

"J. D. Salinger?"

"Who dat?"

"Come on, now. The newest light on the literary scene."

"Writers are boring. All they do is write."

"Editors are boring. All they do is bullshit."

"Moom pitchers?"

"What?"

"Moom pitchers. You know. Like movies."

"Wise ass. Who?"

"Barbara Steele."

"You were better with the cub scouts."

"I don't know. What's opening?"

"Two Brave Men."

"Who's got the lead?"

"Meredith Houseman."

"The girl, the girl. What's the matter with you? Gash!"

"Linda Forbes."

"Time did her last year."

"What else is there?"

"Up the Stairs."

"Up your ass."

"Jane Robbins?"

"Newsweek did her."

"How about Rock Hudson?"

"Stark Naked."

"Harold Tribune."

"I know, I know. Hey, Scott Tissue?"

"So, where are we?"

"Mad Ave., buddy boy."

"Houseman?"

"Gash, I said."

"How about Houseman with a background showing all his leading ladies. That way you get about six girls for your one quarter."

"Houseman any good?"

"He's all right. Ladies like him. Clean smile and all that crap."

"OK, so Houseman, and then the transcontinental TV hookup or the Jap treaty. OK?"

"Sure. Say, how about a piece on athlete's foot in medicine. Inside, I mean."

"We can art it with your foot, I suppose?"

"Up to the knee. But seriously . . ."

"Sure, why not? Let's do it."

PROSTRONG EXMOVIES. COVER UPCOMING ON MEREDITH HOUSEMAN PEGGED ADOPENING TWO

BRAVE MEN. NEED FULL BIOPERSE ETBACKGROUND. INVU. COLOR QUOTES. HOUSEMAN NOW IN MONTREUX. MAILER BY 9/30. ART POUCHLY TO PHOTO BY 9/27. REGARDS. TOURNEUR.

The Western Union machine punched the message out on the yellow paper, and Claude brought it into Jocelyn's cubby. She looked at it, tapped her front teeth with the end of her ballpoint desk pen, and smiled.

Houseman had marked the moment of her move from research into writing, from the old job to the new one with *Pulse,* from her apprenticeship to her standing as full journeyman journalist. He had not had anything directly to do with it, but he was, nevertheless, a memento of her moment of success. It was the war that had actually enabled her to buck the odds—the magazines' dislike of women writers—changing those odds by gobbling up all the men. And she had hung on, so that when the war ended, that old dislike of females had helped her, too, enabling her to get out of the home office and out to a bureau. To Paris. Not too tough to take. The Paris bureau was a nice place to work. It was busy, but that was fine, because everyone had too much to do to look over anyone else's shoulder. And each of them had a beat. Jack Shaw covered politics. Marvin Federman covered business, economics, and the Marshall Plan. She and Harvard Wetherill covered back-of-the-book stuff—religion, education, science, sports, and culture. Movies, for instance. It had never occurred to her that she might one day have to go out and interview Houseman. She was not sentimental that way. But now it seemed a fine idea. How long had it been? Thirteen years? She was curious to see how he had weathered in that time.

She went into Shaw's office to tell him about Tourneur's query and to set up with him the dates for the Montreux trip.

"Any time you like," he said.

"Tomorrow?"

"Fine," he said. "Have fun."

"Thanks."

She went back to her cubby, picked up the phone, and called Meredith Houseman in Montreux. "Meredith?" she said. "Jocelyn."

"Jocelyn?"

"Jocelyn Strong?" she said, with a questioning inflection which managed to say very effectively, "Surely, darling, you remember *me*."

"Oh, yes. Sure. Uh, how are you?"

"Just fine thanks," she said, paused for a fraction of a second to let him squirm just a little more, and then let him off the hook, saying, "Actually, I'm calling for *Pulse*. They want to do a cover story about you, pegged to the opening of *Two Brave Men*, and I've been asked to come down and talk to you. When would be convenient?"

"Come down here?"

"Yes. If you don't mind, that is."

"No. I don't mind. I mean sure, fine. Any time. We'll be here another three weeks or so."

"Tomorrow?"

"Fine. Sure."

"It'll be nice to see you again," she said, choosing her words carefully. "Nice" was wonderfully prissy, so coy, so very bland, and yet so catty. Not that she had anything to be catty about. It was just the fun of it, the game, the pleasure of pure play.

"Carlotta and I will be glad to have you. You'll stay with us, of course."

"I can put up at a hotel if you'd prefer. *Pulse* pays, you know."

"No, no, I wouldn't hear of it."

"Well, if you don't mind, it would make things easier."

"Don't mind at all."

"Good. Wonderful. I'll get to Montreux sometime tomorrow evening."

"Call us when you get in. I'll send the car."

"Lovely," she said. "Will do."

She drew a hundred thousand francs—about three hundred dollars—from petty cash, sent Claude out to get her train tickets, and went home to pack. It didn't take her long to throw a few things together into a light traveling case. She had had sufficient practice at it, and knew what she could get along without, which is the key to successful packing. She was a pattern of brisk efficiency, except for an instant when she picked up her diaphragm. Picking it up was merely habit. But she did pause, just for a moment, wondering if it would get used. But it was only a moment. She tucked it into the case and went to get the steno pad on which she took notes for the files she sent back to New York.

Freddie Grindell sipped a Campari and soda on the terrace that overlooked the lake, and although he listened to what Meredith was saying, his eyes were closed, and his head was turned toward the sun so that his eyelids were beautifully red as the sun shone through them. Still, he was listening to Meredith go on about Venice, rehearsing, really, for his interview. It was silly, actually. Meredith had spent two weeks at the festival and all he had to talk about was the movies. Anybody could go to see the movies. The thing was the people. And Meredith had almost no gossip. Carlotta would have that. It was curious, really, but he enjoyed the company of women immensely more than the company of men. Even Meredith Houseman. Gorgeous, of course, but so dull to have to listen to for long periods of time. He wondered what Carlotta found to talk with him about. Or maybe they didn't talk. Maybe they just fucked all the time. No, he was being bitchy. They found things to talk about. He knew that he and Meredith would find things to talk about, too, if he turned Meredith on. Just the littlest bit. A little bit was supposed to be normal. But he was repressing. Freddie could feel that Meredith was repressing. That was one of the disadvantages of being a notorious queer. Or seminotorious. There were advantages, too. He was a great escort, much in demand at all the best places. What could be safer for a woman's reputation—a woman, say, with a husband out of town, or a freshly widowed widow—than to be seen with Freddie Grindell? But one pays for everything. Here was Houseman, for instance, being almost offensively mannish, businesslike, brisk, as if he were afraid that at any moment little Freddie would come bounding across the terrace to pounce upon his fly. Absurd. As if he didn't know the old bit about not shitting where you eat, which applied to the kinky as well as to the straight. Or even more to the kinky. And this was business.

Not that there was any real work to do. Oh, sure, the studio was all excited and they'd had him fly up from Rome to be with Houseman when the *Pulse* reporter arrived, but all he had to do was to sit around and smile and make sure the reporter was happy. The story would be upbeat and complimentary. Cover stories almost always were. It was as if the cover was such a wonderful accolade that the editors had to keep inventing new superlatives in order to justify their choice of a subject. They turned the thing into a nomination for the Nobel Prize. It was just *Time* upside down. *Time* turned Nobel Prize winners into saps.

So all he had to do was relax. Or was that all? If he pretended, say, that some assassin from *Time* was coming down, stiletto in hand, then the thing he'd have to do would be to anticipate the reporter, imagine the impression that Meredith and Carlotta would make on him, and try to leap through the improbabilities of the editorial process to the finished story. And that impression was puzzling. There was something askew. The surface was perfectly calm, but he didn't believe it. It was too calm. For no reason that he could find to support the hunch, he still had the nagging feeling that something was wrong, somehow, between Carlotta and Meredith, and the surface of good manners was their disguise. For *Pulse?* For him? For each other?

He would have to wait and see. And he would have to hope that he would see it before the reporter did.

He forced his attention back to what Meredith was saying. It was about neorealism and the new Italian movies, and how the Americans ought to be doing things like that. Well, it'd be good copy for *Pulse*. They could present him as the sensitive, intelligent type. And if Meredith had to warm up by rehearsing with him, he didn't mind. He only wished he had one of those reflectors to put under his chin. The rays of the late-afternoon sun really weren't very strong.

Carlotta came out onto the terrace and Freddie forgot about the sun. She would be full of news about what people had got drunk, and who had insulted whom, and who had seduced whom, and whose parties had been terrible and whose had been good—the important news about a film festival. He got up and adjusted the angle of his chair so that he would no longer be facing into the sun. That was just the pretext. The point had been only to get up and yet not to do it in such a way that it would show up Meredith if he didn't get up for Carlotta, which he didn't. Freddie did not do this for Carlotta or for Meredith, but for himself, for the practice. He knew that the other thing that people said about him was that he had the best manners in the world.

But Carlotta did not sit down and tell amusing stories about Venice. She simply announced that Jocelyn was on the phone and was calling from the station.

"I'll go in and talk to her," Meredith said, and he went in.

"Tell me about Venice," Freddie suggested to Carlotta.

She seemed tense. Why? "All the deliciously scandalous things that must have happened."

"Oh, it was about usual."

"That's very vivid."

"I'm sorry," she said. "I was thinking about something else."

"I rather gathered that," he said.

"Actually, I suppose it's your business as much as mine. Or almost as much."

"Your business is my business."

"Not always, but this time it looks as though it is."

"Oh?" he asked. "Let me guess. Jocelyn?"

"Did he tell you?"

"No."

"Then how did you . . ."

"How did I guess? Because he didn't tell me. He hasn't said a word. And yet, obviously, you know her."

"How is it obvious?"

"Well, you called her by her first name. That'd be odd if it were a reporter you'd never met before dropping down out of the sky. And Meredith didn't mention that he knew her, so obviously he doesn't know her casually."

"Yes, well, that's it."

"Long ago?"

"Before we were married. Twelve—no, thirteen years ago."

"But he's told you about it. Or did you just 'find out'?"

"No, he told me."

"Then you have nothing to worry about, I shouldn't think. But I do. Oh, dear."

"You do?"

"If you don't, then I do!"

"If I don't what?"

"Have to worry. Obviously Meredith isn't interested in her any more. He's told you about her. But that'll be obvious to her, too, won't it? And she may not like that. And that'd be bad for the cover story, don't you see?"

"I suppose so," she said.

"Well, it's plain as day. I'm in terrible trouble," he said, with a look of exaggerated distress.

"One of us is," she said.

It was a perfectly plausible rejoinder. A funny traded for a funny. But the look of concentration on her face was not at all exaggerated. In fact, she was trying to hide it. And it was not funny at all.

If she was worried, then there was something to worry about. She was not a silly woman. He noted this and entered it in his personal system of double-entry bookkeeping. He was concerned for her sake, because he liked her. But he was not unaware that if the piece turned out badly he had an excuse now.

It wasn't Jocelyn herself, but the timing of her arrival. That was what bothered Carlotta. Merry's departure, and her discussion with Meredith afterward about the abortion and the hysterectomy were both too fresh for the scar tissue to have formed. There were raw nerves exposed everywhere, Meredith's and her own. And Jocelyn was like salt on the rawness. Even inadvertently she managed to wound. Her comment to Carlotta about Freddie, for instance, had to be innocent because Carlotta could not conceive of her knowing. Could not conceive. Exactly. Exactly. And as a joke, or just as an exercise in idle cruelty, she had quipped, "Freddie is such fun. I think it was a ballerina who told me that she always liked to have a queer around to light her cigarettes and run out for Tampax." And the quick smile and the little tinkly laugh. Oh, it was awful! They had spent the evening in the living room, drinking Cointreau and coffee, and talking. She and Freddie had been at one end of the room, keeping out of Meredith and Jocelyn's way so that they could continue with their interview. And Freddie had babbled on, amusingly, charmingly, and stupidly. No, it was not his fault either. It was just that, perhaps for no reason at all, she had had the feeling that the two whole, healthy people were over there and the two cripples, the two maimed ones, were over here, and that she and Freddie were on the wrong side of the fence. The barbed wire. She remembered reading about Dr. Mengele in one of those concentration camps and how he would nod either to the left or to the right and one way was death and the other way was life—wretched, but still life. And she couldn't get it out of her mind that a Mengele would nod toward life for Meredith and for Jocelyn and toward death for Freddie and for her. And then, at the end of the evening, Jocelyn's nasty little crack.

But it wasn't Jocelyn. She kept telling herself that and believed it, too. It wasn't Jocelyn at all. Which made it worse. Any woman, any competent, efficient, successful woman, coming into the house with all that self-assurance and pertness and at this time would have had the same effect.

And yet despite all this, despite her understanding that it wasn't Jocelyn at all, and that Jocelyn couldn't possibly have meant anything by the remark, she had to answer it. Not just for Freddie's sake, or not even for Freddie's sake at all, but because of the quite innocent aspersion upon herself. She certainly didn't send Freddie out to buy Tampax, for she didn't use Tampax.

It was all perfectly ridiculous, and yet she couldn't just let it pass. So she said, "That's rather a cruel remark, don't you think?"

"I suppose. A little," Jocelyn admitted.

It was enough. She should have let it go, then. But she didn't.

"Well, I don't much like that kind of thing," she said.

"I beg your pardon," Jocelyn said. It was, of course, a declaration of war. Her tone made that perfectly clear. And she made her move with incredible speed. Meredith came back from turning lights out around the first floor, and she asked him for a towel.

"A towel? Sure. But what for?"

"I thought I'd go for a swim," she said. "I mean with the lake right there at the bottom of the lawn, it's so tempting, don't you think?"

"I guess we've gotten used to it," Meredith said. "But sure, why don't we all go for a swim?"

She had no choice but to show Jocelyn that she was not at all concerned, wasn't worried in the slightest. Her trivial challenge was hardly worth picking up.

"No, I don't think so. Actually, I have a little headache, I'm afraid," Carlotta said.

"Freddie?" Meredith asked.

"Now?"

"Why not?" Meredith asked. Carlotta stared at him, and shook her head ever so slightly. No. He caught it. Oh, clever Freddie. Reliable Freddie. That ballerina was right after all.

"No, I guess not."

So it was clear enough. Let them go off together, swim together, have all the lousy opportunity they could want. She didn't care and could prove it. Had proved it. She and Freddie went upstairs, leaving Jocelyn in the hallway waiting for Meredith, who was off getting towels. At the top of the stairway she stopped and listened. Freddie stopped, too. They were eavesdropping, quite openly. Neither had to ask the other to keep still. They stood there and listened to Meredith ask, "What about suits?"

"Oh, really!" Jocelyn said.

She opened the door and went outside. Meredith hesitated for a moment and then followed her.

"Why didn't you let me go with them?" Freddie asked.

"I didn't feel like it," she said.

"I hope you know what you're doing," he said.

"No, I don't. I don't know. And I don't care."

"If you don't care, I don't suppose it makes any difference."

"But I don't not care. I can't not care. I wish I could."

"I hate to be forward," said Freddie, "but would you like to go for a walk?"

"Yes," she said. "It might help clear my head."

She kicked off her shoes, and Freddie took off his, and then they went outside. They were careful to turn the hall light off before they opened the door, so that the shaft of light from the doorway would not give them away. Silently on stocking feet they walked over the well-kept grass toward the lake, but angling left to the clump of mock orange that grew near the dock. At the mock orange Carlotta stopped.

"I'll go ahead alone," Freddie said.

"All right."

She waited. He was gone for a few minutes, and she felt like laughing. It was all so silly, so very childish and silly. But she didn't laugh.

Then Freddie returned. "I'm afraid that we ought to go back," he said, barely whispering, only forming the words with his mouth and letting her lip-read as much as hear.

"No," she said. "Wait here."

"Don't."

"Wait here," she repeated.

She went down toward the lake in the direction from which Freddie had just come. There was a quarter moon, but the faint light was intensified a little by the reflections from the water. Even so, she did not see anything for a while. No, over there, on the grass beyond the dock, there was something white that moved. She went toward it stealthily over the black grass. And then she saw it. Them. And thought how very curious it was that she didn't feel anything more. She kept thinking of what she was supposed to feel, having seen them like that, *in flagrante,* as the elegant phrase had it. But she didn't feel anything except a very mild curiosity mixed with a very slight disgust. It was rather less affecting than the sight that she remembered of a swarm of horseshoe crabs mating one May on the beach in Maine. She stood there, conscious of the faint breeze that ruffled her hair, thinking that they were probably chilly, and then realizing that she ought to feel embarrassment of some kind, but didn't. Mainly because she thought of Freddie hiding behind the bush and what he might be thinking of her, she went back. They returned to the house together.

"I'm sorry," Freddie said.

"Well, it'll be a nice cover story."

"That's not important, is it?"

"You're sweet," she said.

"That's basically my problem," he said.

He went to his room, and she went to hers and lay down. She lay awake, wondering what was the matter with her. She seemed to herself to be some kind of monster. It occurred to her that she could take a gun, run back out there, kill them both, and probably be acquitted because of the blind, nearly insane rage that it would be assumed she must have felt. But there was no rage. There was nothing.

She heard them come in. She heard Jocelyn go up to her room, but Meredith stayed downstairs. Was he afraid of coming up to his own room, and his own wife, in his own bed? Was he waiting until she fell asleep? Or was he feeling guilty? Or proud of himself, like the prize stallion of the pasture? She lay there very still, listening to him. She heard the clink of ice in a glass. It was a long time before she heard anything else. He was coming upstairs. He came into the room and started to undress. How very complicated. He'd had to get dressed so that he could come in here and get undressed. She suppressed a giggle.

"Darling?"

She said nothing.

"Carlotta? Are you awake?"

Nothing.

"Carlotta? Nothing happened. We just went swimming. That's all."

The lying angered her more than the laying. She lay there, silent, and he gave up. He got into bed and fell asleep promptly. Of course. He always fell asleep easily after making love.

It was nearly dawn before Carlotta drifted off.

In the morning she was still depressed. She blamed it on her sleepless night and stayed in bed for a long time. She had the maid bring her breakfast in bed and still did not get up. It would be so nice, she thought, just to snuggle down into the covers and never get up. But there was a knock at her bedroom door. A funny little series of three short raps.

"Freddie?"

"Yes. Are you decent?"

"Yes. Come in."

"How did you know it was me?"

"I didn't. I just guessed."

"I'm afraid I have some unpleasant news for you."

"Surely you jest."

"No. Jocelyn wants to talk to you."

"Oh, God. Whatever for?"

"For the story. What else?"

"Indeed. What else?"

"Well?"

"Not this morning. Tell her I still have that headache. Tell her this afternoon, maybe, or tomorrow. As soon as I feel better."

"OK. I'll tell her."

He did, and came back to tell Carlotta that he had set it up for the next morning.

"Thank you."

"Just doin' mah job."

"You do it very well. But how about relaxing from your job a little?"

"Whenever I can."

"Now. Let's . . . I don't know. Let's play some gin rummy or something."

"Love it. I'll go get some cards," he said.

"Get the vodka, too."

"Now you're talking," he said.

He got the cards and the vodka and they played gin rummy and drank, and Freddie told his amusing stories and made his affable conversation. It struck Carlotta that in a curious way what she was doing was quite improper, at least in appearance. Lying around in bed and drinking with a man in her room. Quite dissolute, really. Or it would be if Freddie were a man. And if she were a woman. She had never been unfaithful to Meredith, mainly because it would have been so easy and so safe. But after several games and five or six drinks, it seemed hideously unfair. She didn't know quite what it was that seemed unfair, but it did. Everything did. That she should be there with Freddie. That Freddie should be there with her. That they should be stuck with each other, two rejects on the human assembly line. It was damned unfair.

"Freddie," she said abruptly, "have you always been queer?"

"I beg your pardon?"

"Or, that's not what I meant. I meant . . . I mean, are you exclusively queer?"

"What brings this on?" he asked, rather coolly.

"I'm afraid I'm being very clumsy about this."

"Yes," he said.

"Come on," she said. "In here."

"In your bed?"

"Is it such a repellent idea?"

"No, of course not," he said. Rather stiffly he stood up and undressed. She wondered if he wasn't still being polite and understanding, good old Freddie. Well, he deserved better than to be sent out for Tampax. He got into bed with her, and she kissed him. He seemed to respond, kissed her, touched her breast, even, if rather tentatively, held her. They embraced and kissed for a long time. She had to play with him, though, to arouse him, to get him hard enough. And then he got into her, and she thought it would be all right. But it wasn't, because he couldn't come, and she realized this and felt sorry for him, felt his embarrassment, felt embarrassed herself for having forced him into this. Into this? Into her. And so they lay locked together in useless, pointless, endless embrace, in passionless passion. He stopped thrusting and just lay there, and she stroked the back of his head and said, "Dear Freddie. Dear, dear Freddie," and she felt him shrinking, shriveling, and finally slipping out of her, and again she said, "Dear Freddie. Thank you."

"Good old Freddie," he said, as brightly as he could. He dressed and left her. She heard him go into his room, and then she heard the shower start. He had hated it. He was trying to bathe himself clean from her. Poor Freddie. Poor dear Freddie. And she had made him do it. What a horrible thing. Had it been out of pity for her? Or had he done it as part of his job? Either way it was just too dreadful, too, too dreadful. She lay there and wondered why she could not weep, why her eyes were dry, what had happened to her so that she did not seem to be able to feel anything any more.

Her body was washed up on shore half a mile or so down the lake. Apparently she had swum out until she was exhausted, and then had just gone under. It was very strange, because she was not much of a swimmer, never had done any long-distance swimming, never expressed any interest in it at all. Even so, accidents of that sort do happen, as the chief inspector of police said.

Meredith was stunned. He walked around as if in a daze and let Freddie handle all the details. Freddie sent out the press releases, arranged for the funeral, took care of everything. Good old Freddie. He also burned the note she had left: "Freddie, I'm sorry. C." He burned it in the ashtray in his bedroom and flushed the ashes down the toilet.

Pulse canceled the cover story. They took the material on athlete's foot, broadened it out a little, and called it "The World of the Fungus" with a microphotograph of colorful fungi on the cover. Jocelyn's file went into the morgue, in a large brown envelope marked "Houseman, Meredith—Actor."

CHAPTER

FIVE

♥ It was Miss Preston's firm conviction that the rich were frequently as underprivileged as the poor, and this conviction was what she invoked in order to balance her dislike for many of her girls. It was good work that she was doing, and that the school was doing—a kind of charity actually. And if the recipients of this charity were often millionaires, they needed it none the less. How many of these youngsters had been entrusted to the loveless ministrations of nurses and governesses! How many of them came from broken homes! How many of them, in the crisis of identity that is part of adolescence, seized upon their wealth as a kind of cloak in which they could hide themselves from themselves! When she considered all these things, she realized how very much they needed the Mather School and her own leadership and guidance. It was gratifying to work with those youngsters she liked; and it was challenging to work with those she didn't. And potentially even more gratifying when she had succeeded in civilizing them, in educating them, in rebuilding them into responsive, responsible young ladies.

Miss Preston considered all these things, composing herself at her desk in her apartment in the main building. On the desk before her was the notation she had made of Mr. Jaggers' telephone call. On the coffee table in the living room there were cups and saucers and a plate full of cookies. Jacqueline brought in the pot of cocoa, put it down on the tray beside the two cups, and announced to Miss Preston that it was all ready.

"Thank you, Jacqueline," Miss Preston said.

Everything was ready. It was a more sensible ritual than the hearty meal that condemned men were supposed to eat. The cocoa and cookies for the daughters of the deceased were tokens of sympathy, gentle hints that life must continue, and, not incidentally, an opportunity for her to reach even the most difficult girls. And Meredith Houseman was one of those most difficult girls. Miss Preston, therefore, was glad—not that Meredith's stepmother was dead, of course, but that she, Miss Preston, would be the one to break the news to Meredith. And perhaps get through to her, see her open up a little, reach her and help her. Of the fact that Meredith needed help Miss Preston was quite certain, and she considered her instinctive dislike of the girl proof. So self-contained, so cool, so aloof! It was incredible in a thirteen-year-old. And distasteful, as the wearing of lipstick or eye shadow at that age would be distasteful.

There was a knock at the door. Miss Preston took a deep breath, got up and went to let Merry in.

"Come in, Meredith," she said. She always called the girls by their proper names.

"Thank you," Merry said.

"Won't you sit down?" Miss Preston suggested. Merry sat down on the couch the headmistress' extended arm had indicated. Miss Preston sat down beside her. The girl looked at her, but the look betrayed nothing, not even curiosity. Polite attentiveness at the most. "I'm afraid I have some bad news for you, my dear," she began.

"Yes?" she asked, but still showing nothing, hardly moving her eyes, her lips, her forehead.

"Your stepmother is dead," she said.

Not a quiver. Nothing but "Oh?" rising, pleasantly modulated. And then, "How?"

"She drowned, I'm afraid."

"Odd."

"Odd? How so?"

"She was never much of a swimmer. I mean she didn't swim much. What did she do, fall off a boat?"

"No. Apparently she went for a swim and got a cramp or something. They're not quite sure. She was alone, you see."

"She went for a swim alone?"

"Apparently."

"Unlikely."

"What do you mean?"

"Nothing. Just that. It seems unlikely," Merry said.

"Oh?" Miss Preston prompted, but the youngster said nothing more. "Would you like a cup of cocoa?"

"No, thank you. The doctor says I should stop having snacks."

"I'm sure he'd understand if, at a time like this . . ."

"A time like this? She didn't like me very much. And I don't think I liked her much at all. Not enough for a cup of cocoa. I don't need it, or anything. I mean, I appreciate your offering . . ."

"Oh, that's quite all right," Miss Preston said.

"Was there—was there anything else you wanted to talk to me about?" Merry asked, after a few moments of silent staring at the empty cups and saucers and the plate of cookies.

"No, nothing else," Miss Preston said. "You may go back to your room now."

"Thank you, Miss Preston."

Miss Preston nodded at Merry. Incredible. No girl had ever before refused the cocoa. She shook her head, puzzled and hurt, and poured a cup for herself.

Merry went back to her room, or, more accurately, their room. She and Helen Farnam shared a double in the east wing. Merry liked Helen because Helen was not like the other girls. Perhaps it was because she was a Farnam or maybe just because she was the kind of girl she was, quiet and a little lumpish, that she didn't pry. She wasn't at all impressed with Merry's being the daughter of a movie star, didn't consider Merry's private life as public property, didn't ask dumb questions or make dumb remarks. She just sat there and was Helen Farnam, as if nothing else in the world could possibly matter. And if you were a Farnam, maybe nothing did.

All of which made it easy for Merry to talk to Helen. And when she got to their room, she told Helen what it was that she'd been sent for. "My stepmother died."

"Oh? I'm sorry."

"Don't be. We didn't like each other."

"Oh."

"And anyway, I think she may have killed herself. I can't imagine her drowning. I mean by accident."

"Oh."

"Miss Preston was funny. I think she was disappointed that I didn't cry or anything."

"Oh? Did she have cocoa?"

"Yes."

"Thought she would. Peg Hamilton got cocoa. When her father died."

"But I didn't drink any."

"Marvelous."

"But . . . I've been thinking."

"Oh?"

"Maybe I should have."

"Why?"

"Well, it isn't really the cocoa I was thinking about. But being upset. I think I ought to seem upset. At least a little. It'll keep the peasants away for a while."

"OK."

"What do you mean, 'OK'?"

"I'll mention to a few big-mouths that you're upset. Then you won't actually have to do anything but be quiet and look moody."

"I do that anyway."

"Then it'll be easy."

"Thanks. You're a marvel."

Helen went back to her homework. Merry thought for a while about what she really felt, which she could afford to do now that the decision about appearances had been made. She suspected that she was probably glad. It was just her father and herself now. And she liked that. But that seemed rather bloodless and cold. Perhaps it was, but she had to admit how with Carlotta gone she didn't even mind being at school. Her father would have had to send her away anyway. Now. She wondered why Carlotta had gone swimming like that and whether she had killed herself. And why. Until the end when Carlotta had sent her away, she had thought Carlotta liked her. Loved her. As she had thought she had loved Carlotta. But . . . It was too depressing. And frightening. She looked across the room at Helen Farnam, puffed her cheeks out the way Helen sometimes did, and decided that that was the way to be.

It wasn't just the loudness of the clock, but the cheapness of it that bothered Meredith. There it stood on the white metal table beside his bed, round and ugly, the roundness and the ugliness proclaiming with every loud tick, *dollar, dollar, dollar*. He wondered where Dr. Marston got them. Liggett's, Woolworth's,

Kresge's would all scorn such a ghastly clock. But there it was, with its two imitation-brass bells at the top—and loud? God, it was loud. Awful. Ridiculous, too, that Dr. Marston should have to import these cheap, loud, ugly, awful clocks from the United States to Switzerland.

The point, of course, was not to think about the clock, not to look at it, or listen to it, or worry about the alarm that was set to go off in an hour. Less than an hour, now. Fifty-five minutes? No, fifty-three. But there he was, looking at the clock again. You could go out of your mind that way. Which was the point, too. The real point. Not his, but Dr. Marston's, and the clinic's and the cure's. That clock. But he wouldn't think about it. He'd think about something else. Anything else.

Or, no, that wouldn't do, either. The way to beat it was to get some sleep. Not think about anything at all, but just sleep, through the ticking of that cheap clock, through the obscenely loud alarm, through everything. Or if not through everything, at least through the hour between the treatments. What wore you down, really wore you down, was the lack of sleep. He remembered reading somewhere that absolute rest was almost as good as sleep. The hell with that. The only thing as good as sleep was death itself. Which would be preferable to this, quite clearly. Without any queston at all. A hell of a way to blow a thousand bucks a week. It was sheer hell and at devilish rates, to boot.

Sleep, however, was out of the question. He tried it, tried very hard, but couldn't. His mind kept racing, trying to block out the persistent *cluckcluck* of the clock. He could not even bury his head under a pillow for the good Dr. Marston had thought of everything and thoughtfully neglected to supply pillows. There was no getting away from the damned clock. It beat on the eardrums like drops in a Chinese water torture. Which was oddly enough, exactly what it was. Chinese torture.

At a thousand a week. Brainwashing techniques from the Korean War, picked up, applied to a useful and socially desirable end, and here he was, volunteering for this. He was crazy. And if he wasn't crazy, he would be soon. He'd have been better off dead.

He thought of Carlotta, who had decided that she'd be better off dead. And here he was, now, wishing more than half-sincerely that he could follow her. But they'd thought of that. No razors, no belts, nothing sharp or heavy or blunt. And of course the door was locked. He couldn't just wander out and stroll down to the lake. Talk about ironies, this was the ideal retribution, wasn't it? If anything could balance out what he had done to her, this did.

But that was just melodramatic horseshit. His being here didn't have anything to do with Carlotta. His entertainment of the idea of suicide was not serious. He knew that. He just hated the clinic and this insane treatment and Marston and the clock, and wished he didn't have to be going through this. But he knew that if he had the chance, he wouldn't kill himself. And that he wasn't even here because of Carlotta, hadn't started to drink because of her death. Oh, sure, that had been part of it, but only part.

He looked around and in the emptiness of the clinic room his gaze fell upon the clock. As, of course, it was supposed to do. And he noticed the time, as he was supposed to do. Continually to be aware of the time. And, Jesus Christ, there were only thirty-two minutes left before she'd be back. The alarm would go off, and the door would open and she'd be there. His stomach churned thinking about it.

It was so unfair. It was all so damned unfair. He could have survived Carlotta, if that had been the only thing he'd had to bear. And he could have survived the idleness, too. But both of them together had been too much for him. And with the idleness came the opportunity. What the hell else did he have to fill up his time with? No movies to make, and no family, no one to talk to. Of course he'd started to drink. If only he'd believed Jaggers and all those assurances about readjustments of the motion picture business. But Jaggers was adamant about holding out for a price. Nothing less than five hundred thousand against a participation in profits. And nobody was getting that kind of money these days. "But they will, they will," Jaggers had said, "and when they do, you'll be the first." And so he'd been idle, waiting for some producer to get desperate enough to pay five hundred thousand dollars against a participation in the profits of a picture. And it wasn't just the waiting, but, in this crazy business, the suspicion, which rapidly grew into a conviction, that he wasn't worth it. If no one wanted to pay it, then he wasn't worth it. That seemed reasonable enough. And he'd started reading plays, but had found nothing. And had started real drinking. Before lunch—hell, before breakfast. And even that was all right. Anyone was entitled to go off on a toot for a while. But suddenly Jaggers had come up with the offer. Some nut was desperate enough to want to pay the price. And Meredith Houseman was worth it. Some nonsense about an anamorphic lens and a new ratio on the screen, wide, wide, wide. And he'd had to sober up. And couldn't. Not that fast. And they weren't taking any chances. The reason they'd wanted him in the first place was that they weren't taking any chances. Big names on the marquee, big budget, big everything to make the risk as small as possible. And still it'd be risky enough with the new process, the new lens, the new cameras. What director knew how to use it, how to frame a shot, even? And the studio had insisted that he take this crazy, inhuman, brutalizing cure, guaranteed by the North Koreans and the Chinese Communists to be enough to make any man do anything. Renounce his country? Sure! Renounce even his bottle.

But it was no good feeling sorry for himself. He had

gone through that before, with bottle after bottle of booze. He had thought about Carlotta, and the guilt he had felt when she had told him of his part in her hysterectomy, and how he had refused to accept that guilt, had gone off with Jocelyn to defy the guilt, to hide from it in the darkness and the warmth of her embrace. Worst thing he could have done, of course. But then, how could he have known how Carlotta would take it, how she would have been hurt, and what she would think? How could he have known that she would swim out into the lake that way?

So he had gone the other way, and, instead of fleeing from the guilt, had clung to it, as he would have liked to be able to cling to Carlotta herself. Clung to it and to the bottles that helped him feel it. Which was what brought him here in the end to Dr. Fu Manchu Marston's Chinese Torture Clinic and that lousy clock. That cheap, lousy, son-of-a-bitching clock. Which had to be broken. Couldn't possibly be telling the right time. Could it really be only five minutes now? Just five?

Well, the hell with sleeping. He lit a cigarette with the electric lighter—like a car lighter—that they let the patients have so that they couldn't try to burn themselves to death or burn themselves badly enough to get out of the clinic and go to a hospital. His stomach was writhing. It was such a stupid, such an obviously stupid kind of cure. Brainwashing, indeed. And so damned unnecessary. He'd had enough as it was. Five days of this madness. Or was it six? Anyway, an eternity. Enough to know what it was like. And they could just write into his contract that if he took a drink while the movie was shooting, he'd have to go back here. That'd be enough to keep him off the stuff. That'd be enough to keep him off food and water. Off breathing. He wondered if he could bribe the nurse into sending a letter out for him to the studio or to Sam. Sam could fix it. Sam could fix damned near anything. And if he could get him out of this, he could have twenty percent, fifty, a hundred and fifty percent of anything he ever made, forever. Without ever doing another thing. Just for this. This one little favor. And it'd be worth it. Lord, yes.

He puffed on the cigarette again. It was like smoking straw. What the hell was the matter with those cigarettes? No, it wasn't the cigarettes, it was him. His mouth was dry. His stomach was in knots and his mouth was dry. His tongue felt like a shoe that had been kicked into the back of a closet somewhere and left there for years and then, for no reason, put into his mouth. And it wasn't even his own shoe. It felt like a size 14 EEE. He looked at the clock again. There was no more time left. But the alarm hadn't rung. Cheap, lousy clocks. He sat up on the edge of the bed and looked at the clock. It would ring now, any second. But it kept on ticking. And that was as bad, the waiting for it, as the fear of it was. He wished it would ring so that the awful business would be over, for an hour at least. Maybe in the next hour he could get some sleep. Some hours, of course, just from the sheer exhaustion of it, he did sleep. But that was almost as bad, because then the hour went by in what seemed like two or three minutes. And bang, there it was. Or, not bang, but ring. And there she was again.

Finally it rang. He reached out and pushed the little button to stop the clock, then remembered that the button was gone. The nurse had the button. So he sat there and waited, listening to the cheap loud ring of the cheap loud clock. And then the nurse came in and stopped the clock. And she took the bottle of Black Label out of the cabinet in the table under the clock and poured a double shot of whiskey into the tumbler. She added the ice and poured the Evian water into it to make the perfect highball. There wasn't a bar in Europe or the States that made a better highball than Dr. Marston's nurses.

"Here you are," she said brightly. "Time for your drink."

He accepted it meekly. He had tried fighting. That did no good. The two goons outside had simply come in, held him down, and forced the whiskey down his throat. So he took it, raised the glass in a silent toast, and drank it down. It was awful. Just torture. It was like drinking toad piss, only worse. The worst thing that anyone could think of. She took the glass, then waited, and in a matter of seconds he started to work. The Antabuse caught the liquor and sent it back, never missing. It was like playing tennis against a backboard. He retched, then again more violently, then vomited, and continued to retch and heave, even after his stomach was empty, unreasonably, helplessly, violently. Then the nurse handed him the mop and watched him while he cleaned up his own mess. That was part of the treatment, too. And then she gave him his pill and a little of the Evian water. The Antabuse pill. Or maybe not, this time. The treatment, according to Dr. Marston, was to substitute, after a while, placebos for the Antabuse. Eventually the mere routine of drinking and immediate vomiting would set up a psychological connection every bit as reliable as the Antabuse. And the smell of liquor would be intolerable to him. Forever. He hadn't been there long enough, he didn't suppose, to rate a placebo. It was still Antabuse. He swallowed the pill with the water, then finished the water to get the taste of the vomit out of his mouth. Then the nurse reset the alarm clock and left. He lay back on the bed, exhausted, and tried not to listen to the ticking. If only the clever bastard had used quieter clocks . . .

The natives, as Helen and Merry sometimes called them, were restless. Not that they had any business to be excited by the prospect of a visit to the school by Meredith Houseman or even to be interested, but Heidi

Krumrind, the most native native of them all, had overheard Merry's telephone conversation with her father and had gone blabbing all over the whole school with a big, idiotic grin that displayed an awesome set of braces, saying that she'd heard from Merry herself that *he* was coming. Well, strictly speaking, literally speaking, it was true enough. But the implication—that Merry had told her, had deigned to speak to her, about anything at all—was not true, and Merry was annoyed.

"It's exactly what you'd expect from the Krum," Helen said, "and not worth a thought."

"I know. And I'm not giving it a thought. But it's like a mosquito bite. That's not worth a thought, either. But it's a nuisance."

"I know. But don't sweat it," Helen said.

"I never sweat," Merry said, in a playful, fake-arch way.

And certainly, as far as outward appearances were concerned, it was quite true. The poise and assurance which are supposed to be the products of a good private secondary education could hardly have found a better exemplar than Merry. She was bright and pretty and popular, and she knew that she was all of these things. But she was also Meredith Houseman's daughter and had had to defend herself from the others, from their too quickly proffered friendship, from their occasional displays of enmity, the other side of the same coin. And the more defenses she managed to construct the more glamorous and exotic she seemed to become in the eyes of her schoolmates, to whom any kind of self-possession or self-awareness seemed at the time enviably sophisticated and yet contemptibly snobbish.

She was, of course, excited by the prospect of her father's visit. She was now sixteen years old, and a few months into the eleventh grade, and had seen her father only twice since that summer they had spent together—with Carlotta—in Switzerland. Her summers she had spent at a special camp in New Hampshire, where a friend of Sam Jaggers ran a very good program of music and dance. Her vacations she had spent with the Farnams in Darien or Palm Beach. She did not feel especially sorry for herself for having been deprived of her father's company for those years. She knew that Vicki Dalrymple's brother had been sent away to school when he was four years old and the Dalrymples were in India. And he hadn't seen them again until he was sixteen. Vicki had told her about it once. The Dalrymples had gone up to Andy's school, and Andy had come running to his aunt and uncle, had embraced them, exclaiming, "Mom! Dad!" and had had to be told, as gently as possible, that, no, he'd picked the wrong pair, that his mother and father were the other two. It was just one of the burdens of empire, or whatever they called it. And her life had its burdens, too.

There would be, at any rate, no difficulty for them in recognizing each other. She looked different, of course, very much different from the way she had looked the last time he had visited her. All her roundness was gone, and through careful, even fanatic, dieting she had achieved a splendidly sylph-like figure. She had grown an inch or two, and she had that kind of glamorous emaciation that gives the best models their charm. But in all the growing and slendering, in all the loss of that unfortunate pudginess which had settled about her a few years before, there was a new clarity to her features, which were his.

She had no fears, therefore, that they could fail to recognize each other. In fact the only thing she was at all concerned about was the impact of the moment of their meeting. She did not look forward with great enthusiasm to a moment of poignant drama. It wanted to be casual, easy, natural, like the meetings of those peasants with their parents, those hard-working pharmacists or country lawyers or middle-echelon executives of large corporations. She even envied the easy insignificance of those moments, the casual hellos, the affectionate kisses, the modulated affection of their greetings, as if they had been apart for only a month or so.

She did not wait for him, therefore, in the main parlor or look out for him through the large bay window that commanded a view of the drive from the front gate of the school. She stayed in her room, pretending to read, waiting for the *gauche* shriek of someone like the Krum that would announce that a limousine had arrived and that *he* was here!

It was not, in the event, quite that bad. It was Vicki Dalrymple who came to tell her that her father was downstairs, and Vicki had some idea of what it meant and of what restraint was appropriate. There were clusters of girls downstairs pretending unsuccessfully that they were not there to ogle and stare, but Merry didn't care. Her father was there to see her, and he called out to her, "Merry! Oh, Merry, you're gorgeous," and held his arms out, and she ran to him, and he hugged her in front of everyone, and she just didn't care. It was too wonderful, too splendid for anything to be able to mar it, anything—even the wide eyes of the Krum or all the peasants together, feasting on the greeting of their most special classmate and her super-special father. It was just so great that nothing could hurt it. Nothing could even touch it. And he was wonderful. He held her, kissed her on the forehead, and then looked up, waved at all of them, and gave Merry his arm. She took it and, on his arm, walked out of the building and into a technicolor sunset.

Well, not a technicolor sunset, maybe, but the gardens. The Marvell Garden, as the school called it, or the Marvin Gardens, as the students referred to it. The school's designation was taken not from the game of Monopoly but from the poem of Andrew Marvell, which the students were required to memorize in order to earn the privilege of walking in its paths, among its well-kept formal beds.

Here at the Fountains sliding foot,
Or at some Fruit-trees mossy root,
Casting the Bodies Vest aside,
My soul into the boughs does glide:
There like a Bird it sits, and sings,
Then whets, and combs its silver Wings;
And, till prepar'd for longer flight,
Waves in its Plumes the various Light.

"Not inappropriate for a garden in a school like this," her father said.

"Actually, it's the lines that come next that make it appropriate," she answered and quoted, "Such was that Happy Garden-state,/While Man there walk'd without a Mate . . ."

"I see what you mean," he said. "But tell me about you."

"I don't know. What's to tell? My life is sort of what you'd expect. You see the school. You see me. You can put them together and figure it out. I'm doing pretty well I guess. My grades are good, anyway, and I have a few friends."

"Good," he said. "I'm glad."

He stopped to look at a rosebush that had put out a few late blooms, all the more beautiful and all the more touching because of the lateness of the season and the hopelessness of that last flowering. Those blossoms could never possibly come to bear.

There were questions that Merry wanted to ask him, but she hesitated. It was terribly unfair, but she kept framing the questions in her mind and then abandoning them, because they were exactly the kind of questions that the peasants would ask her—if they dared. It was as if she were not in the garden alone with her father, but somehow a little removed, watching herself, watching her father and herself, and passing judgment upon the style and taste of each gesture and each word that passed between them.

"How did the picture go?" she asked. It was unsatisfactory. The question had the proper distance to it, was neither excessively prying nor excessively personal, and yet it was a question that any reporter, any interviewer would have asked.

"All right," he said. "Better than it had any right to do. It's dullish in places, but it looks quite handsome. Like a painting. The width, I suppose, does that. It has the look of one of those great historical monuments of David."

"I—I didn't mean just the picture. I meant you."

"Oh, all right, I suppose. It was very slow going."

"I meant the drinking."

She looked away. That had gone too far the other way. And was prying and impertinent. But she was damned if those stupid, fatuous slugs, because of their very stupidity and fatuousness, should enjoy a greater degree of candor and openness with their parents than she could manage with her father.

"You know about that?"

"Mr. Jaggers wrote me about it. He thought I'd be less upset by that than by your unexplained silence."

"Well, if that's what he thought . . ."

"He was right," she said.

"Yes, I suppose so," her father said. "Well, anyway, that's all over with. I took a cure, you know. And it worked. It does work. I can't touch a drop of anything except an occasional glass of champagne. Everything else makes me violently sick. Even the smell of it. A week or two after I got out of the clinic I was riding in a car with one of the executives of the studio who'd had a beer with lunch. They had to open the window, and I could hardly stand it even then. Just the smell of the beer on his breath."

He was wonderfully conversational, easy, and even

funny as he talked about it, and for a little while Merry was not off in the bushes observing the father and the daughter, but was wholly there beside him, listening and answering and sympathizing as far as she could.

"Was it because of Carlotta?" she asked.

He looked at her, held out his hand and touched her cheek and her upturned chin, thought for a moment, and then said, "Oh, Merry. I think I'd better wait on that a little. We'll talk about it one day. We will, I promise. But I think it'd be better if we waited until you are a little older. It'd be terrible if you didn't understand, now, and terrible if you did. Forgive me?"

"Yes, Daddy." Forgive him? She was exultant, deliriously happy that he could treat her that way, as a father ought to treat a child, and that for the moment at least, and at least with him, the terrible responsibilities of correctness and sophistication had been lifted. She felt the kind of relief a sailor of a small boat feels when after maneuvering through high waves and heavy weather he reaches a sheltered cove. It is not yet his own mooring in his own harbor, but it is a respite and altogether wonderful.

They took another turn around the garden, looking at the gay-feather and the Japanese anemone, the Michaelmas daisies and the autumn crocus, and the first of what would be a marvelous profusion of white and orange and rusty-red chrysanthemums.

He asked her, when they neared their starting point on the great circular path, what she'd like to do for the rest of the afternoon. She told him she didn't care. She was happy just to be with him. He suggested a picnic.

"Oh, yes. That'd be perfect. It's such a fine day!"

"Is there anyone you'd like to take along? One of your friends, perhaps?"

"Well, Helen Farnam, maybe. She's my roommate."

"Yes, I know. I was hoping you'd suggest that she come. She and her family have been very good, having you for vacations, haven't they?"

"Yes, they have."

"Go get her, then, and we'll get going."

It was a fine picnic. Meredith had brought along a hamper from Vendôme full of pâté and cheese and fruit and jars of little babas in rum and iced splits of champagne. They drove out into the country in the limousine and picnicked near a brook, and then they drove back to school. Merry and Helen both thanked Meredith, and both kissed him good-bye and told him what a super time they'd had. And, indeed, they'd had such a fine time that they forgot themselves and even told several of the peasants all about it, mentioning even the champagne, which produced, invariably, the wide-eyed awe the two of them would have liked to be able to express themselves.

That *The French Revolution* seemed at the time a speculative venture, and that the fate not only of the studio but of all the studios seemed at the time to be in doubt and to hang upon the success or failure of that picture, is difficult to believe now. But there it was, a pile of film cans, in which there was, as Martin Siegel said in his characteristically evangelical way, "Nothing. That's right, gentlemen. Nothing. A length of film, yards of it, maybe half a mile of it, and on that film little images, all of them distorted so that you can hardly see what they are except through a peculiar and very expensive lens. And the images, too, are nothing. Nobody looks at them. What we are selling is light and shadows, the frailest, the most insubstantial things. Don't think of it as anything more. Forget the hardware, the props, the costumes, the buildings we built, the cities we built. They've all been torn down anyway. Forget the millions of dollars which these images cost us to make. Forget, if you can, the company and the industry—about which nobody really cares. But think of the light and shadows, the play of man's fancy and imagination over the pageant of his past. This motion picture represents more than an investment, more than a process, more than a series of images and a narrative line. This motion picture represents an affirmation of the spirit of mankind and our faith in that spirit. In these cans, gentlemen, is man's dream of freedom. Of liberty, fraternity, and equality. Nothing less! And that's what I want you to go out and sell. I want every theater owner and exhibitor to feel that when he dies and stands before St. Peter at the gate of Heaven, and when his life is being judged there, he shall be able to say sincerely and in all modest pride, 'I was the first man in my district to show *The French Revolution.*' "

Siegel sat down, took a four-dollar Sulka handkerchief from the breast pocket of his custom-made shantung suit, and wiped away the tears that his speech had brought to his eyes.

The other executives in the room—vice-presidents in charge of promotion, publicity, sales, and production, and their assistants—looked variously solemn, inspired, deeply moved. One, who had been about to light a cigar, held the cigar and the opened, gold Dunhill lighter in front of him as though transfixed or at least as though posing for a commemorative waxwork. Another looked up toward Heaven or, anyway, toward the ornamental molding of the bizarre, neo-Egyptian decor that Siegel's father and predecessor had installed at a more optimistic moment in the company's fortunes.

"All right," Siegel continued. "Now tell me about the opening."

The vice-president in charge of publicity described the plans for the opening. It was to be a benefit for the Heart Fund.

"Yes, good," said Siegel. David Siegel, after all, had died of a heart condition.

The vice-president described the television coverage, the after-theater party in the Astor grand ballroom, the tumbrels which would precede the limousines down Broadway. . . .

"It's taking a chance, Sol," someone said. "You don't want people to think that audiences are going to die. . . ."

"It's showmanship," the vice-president in charge of publicity answered. "And it's part of the theme. This is one of the invitations," he said and produced from his attaché case a small gilt guillotine. He handed it to Martin Siegel.

Siegel took it and put it down in front of him on the desk, which was as large as a Ping-Pong table, but heavier, made of massive, intricately, hideously carved oak. He played with the little toy, looked up, and announced with all the delight and wonder of a small child, "It works."

"Not only does it work," said the vice-president in charge of publicity, "it cuts cigars!"

"Great! Just great!" said Siegel. It was one of those times, they all agreed later, when he sounded just like his old man.

Melissa Filides, the Greek shipping heiress, gave her guillotine to her maid, who had children she thought might like it as a plaything. It was a perfectly dreadful little object, but quite in keeping, Melissa thought, with this whole dreadful business. The motion-picture company was spending absurd amounts of money. That was no concern of hers, for the agreement had been that a lump sum would be turned over to the Heart Fund by the company, which sum had nothing at all to do with the expensive tickets. What the motion-picture company got out of it was the television coverage, at far less cost than they could have managed in a straightforward way by simply purchasing the time and running commercials. The Heart Fund stood to benefit, by perhaps a third of the difference, but it was still a great deal of money. And for that money, Melissa had agreed to give her name to the proceedings and her presence for the few undoubtedly dreary hours that it would take. She would sit through their tiresome movie, and then go to their vulgar dinner at the Astor, and then a hot bath and bed. True, she had been quite successful at the Colony, describing her patronage of this film about the Revolution, but it wasn't worth it. It just wasn't worth it. And this last piece of news was the very final straw. That they should presume, themselves, to arrange for her escort was bad enough. But that they should provide, among all the possible people in an ill-assorted world, an actor, no doubt as stupid as he was handsome, vain and boring, and requiring catsup with anything he put into his mouth—well, it was just too much. Not that Meredith Houseman would be quite that bad, but very nearly, very nearly. He came, she believed, from Montana. . . .

"There," Colette said, "it is done. Is good, mademoiselle?"

"Yes," Melissa said, studying her reflection in the mirror of her dressing room. The dress was by Givenchy, a stark white satin gown that draped in classic severity. It fastened over the left shoulder with a diamond-and-emerald sunburst and, like a toga, left the other shoulder bare. Matching the emeralds in the sunburst there was a pair of emerald earrings, small and rather modest looking. They had been a gift from her father on the occasion of her twenty-first birthday.

"You look magnificent," Colette said.

"Yes." Melissa nodded.

Colette opened the door for her, and she made her entrance into the living room, where Meredith Houseman was sitting and waiting. He got to his feet instantly and rather gracefully.

"Mr. Houseman, how do you do? I am Melissa Filides."

"How do you do," he said, with a slight, quite correct nod of his head, an indication, really, of a bow. Melissa detested those Americans who insisted upon shaking hands with women.

"I'm sorry to have kept you waiting. Maurice got you a drink?" she asked. She looked at the table beside the chair in which he had been sitting.

"Just vichy," he said. "I—I don't drink anything except champagne, I'm afraid."

"What's to be afraid of? My father was like that. We have time yet for a drink, do we not?"

"I think so," he said.

"Good," she said. "Maurice, champagne."

She did not have to raise her voice. The kitchenette was just off the living room of her suite in the Hampshire House. She owned the suite, occupying it only during November and letting the hotel rent it during the rest of the year. There was, that way, not only a considerable saving, but the assurance that each November her suite would be there, ready for her.

Maurice appeared with a bottle of Taittinger '47 and two iced tulip glasses, each one three-quarters full.

Melissa raised her glass and said, "To the film, I suppose."

"To a pleasant evening," Meredith answered. He was not, after all, absolutely impossible. It might, she decided, be not such an unpleasant evening at that. She had expected, of course, that he would be an attractive man. These movie people had to be. It was their business. But the way in which he fulfilled her expectation was neither tiresome nor cheap. He did not appear to be fashioned out of plastic, as so many of these people did when one saw them on the screen.

When it was time to go, he rose, again gracefully and easily, took her cape from Maurice and helped her into it, and gave her his arm.

"Well, off to the movies," he said. "You know, one of the screenwriters told me that Burke had a wonderful comment about the Revolution. Or maybe it was a comment somebody else made about Burke's view of the Revolution. I don't remember. But it was a fine remark about looking on at France and mourning for the plumage while the bird was dying. I hope that there will at least be some pretty plumage from time to time and that you won't be entirely bored."

How had he guessed that she looked forward to the picture with so little enthusiasm? Or had he guessed? Was this, perhaps, his own sentiment? She smiled at him, as if they were sharing some wonderful private joke.

The film was a great success. At any rate, there was cheering and applause when it was over—which was hardly surprising. The audience was packed with employees of the studio, stockholders, and their families and friends. It did go on to be one of the all-time high-grossing pictures, but the novelty of the wide-screen process, the sheer size and scale of the picture, the huge advertising campaign, and the feeling of some of the important critics that the industry depended upon the success of this film and their resultant exaggerated praise, all had more to do with its success than any artistic excellence. Still, it wasn't a bad movie. There were lots of fights and lots of executions, and lots of love scenes. It was odd, Melissa thought, to sit beside a man in a theater and watch him at the same time embracing another woman.

He was very smooth about it. A lot of that smoothness, she supposed, was the effect of the editing and the cutting and the lighting and the direction, but even while she made those intellectual qualifications to herself, she still felt the physical impact of it. Or the impact of the combination of the image in front of her and his real presence beside her.

"Arduous work you do," she whispered to him.

"Yes," he said, "but it pays well."

But even their joking did not entirely dispel the effect. She found herself looking at him in furtive little sideways glances. And she was relieved when the scene on the screen changed to more bloodshed.

After the film was over and the applause had died down they went out into the throngs on Broadway, past the gawking crowd of spectators on the other side of the police barrier and across the street to the Astor. It was curious, Melissa thought, to be with Houseman out in the streets, in the crowds, after the movie they had just seen together. The stares, the whispers and shouts, the calls of greeting from the jostling mob at the barricade resembled some of the scenes of the film, and it was rather comfortable to be next to the center of attention for a change, instead of as one of the world's richest women, exactly at the center.

The grand ballroom was packed, not only with people but with the television cameras and their cables, the hot, bright lights, and little enclaves of technicians and engineers. It hardly looked like a setting for any sort of party, but more like a set. They were seated at the head table and Meredith ordered champagne. There was little opportunity for talk, because one person after another came up to congratulate Meredith on the film, or to meet Melissa and congratulate her on the party and the coup for the Heart Fund. Finally, in a momentary lull, Meredith suggested that it might be something of a relief if they were to get up and dance.

"Yes, let's," she said gratefully.

So they danced. And they continued to dance—waltzes, fox-trots, tangos, even a Charleston. She was delighted to find that he was such a light, pleasant, accomplished dancer. That was her first observation. But very soon thereafter, it became a kind of competition between the two of them, as they danced ever more strenuously, ever more closely, ever more extravagantly. Neither of them wanted to go back to the dullness of the head table and introductions and congratulations and thanks, but more important, neither wanted to admit to the other that there was even a possibility of fatigue. They were too graceful, too perfect, too ethereal to admit to such mortality. And it was marvelous to dance with him, knowing that every eye was on them, not only in the ballroom but in living rooms and bedrooms all over the country, through that monstrous machine that the television people continually pointed at them.

But that was not yet all. More than the mere pleasure of his accomplished dancing, and more than the excitement of their musical athleticism, and perhaps growing out of both, there was an intense physical awareness she felt of his male body, which thrilled her. And this was more startling, more exciting, more marvelous than anything she could imagine. They danced slow and he held her close, or they danced fast and she felt his glancing touch, his lightness, and burned, burned.

"You are a very exciting man," she said between numbers. And then, hardly aware herself of what she was about to say, added, "How long do we have to stay here with all these people?"

"Let's go now," he suggested.

"But they have just begun to serve dinner. . . ."

"Are you hungry?" he asked.

"No," she said. Not for the dinner anyway.

They left abruptly, not bothering to say good-bye to anyone. She felt like Cinderella fleeing from the ball, but this time the prince was with her, and together they got into the limousine and went back to Melissa's suite at the Hampshire House.

Colette and Maurice were waiting, of course. Colette always made tea and toast for her mistress at bedtime. Maurice opened the door and took Melissa's cape.

"Champagne," she ordered and then added, *sotto voce,* "and then you may go."

"Oui, mademoiselle."

"Bon soir, mademoiselle," Colette said.

"Bonne nuit," Melissa answered. "That will be all for tonight."

"Mais, mademoiselle . . ." Colette started to say.

Melissa narrowed her eyes and glared. "I said that will be all!"

Colette left for the servants' quarters. Maurice put the champagne on the coffee table, said, *"Bonne nuit, mademoiselle, monsieur . . ."* and followed his wife.

"I must apologize for my servants," she said. "Usually their function is to keep men away from me. To discourage visitors. And they are very faithful. But unfortunately they are not very adaptable. Unzip me, please."

He assumed that she was going off to her bedroom to change, to slip into something a little more comfortable, as the saying goes. After all, she had just dismissed her servants, and it seemed plausible that she needed some help undressing. It was unusual, perhaps, but possible. He pulled the zipper down the back of the dress.

She turned, gazed at him for a moment, and then let the top of the dress fall. She wore no bra, for the Givenchy dress had its underpinnings built into it. She held out her slender arms and he kissed her.

"Get the champagne," she said huskily, and she broke away from him to disappear into her bedroom.

He picked up the small silver tray and followed. She was already naked when he came into the room. The bed, of course, was turned down. He put the tray down on the night table and undressed while she watched him from the bed, where she lay propped up against the pillows, her arms folded across her delicate, diminutive bosom.

"You undress very well," she said. "I've often wondered why there aren't male strippers."

"Perhaps if there were more women like you, there would be."

"Like me? But how little you know me. Come. Hurry."

He stepped out of his patent leather dancing pumps, drew off his socks, and took off his shorts. Then he joined her in the bed. They kissed passionately and touched each other, delighted and amazed to be together there and to have each other's bodies to touch and explore. Meredith kissed her again and started to climb on top of her, but she pushed him back.

"No, not yet. Don't rush so."

"Rush? But I thought you were in such a hurry."

"In a hurry to get into bed," she said. "Not to get out again."

"But I—" he started to say.

"Please," she said. "Slow, slow, slow."

"All right," he said. "Why not?"

They lay there together for a long time. He touched her breasts, ran his fingers in light, delicate circles around her nipples, ran his hand down the flatness of her belly and brushed over her hair, as if almost inadvertently and only on the way toward the smoothness of her inner thigh. And she touched him, stroking his chest and his thighs and occasionally letting her hand come to rest on his penis, but lightly, almost timidly.

Finally he could bear it no longer. "Oh, Melissa," he groaned, and this time, as he mounted her, she made no protest. Or if it was a protest, he could not tell whether it was meant to be heeded or not. Over and over, in a barely audible high voice, she repeated, "Oh, oh, oh, oh," and again, "Oh, oh, oh, oh."

It took a long time before he could make her come. At last the light little "Oh, oh's" changed to a longer, higher "Oooooooooo," and in the excitement of her coming, he came, too.

They lay together, sharing their exhaustion as they had shared their passion. And together they revived a little, and she asked him for some champagne.

He poured it for her.

"None for you?"

"No, I've had enough. I don't drink much."

"You're lucky."

"You think so?"

"Yes. No. I don't know. No, I'm lucky. Do you know that you are the first man I've gone to bed with, really?"

"No."

"You don't believe me?"

"No."

"Well, it's not true. In a way, though, it is. You are the second man. The first was my cousin, Nikos. I was eleven. He was then, I think, thirty-two."

"How awful."

"Yes. I have not since then been to bed with any man."

"Well, maybe I will have some champagne after all."

Four days later they decided to get married. They were in bed at the time. Melissa picked up the phone and sent a cablegram to her mother in Paris. Meredith called Merry at school, but was not allowed to talk to her because she was in gym. He left a message with Miss Preston.

Had Miss Preston been a little more clever, or a little more understanding, or even just a little luckier, she might have realized that this was the time for her assault with the cocoa and sympathy. But all she did was mention it to Merry that afternoon after chapel, and congratulate her. As far as Merry was concerned, it was like being congratulated for having cancer. Without even smiling, she said, "Thank you, Miss Preston," and continued on toward the dining hall.

Miss Preston was appalled. She had never in her life seen such a cold, unemotional girl.

Merry was hardly unemotional, however. The only thing was that she did not want to let anyone know quite how smitten she had been, that she had fallen in love with her own father, and how sick at heart she was that he had married another woman. She could not even share her feelings with Helen, whose parents and stepparents, and even step-stepparents now, were getting divorces and remarrying about every other week. In fact, she did not permit herself to think about it much, at least during the daytime, when the expressions that such thoughts might bring to her face would be more than she cared to reveal to any of her schoolmates. No, she waited until night, and lights out, and in the warmth and comfort and, above all, privacy of her bed, considered what to do.

The next day was a Wednesday, which at the Mather School meant a half holiday. There were classes in the morning, but after lunch the students were at liberty. It was a time to relax.

Merry went downtown, went into the five-and-ten, and bought lipstick, eye shadow, and rouge. This was a violation of the rules of the school, which forbade the girls to wear makeup or to keep it at school. She also bought a small jar of cold cream and a box of tissues, which were perfectly legal.

She took her package with her to the railroad station, which was a suitably anonymous place, and where there was a ladies' room. In the ladies' room, she put on the lipstick and the eye shadow and touched her cheeks with the rouge, which she blended in carefully. Then she threw the lipstick, eye shadow, and rouge away, but kept the tissue and the cold cream.

Then, all made up and obviously not a member of the student body of the Mather School, she went to a liquor store half a block from the railroad station and asked for a fifth of Black Label Scotch. It was the only brand she knew.

"You eighteen?" the man behind the counter asked.

"That's the nicest question anybody's asked me today," Merry said.

"Well, are you?"

"Of course I am."

"You got a driver's license?"

"Yes," she said, thinking fast, "but it's in the car. That's my car there, across the street." She pointed vaguely across the street.

"Oh, OK. You know how it is. I gotta ask, you understand."

"Yes, of course."

He handed her the fifth of Black Label and she paid him. Then she went back to the railroad station, into the ladies' room, and, with the tissues and the cold cream, removed the makeup. Then she went back to school. She hid the bottle of Scotch in her laundry bag in the closet.

She waited until after dinner before she began to drink. Helen was studying in the living room of their little suite, and she was quite used to Merry going off to bed to read there. So there was nothing at all unusual about Merry's retiring to her bedroom cubicle. She even had a book in bed with her. But under the bed she had her bottle, too, and her plastic toothbrush glass. She drank the whiskey neat, there being neither ice nor water nor soda available. It kind of burned as it went down, but then the burning feeling turned to a glowy feeling, and it wasn't bad at all. But the point now was to get drunk, and even if it had tasted terrible she would have continued. It took her a little less than an hour before she felt that she was honestly drunk. Her cheeks felt quite rubbery, and her tongue felt thick and not quite right. And she felt a little silly, too, but pleasantly silly. Irresistibly silly.

She looked at the clock on her bureau. It was twenty-five minutes to ten. She got up, stumbled, laughed, and then went out into the living room.

"Are you all right?" Helen asked.

"Yes. Why?"

"I don't know. You look funny."

"You look funny, too."

"I didn't mean it that way," Helen said.

"I know," Merry said. She started out of the room.

"Where are you going?"

"Where would I be going?" Merry asked in return. Not even now did she want to say anything to Helen. And it was sad to realize that she didn't feel like confiding in her only friend. But she didn't. And Helen, she supposed, would have to suppose that she was just going to the bathroom.

She went downstairs and across the grand entrance hall of the school to Miss Preston's door. She knocked, using the miniature door knocker. Miss Preston opened the door herself.

"Yes, Meredith?"

"I want to report myself, Miss Preston."

"Oh? Report yourself for what?"

"For drinking."

"You've been drinking?"

"Yes. That's why I want to report myself," Merry said, suppressing only with difficulty a fit of giggles.

"But I mean just now. You've been drinking just now?"

"Yes."

"Where?"

"What difference does that make?" The giggles were growing more difficult to suppress.

"I'll ask the questions, young lady, if you don't mind. Where?"

"In my room."

"What about Helen?"

"What about her?"

"Has she been drinking, too?"

"No, Miss Preston." What an absurd question for Miss Preston to ask, Merry thought. Helen drinking? And how ridiculous she looked, stern Miss Preston swaying back and forth. Or, was it she, herself, who was swaying? She felt odd, terribly terribly odd. "May I sit down, Miss Preston?"

"Yes, of course. Did she know that you were drinking, Meredith?"

"No, Miss Preston."

"Where did you get it?"

"The whiskey?"

"Whatever it was. Where did you get it?"

"I bought it today, downtown."

"At which store?"

"I'd rather not say."

"That's not unreasonable, I suppose," Miss Preston admitted. She thought for a moment, and then she asked, "Why were you drinking?"

"Because I wanted to."

"Why?" Miss Preston snapped.

"To get drunk. Why else would . . . I don't see what difference it makes."

"I don't believe, Meredith, you are in a position to see anything at the moment," Miss Preston said. She picked up the telephone, and while she held the receiver with one hand, flipped through a card file with the other. She found Merry's card and started to dial.

"Hello?" she said, after a while. "This is Miss Preston at the Mather School. Is this Mr. Jaggers?"

There was a pause. Then she continued. "No, she's all right. I mean, she has come to no physical harm. She has, however, violated one of the school rules. . . ." Pause. "Yes. I'm quite sure. And I thought it might be the best thing if I were to talk with her father." Pause. "Yes, right now, if that's at all possible." She listened to Mr. Jaggers for a moment, and then picked up a pencil, a small gold Cross pencil, and wrote another number on Merry's card.

"Thank you very much indeed, Mr. Jaggers. . . . Yes, I understand. I am as sorry about this as anyone. . . . Yes, thank you again. Good-bye."

Then she dialed the other number and asked for

Meredith Houseman. Evidently she was asked to give her name, for she said, "Agatha Preston of the Mather School. . . . Yes, that's right. Mather, as in Cotton Mather. M-A-T-H-E-R. . . . Yes."

Merry listened as Miss Preston explained to her father about the violation of the rules of the school and the necessary consequences. Or if she did not actually listen to the words, which were all perfectly predictable, then she listened to the music, to the tone of voice, the ingratiating singsong which gave an odd lilt to the clipped diction, and then the voice stopped and Miss Preston started to listen. Only idly did Merry wonder what it was that her father could possibly find to say. Not that it made any difference, of course. How could it?

But it did. Miss Preston's demeanor had changed, and she was saying now, at irregular intervals, "I see. I see. Yes, I see," but angrily, even furiously, with her lips pursed and her eyes narrowed. "This is outrageous, Mr. Houseman," she said, after a slightly longer pause than usual. And then, "Well, I shall give this all some very careful thought, and I shall inform you of my decision, through Mr. Jaggers, if that will be all right." Pause. "Yes, I'm sure you would, but I was thinking of myself. I'd prefer to deal with Mr. Jaggers. And I do hope you'll forgive me for troubling you with what seemed to me to be an extraordinary and very pressing problem. Good-bye."

She had practically spat her farewell into the phone. And she had slammed the receiver down onto the cradle with a force that betrayed rage such as Merry had never seen her express before. She looked at Merry, sighed—or perhaps it was only a deep breath that she took to regain her self-control—and told her what her father had just said.

"I am afraid," she began, "that the talk I just had with your father was most unsatisfactory. What he told me was not, I am sure, intended for your ears, but I think I'm going to tell you just the same. I think I ought to tell you."

But having said that, she fell silent and seemed to reconsider. Or perhaps she was just trying to frame it properly, to translate it from Meredith Houseman's style into her own, or into a style that would be appropriate for the conversation of a headmistress with a pupil. Merry waited, curious, and yet still largely indifferent. She could hardly expect that after all the talk was done with, it would make any difference at all. This was only the lecture she knew she would have to endure, and had been willing to endure, just as she had been willing to endure the taste of whiskey—whether she liked it or not—to accomplish her purpose.

"He said," Miss Preston continued, "that he was not surprised. He even laughed. I told him that you were here in my suite and that you were drunk, and he laughed. And he told me that he was a drunk, and that he believed your mother was a drunk, and that it was only reasonable that you should turn out to be a drunk, too. And he suggested that it was only natural that the school should want to bounce you, but that there were other schools, and that sooner or later you'd probably get through one of them."

Merry lowered her head. She did not want Miss Preston to be able to see her face.

Miss Preston, however, did not leave her alone. "Look at me," she said. "Meredith . . . Merry, please."

Merry looked at her.

"It's a terrible thing. And I hardly know what to do. But I do know what not to do, and I think that I will not have you expelled. Will not expel you. I want you to stay here in the school, and I want you to consider what your father told me over the telephone, to consider whether that's the kind of life you want for yourself, and the kind of thing you want to allow to be said about yourself. Is it?"

"No, Miss Preston."

"Of course not. I shouldn't have thought so. Now go into that room, my guest room, and go to sleep. I don't want you back in your room in your present condition. Tomorrow morning, during breakfast, you'll go to your room and dress, and if anyone asks, you shall say that you didn't feel well and you spent the night in the infirmary. It's a great burden that your father's career and your father's life have placed upon you, and an unfair one, too. And this once, I think, I ought to see my way to giving you another chance. One more chance. Do you understand me?"

"Yes, Miss Preston."

"All right then," Miss Preston said. "Go on to bed."

"Thank you, Miss Preston."

Merry went off to the guest room and went to bed. Agatha Preston sat up for a while and read, or pretended to herself that she was reading. Actually, she listened for any hint, for any sound . . . and with no idea what it was that she was listening for. But after a while, after perhaps ten minutes, she did hear it. It was muffled. The girl was trying to muffle it, but even with her face buried in the pillow, the sobs were audible to one who was sitting very still and listening for them.

But even having heard the sobs, Miss Preston could not be quite sure whether they were sobs of gratitude, or of humiliation, or of rage that her obvious little plot to get herself expelled had failed. They were, she thought, most probably a combination. But even so, even so. It was, at last, a beginning. A place to stand. She recalled Archimedes' words "Give me a place to stand, and I can move the world." Could she move Merry? She was not anywhere near that degree of optimism. But neither was she entirely without hope now.

CHAPTER

SIX

♥ Merry had no idea whatever that her father had meant well. His manner of dealing with Miss Preston had been peculiar, but it had worked. Meredith, in bed with Melissa at the Hampshire House, had been happy enough and had felt good enough to venture the one long shot that might keep his daughter in school. He could not have said why he expected his maneuver to work, much less how he expected it to work, but it felt right, and whether it is that happy people are more in tune with the pulse of the world's workings or that people who are happy are blessed, or lucky, it is nevertheless true that he had the confidence at that moment to trust his impulse. And Miss Preston did do what he wanted her to do and kept Merry at the school.

To Merry, though, it seemed utter abandonment. She had known that her father would have no moral views about drinking and would not take very seriously the news that his daughter had, for the first time in her life, got drunk. But she had not expected him to go quite as far as he did. He had seemed to dismiss it entirely and her with it. And she concluded that she was unimportant to him. It was a not altogether improbable misunderstanding. And even if Meredith had known about it, there would have been very little he could have done. It would have been foolish for him to write her or telephone her and explain how he had manipulated her headmistress. She was only a youngster, and it would have been dangerous and unwise to undermine entirely her respect for all rules and authority. But he didn't know, and it never came up.

One of the reasons that Meredith never suspected his daughter's real feelings was that her response was difficult to interpret. She applied herself to her studies, improved her marks, made a few more friends among her schoolmates. Miss Preston was entirely pleased and even wrote to Mr. Houseman to say that his daughter seemed to have improved markedly since the unfortunate incident of the preceding term. Miss Preston's motive for writing to him was only partly to inform a parent of a student's progress. She was also boasting a little of having redeemed an all but lost child, and flaunting her success in that actor's face. Not that she would have put it that way, even to herself, but that was the effect of it. It did make her feel very good indeed to write that letter and put it in her Out box.

It never occurred to Miss Preston to wonder at the determination and seriousness that Merry displayed. For her, determination, no matter where it came from, and seriousness, no matter what its object, were entirely good things. They were natural to her, so she thought they were quite natural and appropriate to anyone, and universally desirable qualities. Merry was applying herself, and Merry, she thought, was therefore all right. The fact was that Merry's hard work, her careful cultivation of the friendship of faculty members and fellow students, her display of all the virtues in Miss Preston's heaven were manifestations of something very like cold rage.

Merry continued through the school year in this manner, earned fine grades—she was, after all, a bright girl—and then in the spring wrote a letter to her father asking him if it would be all right with him if she spent the coming summer with her mother. The letter was full of fine reasons, good character, delicate sentiment, and leaden sincerity. Meredith was appalled. Not only had Merry asked to spend the summer with Elaine—which was bad enough and a slap in the face—but she had been a prig and a priss about it, unanswerable and insufferable. He felt awful, and thought that he had somehow lost Merry, and had stood by while she lost herself, her lightness, her vivacity. He felt like a heel, which was exactly what Merry wanted.

At the beginning of June, then, she flew out to Los Angeles. Elaine and Harry were waiting for her behind the barrier, with Lyon beside them. Merry recognized Harry first. He looked almost exactly the way she remembered him. He was a little gray around the temples and a little fatter maybe, but he looked like himself. Her mother had aged, though. In the seven years that Merry had been gone, her mother had turned into a middle-aged woman, thin, fluttery, nervous, and rather drawn. Lyon, of course, was totally different. He had been five years old the last time Merry had seen him and he was twelve now. He was tall and looked as if he would be quite handsome in a few years.

Merry waved, hurried as fast as she could through the crowd of passengers, and kissed her mother, and Lyon, and Harry. Harry and Elaine both exclaimed about Merry's good looks, not so much to Merry as to each other. It almost got to be a little embarrassing. Lyon just grinned, which was easier to take, and suggested that they go to get Merry's baggage, which was sensible.

It took ages for the bags to get from the plane to the baggage-claim area, and Merry realized that it was unfair to make the comparison, but that it was unavoidable: Life was really so much easier if it could be arranged the way her father's was, with people around to speed up things like luggage, or to wait for them and take care of them and save you having to bother with them yourself. But she knew, too, that what she really meant was that she was eager to get going, to get out into the car and to get home, to see what their new house was like, and what they were really like. What could you tell about anyone in an air terminal?

The house, as it turned out, was quite comfortable. It was rather grand, a great Tudor structure with a large round turret and dark beams in the stucco. It was high on a hill in Pacific Palisades. Harry Novotny had done well for himself, or the world had done well by him. The new television shows, with talking dogs, horses, porpoises, and mules, had kept him busy. His luck had been simply to be there at the right time and to have a little capital to expand at just the appropriate moment. The fifty thousand that Jaggers had sent the Novotny family seven years before had grown into a lot more. Merry was entirely pleased, and a little puzzled, too. She could not quite remember her reason for running away. She wondered what her life would have been like if she had stayed. It all seemed so terribly whimsical and chancy.

She got on well with them at first. Her mother was glad to see her, and affectionate and interested in her. During the first few days of her visit, Merry noticed that her mother drank a little too much, but she never seemed to be drunk. Only a little wobbly in the late afternoon and early evening. Harry seemed to make up for it, though. He was as charming as he could be and more lively than she remembered him. He took her to his menagerie to see the animals. He took her for rides along the ocean. He brought home a bag of charcoal and barbecued steaks outside on the grill, which was, Lyon said, something he hadn't done in years. He seemed most intent on making her stay a pleasant one.

She might have preferred it, actually, if his friendliness had found some slightly different form in which to express itself. He affected the cuddly uncle and was forever putting his arm around her shoulder, or patting her on the backside, or pinching her cheek and saying, "How's my little beauty this morning?" or "How about a picnic in the mountains, gorgeous? Just the two of us. What do you say?"

To the suggestion of the picnic she responded with enthusiasm, but insisted that Lyon come along. She remembered that she had liked Lyon, and she still liked him. More than ever. He was a quiet kid, and his father seemed to ignore him most of the time, and their mother seemed to ignore everything most of the time. She felt sorry for him a little, and they played chess in the evenings, or two-handed casino. And she insisted that he come along on these little excursions that Harry was always thinking up.

As it turned out, it was lucky that she had been moved to do so.

She had been at the Novotny house for just over two weeks when Harry made it clear one evening that his affection was not merely avuncular. They were watching television. Elaine had fallen asleep in her chair and Harry took her upstairs and helped her to bed. Then he came down, went to the kitchen, brought back two bottles of beer and a plateful of ham sandwiches, and sat down next to Merry to watch TV with her. What could be more cozy and familial?

The only trouble was that Lyon was in bed. He was, after all, only twelve. And Elaine was in bed, too. There were just the two of them. He gave Merry a beer, because there isn't anything in the world that goes better with ham sandwiches, he said, than a nice cold beer. She accepted the beer and felt very grown-up indeed, sitting beside her stepfather and drinking a beer. They drank the beers and when the glasses were empty Harry went back to the kitchen and got two more bottles. They drank those, too.

It was after the beers that she began to feel a little funny. It took her a long while to realize what it was that was unsettling her. Slowly it dawned upon her that whenever she looked around at Harry, she saw that he was looking at her. She watched the television program for a while—it was an old movie, with Dane Clark in it—but every little while she would look around, not turning her head even, but shifting her eyes a little. And every time she looked, there he was looking at her. Staring, really. And then, even when she didn't look around, when she wasn't checking, it seemed to her that she could feel his stare, as if it had weight. She tried for a while not to think about it and not to let herself worry about it, but that did no good. It was perfectly true, and he was staring.

Then he put his arm around her shoulder. He tried to pass it off as just another stepfatherly gesture, asking her if she was "comfy," but his voice sounded odd, as if it came from the works of some kind of intricate doll.

"Oh, yes," she said. It seemed to be the only possible thing to say. She couldn't very well ask him to take his arm away from her shoulder. It would have been too blunt and too definite. She was not, after all, absolutely certain that her suspicions were not groundless. And all he had done, and she hoped all he intended to do, was to put an arm around her shoulder.

But that thought was terribly disturbing. The very fact that she was hoping that he wouldn't try to do anything else, or anything more, raised the possibility that he would. And the possibility seemed to be a probability. And when he started stroking the back of her neck with a fingertip, a certainty. An absolute certainty.

It was just awful. And the worst part of it was that

she had nowhere to go. Oh, certainly, she could invent some pretext for getting out of the room and away from him this time. But her father was in Europe with Melissa, and her mother didn't seem to care about anything much. It was outrageous. And the rage that she felt was something of a tonic. She had run away before and she could do it again. But the effort of it, the necessity of it, the sordidness of it all were tiresome. And tiring. It was literally tiring to think about. She felt as though she were not merely contemplating running, but had actually been running, for days, for weeks, breathlessly and furiously.

But she had not been running at all. What she had been doing was precisely the opposite. She had been sitting very still, not moving, hardly even breathing, in the vain hope—she knew even then that it was vain—that he might not notice her or, noticing her stillness, might get bored or discouraged. Or feel like the crumb that he was.

It didn't work. She hadn't expected that it would, had known, actually, that it wouldn't, and that, had she been able to remain as still as stone, even that would not help. But she understood suddenly the odd myths she had had to study at school, which had seemed so bizarre to her at the time. Those Greek maidens who were always turning into birds, into trees, into springs, into flowers . . . She wished she could.

The hand moved. He was no longer stroking her neck but her upper arm. Idly, absently, as if to suggest that he was not quite aware of what it was that he was doing. The upper arm, and then the inner part of the arm, and she knew, oh, she knew beyond any doubt or hope that it would be her breast next, and that those stubby fingers would be touching her breast in another few seconds or few minutes. Whenever he felt like it. Why didn't he go upstairs to her mother? What a horrible thing that would be to ask him. And satisfying, too. She wondered what he would say. She wondered if she had the nerve to ask him.

And then the fingers moved, ever so slightly, as if the intention was only to continue stroking her upper arm, and quite by accident they brushed against her blouse. She felt as if a bug were crawling on her.

"Please, Harry. Don't . . ." she said.

"Don't what?" he asked, as if he had no idea what she was talking about.

"Don't touch me that way."

"What way? What do you mean? What way?"

"You know," she said plaintively. And then again, more calmly, "You know."

"No," he said angrily. "No, I don't know."

But before she could answer, before she could frame the words that would be at the same time tactful enough and yet firm enough, he leaned toward her, reached around with his other arm to hold her, and tried to kiss her. She averted her mouth, but he kissed her anyway, on the chin, on the cheek, on the lower lip, following with his mouth, chasing, while she turned her head this way and that, fleeing from his kiss. And all the time he held her in a grip of iron.

"Stop! Stop it! Harry, for God's sake, please stop it. Let me go," she pleaded.

And suddenly, for no reason that she could imagine, he did. And she fled from the room and ran upstairs to her room. She lay down on her bed, listening, wondering whether he would follow her, whether he was following her even as she lay there, but stealthily, so that she could not hear him. She wondered whether she dared get undressed to go to sleep. She thought of herself asleep where she was in the room in his house, and wondered whether she dared sleep. There was no key in the empty door lock. Would he come in to continue to pursue her, to molest her further. . . . It was horrible, horrible.

Deliberately she tried to calm herself. She could

scream. Lyon was asleep in the next room. And her mother, her own mother, was asleep in their room, in her and Harry's room, at the end of the hall. They would wake up, she thought. And that was all she dared think, because she knew, even without thinking it out, that if Harry attacked her there would be nothing that Lyon or her mother could do, even if she screamed and woke them, and they both came in and wanted to help her. But she didn't think that Harry would. She wasn't sure, of course. And she had no idea why she thought so, but she did think that, for that evening anyway, he would leave her alone. Just before she fell asleep, she realized that she could always call Sam Jaggers. And that made her feel better, safer, and calm enough so that she could, after a while, drift off into a troubled sleep.

Her first thought when she woke up the next morning was that she would try to keep Lyon with her as much as possible. While she was around the house, anyway. And she would try to be around the house as little as possible. Neither scheme seemed foolproof. But the thought of Mr. Jaggers, off in New York, was enormously comforting.

Although hardly a passionate athlete, Merry decided to join the Beverly Hills Tennis Club as an associate member and to take tennis lessons there. Her game, she explained, could use a little polish. Her real game, however, was getting out of the house, and the tennis lessons were as good a way of managing that as any she could think of. For one thing, she could go to the club as often as she liked to play tennis. Then, while she was there, she could meet people—other people her own age, whom she realized she missed. She had to create for herself an active social life, the more demanding the better. And the members of the Beverly Hills Tennis Club—to which her father belonged, and to which she had the right to apply for an associate membership—would all be appropriate people for her to be friends with. All she had to do was to find a few whom she could stand.

It was easier than she had feared it would be. She was both surprised and delighted to find, after all those years, that her situation was not unique, that there were other children of other movie stars, with whom she felt immediate bonds of sympathy and understanding and who felt the same sympathy and understanding toward her. They knew all about being a celebrity in school for nothing at all they had done themselves but only because of who their parents were. They knew about the shifting domestic arrangements, the geographical whimsy of homes and careers, the years of loneliness at schools and camps, the piles of money and the pinches of affection. And they welcomed Merry into their midst as openly and as eagerly as a settlement of British colonial officers would welcome a new British family to their sun-baked island, or a gathering of deposed kings and archdukes in Lisbon would welcome the newest victim of yet another revolution.

They were in many ways a strange group, but then they had all led strange lives, had been exposed to the surrealist glitter and to the infernal greed and selfishness of Hollywood from their earliest years. There wasn't a one of them who hadn't known exactly how well or badly his father or mother was doing in the business simply from the birthday-party invitations they got or failed to get.

These children's parties were, like all parties in Hollywood, a kind of stock exchange. The parents came, too, and they were there to make deals, to insinuate themselves, or to join the others in the rich feasting upon a shred of some shattered career. But, almost incidentally, the children got to know one another. Often they hated each other at first, but just as often they found that they had outgrown everyone else, the other, ordinary kids who were less cynical than they, less rich and less battered. What could they talk about with such innocent youngsters?

It was through the pro that Merry met Pam Gerrard, the daughter of the director Walter Gerrard. They played tennis together a few times, and then one day Pam suggested that after their game they have lunch together. From that point on it was easy.

They were all there. There was Lila Frampton, the daughter of the singer, and Bill Hollister, whose mother had been one of America's sex symbols and still was, so that Bill's very existence was an embarrassment to her and to the studio. What kind of sex goddess has a seventeen-year-old son? And there was Ronny Golden, the son of the great comic. Or he had been great once. Now he worked on television, throwing pies around in between the cartoons in the afternoons, and he drank a lot. And there was Harry Green, whose father was the producer of all the Dracula movies, after having produced Brecht in Berlin. And Jill Morgan, the granddaughter of the dancer. And Ed Kent, the son of the singing cowboy. And of course Pam and Merry.

They were at Bill Hollister's, because his mother was in New York for a two-week series of conferences with the studio brass, and the great big house and the great big pool and the great big bar were all there, feeling sad because nobody was using them.

What amazed Merry was not their indifference, their cynicism, or their amused distaste for everything and everyone, but her own innocence. She had never examined her own position, had never realized the extent to which her own life was affected, had to be affected, by her father's career. None of these people had any ambition, but then they all had trust funds of substantial size, and no worries about money for as long as they lived. Or even momentary worries. Bill Hollister's father, who did nothing but produce his wife's movies—co-produce, actually; he always got someone else to do the actual work, sign the contracts and checks, and make the phone calls and write the letters—didn't like to be bothered with anything so demanding as a weekly allowance for his son, household money for the servants, pin money for things like the paper boy or the cleaner. He simply kept a couple hundred dollars in small bills and change in the upper-right-hand drawer of the Regency desk in his study. It was like a faucet, and anyone who was thirsty was to go and get a drink. He didn't like to be bothered with specific requests. He looked in the drawer from time to time, and if it wasn't full, filled it.

But the Hollisters' method of money management was merely a picturesque example of the general unreality of money that they all felt, because their parents all felt it. Merry was fascinated by them all. She had gone to the beach with them, and driven along on the Palisades Highway to look down on the sand and spy out the sleeping bags they were always sure to find, writhing like beached dugongs. There was a striking detachment in their observations of these matings that was as interesting to her as the matings themselves. They took nothing seriously—not even sex, which, in their parents' lives, was something like motherhood and the flag—one of the great, solemn, sacred things. But to these youngsters even that solemnity was intolerable. Besides, they knew what came of it. They knew about the affairs, the divorces, the paternity suits, the irregular ménages that had wrecked their own childhood, and while they were not blaming anyone or anything—because to do so would be to be stuffy and self-righteous—they were not going to swear allegiance, either, stiff at attention, with a hand over the genitals. It was all too silly.

On the other hand, they certainly did not despise sex. At the pool at the tennis club that morning, Ronny Golden had mentioned an article he'd read in the Los Angeles *Times* about a crackdown on a ring of pornographers in Chicago. The intriguing part of the story was the amateurishness of the ring, which was made up not of professional pornographers but of quite ordinary people, mostly married couples, who were exchanging Polaroid photographs of each other.

"Why Polaroids?" Pam asked.

"Well, it's obvious, isn't it?" Harry replied. "With an ordinary camera you've either got to take the film down to the drugstore, which isn't terribly likely, or you've got to have your own darkroom, which is a nuisance."

"You mean the drugstores won't develop pictures . . . like that?"

"No," Harry said.

"That's lousy," Ed Kent said. "I mean, if you stop to think about it, it's really lousy. Say a guy is married and he and his wife want to take pictures of each other. They ought to have a right to do that."

"Why would they want to do that?" Pam asked.

"I don't know. But why shouldn't they be able to?" Ed asked.

"I can imagine that a man and his wife would want to have pictures of each other so that, when they got old and wrinkled and—well—ugly they could look at the pictures," Lila suggested.

"It doesn't even have to be anything as remote as that. There are voyeurs in the world, you know," Ronny said.

"What are voyeurs?" Merry asked.

"People who like to watch," he answered.

"Doesn't everyone?" Bill Hollister asked. They all laughed, and then dropped it for a while.

It was later, in the locker room, when the boys were dressing, that Bill asked Harry and Ed whether they thought he ought maybe to get a Polaroid.

"Sure, why not?" Ed said.

"What? What?" It was Ronny, coming out of the shower. "What are you cooking up now?"

They were down in the cellar in a large, paneled playroom Bill's father had had built. There was a long bar at one end of the room, and there were pinball machines, and even a slot machine, at the end of the bar. The rest of the room was open for dancing, but lined with large red leather couches. On the walls were heads of moose and deer and antelope that the elder Hollister had bought from a Los Angeles taxidermist.

They sat around and talked, danced occasionally, or just sat there with a drink in one hand and tapping the fingers of the other to the rhythms of the music. It was actually a little boring. But that had been planned. It was Ronny's idea that a little bit of boredom at the beginning of a party could be a good thing. Whatever you suggested would then seem all the more attractive if only because something is always better than nothing.

Bill waited until the interval between two records and then mentioned to Harry and Ed, as if it were news, that he'd bought a Polaroid that afternoon.

It was like turning a switch on a cleverly designed machine. Everyone was interested. The girls were interested, and the boys were interested in their interest. The conversation moved smoothly from a reprise of the crackdown in Chicago, to a proposal that they take some dirty pictures, to a hesitancy on the part of Pam and Merry and Jill. Lila was all for it, but then she was all for anything, and mainly for Bill. But that moment of hesitation had been foreseen, and the answer to it was that they should play strip poker first—which implied that not all of them would be stripped, and not all of them would be taking the pictures, or posing for them. It wasn't a sound, solid excuse, but as Ronny had explained earlier, before the girls had shown up, it didn't have to be. All it had to be was a pretext that the girls could use to talk themselves into it. And they did.

They began to play, and even then Ronny's scenario held good. Jill lost a shoe, and then Lila, and Bill and

Ed, and then Lila lost her other shoe, and Ronny lost one of his. It went on that way until the eight of them were sitting around in various stages of undress at the intersection of what were really two different games. The winner, in theory, was Ed, who had lost only his shoes and socks. But he was the loser, too, for the object of attention, and the object of the game, was nudity, and Lila, who was clad only in a bra and a pair of panties, was winning as much as Ed was. It was, as Ronny said it would be, a case of clinically induced mass hysteria. Lila, of course, was embarrassed to be the first to have to strip off anything vital, but she did. In a couple of hands in which Ronny lost his shirt and Merry her skirt, Lila sat there smoking, flicking her cards nervously with a thumbnail, and licking her lips, which seemed suddenly to be very dry. And then she lost and had to take her brassiere off.

Nobody said anything, or even seemed to stare, but they all looked, and she was as suave and dignified about it as she could be, not even trying to cover her breasts with her arms, which she could have done by holding the cards up in front of her face. To have done so would have been to violate the code which they had all set up for the evening by having agreed in the first place to play the game.

But the game wasn't even the main object. Nobody yet had mentioned the Polaroid camera that Bill had left at one end of the bar. No one had even alluded to it. But it was there in all their minds, at the same time exciting and frightening.

They played a few more hands. They were playing with lots of wild cards, in a futile attempt to keep some interest in the game itself, in the play of the cards. Deuces and jacks and the king with the ax. Deuces, treys, and one-eyed jacks. Red fives and black tens. And there were lots of straights and flushes and four- and five-of-a-kind hands. But nobody cared. What they watched was Merry taking off her slip, or Pam taking off her bra, or Harry taking off his trousers. And Lila, at last, the first to strip down altogether, standing up, pushing her underpants down past her hips, and then stepping out of them. Her nakedness was an incentive to the play, to the stripping, to the progress of the evening toward the camera on the bar. Lila had dark hair, and the darkness of her pubic hair made her look, if anything, even more naked.

Merry was enormously relieved at not having to be the first one to strip. She was sure that she couldn't have managed it at all, but would have run out of the room and out of the house. The idea of having to take one's clothes off while everyone else was dressed was utterly terrible. Or was it? In a curious, incredible, improbable way, she realized that she was, at least partially, looking forward to taking off her clothes, too. Her body was as good as Lila's, certainly. And being, at the worst, the second girl to strip, she would have company, and a kind of support.

"Pretty as a picture, isn't she?" one of the boys asked.

"What about that?" another asked. "Why don't we take some?"

"Pictures?"

"Sure. I think that next time Lila loses, she ought to have to pose for a picture," Ronny suggested. "Does that seem fair?"

They agreed that that was fair.

"Talking about fair," Pam said. "I've been wondering why it is that you can only lose in this game. I mean, the point is to see who loses the slowest. But you can't win. What if Lila won the next hand? Shouldn't she get to put something back on?"

"No, that gets too complicated. If she won, she wouldn't necessarily be winning her clothes," Harry said. "She might win a whole mess of socks, say, or a couple of belts. It would depend on what was bet. This way it's sort of like a game I was in last winter. We all went out to the beach and built a huge bonfire, and we played strip poker, and the loser of each hand had to throw one article of clothing into the fire. We had a hell of a time getting home, I'll tell you."

"Come on," Lila said. "If you're playing, then play."

"What's the matter? Feeling lonesome?"

"No, just a little silly," she said.

"Relax, dear, you look great."

But they dealt another hand and started to play again. Harry lost his undershorts, and he was naked now, too. Merry tried not to stare at him, but she could hardly help it. It was odd the way boys were built, she thought. She wondered how it felt to walk around all the time with all that hanging down between their legs, and how they could do it without getting aroused all the time. But on the other hand, for all she knew, maybe they were.

There were a few more hands. Merry had to take her bra off, but it wasn't so bad. For one thing, Lila was naked, and Pam had taken her bra off a long time ago. And then, for another, Merry's breasts were bigger than Pam's, but not so big as Lila's, and she was glad to be sort of in the middle. She felt a little less noticeable that way. At the same time, she was beginning to feel a distinct thrill every time one of the boys looked directly at her naked breasts. She looked down and saw that her nipples were hard and swollen.

Ed lost his shorts. And then Lila lost again, and they had to stop playing to take a picture of her.

Bill had already loaded the camera, but it took a few minutes to get the flash attachment on, and then, when the camera was ready, they had to decide what to do with Lila. How to pose her.

"Alone or with somebody?" was the first question that had to be answered.

"How about alone this time, and with somebody next time?"

"But with whom?"

"How about from now on we play high-low, and the high hand and the low hand pose together?"

It was agreed that that's what they'd do.

But that still left the posing of Lila. They had her sit on one of the couches. They tried it with her lying down on one of the couches. But, as Bill said, "It's all right, but it's not great!"

Finally, they had her lie down on the floor next to one of the couches. She lay on her back, crooked one arm under her head, stretched out the other arm, and bent one knee to the side. Bill stood on the couch above her and shot downward.

"You closed your eyes!" he said.

"It was the flash."

"Well, let's see what we got."

Bill pulled the tab of the film, waited sixty seconds, and then pulled the backing off the film to reveal the picture.

"Sensational!"

"A little too light, don't you think?"

"Who notices about too light? Just so long as you can see her."

"Let me look," Lila demanded. They handed her the picture, carefully holding it by the edges and warning her to hold it the same way. She didn't say a thing, but just stared at it, both delighted and a little bit shocked, too. "It looks like . . ." she began, but then stopped.

"It looks like you've just had it."

"From a whole army."

"Back to the game, back to the game!"

But first there was the new question to be resolved—what to do with the pictures. There was after all a picture now, still wet from the fixative coating from the little squeegee and curled from the wetness and from having been pulled out of the camera. But to whom should it go? It was suggested that the subject of the picture assign it. But what would they do with pictures in which there were more than one subject? They could play poker for them, someone offered. But, no, it might work out that one person would wind up with all the pictures, or with most of them. And, if for no other reason than the safety of the thing, it was essential that all of them should have a selection of the pictures. At last the decision was made that all the pictures should be kept together, mixed up, and dealt out, face down, at the end of the evening. That way it would be entirely random and entirely fair.

They continued to play cards, but there was no real interest in it any more. It was only a matter of time before they would all be stripped and, anyway, the point now was the taking of the pictures. So they all stripped and sat down for a new hand, for the pictures, playing for the privilege or the obligation of posing for the Polaroid. They played high-low, and this time there were no wild cards. The game was interesting again. It was Pam's deal, and she dealt out the seven cards quickly and smoothly.

"Now what do I do?" Merry asked.

They explained it to her. She could declare either high or low. If she declared high she would take the five cards that made the best hand; if she declared low she would take the five cards that made the worst hand—ace, two, three, four, six, of mixed suits, for instance. That was assuming that she was trying to win. If she was trying to lose, she would take the best hand she could make and declare low, or the worst hand and declare high. It was, they all agreed, deliciously complicated.

Merry had three eights among her seven cards. That was a pretty good hand. So she took the three eights and declared low, figuring that she would be sure to lose that way. But nobody else at the table had a hand anywhere near that good, and they were all trying to lose, too, and all declared high. Which meant that Merry had won the low spot. Ed Kent won the high spot with a jack-high hand. Everyone put the cards down. Bill picked up the camera and held it while Harry and Ronny looked at the instruction book and fussed with the controls on the front, talking of lightness and darkness and distance from the flash.

"OK. On the couch, I guess, huh?"

"Yeah, on the couch."

She sat down on the couch and Ed sat down beside her. She looked at the camera in order not to look at him.

"How about a kiss?" one of the girls suggested.

"No, too obvious. It ought to be more stylized. Look at the way Merry is looking at the camera. Like that. But hold each other."

"Hold? You mean I should put my arms around her?" Ed asked.

"No, no. That'd be like the kissing. Look straight ahead, and with one hand hold her tit. And you hold him."

Timorously she put her hand out and closed her fingers around his penis, now erect, thinking all the time that at least she didn't have to look at it, as if it couldn't possibly be happening unless she saw it happening. But all she saw was the camera, and Bill moving closer with it, and then backing up a little, and then moving closer again.

"Smile," he said. "Say cheese."

She smiled. The camera flashed. She let go. It occurred to her that she had hardly even been aware of his hand on her breast.

They pulled the film out of the camera, waited the sixty seconds, and then peeled the print.

"Great! It's Grant Wood gone porno!"

"The light's much better this time."

"Pretty funny."

Merry looked. It was incredible. Involuntarily she wiped her hand against her thigh. The picture fascinated her. It was exciting to look at herself and see how very sexy she was. And she wondered whether Ed wasn't embarrassed by having an erection like that. It was so visible.

The picture-taking continued. They abandoned the cards altogether, and now they just took pictures. Bill and Lila, lying on the floor together, each with a hand on the other's genitals. Harry and Pam, with Pam sitting on Harry's lap, and their arms around each other. Ronny between Jill and Lila, with both of them holding him as if he were a baseball bat and they were captains of opposing teams choosing for first ups. And then Merry between Ronny and Bill, with each of them holding a breast, and with her holding both of them, one in each hand. And then Lila and Pam kissing each other and holding each other's breasts. And then Lila and Bill, with Bill on top of Lila as if they were actually doing it.

There was the usual fiddling around with the camera to get the best angle, and then finally, when the angle was right, Ed, who was taking the picture, said, "OK, look passionate, kiddies. Look as if you're really screwing her."

"He is!" Lila announced, rather calmly.

"Jesus Christ! He really is!"

The camera clicked and the flashbulb flashed. The picture was disappointing. It didn't show as much as they had hoped. It didn't show much at all. Just from looking at it, you couldn't have known it was the real thing at all. But it was the real thing. They had all heard Bill groan during the quiet sixty seconds that the film took to develop. And there were a few laughs, and somebody even clapped. But then they peeled the print away from the negative part of the film pack, and all it showed was the two bodies, one on top of the other.

"Come on, let's go," someone whispered into Merry's ear. It was Pam. "Come on," she said again, still whispering, but insistently, pleadingly. Merry was rather relieved that Pam had decided to go. She knew that she should have decided that a long time ago. It was just that she was shy. Which was pretty funny in a way. She nodded, yes.

She followed Pam across the room to the other couch, near the bar, where their clothes were.

"Hey, where are you girls going? The fun's just beginning!"

"Aw, Pam, come on."

"Don't go yet. Let's at least finish the roll."

"Yeah, the roll!" somebody echoed, and the rest laughed.

"I promised I'd get Merry home by midnight, and it's nearly one now," Pam explained.

"Well, then she's already in trouble."

"We should have gone an hour ago."

"Oh, come on!"

"No. I can't. Her stepfather is a monster, anyway."

It wasn't their arguments or their protestations, but the fact that they had put their clothes on that sealed it. There seemed to be no hope at all of getting them to undress again.

"Well, I guess if you've got to. But take a couple of pictures."

The pictures were arranged, face down, on the bar. Merry and Pam each took two. Merry didn't even look to see which ones she had chosen until they were in the car. She had got the one of Lila and Pam, and the one of herself and Ed Kent. She put them into one of the side compartments of her purse.

"Son of a bitch!" Pam said.

"What? Who?"

"Bill."

"Oh?" Merry asked.

"Doing a thing like that right in front of me."

"Yes," Merry said. She had no idea what, exactly, was bothering Pam. They'd all been doing all of it together. And while she was glad to be in the car going home, she thought it had been pretty exciting.

The law about every action having a reaction of equal force and in the opposite direction does not apply to human behavior. With human actions there is frequently no reaction at all. But somtimes, even more tantalizingly, more frustratingly, there is some sort of reaction, of unequal force and in some improbable direction. In this case, the reaction to the evening in the playroom came through another party, a going-away party for Tony Hardison, who was leaving the faculty of the film department at UCLA for the faculty at NYU. He was a person of almost no importance. The party was hardly the great social occasion of the season, but only a gathering of disparate people in a small rented house of vaguely Moorish design in a cheaper section of Brentwood.

What made it important was Sandra Kellman's invitation to Bill and Ronny and Ed, at the paperback rack of a Schwab's drugstore one afternoon. Bill went home and called Pam to invite her to this blast he'd heard about. She declined him, quite coolly. Then he called Merry, invited her, and she accepted. As soon as he'd hung up, she called Pam to make sure that Pam didn't mind, and even offered to have a headache or something, if she wanted her to. Pam told Merry to go ahead and have fun, if she wanted to. But she was through with Bill Hollister. News of the party got around. The fact that Bill had called Pam and had been turned down, and that he'd called Merry and was taking her, was a part of the news. Lila Frampton heard about it, thought about it for a while, brooded about it, decided that Bill Hollister was a son of a bitch and Merry Houseman was a pain in the ass, and admitted to herself that she had been betrayed. She was not quite sure just how she had been betrayed, but the feeling was inescapable. What kind of an impossible bunch of people were they? They had made her feel ridiculous. And cheated. It wasn't that she had gone too far at that picture-taking session, but that they had all stopped short. And now Bill Hollister was taking Merry to the party, and not her.

None of this was articulated in just so many words. It all welled up, and the pressure built, until she felt she had to do something to get back at someone. And in almost a random way she picked Merry. She knew Merry less well than Bill or Pam. And besides, she hadn't quite given up on Bill Hollister. Getting at Merry the right way would clear the field for her with him. But that was only a secondary reason. It only occurred to her after she had taken the envelope down to the corner and dropped it in the mailbox. And it only seemed to make it all the better.

Inside the envelope was a picture of Merry, naked, sitting between two young men. In each hand she held the penis of one of the young men. Each of them was holding one of her breasts.

The envelope was addressed to Mr. Meredith Houseman, The Excelsior Hotel, Rome, Italy.

It wasn't so much a party as a mob. The small living room was packed with people. So was the dining room. It took literally five minutes to get from the living room into the dining room, where there were bottles of liquor set out on a table, and back to the living room again. The trip would hardly have been worth it if it hadn't been for the heat. The very body heat of all those people overwhelmed the air-conditioner, and one had to set off for the liquor table or perish of thirst.

All that would have been tolerable if it had been a good mob, a mob that knew each other, or at least had something in common so that they could get to know each other or might care to try. But Tony Hardison prided himself on knowing different kinds of people. Academics and nonacademics, film people and athletes, writers and plumbers. In a way he'd made a small academic career out of it, because the people at the

University assumed that his connections with the commercial film world were important, and a kind of endorsement of his credentials. The commercial film people, similarly, respected his academic connections. It was a nice little tightrope he managed to walk. But it made for lousy parties.

Merry was bored out of her mind. She was sitting on a bridge chair, by herself, in a room full of people, none of whom she knew. The bridge chair was just next to the air-conditioner, and it was one of the few places in the room that was even bearable. Bill had set out for the dining room to get fresh drinks, and he seemed to be taking forever to come back.

"Jesus, it's hot."

"I beg your pardon," Merry said.

"I said it's hot."

"I know. I was only wondering whether it was me that you were talking to."

"Yeah, I guess so. Have a drink?"

"A friend just went to get me one."

"It'll take him a while. It took me a while to get these. And the girl I got this one for has disappeared. You take it."

"Thanks," Merry said, and she took the drink.

"You a friend of Tony's?" he asked.

"No. A friend of a friend, only."

"Then you're closer than most. We met in a bar once. Six, maybe eight months ago. And he wrote my name down in a book. A week ago he called me to invite me to this. Crazy."

"You must have made some sort of an impression on him," she said.

"An impression on an IBM machine. I was drunk, and I let it out that I was a technical adviser on movies."

"Oh?"

"Action stuff. Used to be a stunt man. Now I just figure them out and hire the guys to do the work."

"And that was why he invited you?"

"Yeah. I wouldn't have come, but . . . As a matter of fact, I don't know why I did. My name's Denver James."

"I'm Merry Houseman."

"Oh? I once doubled for your father. I forget what picture."

"Oh?" It was odd. His hair was black, and he had a square, chunky body. He looked nothing at all like her father.

"It doesn't matter. It's hot as hell in here, isn't it? How about you and me go for a ride somewhere?"

"No, I think not. My friend will be coming back any moment."

"The kid?"

"I'm sorry?"

"The kid you came in with. He's talking to some dame with hair down to her ass and beads the size of eggs. In the dining room."

"Well, it's a party," she said. "That's what people do at parties, isn't it?"

"Yeah, that's what people do," he said, but he said it with a suggestive quality in his voice, a barely hidden leer that Merry didn't care for at all.

"Excuse me," she said. She got up and wove her way through the crowd toward the bathroom. She was not exactly running to the bathroom to hide, but only to put some cold water on her face and cool off a little. Getting away from that man was only incidental.

The bathroom was hardly an ideal refuge. At the sink there was a girl putting in a contact lens that had fallen out. Another girl was puking into the toilet. She left the bathroom. In the hallway she saw that Bill Hollister was indeed talking to some girl with hair down to her ass. And Denver James was waiting for her. He had picked up the drink she had left, and was holding it.

"You forgot this," he said. "When you're running away, always walk. That way you won't trip."

"I wasn't running away."

"Good," he said. "Then why don't we run away now? It's just too damned hot in here."

She thought about it for a moment. It seemed almost to be a dare. It was corny, but there it was. "All right," she said. "Let's."

His Bugatti was parked outside. He drove fast but well, westward toward the Pacific. At the ocean he turned south, went through Santa Monica and on toward Venice. He had turned on the radio, and he tapped his fingers lightly in the rhythm of the music. He didn't say anything, and Merry didn't say anything, either, but the silence was clear enough. Sooner or later, she knew, he would make his pass. It was there, like the ocean, surging and falling on the sand. It didn't need to announce itself, or make conversation. It was just there. Not that it was at all important. Somehow, it just didn't seem to be all that big a deal any more. She remembered Bill screwing Lila that way, and didn't care. That was the funny thing. That she didn't care. Well, as far as this Denver James went, she was willing to go along. She'd try to stop at some reasonable point, but she just wasn't sure whether there was a reasonable point, or if there was, where it was. It seemed odd, now that she thought of it. Her flight from Harry Novotny's ridiculous little bit in front of the television set had brought her to this. Denver was probably about the same age as Novotny. Better-looking, of course, but even that didn't make much of a difference. She wondered if anything did.

He turned off the road and pulled to a stop at a little platform that overlooked the water. Merry was sure that it would come now. Maybe he would smoke a cigarette first. She hoped he wouldn't, mainly because she realized that she'd just as soon get it over with. But he neither lit a cigarette nor made any advance toward her. He just sat there for a while, looking out at the water. Then he asked her, "You want to come inside?"

"Is this your place?"

"That's right."

She opened the door and got out of the car. He got out from his side and led the way into the little beach cottage.

It was a pleasant little place, only two rooms, but the obviousness of it was disarming. It was, without any possible mistake, a shack for shacking up. There was the living room and the bedroom, and a small bathroom, and a smaller kitchenette. In the living room, the only comfortable place to sit, the necessary place to sit really, was the studio couch, which provided a view, through the picture window, of a stretch of beach and a vista of ocean. Merry sat there.

"Would you like a drink?" Denver James asked. "Or beer?"

"A beer, thanks." One of the good things about not fooling around and not playing games with the sex part of it was that she didn't have to play games with anything else. If she'd felt like one, she could have asked for a Coke, without worrying about whether it was childish or grown-up. All that was beside the point, which was a relief.

He sat down next to her and they drank their beers. It was what Novotny had done, sitting with her and drinking a beer. But this was different. She could feel how different it was. It wasn't anything fearful or nervous. He was just taking his own sweet time. He was drinking his beer and enjoying that, and he'd get to her later. When he felt like it. There wasn't any of that hesitation that gives rise only to hesitation. He kicked off his shoes, and unbuttoned his shirt. He had that kind of confidence. And he scratched at his chest a little. And took another sip of beer. Merry kicked off her shoes, too, and tucked her feet up under her.

Even after the beers were finished, he sat there

smoking and looking out the window at the sea. Then he put out the cigarette, stubbing it out carefully, and even explaining, as he did it, "I hate the smell of them when they smolder in ashtrays."

Before she had time to agree with him, she saw that he was drawing close to her. He took her in his arms, held her, kissed her, and then started undoing the buttons of her dress. He undid them all, and then got up to take his own clothes off. She undressed, too.

Even more than at the session in the basement with the cards and the camera, she felt a tingling of excitement as she removed her clothes. It was, she told herself, anticipation. It had to be. She could not have imagined anything else. The darker truth—that her presence in this room was a consequence of her having posed for the pictures and that it was the nakedness that was primary and the mating secondary—would have required an analyst to formulate. And even then, she would not have accepted it.

Still, there was a falling off, and a momentary cooling as she turned to look at him, framed, for an instant, in the glare of light that came through the doorway to the bathroom. He threw the studio couch cover onto the floor and lay down beside her. He held her for a while, and kissed her, and then went into her. It wasn't like it was in novels at all. It didn't hurt so much as they always say it does. And it wasn't great and glorious and beautiful the way they say it is. It wasn't much of anything.

He was slow and easy and gentle with her, and it was mildly interesting to feel him ejaculate the warm, wet fluid into her. But it wasn't very exciting.

It was only the second time that she liked it. It was odd, but she hadn't expected a second time. She thought that people just did it once and then it was a new chapter. Or they went to sleep. Or he would take her home. But they lay there together, and he ran his fingers over her, and touched her. And she ran her fingers over him, because it seemed somehow to be the polite thing to do. And she watched him as he began to get hard, and saw how he got bigger, and hardened, and the way his penis started to twitch, and grow, and then stretched out along the flesh of his thigh, and then grew more, and moved like the hand of a clock until it pointed to his navel, straight up, and then raised itself from his abdomen. And he went into her again, and this time it was exciting. It still wasn't the big thing, the great climax with fireworks and drums and pounding surf. But it was good. And when it was over, she said that she'd better be getting home.

They got dressed and he drove her home. She had to tell him how to get there, but that was all they talked about on the way back. They pulled up in front of the house.

"I don't think I can invite you in," she said. "I'm sorry."

"That's all right," he said. "Hell, I've already been in, haven't I?"

She smiled. It was funny, after all.

"That's better," he said. "A little smile never did anyone any harm, now, did it?"

"I guess not," she said. She noticed that he was smiling. "Good night," she said.

She got out of the car and went into the house, as quietly as she could.

In the Bugatti Denver James lit a cigarette. She was gone, but he was still smiling. He was remembering another night, years before. What the hell was her name, he wondered. Ellen? Helen? He sat there, outside the house, until he remembered without any effort. The trip to Mexico, and all of it. This kid's mother. It was kind of funny. It meant that he was getting on, getting old. But he knew that anyway. And he couldn't imagine a better way to do it. No, sir.

He started the car and drove back to the cottage.

Three days later Merry left Los Angeles. Her father had called Jaggers, who had called Wemmick, who had come to the Novotny house to tell the Novotnys that Mr. Houseman didn't approve of the company that Merry seemed to be keeping, or of the apparent lack of supervision on their part. He waited while Merry packed, and he drove her out to the airport. On the way he asked her about the pictures, how many of them there were and who might have them.

"That was the only one," she said. "There were two. I mean, there were two that I was in. I have the other one."

"Burn it," he said.

She waited for the lecture. It was a long drive to the airport, and it looked as though it would be one long lecture. But all he said was, "This kind of thing can be expensive, you know."

"I know, now."

"Good. We won't always be this lucky."

She didn't answer. No answer seemed to be necessary.

At the airport he told her that Sam Jaggers would meet the plane. And that she would spend the rest of the summer with him.

"All right," she said.

"Actually, I think you'll like him. He's a fine man."

"I do like him," she said.

He smiled, said, "Good-bye, Merry," and went back to his car.

Merry spent the summer with Sam and Ethel Jaggers. She lived with them and spent the days teaching rhythm and dance to five- and six-year-olds at the Ethical Culture School Day Camp in Riverdale. The school bus left from Sixty-third Street and Central Park West, only a few blocks' walk from the Dakota, on Seventy-second Street, where the Jaggers had an apartment.

On September first, her seventeenth birthday, the

Jaggers took her out to dinner at the Chambord. Before dinner, they ordered champagne cocktails, not only for themselves but for Merry, too. She would have felt very grown up, except that it was too late for that now.

CHAPTER SEVEN

♥ Merry's return to the East was more than an airplane flight that could be measured in thousands of miles. It was a change of worlds. Behind her, receding at incredible speed, the whole crazy world of Los Angeles, with its barbaric foliage, its uncertain geology, its gaudiness, diminished into a bad dream, and then into the recollection of a bad dream. That strange things had happened to her there, that she had herself done unlikely things, seemed perfectly normal. It was a kind of looking-glass world, anyway, there, where one lost all bearings and all patterns of appropriate behavior. Not even Alice, who had seemed to be a perfectly well brought up little girl, of a perfectly ordinary family, had been able to carry her sanity with her when she had ventured down into the rabbit hole, or through the looking glass. And it had been like that for Merry. Novotny's advances, the incredible evening in the playroom, the improbable evening with Denver James, all seemed to her to be encounters with new and less pleasant versions of Tweedledee or the Mock Turtle.

Jagger's world was so astringently, so bracingly real. And the buildings of New York were so stable and so weighty. There couldn't be, in New York, any of those bizarre landslides one kept reading about in Los Angeles, in which a palisade would suddenly fall into the Pacific, taking with it six or eight houses. There were geological faults out there. Nothing was certain or definite or reliable out there.

But even New York seemed busy and distracting in retrospect when she considered it, as she did every now and then, from the safety and security of her room in the Mather School. She knew that she was putting a great deal of faith in small things, but her knowledge of what she was doing did not interfere with her doing it. The comfortable continuity of the pattern, say, of the cover of her new math book, just like last year's but in a new color, was indescribably soothing. She arranged her textbooks on her desk with sacerdotal care, promising herself that this term she would study hard. She would really work. It was a kind of sacrifice that she promised to the household gods of her dormitory room, in exchange for which she hoped that those gods would afford her their blessing and their protection.

Helen Farnam thought it was all perfectly natural. She was not, anyway, the kind of person who would ask questions, but in this case there didn't seem to be anything unusual or remarkable. Sure Merry was hitting the books, but this was the term to do it. It seemed to Helen to be a pretty good idea. This was the time to shine, and improve like hell for the college-entrance people. This was the last term they'd see on the records that went in with the applications. Helen's explanation, and the reasons she adduced, were all sensible. But they had never even crossed Merry's mind. All she thought about was that nothing could reach her, nothing could touch her here.

If only he had not torn it up, but had left it about so that she could look at it, it might have been different. She could have stared at it until it got boring, until she had somehow exorcised it, and had conquered it. But destroyed as it was, it was all the more powerful, for it was no longer a simple piece of paper, but an image in her imagination. It was just bad luck. Melissa could not possibly have asked him not to destroy it, without revealing too much. For to have revealed anything would have been to reveal too much. And, thinking about it, she knew that there was nothing she could have done to prevent him from tearing it up and setting fire to the fragments in the ashtray of the study in the villa. She had thought, when he took it with him from the hotel to the villa where they went for weekends, that he was going to keep it, to tuck it away somewhere where it would be safe. And it would have been safe that way. Far safer than it was this way, committed to her memory. It was something she thought about rather more than she would have liked.

She could understand the reason. It was the resemblance between the two of them, the striking resemblance which was so invidiously alluring. She was sufficiently aware of her own nature to know that the incredible translation of the same features to a female body, softer, smoother, rounder, and less frightening, was what had captured her fancy so. She liked Meredith and even loved him. More than she had ever expected to love any man, she loved him. She had married him thinking, with at least a part of her mind, that it was better to have been married and separated than never to have been married at all. It solved so many problems. One was no longer a spinster, which was such a terribly unattractive word. So even if it didn't work out, it would be worthwhile. And so very clean, too, because he was obviously not interested in her money, or in any of the other absurd things for which she had to look out so carefully. And it had been better than she had hoped, because they were not together all the time. He had to run off to make his movies, and to have conferences with studio people, and to discuss his business ventures with his agents and managers. It wasn't one of those dreary little marriages where the wife is always taking off her nightgown to put on an apron, or the other way around. He was good fun and pleasant company and, like the best company, not too oppressive by his hovering around. She had begun to think that it might go on for quite a while, even indefinitely. But then that picture came, that absurd amateurish picture of Merry.

She had seen it only twice, and then it had been torn and burned, but she remembered it. It had been etched into her mind as with the acid of a photoengraver. And she first became aware of how much it meant to her when she noticed that she felt a certain resentment toward Meredith for having burned it. It was his daughter, and his daughter's picture, and of course he had the right to burn it. To eat it if he wanted to. But it was her picture, too. Deeper and more important in her life than anything he could imagine. Precisely because she liked him, and because she had had a better life with him than she had expected, the picture of his daughter, his double, his mirror image, haunted her. Even when she managed to forget about it, it came back, and at the worst moments. In bed with Meredith one night, she had touched his cheek. It had a day's growth of whiskers on it, because they had been out sailing in the Tyrrhenian Sea for the weekend, and she had all she could do, feeling the stubby growth of the whiskers, not to show her distaste. Men were so hairy, so hard and bony and hairy. And then suddenly she remembered the picture of another Meredith, who looked like this one, who *was* this one in a way, but refined, like a chemical that has been repeatedly distilled, purified into the smoothness and the silken softness with which she was more comfortable and more familiar.

She suggested that perhaps they might go to New York a little earlier than she usually went there, even as early as late September. "No one will be there, darling, and we'll have the whole town to ourselves," she explained. "New York in September? I can hardly imagine it. It must be a little fishing village."

Meredith assured her that there were people in New York even in September. Nobody she knew, perhaps, but people.

And he said that, yes, they'd go early, so that she could see it.

The probabilities were all against it. She reassured herself with the thought that, almost assuredly, Merry would be one of those boring American girls who nourish themselves exclusively on Life Savers and milk shakes, who have nothing original or interesting or remarkable about them, whether in their thoughts, their feelings, or their perceptions. And she even hoped that Merry would be one of those girls, for then she could dismiss her and be rid of her. No matter what she looked like, and no matter how attractive she was or how like her father she was, unless she was truly *sympathique,* there was nothing appealing or interesting about a seventeen-year-old girl. And women are much more sensible than men, anyway, not being so easily swayed by a well-sculpted cheekbone, or a graceful brow, or a limpid gaze. Such charms are by no means negligible, but they are only secondary. A woman learns, from looking into her own mirror, how little appearance is to be trusted, how little the eyes reveal of the soul.

Meredith had to go to the coast. There was some enormously large, enormously complicated business about making films in Spain to liquidate blocked pesetas, which couldn't have been more dreary. But there were very large sums involved, and there was a great deal of planning and discussion that had to be got through. Meredith was kept very busy. That part of Melissa which was frankly scheming about Merry couldn't have been more pleased. The plans were that Meredith would stay in town for the weekend and that Merry would come down from school to see them. And to meet her new stepmother. And then he would go on to the coast. She couldn't have arranged it better if she'd tried. On the other hand, she wondered what she would do in the event that Merry turned out to be dull and ordinary and boring. Shop? See friends? But who would be in New York whom she knew, and whom she could stand?

As it turned out, she was able to stand Merry. More than she hoped, and more than she feared, Merry was an extraordinary girl, a beautiful girl, and so beautifully fragile. She did, indeed, look like her father, but there was a quietness about her which was not mere manners but something physical, like the quietness of an animal, of a fawn, say, who freezes and relies on its dappled camouflage in a time of danger. Oh, she was a sweet, delicate thing, but not maimed or cowed or defeated. Not yet, anyway. It was apparent that she loved her father very much. Even too much. And she was trying very hard to like Melissa and to make Melissa like her. Melissa could tell all of that within five minutes, by the girl's carriage, by the way she leaned forward on a chair, by the way she craned her graceful neck forward just a little and listened so attractively, with her lips just slightly parted.

"You are at school now for good?" Melissa asked.

"For good? I'm sorry. I don't understand . . ." Merry said.

"They let you out sometimes? As now? Or must you stay there always?"

"Oh," she said. "We're allowed to come home on weekends. Seniors are. Or to visit at the homes of classmates, if there is a written invitation. And seniors are allowed to go to a college for a date with a boy, if there is a group of three girls from the school."

"But you could come here on weekends, couldn't you?"

"Yes," Merry said.

"You must do that. It will be a good change for you."

"I'd like that," Merry said.

It was easy enough. It seemed to be for Meredith's benefit, and Meredith, who was sitting opposite them on the other love seat, smiled approvingly. The effect was altogether gratifying, for Merry could not but notice, and would have to think that Melissa was trying to please as much as she was herself. Which was a bond between them. The feeling of being on probation, of being a little uncertain about one's position, had the double effect of making one at once more alert to these tonalities and more vulnerable, more open to this kind of indirect advance.

"I'd like that very much," Merry said again, as if it were a favor that she was doing for Melissa, helping her out in front of Meredith. And that was good, too. The generosity she had displayed meant that she didn't dislike Melissa. And there is no better way of making a friend than allowing someone to do a small favor for you.

For the rest of the evening Melissa settled back and withdrew into the background, leaving the father and the daughter to talk together. She could not hope to compete with Meredith, nor did she mean to try. At eleven-thirty, she brought a kind of coziness to the end of the evening by ordering cocoa, which they could all three drink together. And then they went to bed.

Meredith had to get to the airport fairly early the following morning. And Merry was supposed to take the train back to school right after lunch. They all got up early and had breakfast, and Meredith went off to the airport in the limousine. She and Merry were left alone.

She was tempted to talk to her, to ask her about herself, to find out as much as she could about what her life had been like. She was pleased with the freshness and the apparent innocence of Merry's features, but she was not inclined to stop there, as other people might have done. If for no other reason than that she remembered her own childhood, and how much she had managed to hide under a smooth skin and a clear eye, she was prepared to allow to Merry at least the possibility of some sort of experience. There was, she knew, that extraordinary photograph. But what her experience had been, whether fortunate or unfortunate, helpful or harmful—to Merry and to her own designs upon Merry—she had no idea. And she was eager to find out. But she knew, too, that it might be ruinous to pry. Confidence must be earned. She suggested that they go for a walk in the park. Merry agreed, and they went downstairs, crossed Central Park South, and started north.

They didn't talk much but walked briskly, enjoying the crispness of the late-September morning and the loosening of their muscles with the exercise. The second wave of fatigue, the real fatigue, did not hit them until they were all the way up to the Seventy-second Street crosswalk. They sat down on a bench to rest.

"It's a large park," Melissa said. "I've never walked this far up before."

"I have," Merry said. "This summer. I lived in that building there, with Sam Jaggers. He's Daddy's agent. Or lawyer. Or both, I guess."

"Yes, I know. I thought you were in Los Angeles," Melissa said, lying, to see what Merry would say.

"I was. But I got into some trouble out there. And I came to New York," she said. She looked at Melissa, rather surprised that her stepmother hadn't heard about it.

"Oh?" Melissa asked. But Merry said nothing. She was not yet ready to confide. Just before the pause got to be too long, at which point it would be prying, Melissa continued, "Then perhaps you'd like to stop in and say hello to the Jaggers. Did you like them? Did you have a good time there?"

"Oh, yes. They're wonderful. And . . . I'd like to stop in, if you wouldn't mind."

"Not at all. Why should I mind? Let's call them first, though. There's a phone booth somewhere, I suppose. There always is."

They called up, and then called on the Jaggers, with whom they had a second breakfast. Then they went back to the hotel, and Merry went off to the station to catch her train.

It had gone rather well, Melissa thought. Her pretense of ignorance about Merry's escapade in Los Angeles was especially pleasing. When Merry confided all that to her, it would be an unmistakable sign that a certain degree of intimacy had been achieved. She decided that she liked Merry. The girl had a sense of herself. Like a cat. The fawning affection of dogs was dreary and tiresome, Melissa thought, but cats and kittens were interesting, perhaps because of their reserve. One had to earn their approval.

The following weekend she drove up to the Mather School in the Ferrari. It was a surprise for Merry, and she was gratifyingly pleased.

"But it's such a long ride!" Merry said.

"Ah, but you see, I have all the time in the world. And I like to drive. And I see some of the country. The Hudson valley is quite beautiful, and I am, I suppose, something of a tourist. And I have a new car, which has just been delivered, and I wanted to drive somewhere. I thought it might be pleasant to drive up here to see you."

"A new car?"

"Yes, a toy, really. If you like, we could go for a

ride. I am told that the Mohawk Trail is very attractive at this time of the year."

"I'll have to get permission," Merry said.

"Permission?"

"From Miss Preston. The headmistress."

"We'll ask together," Melissa suggested. "Unless you'd rather do it alone?"

"Oh, no, together," Merry said. "Miss Preston would want to meet you, anyway."

That was good, Melissa thought. They were already allies, suppliants together to the authority of the school's rules. It was not by itself very important, but the cumulative weight of all these little things together would sooner or later make itself felt.

They went to Miss Preston's office, and Merry introduced her stepmother to her headmistress with rather a note of pride, Melissa thought.

"Miss Preston, I'd like you to meet my stepmother, Mrs. Houseman. Melissa, Miss Preston, our headmistress."

"How do you do?" Miss Preston asked. "It's a pleasure."

"How do you do?" Melissa returned. "The pleasure is mine. Merry has spoken of you with great admiration."

"I'm very glad to hear it," Miss Preston said.

Miss Preston was pleased to meet Melissa, and made it evident. Melissa wondered why. Could it be that she approved of a stepmother for her pupil? Or that she was impressed at meeting one of the richest women in the world? Or was it something else?

Miss Preston must have been, at one time, an attractive woman, and yet she was *Miss* Preston. There was somehow, in some way, a vibration, an intonation, a resonance, however faint, that led Melissa to suspect that in another country, and at another time, Miss Preston might have been courting her, rather than herself courting one of Miss Preston's students. They gauged each other, were pleased with each other, and yet the least bit uncomfortable because of that recognition—which was, Melissa knew, surely mutual. They chatted for a few minutes about the beauties of the fall foliage in the surrounding countryside, and then Melissa asked with all the casual charm of which she was the assured mistress whether she might take Merry for a ride to see some of the countryside.

"It's a little irregular," Miss Preston began. "Applications for day excuses are usually supposed to be filed by Thursday noon."

"My visit was a spur-of-the-moment thing. Merry didn't know," Melissa said, smiling.

"Of course. I don't see why not. You'll try to have her back by six?"

"Certainly by then," Melissa said.

"Have a good time," Miss Preston said.

And it was done. They said good-bye to Miss Preston and went through the entrance hall out to the car, where the small red Ferrari gleamed in the noon sun. Melissa started the car, gunned the motor, and then drove off, with Merry beside her, positively aglow with the pleasures of liberty from school, of the powerful car, of the brightness of the day, and of Melissa's company.

"The leaves have not yet begun to turn color," Merry said, after they had been driving for a while on a winding country road that led in the general direction of the mountains and of the Mohawk Trail. "It will all look quite different in a few weeks, yellow and red and orange."

"It's nice now," Melissa said. "The richness of the country, and the prodigality of it amazes me. I, I am often overwhelmed with a feeling of uselessness when I think about this land, and of those who work with it. Yes, really, I am useless."

"But Valéry says that the great value of poetry is its uselessness."

"And who cares for poetry?" Melissa asked, proving her point with the question. And then she turned the subject to Merry by asking, "Do you read Valéry?"

"A little. At school."

"Do you like him?"

"Oh, yes. Very much."

"I used to."

"Used to?"

"I suppose I still do. But I haven't read a word of his in years. Alas! Perhaps I should. To remember."

"I just loved that marvelous thing he said about his smoking: 'I like to keep a little smoke between me and the world.' Or was that Verlaine?"

"I don't remember. But it's a nice phrase. I was rather like you, you know."

"Were you?"

"I think so, yes. My father was something of a glamorous figure, too, if in a different way. He was extraordinarily handsome and, as you know, very rich. He had a stable of race horses, and his yachts, and many mistresses. But the effect on me was a little unsettling. I was a lonely girl, very much in love with my father, and almost never with him. Or when I was, I hated it, because there were other people there who had less right to his attention, I thought, than I did, and who got more of it. I'm not presuming, I hope, on your privacy, or on your feelings?"

"Oh, no. In fact, when I asked if you really thought you were like me, I was . . . well, I was pleased. Because if I was—if I am like what you were, then there's hope for me."

"Of course there's hope. And more than hope. A certainty that you will grow up, and leave school, and be a woman. And a splendid one, I should think."

"Perhaps."

"Of course. Don't worry about it. Tell me what happened in Los Angeles."

Merry was silent.

"Nothing is that awful," Melissa suggested.

"You don't know—"

"But I do. I told you that we were very much alike. Do you know—but of course you don't—that I was raped by a cousin of mine when I was eleven years old?"

"But that was something that was done *to* you. It wasn't your fault."

"But you see, it was. Partly, at least. I had led him on."

"But you were only eleven."

"And you were only sixteen. What's the difference? Is it so large really?"

Merry considered Melissa's question, and then considered Melissa. She pretended to be looking out at the view. They were parked in one of the turnoffs of the winding road which is the Mohawk Trail, and below them, stretching away into the fuzzy green distance, a long, gently undulating valley lay in all but incredible serenity. Merry stared out at it for a while, and then, still staring, not looking at Melissa, she began to tell her about what had happened to her in Los Angeles. She told about Novotny, and about the gang she had been seeing and playing with at the tennis club, and about the pictures they had taken that night. And she told about the last night, the night with Denver James.

She had no clear idea why it was that she was telling all this to Melissa. There was no reason she could think of. And there was every reason not to. Melissa would be disgusted, or shocked, or even merely displeased, and she would lose the friendship and the warmth that had been proffered. She was sure that that was what would happen.

But it didn't. Melissa listened, smoking a cigarette and saying very little. But she seemed, somehow, to understand, and even to sympathize. There was no lecture, no condemnation, nor even any feeling of constraint, but only, at the end, her head shaking, and a sigh, and, "Oh, you poor, dear girl." And she drew Merry to her, and held Merry's head on her shoulder and stroked her hair.

No one had ever been so good to her before. Not her own mother, or Carlotta, or her father, or anyone. She was so happy, and so relieved, that she wept. And still Melissa held her.

After a while Melissa found a handkerchief, gave it to Merry, and suggested that they had better be getting back if they didn't want to make Miss Preston angry with them. They drove back to school, and as they approached the gate, Merry asked if Melissa would come up again.

"Of course," she said. "And you must come home for the weekends, too. Next weekend?"

"I'd love it."

"So would I."

Merry couldn't thank her enough. There was just nothing she could say. She leaned over, kissed Melissa on the cheek, and disappeared into the Mather School.

Melissa sat there in the car, looking at the door through which her stepdaughter had disappeared. She sighed. And then she started the Ferrari's engine and drove back to New York. It was not a triumph. It had gone far beyond that now. There was no question of seducing the girl, but of comforting her. It had been quite true, and she had meant it when she had suggested that they were very much alike in some ways. And the comfort they could bring to each other, the soothing of each other's hurts from the sharpness of the world, would be a beautiful thing.

She drove very slowly, which was unusual for her. She knew that she would get to New York soon enough, and begin the week of waiting that would be unendurably long. Each minute she delayed on the road would be a minute less of that awful waiting.

It was a remarkably simple idea, and the only mysterious part of it was that nobody had ever thought of it before. In small ways, of course, it had been done. Every now and then, when an accumulation of some frozen currency got to be large enough, there would be a meeting about it. Either a frozen currency or a worthless one. Like Egyptian pounds. Who the hell wants Egyptian pounds? Nobody! The discount rate is robbery. But some assistant accountant, or a nephew of an important executive on the wife's side, had figured out that BOAC accepts Egyptian pounds, because they have an installation in Cairo, have a payroll there, and have a way of spending that disesteemed currency. The assistant accountant told a friend, who called up a relative, who sent a memo to an acquaintance in the publicity department, where it was lost. But the man in publicity remembered it, and several months later suggested it, and got all the credit for the suggestion. The suggestion was simple: that they do more in the way of press junkets, using BOAC and paying BOAC in Egyptian pounds. It was like paying them with the comics from Fleers Double Bubble Gum. It was practically free. And the tax write-off, as a legitimate expense on advertising and publicity, made it all the more sensible. On the tax sheets it counted as if it were real money. So they started running junkets, and the man in publicity got a promotion, a raise, a transfer to the Paris office, where he was made Deputy Chief of European Publicity. The accountant got nothing. The nephew got a good lesson in how not to get ahead in the movie business.

But he tried it another way. He went to his uncle, Harvey Fuld, and told him that he had figured out a way to make a great deal of money.

"Sure, kid, sure. But the best way for you to be making a great deal of money is to be my nephew, and stop it with the thinking."

"Remember the idea about the junkets and the Egyptian pounds?"

"Yeah? So?"

"That was my idea."

"Oh?"

"Here's a copy of the memo I sent."

It wasn't a copy. He had written a new one, dating it back to about the right time, and had thrown away the original. Anyone can make a carbon, he had decided. Any time.

"Anyone can make a carbon," Fuld said. "Look, what are you sweating it for?"

"For your attention."

"So? Three minutes. Talk."

The idea was that they should make movies in Spain. Huge movies. Multimillion-dollar movies. The studio's earnings in Spain were consistently high, and they had a fair pile in blocked pesetas. But if the studio had all this money there, then there must be other companies that had more. And they could invest in the films, spending the pesetas in Spain and getting the money back in other, more desirable currencies. All the films had to do was break even. All they had to do, really, was to make back 90 percent of the investment, and it would still be a good deal, because the 10 percent loss would be a lot less than the discount rate that they'd have to pay any other way. "We can take out six, eight, ten million dollars at a time."

"You're crazy."

"Why?"

"What's in Spain to make movies with?"

"Everything. Mountains, deserts, plains. And cheap labor. We could build sets there for next to nothing."

"Unions?"

"Government unions. If the government is willing to go along with it—the Spanish government, I mean—then we have no union problems. At all."

"How do you know all this?"

"I've been reading."

"Oh, you college kids. Reading. If it's in a book,

then everybody knows about it. And what good can it be? But go. Go to Spain. Look, see, talk to people. And then come back and talk to businessmen here who have all that money there. If there are any. And come back to me in two months."

So Norman Fuld went to Spain, and talked and looked and figured. And came back to the United States, and went to New York, to Pittsburgh, to Detroit, to Wilmington, to St. Louis, and talked to businessmen who had dealings with Spain. And then back to Los Angeles and Uncle Harvey. And became a producer.

It took a year and a half for Norman Fuld to arrange for the first picture. It had to be sure fire, to warrant the investment of ten million dollars. First there was a treatment, and then a first draft of a script, and a second and third and fourth draft. And then he had to go out and sell the script to the businessmen, who were even more cautious than the bankers who usually finance Hollywood films, because they had had less experience, and were afraid of such a speculative and insubstantial business. But even to the appliance men and the steel men and the chemical men Norman Fuld was able to point out that in *Nero* there would be the burning of Rome, and the destruction of the Temple in Jerusalem, and the torture of Christians in the Colosseum—something for everyone. But he had to get names, too. And among the names that he wanted was that of Meredith Houseman.

The discussions took a long time. Houseman would talk with Norman Fuld, and then go back to talk to Jaggers and Wemmick. Jaggers would talk to Fuld. Then Fuld would talk to his Uncle Harvey, and Uncle Harvey would talk with Wemmick. And then it would start over again, with Houseman and Norman Fuld. It was indeed a complicated arrangement, and it took time. Meredith had been out in Hollywood for two weeks already when he called Melissa, as he did every night, and announced that it would be at least another two weeks.

"Are you all right? Do you want to come out here? Shall I fly back for a weekend?"

"No, I'm fine," she said. "I don't think I want to come out there. Do you mind awfully?"

"I don't mind," he said. "Whatever pleases you, darling."

"Let's just wait it out then, shall we?" she asked. "Anyway, I'm amusing myself."

"Oh?"

"Oh, yes. Merry's coming down from school this weekend."

"Oh, that's wonderful. That's really very sweet of you."

"Not at all. I like her."

"Nothing could make me happier. Except to see you."

"Soon, soon."

"As soon as these talks get done with."

"Call me tomorrow?"

"Of course."

"Good night, darling."

"Good night."

As she hung up, it crossed her mind that some things seemed very nearly irresistible. She would have Merry all to herself for the whole weekend. It was a delightful prospect.

She could not say a word, and if she could not speak it was at least partly because the whole thing was unspeakable. She was surprised, even shocked. But not offended, nor did she want to give offense. It all seemed so natural, even though, of course, it was supposed to be the very opposite, the absolutely unnatural thing. But it was so comfortable that she could not believe any of the fragmentary thoughts that illumined the darkness of her mind like the momentary flashes of heat lightning on a close summer night.

She had been sitting on Melissa's bed talking. She had come to New York and had had a fine afternoon with Melissa, shopping, having tea, visiting the Museum of Modern Art, and then having dinner. And they had walked along Fifth Avenue after dinner and looked at the displays in the windows of the stores, and had come back to the hotel suite, feeling good and glowing and close to each other. It was the natural thing to continue to talk, in the living room first and then, after each had slipped into something more comfortable—Merry her plaid flannel bathrobe and Melissa an exquisite French silk negligee—in Melissa's bedroom. Merry was sitting on the bed and Melissa was stretched across it, and they were talking only intermittently, but communicating somehow, even in the interstices of silence. Melissa propped herself up on an elbow and began stroking Merry's hair. And then she kissed Merry on the lips.

Which brought it all out there, for some kind of comment, for some reaction, for some response or even a lack of response which would imply an acquiescence. And Merry's thoughts raced impossibly, like a motor out of gear, while Melissa waited, giving her all the time she could possibly need, not forcing her, not pushing her at all. And Merry realized that, too, and was grateful and all the more anxious not to say anything or do anything that would hurt Melissa, not to repay such tenderness with pain.

Out of context, out of syntax, the words presented themselves like lewd scrawls on subway walls. Lesbian. And it was that. Incest. She wasn't sure, but it probably was that, too. And yet, perhaps because of their isolation, their lack of context or syntax, they had neither force nor relevance. There was nothing in them to balance the gentleness which was between them and all around them and beneath them, like the bed itself.

"Well?" Melissa asked, gently reminding her that it was up to her now. And Merry appreciated that, too, understanding immediately Melissa's refusal to push her and her scrupulousness in allowing Merry to decide for herself whether to get up and exit gracefully or to remain.

She turned to Melissa and returned the kiss.

She had thought that that would settle it, but it didn't. Or somehow it seemed that it hadn't. For Melissa did nothing more than kiss her and continue to stroke her hair as she had done before. Merry was convinced that she must have misconstrued everything, must have been leaping to conclusions about Melissa, because of the relative calm of their merely affectionate embracing. It was too pleasant, too delicate, too sweet for all that tortured thinking and all that fear. But then Melissa moved her hand almost inadvertently from Merry's hair to her shoulder and from her shoulder to the opening of her bathrobe to her breast, which she caressed with the gentleness of a butterfly on a flower. Merry lay back on the bed and closed her eyes, luxuriating in the tingling that she began to feel. Then Melissa, who had unclasped the single catch of her own peignoir, kissed her again, this time with more ardor, and Merry, who did not know exactly what to do, what the rules were, what the proprieties could possibly be, reached out to touch Melissa's breasts and found that this was more exciting than anything that Melissa had done to her. She had been kissed before, had felt caresses of her breasts before—although never with such finesse as this. But she had never touched another woman's breast, had never felt the weight of one, the firmness, or the softness, or traced the Oriental opulence of its curve with a fingertip that positively burned with sensation. The strangest, the most exciting part of it was that she could touch Melissa's breast and feel, with her own body, on her own breast, what the touch must be like. That was it. The very strangest part of it was how unstrange it was, how wonderfully natural and easy.

She hardly noticed that Melissa had moved her hands again, from her breasts to the nape of her neck and then down her side and across the flatness of her belly. And then the thighs, with a hand as cool as a spring breeze, as smooth as water, as soft as one's best dreams. And then she was no longer stroking her but kissing her, too, all over her body, and Merry was about to stop her, because now she was not being merely agreeable and returning tenderness for tenderness, but was excited and thoroughly aroused and wanted her to kiss her there, and the realization that that was what she wanted frightened her. But she could not shape the words, could not find the voice to speak, could not do anything but moan softly, and then it was too late to do anything but moan, less softly now, but louder and louder, until, without being able to help herself, she was crying out in an agony of pleasure as the sharp tongue flicked again and again, searching and at last finding the supreme shudder at the core of her being.

It was an awakening, a gradual process of discovery and of self-discovery, supported by Melissa's consummate tenderness. As she explained to Merry, who had asked quite fetchingly if what they had done wasn't wrong, "Nothing that is done with tenderness, with affection, with love is wrong. It is only harshness, and coldness, and cruelty that is wrong."

And she kissed Merry again, for the honesty of her question, and opened a half bottle of champagne to celebrate the acceptance of the answer she had given. They drank the champagne and then turned out the lights. They lay in each other's arms until it was very late indeed.

It was a perfect weekend, and Sunday afternoon, when Merry left to catch her train back to school, there was no question in either of their minds but that she would come back the next weekend and every weekend for the rest of the year.

"I'll see you Friday, then," Merry said.

"Of course, dear."

"I'll miss you."

"And I'll miss you. Have a good week."

"You, too."

"It'll be miserable."

"Yes."

And then they kissed, and Merry went down to the limousine to go to the station.

But Meredith came home the following Friday, Norman Fuld having finally agreed out of desperation to meet his terms. Meredith arrived at noon, and Merry came in at eight-thirty that evening. He was feeling good, even jubilant, over the success of his negotiations, and he was pleased that Merry and Melissa were getting on so well and that she had come to visit for a second weekend in a row. It appeared to be a normal household for a change, run the way other households were run, or the way he imagined that they were. They all went out to have a late dinner at "21" and then they came back to the apartment in the hotel. Meredith said that he was exhausted after his trip and wanted to get to bed early. What he really wanted was Melissa, from whom he had been separated for three weeks. But she said that she had a headache and a touch of nausea.

"From '21'? They'd be mortified!"

"I'm sure it wasn't the food. I must have picked up a bug of some kind. I'm sorry, darling."

"So am I."

Meredith went off to bed, and if he was disappointed, that was all he was. Melissa stayed up for a while, "until the nausea passes," and she felt relief that she would not be violating the bond between herself and Merry. It was Merry's feelings that she was thinking of, or perhaps her own, too. Or her own idea of what she should like Merry to feel in this odd and singularly delicate situation. Merry was not quite so finely aware of the subtleties of what was happening, but she felt vaguely uneasy and restless. She could not sleep. She lay in bed awake, trying to sleep, but she only tossed and turned on her pillow. It was nearly three in the morning before she drifted off. Melissa fell asleep on the couch in the living room a little later.

But the problem was not yet solved or not permanently solved. It would be difficult, Melissa thought, when she considered her position the following morning, to repeat the same excuse that night. At the same time, some excuse, some pretext would be necessary, for it simply did not feel right to make love with Meredith while Merry lay in the next room alone. It was not that Melissa thought it would be a matter of infidelity to Merry—for she did not think in such terms—but it would be disturbing, and even disgusting. It would be wrong. She remembered what she had told Merry the weekend before, that nothing could be wrong if it was warm and tender and loving. But life wasn't that simple somehow. One couldn't merely trust to one's feelings about things. Or perhaps one could. Because this felt wrong and therefore had to be wrong. She could not possibly sleep with Meredith while Merry was in the house. The only thing to do, then, was to get Merry out of the house. For her own sake. And for all their sakes. But how could she manage it on a Saturday? It was ridiculous that at moments of such importance absurd and trivial things like the schedule of a school could be relevant, but there it was, looming up before them all, Miss Preston's idea of what a weekend was. Weekends began after a pupil's last class on Friday and ended Sunday at six in the evening. It would look odd for Merry to return on a Saturday. She supposed it would be allowed, but there was such a weight that lay against it, like something blocking a door in a nightmare. She would have to tell Merry, explain to Merry . . . What? She ran over several possible lies, but all of them sounded impossibly flimsy. They had suddenly been called away to visit some producer. They had been invited to Palm Beach. They had to go . . . But no, anything that she made up reeked of falsehood, and Merry would conclude, would have to conclude, that Melissa wanted to get rid of her in order to be alone with him, that it was not at all that she preferred him to Merry, but that it was impossible, simple impossible, with all three of them together. Now. She hoped, of course, that she could work it out, that there could be some *modus vivendi* that would present itself. How had she overlooked the inevitability of this embarrassment? But she had overlooked it. Or had not bothered to look at anything but at Merry. And now she had to risk breaking Merry's heart. If only she could just explain it all to Merry . . .

But why not? She was a bright girl and more important, a sensitive girl. Surely she would understand how Melissa was in an impossible situation and could not lie in Meredith's bed while Merry, sweet Merry, wonderful Merry was in the next room, where she would rather be. Yes, if she was going to be honest with herself, she had to admit that. And did, freely, gladly, hoping that Merry would believe it, too. Because it was true.

There was an enormous difference, however, between having decided to tell the girl and actually telling her. It was a fearful thing to bring herself to do. She was afraid of getting it all wrong. But somehow, somewhere, in the midst of all that love, words would come. She had to trust that that would happen. Or just lie in bed, watching the clock's hands turn maddeningly quickly toward nightfall. Colette had come in that morning, had found her sleeping on the couch, had waked her with great diffidence and an expression of sympathy, and asked if perhaps her mistress didn't want to go to bed now. And Melissa had gone into the bedroom, to the bedroom of her own apartment, tiptoeing as if she were a burglar, to crawl into one of the big double beds. Neither she nor Meredith had ever used the second bed in the bedroom. Until now.

She fell asleep and refused to be waked even when Colette came in with a hot cup of the Mocha and Java coffee that she liked, a little after noon. She had drunk half the coffee and thanked Colette, but had told her to say that her mistress was still not feeling well and would like to sleep yet a little longer. It was only a postponement, but even a postponement was welcome. It would, at least, give her time to think.

But now, having lain in bed for yet another hour and having considered it from so many different angles that she was nearly dizzy with thinking about it, there seemed to be only one possible thing to do, the one thing that would not hurt anyone, neither Meredith, nor Merry, nor even herself. She would try to tell Merry the truth. She called for Colette, who brought her another cup of coffee, and she asked her whether Mr. Houseman was still in the apartment.

"No, madame. He has gone out. He did not tell me where he was going."

"And Merry?"

"She is here."

It was too soon really, but it was a good chance, and there might not be a better one. More thinking about it would only make it more difficult, anyway.

"Ask her to come in to me, would you?"

"Yes, madame. Shall I bring more coffee?"

"No, thank you. I'll be getting up in a few minutes, and then I'll have some more."

"Yes, madame." Colette went to call Merry.

"Are you feeling better?" Merry asked from the doorway, even before she had really come into the room.

"Yes," Melissa said. "Or, no. Not better, but fine. Perfectly well. There was nothing wrong with me last night."

"But I thought . . ."

"There was nothing physically wrong with me. But I could not . . . I could not properly welcome your father home, with you in the apartment. I mean to say that when you are here, then only you are here. I can think only of you. And so I pretended, last night, to be sick. But it isn't fair. To your father or to you. And . . ."

"I understand."

"You do? But how can you?"

"You want me to go, isn't that it?"

"Yes. But I must be sure that you know why I want you to go. That I don't want for you to go at all, but that you have to go, I have to ask you to go, for my sake, because I love you so."

"I know."

"Do you?"

"I think so. Partly. Enough. I—I love him, too. He's my father."

"Yes."

"And I'll go."

"There will be other weekends," Melissa began, but Merry interrupted.

"Not like last weekend."

"Oh, yes. Yes, there will. Your father travels. I can come up to school."

"No, for your sake, no. And for mine."

"Oh, Merry, Merry," Melissa moaned.

She could not remember later whether she had reached out her hands to Merry, or whether Merry had leaned over toward her first and she had reached out her arms only then. Or perhaps both happened at the same time. She simply could not remember. And it was important to remember, because if she had not reached out her arms, or if Merry had not leaned over, then everything might have been all right, and nothing would have happened. Nothing would have happened at all.

But however it was, they had kissed and had kissed with great passion and feeling and for a long time.

Longer than she had realized. And longer than she could explain. For Merry had not closed the door, or perhaps she had closed it and he had opened it, but there it was, open, and there he was, Meredith was, looking at them, watching them.

"We were saying good-bye," Melissa said, as soon as she noticed him.

"Oh?"

"Merry has decided to go back to school. To cut her weekend short and go back to school."

"Oh?"

"Isn't that right, Merry?"

"Yes, that's right."

"Then perhaps you should go."

"I remembered I have a paper due on Monday and I forgot to take the books with me. So I really do have to go back."

"Yes, all right."

And Merry left the room to go and get her things together and go back to school. Meredith came into the bedroom, closed the door behind him, and asked, "What the hell is going on?"

"Nothing, darling. What do you mean?"

"With Merry. You know damned well what I mean."

"She's going back to school. That's all."

"Back to school? Just like that?"

"There was a paper—"

"There was more than a paper. . . ."

"What are you talking about?"

"You know perfectly well what I'm talking about. And it makes me sick. Much sicker than you were last night. Or pretended to be. Jesus Christ, how could I not have seen it before! How could I not even have suspected it, or thought of it? I guess because it was just unthinkable. Unthinkable and plain lousy."

"I don't know what you mean," she said.

She had resigned herself to a scene. She knew that

sooner or later she would have to break down, admit it, and cry. And she wondered what would happen then. Would he storm out of the room and out of her life? Or would he beat her? Or would he, perhaps, just possibly, forgive her? Or understand? Or forgive and understand? She had begun to be a little hopeful, because he had said nothing for several seconds. But then she noticed—and it seemed only curious, an odd and inexplicable thing—that he was taking off his shirt. And his shoes. And his trousers. And then suddenly she knew, and she started to say, softly, because it didn't make any difference, because she didn't have any hope of its making any difference, "No, no, no, no, no," but he took off his underclothes and advanced toward the bed. And still she said, "No, no, no," until he slapped her. And then she was frightened, and she got out of the bed, but he grabbed her arm and twisted it, and it hurt, and she cried out, but he continued to twist it, so that either it would break or she would have to fall back on the bed, and she did fall, she fell back on the bed, and he fell on top of her, and slapped her again.

"Don't, Meredith. Don't. It's a cruel thing. . . ."

"You deserve it."

She stopped protesting, because of the words he had used. She remembered, as one recalls a vivid lesson from school years and years back in the dim distance, her cousin, who had spat out at her the one word "Deservedly," and she had stopped struggling then, so that he would not hurt her, but he had hurt her anyway, hurt her with a searing pain that she remembered ever after as the harshest, cruelest, hardest thing she had ever had to bear in her life. And now, after his "You deserve it," she also stopped struggling, and he tried to hurt her and did, not as much as her cousin had hurt her, but enough, enough to make her whimper in pain, and in pain mixed with pleasure, and then, oddly, abruptly, suddenly, marvelously in pleasure, pure pleasure, pleasure she could not have imagined, and she cried out for the pleasure, shrieked out long, high, piercing cries of joy. She had never known anything could be this good, could be this sharp, but with a sharpness of pleasure that was like pain, but more consuming, deeper, higher, and—

But then he let her go. He just let her go, and climbed off her, and off the bed, and started to get back into his clothes.

And in the next room Merry, who had been sitting on the bed with her overnight case all packed, heard that the cries had stopped, and with the tears streaming from her own eyes for the pain of the woman in the next room with her father, she fled from the apartment, and she was still crying when she got to Grand Central Station. She could not get her tears to stop, really stop, until she was past Poughkeepsie.

That it was Fathers' Weekend was merely ironic. Merry's father wasn't there. He was off in Spain making a movie. But Merry was just as pleased, for her whole involvement in the play, the refuge in the sheer brutal work of the rehearsals and the memorization, had been an attempt on her part to obliterate even her thoughts of him. But it was a curious way to try to do it. Even she had to admit that. For one thing, the theater was an odd place to hide in, especially if what she was trying to hide was her connection with her father, the actor. But in another way it was quite all right. It didn't matter what everyone else thought. Out in the audience they might be looking for similar kinds of gestures, similar expressions or poses to which they could point and say the obvious thing—that, yes, she certainly was her father's daughter. But up on the stage she was trying to be someone else entirely, not her father's daughter, or herself, but Rosalind, looking for her father in the forest of Arden. On the stage in *As You*

Like It her father was the old duke and was played by Helen Farnam, who had a deep voice and was tall.

Jaggers had come up, of course. And he was her father's agent, but she liked him anyway. Or perhaps she liked him because of that. Sometimes, late at night, it seemed to her that she had two fathers, or a father who could split apart and be like Dr. Jekyll and Mr. Hyde. Jaggers was the Jekyll. The other one was the Hyde. She was glad he couldn't come.

She had joined the dramatics club mainly because Helen had joined it. "I've got to have some extracurricular activities," Helen had announced one day and had joined the dramatics club because it looked pretty easy. But it had turned out to be very hard work, and that had appealed to Merry. She needed something to take up every last bit of the little slack that the teachers' assignments left in her day, something into which she could throw herself in order to forget herself. And so she had joined, too.

It was well into the fall term, but they had made an exception for her and had allowed her to join because—well, because she was Meredith Houseman's daughter. In a way she had used her connection with her father in a reverse way, explaining that she had been timid of the stage and acting and anything that had to do with the theater because she was his daughter, but had decided that it just wasn't fair for her to be cut off that way and never to have allowed herself a chance to try. And they had agreed with her and had welcomed her.

What they hadn't known about was the letter from Melissa. It was a kind of love letter. She had, anyway, expressed in it her love for Merry. But it had been a letter of parting, too. They could not see each other again. Meredith had threatened to have Melissa committed to a "rest home" if she tried to see Merry again. And it was also a letter of news. Melissa was pregnant. Merry could not remember the letter very clearly. She had burned it and had later regretted having burned it. But the confused recollection was accurate enough. It had been a confused outpouring of grief and rage and frustration and love.

During the fall term Merry had limited herself to the technical side of things, but after the Christmas vacation she had decided to try for a part. And if she was going to try for any part, it might just as well be a big one, she thought. She had been "home" for Christmas, if you can call the Hampshire House home. Meredith had invited her down to spend the holidays with them and to say good-bye, for he was going off to Spain to make the film of the life of Nero, and Melissa was going off to Paris to be with her family and await the birth of their child. But the real point of the invitation had been for Meredith to show Melissa off to Merry. Melissa had not borne up very well during the first trimester of her pregnancy. She had had morning sickness and had been unable to hold down very much food even in the afternoons and evenings. She vomited almost continually for the first couple of months, and it was, the obstetrician had said, almost as if she wanted not to have the baby. It was a glum week. On the twenty-sixth he flew to Madrid, and she flew to Paris, and Merry went to stay with the Farnams until the third of January.

A week later she wrote her name down for the tryouts. And she got the part. The lead! Rosalind! The girl who is looking for her father, and who, during the search, disguises herself as a boy. It was a goddamned psychodrama, but there was no one with whom she could share the joke. Or maybe it wasn't a joke. Maybe it was a blessing in disguise, even if the disguise was jester's motley. At least she understood the character. And she played it. Somehow, into the fun and froth of *As You Like It* she managed to get a little weight, a mere suggestion of the distillate of the experience she had recently gone through and which had proved to be improbably appropriate. She was a great success. Mrs.

Bernard, the drama coach, told her at dress rehearsal that she was just wonderful and asked her if she had ever given a thought to going into the theater. She had meant it, perhaps, as a compliment to give Merry a little extra confidence for the trial of the following day, when she would face an audience for the first time in her life. But there was something earnest in her expression and intonation. The question, anyway, deserved an answer.

"Yes, I've given thought to it."

"Oh?"

"And I don't think I'd want it."

"You might think about it some more."

"It's my father's life. I don't want it for myself."

"Are you sure you aren't running away from it? You really do have talent, you know. And of course you'd have the connections, the name."

"But that's just it. I shouldn't want to use the name. And I'd be crazy not to. And I don't want it."

"Well, then," Mrs. Bernard said, "what do you want?"

"I don't know."

"Whatever it is," the older woman said, "I wish you well."

"Thank you."

"And break a leg tomorrow."

"What?"

"Break a leg. Surely you've heard that expression?"

"No."

"From your father?"

"No."

"Odd."

"What does it mean?"

"Luck. It means good luck."

"Thank you."

The next day, the fathers appeared, and Jaggers appeared to play the part of Merry's father, and then she left him to get made up and into her costume to play the part of a girl looking for her father. And she was just nervous enough, and yet in a strange way just calm enough, to do it exactly right, better, much better, than at the dress rehearsal. And it went wonderfully. The audience laughed and applauded, and it was like drinking champagne to hear them—but better, as if one ignored the gross liquid and drank only the pure bubbles. And at the end she came out to say the little epilogue speech, and the final ovation for the play and for her rang in her ears.

It was still echoing in her mind's ear when, later on that evening at the cast party, Jaggers asked her if she wanted to go to Spain that summer to be with her father.

"Does he want me to come?"

"Yes, of course."

"Then why didn't he write to me and ask me?"

"I think he was afraid you might say no."

"So he left it to you?"

"Yes, I'm afraid so."

"Well, I don't want to."

"But what will you do, then?"

"I thought I might go to some camp to be a dramatics counselor. Something like that. I mean, I've had a little experience now. That job at Ethical last summer, and this now."

"You're not old enough."

"But—"

"They want college juniors."

"Oh."

"But if you want, I can get you into a junior theater. The Cape Cod Junior Theater. They do children's plays. You could be an apprentice there. I have a friend there, and I'm sure I could arrange it for you."

"Would you?"

"If that's what you want."

"Oh, yes. Yes. I loved it tonight. That's what I want."

It was only later that she realized that she had done exactly what she had told Mrs. Bernard she would not do. She had used her name and her father's connections to get what she wanted. In the theater.

After the cast party she went up to her room and found a telegram on the floor. It had been slipped under the door. She ripped it open. It was from her father.

DEAREST MERRY: BREAK A LEG. LOVE. DAD.

The tears rushed to her eyes. She wished that he had been there, after all.

CHAPTER

EIGHT

It was an old clapboard building that looked as if the architect had started out to build a barn and had changed his mind halfway through and made it a church instead. Actually, it had been a Grange hall once, but the Grange had given up the ghost and the building had been left vacant, then put up for auction for the back taxes, and the Cape Cod Junior Theater had been born.

The building was still undecided about what it wanted to be, and the two large painted jesters that supported the sign proclaiming "Cape Cod Junior Theater" made it look even more absurd, like an old lady who has drunk too much Christmas port and has decided that, yes, she's going to show the youngsters how to tango. All the money that had been spent over the years, the proceeds of ticket sales and the membership dues and the gifts, had been spent, probably sensibly, on more relevant things like lights and light boards, sound equipment, and the practical hardware of theater, so it was less embarrassing than it might have been. The old lady could tango pretty well, after all.

Merry was a little put off the first time she saw the building, but she soon learned that there was hardly time to sit around and contemplate its architectural peculiarity. The work was frantic, all but continuous, and quite wonderful in its way. There were four productions during the summer, each running for two weeks. And the day that the first play opened, the second started rehearsals, so for six of the eight weeks of the season, the theater was running a double schedule. Or actually a triple schedule. In the mornings the children of the surrounding communities came for drama workshop and technical workshop, the youngsters learning about mime and diction and how to walk across a stage, and ten- through fourteen-year-olds learning about lights and makeup, stage design, and set decoration. Then in the afternoons there were rehearsals, usually from two to five. And then at seven there was the makeup and costume call for the eight-o'clock performance. And even after the performances, at ten o'clock, there were rehearsals again, because there were always people who couldn't make afternoon rehearsals—townspeople who had jobs, or some of the apprentices who worked during the day making pizzas or mowing lawns or hauling canned goods around the supermarkets. Merry didn't work because she didn't have to, but that meant that she could spend more time at the theater, and there was always something to do, and usually there was more than it seemed could ever get done.

With considerable animation, Merry explained all this to her father. She was delighted that he had come, and flattered, too. She knew that he had not flown back from Spain just to see her performance. He had told her about the meetings in New York. But he had come up from New York—and just to see her. It might as well have been from Spain.

All her doubts were gone, dissipated as easily as the early-morning fogs on the Cape were dissipated by the sun. She had been rather glum at the Hyannis airport, waiting for his plane. Her whole summer, and the delicate balance she had achieved, had been threatened by her father's phone call and the news that he was coming up to see her, for she had very carefully avoided being Meredith Houseman's daughter, had alluded to him as infrequently as possible, and had tried very hard to be just another apprentice in the hope that she could make it on her own, succeeding or even failing on her own terms. This had been difficult to do, but not impossible. The other apprentices, and the directors and teachers, too, had taken her behavior for a kind of modesty, which was not exactly right but close enough. At any rate, they had cooperated with her and tried to make nothing more of her famous father than she did.

But now he was here, had appeared, and would be attending the dress rehearsal of *Alice in Wonderland,* in which Merry was playing the White Rabbit. There would have been nothing extraordinary about this if Meredith Houseman had been anyone else in the world. A doctor, say, or an accountant. But being the man he was, the celebrity, the famous actor, the glamorous Hollywood star, he would have to be the center of attention. Merry had been thinking about that and had found herself moving in a peculiar way from a simple resentment of her father's celebrity to an acknowledgment of his helplessness in the situation and finally to a feeling of loneliness. His visit could not but sever the delicate web she had spun, could not but subject her to a glaring light of attention which would nullify the protective coloration she had so carefully tried to assume.

She had got about that far when the plane landed,

and her father had come off the DC-3 to the usual stares of the inevitable gawkers. He had smiled, waved, and then walked quickly to her, to kiss her on the cheek. She was glad to see him and she said so. And she realized that it was the failure of the Junior Theater she feared, not his. He could not help but shine. If they were dazzled, it was their own eyesight and their own habitual obscurity that were to blame.

On the ride from the airport she told him about the theater, and he told her about Spain and the shooting on *Nero*. They were not at all comparable, but he made them seem so, made it appear as though one professional were talking shop with another.

They stopped for lunch, and during the meal they continued to talk like two old friends, both of whom were used to the long separations and sudden intimacies of life in the theater. It was just fine being with him again. And then, just before the coffee came, he told her quite casually that Melissa had had a stillbirth in Paris, and had initiated proceedings for a divorce.

"How do you feel about it?" Merry asked.

"How should I feel? It's over. I don't need a judge to tell me that. Neither does she."

It seemed blunt and almost cruel, but sensible. And he was so cheerful that she could not be broody or depressed.

"I guess there's just us now," he said. It was exactly what she had been thinking.

The exhilaration of the dress rehearsal met the peculiar and unexpected calm that Merry felt because of her father's visit, and the effect of the meeting was that of a waterfall's turbulence meeting the calm water of a mountain pool and setting up a curtain of mist which, in the right light, discloses a rainbow. The rehearsal went well. The complicated dance step Merry had to do after she sang her song went perfectly. There were roughnesses, of course, but it was only a rehearsal. Mary Ann Maxwell, who played Alice, was less good than she should have been, but as she explained to Bill Schneider (who told Merry), she was awfully nervous with Meredith Houseman out there in the house.

After the rehearsal there was a picture call for the photographer. Meredith waited in a back seat. Merry was eager for the picture-taking to be over, so that she could leave with her father and spend some more time with him. But Lloyd Cook, the director, had the bright idea of asking Meredith if he would mind posing for just one shot with Mary Ann and Merry.

"It'd be wonderful publicity," he said, as if Meredith were some kind of moron who would not otherwise have realized this. But there was no graceful way to decline. Merry saw that and understood that there was nothing else her father could do. It wasn't the posing that bothered her, or the exploitation by Cook of her father's face and the fact that he had visited the rehearsal. What bothered her was that up on the stage in the tea-party set, after the photographer had arranged them in the obvious way—Meredith in the middle and Mary Ann and Merry on either side of him—her shoulder itched. She thought it was probably a mosquito bite and she scratched it. But she caught it the wrong way and it hurt, so she turned to see if she had opened it and if it was bleeding, and the turning of her head came at just the right moment, so that she was able to see that her father's hand—the other one, the one with which he was holding Mary Ann—was not around Mary Ann's waist at all, but lower, so that he was in fact holding her by the buttocks.

The bulb flashed, and the photographer said thank you. Her father nodded, smiled, and said, "That's quite all right," but it wasn't all right. It wasn't all right at all. It wasn't just the mosquito bite, but everything, everything had opened up, had been caught the wrong way and hurt now. The feeling of closeness to her father was all gone. And his betrayal of her (for that was what it seemed) reminded her of her own betrayal with Melissa. How calmly she had taken the news! How easily she had dismissed the report of the stillborn child and Melissa's evident unhappiness in Paris. How eager she had been, at any cost to anyone, to claim her father for herself, as exclusive property. But it was impossible. There would always be ambitious creeps around like Cook. And like Mary Ann Maxwell. Although Mary Ann had done nothing. (Did Merry really expect Mary Ann to cry out, "Get your hand off my ass!" right there in front of everyone, and to Meredith Houseman?)

They went across the street afterward to the Rexall drugstore for sodas. Merry and her father, and Cook and Mary Ann, and Schneider, and Sarah Evans. Merry felt terrible. She had lost even the pretense of anonymity she had tried to establish. And she had not gained a thing. Not a damned thing. She heard her father explaining to someone that he had to go back to Boston that night to catch a plane for Madrid, and realized that it just couldn't be soon enough to suit her.

Two days later the picture came out in the *Standard-Times*. Her father was looking at Mary Ann, who had a drippy, Gee-isn't-he-terrific look on her face. Merry didn't mind that so much. What had bothered her was the fact that, in the flash of the bulb, in the frozen instant of the camera's vision, she seemed to be looking at her father with the most profound admiration and love that anyone could imagine. It made her positively sick. Deliberately, as an act of defiance to her father and to the stupid inability to learn anything that she saw in herself, she cut it out and taped it to the wall above the bed. It was the first thing she saw every morning and the last thing she saw every night. It was the whetstone to her anger, which she kept perpetually sharp.

Two weeks later she had a long-distance telephone

call from her mother in California. Her mother told her that her stepfather, Harry Novotny, was dead.

"Oh? How? What happened?" She wasn't sure that that was quite the right thing to say, but it sprang to her lips and across the wires before she could compose herself.

Her mother burst into tears and then recovered herself. She told Merry that Novotny had been slashed to death by an ostrich. Merry remembered, with preternatural clarity, the way her stepfather had treated the animals, and the way he had boasted of it: "You got to beat them animals good. Mice? Good Christ, we must have gone through a hundred mice before we could get that cat to jump over them. So we stuffed the cat's mouth full of gauze and beat that cat. Oh, boy, did we wallop that cat!" But there would be no more walloping. The ostrich had evened the score. There was no bitterness or rancor in her observation. It merely seemed to her that this was the way it was, perfectly reasonable and perfectly understandable. There was a mathematical precision to it. Or if not quite an even balance, then a small remainder for her. For her own score was settled, too, or expunged. First Melissa and now Novotny, her two stepparents, parallel like the lines in a geometry theorem, and like those lines, they had met at infinity—which was, anyway, much beyond Merry's horizon.

"How awful," Merry said. "I'm sorry."

"They just called me up from the studio and told me, the way I'm telling you. It was awful."

"How is Lyon taking it?"

"He's being very brave. He's a fine boy. A real comfort."

"I'm glad."

"Merry?"

"Yes?"

"Can you come out?"

"To Los Angeles?"

"For the funeral."

"I don't know. I—I'll have to ask Mr. Jaggers."

"For permission? To come to your own stepfather's funeral?"

"No, no, Mother," Merry said. Her mother had begun to bawl and Merry couldn't stand it. "For the money. To fly out."

"Oh, yes, surely. I'm sorry. I don't know what I could have been thinking of."

"It's all right. You're upset. I understand."

"You'll let me know?"

"As soon as I know. When is it?"

"The day after tomorrow."

"I'll let you know tonight or tomorrow morning. As soon as I know myself."

"Thanks, Merry."

"Of course, Mother."

"You're a wonderful daughter."

"Thanks, Mother," she said. It was embarrassing and very unpleasant, and more than anything she wanted to terminate the conversation. "I'll call you back as soon as I hear. Good-bye."

"God bless you."

"You, too," she said. She hung up before her mother could say anything more.

She was on the phone for another half hour. She had to call Jaggers in New York to ask him if she could go to Novotny's funeral. And then she called her mother back to say that she would be coming out and to tell her what plane to meet. And she called the producer of the Cape Cod Junior Theater to tell her that she had to go out to California.

If she had said just that it would have been all right. But she hadn't realized how it would have to sound to a stranger, and quite without thinking, mentioned that it was her stepfather's funeral, and that he had been killed by an ostrich.

"A what?"

"An ostrich."

"What is this? Some kind of a joke?"

"No. Not at all. Really."

"Merry, this is in terribly poor taste."

"He was killed by an ostrich. He was an animal trainer."

"Oh, come now. Be serious."

"I am being serious. I swear."

"All right, Merry. I understand. Have a good time at the funeral. I'll see you tomorrow."

Before Merry could tell her again that she wouldn't be at the Junior Theater any more, would be going to her stepfather's funeral, and that he really, honestly, actually had been killed by an ostrich, the producer hung up. And Merry was left with the dead phone in her hand. And it was, after all, an improbable thing to call up and tell someone. She could send the producer a copy of the obituary when it came out in one of the Los Angeles papers. Or in *Variety*. That was the best part of the whole thing. She just wished she could see the woman's face when she read the obituary and remembered what she'd said to Merry on the phone. It was one of the funniest things that Merry could remember.

The funeral, however, was even funnier. It was a fairly showy funeral, which was what Harry Novotny would have wanted. Perhaps he had made the arrangements himself, selecting the service and the casket and the plot before he died. She certainly hoped so. It was absolutely impossible to think that her mother had picked it out. There was lots wrong with her mother, but Merry just couldn't believe that she was as bad as this. The climax of the memorial service was the release of a hundred doves, which were supposed to symbolize the release of Novotny's immortal soul from the prison of his body, but which were not quite right considering that he had been killed by the kick and slash of an ostrich's claw. There was a gasp from the assembled mourners, which could have passed for a gasp of amazement but was more probably one of shock. And then Merry and then Lyon and Elaine climbed into the Cadillac limousine, behind which the other cars followed in the procession from the funeral chapel to the plot—a trip of no more than four hundred yards.

At the graveside there were more prayers, but Merry kept looking up into the trees, where every now and then she could see one of the doves, sitting there tamely. She wondered whether after the funeral was over there wouldn't be someone who came to catch all the birds, put them back into their cages, and use them again at another funeral. At hundreds of funerals. It was so absurd and so pathetic that she could hardly remember that she had disliked Novotny. Nothing about him seemed to make all that much difference any more. It was incredible that he could ever have made much of a difference to anyone.

And yet her mother was crying. Not extravagantly or uncontrollably, but Merry was more inclined to believe in the restrained sobs that broke, every so often, the quiet melancholy of her mother's demeanor. She wondered whether her mother had ever loved this man, or was now feeling guilty because she hadn't. She just had no idea. And she felt a little guilty, too, to be thinking in this way on the grass beside the open grave. The worst part of the funeral, she decided, was that it was so interesting. But perhaps, she thought, that was because she had never been to one before.

After the funeral Merry resolved to stay in Los Angeles until the beginning of school. She hoped that in three weeks, when she was supposed to appear at Skidmore, her mother would have recovered from her depression. Elaine had not been much of a mother, but then Merry had not been much of a daughter, either. It was the very least she could do, to stay and give what comfort she could.

During the next several days she tried everything she

could think of to help her mother begin to adjust to Harry's death. She suggested walks on the beach, automobile rides in the desert, but Elaine refused to be diverted from the fascination of her grief. She sat in the living room, all in black, on the hottest days, refused almost all food, and would talk of nothing but Harry Novotny and what a good man he had been.

Merry found her mother's company exhausting and her conversation depressing and distasteful. With the running of the household on Merry's shoulders, and the constant demands made by the stream of guests who came to pay condolence calls, she was extremely tired, but even so she could have endured it all. She had had no previous experience with mourning, and she assumed that this was what it was always like.

For herself, she had Lyon's company. He was thirteen now and, while still lumpish, had occasional flashes of wit that amused her. It was, moreover, something of a bond between them that they could see the utter falsity and theatricality of Elaine's continuing eulogy for the good man whom she claimed to mourn. He had not been like that at all, but an indifferent father and, in his later years, a lecher and a drinker. And his indifference to Elaine had grown more and more pronounced in his last five years.

Merry could have stood it all, except for the three "harpies" who came singly or all together every evening to condole and to pray with Elaine. Her mother was curiously evasive about their presence and avoided Merry's questions, and Merry could hardly push her inquiries or press her mother for an answer. But quite inadvertently Elaine revealed something about them one evening when, after they had left, she asked Merry, "Do you believe in life after death?"

"I don't know, Mother," she answered, with more tact than truth. She didn't believe in it at all.

"There is," her mother said as if it were terribly

obvious, and in the same tone she would have used had she been telling Merry that of course it was Thursday.

Merry let it pass, but the following evening she made it a point to leave the room when the three women arrived, and to listen from the stairwell to their conversation. After a few moments of polite chat, one of them asked, "Will you join with us in prayer, sister?"

Merry could hear the rustle of their clothes as they knelt to pray, and the cadence of their indistinct supplications. She couldn't stand it. She fled to her room.

She realized that she was of no use to her mother. She would not accompany her mother into the fantasy she had found for solace, and there was no other kind of sympathy or even company that her mother would accept. And she hated being there, and having to witness in silence all this maudlin, offensive show of grief and religion. But where could she go? There were still two weeks to kill before the opening of the fall term at Skidmore, and there was something pathetic about the idea of going to Saratoga Springs early like some orphan child who had no home. She was too old to sail blithely into the Jaggers' apartment in New York, but not old enough or confident enough to take a hotel room somewhere and wait out the two weeks alone. Helen Farnam was still in Europe and would not return until two days before Radcliffe began. And her father was in Spain, working on *Nero*.

The picture of her father she had kept over her bed on Cape Cod had not only served to maintain her anger, however, but had also in part aroused her curiosity. She knew nothing about his life; or about their roots, whatever they had been—except that her grandmother was still alive. Out in Montana. And her great-grandmother, she thought, was alive, too.

It had been by a process of elimination that she arrived at the idea of going to Montana, but having thought of it, it seemed to her a not at all unattractive prospect. But she could not just appear there without warning. For all she knew, her father had been disowned, disinherited, disclaimed. He never spoke of them. What could they think of him? What welcome would she get?

Sam Jaggers would be likely to know. She went to her mother's bedroom, closed the door carefully, and called Sam Jaggers in New York. It took her a few moments to get through to him.

"Hello, Mr. Jaggers, this is Merry Houseman."

"Hello, Merry, how are you? What can I do for you?"

"I'm here with my mother in Los Angeles, and she doesn't need me any more."

"Oh?"

"And, well, actually, I can't stand it any more."

"I see," Jaggers said. "And what would you like to do? We're going off to Lake Louise for a couple of weeks. Would you like to come with us?"

"That's very kind of you," Merry said, "but I thought I might go to visit my grandmother in Montana. That is, if you think she might like to see me."

"Why not?"

"I don't know. I don't even know where she is," Merry said. "Does she know I exist?"

"I imagine so," Sam said. "Just a moment."

She held the phone while he flipped through a desk file of some sort, while muttering indistinctly to himself.

"Ah, yes, here it is," he said after a few moments. He gave her the number. "Spoon Gap 10. Tell the operator to route it through Butte."

"Ten? What kind of phone number is that?" Merry asked.

"Well, it's easy to remember;" Sam said.

"You wouldn't like to call her for me, would you?" Merry asked.

"No, I'm not her granddaughter," Sam said, and laughed gently. "Do you need any money?"

"I don't know," Merry said.

"I'll put five hundred in your account."

"Thank you," Merry said. "And have a good time at Lake Louise."

"Enjoy yourself in Montana," Sam said.

It was not so much a visit as a pilgrimage. And on the part of the women who met her at the bus stop, it was not so much a welcome as an acknowledgment. They introduced themselves and performed the rituals of courtesy, but below that simple surface there were odd currents, eddies, and undertows. There was Ellen, her grandmother, her father's mother, and in the car, wrapped in a blanket even though it was still summer and still warm, was the other woman, incredibly old, Merry's great-grandmother, Martha. Minnie, the dark one, who was part Indian, was the servant.

They drove through Main Street, which for two blocks had stores and a post office, and the garage. Houseman's Garage. Her grandmother told her that they'd bought that in the thirties, in the Depression. Sam had. "He was your grandfather. He died," she said. But before he had died he had bought up most of Spoon Gap. A half interest in almost every business in town. From the hardware and feed store he had branched out, bought and bought, and then died, leaving the women behind him to enjoy the fruits of his labors.

The car did not stop in town, though. It went on, up into the gap and into the hills, to the old ranch where the women lived now. "Your great-great grandfather started this ranch. Homesteaded it. His name was Amos Houseman, too."

"Too?"

"Your father's name is Amos. Didn't you know that, child?"

"No," she said. "I didn't."

"Well, it is," Ellen said.

"It is," the very old woman wrapped in the blanket said.

Merry nodded and smiled.

The car turned off the road and went through a stone gate and up a steep driveway to the ranch house. It had been kept in good repair or, more probably, restored. Certainly, money had been spent on it over the years. There was a new kitchen, and all the plumbing was modern and new. The living room was much as it had been, with the great stone fireplace taking up a whole wall. Through the window there was a fine view of the mountains beyond—two mountains and a third towering peak visible between the first two, off in the distance.

Merry stayed there for ten days. There was little conversation, for on the simple surface there was nothing much that she had in common with the two women, nothing she could talk about to them or they could talk about to her. But it felt good, and there was a kind of intimacy that she felt. She could not explain it, could not have said what it was or how it worked, because she did not know about their lives, had never heard the story of Amos Houseman and the stranger who came through Spoon Gap to beget Sam upon Martha and die at Amos' hand. Nor did she know what Ellen's life had been, living with Sam during all those years of propriety and vengeance. They were through with it all now. They had suffered from their men, and had endured and outlived them. And in Merry they saw themselves, young again, beautiful again, and vulnerable again. And there was a kind of gentleness and a kind of respect that they gave her, and that she returned, even though without knowing why, or how it had welled up.

Merry was all the more pleased to realize that the feeling of intimacy seemed to be mutual. They were sitting in the living room one evening, around the fireplace. Merry was turning the pages of a magazine. Ellen was working on a comforter, knitting the squares and every now and then dropping a finished one into a basket. Martha stared into the fire. It was after Ellen had completed one of the squares that she asked Merry whether she might like to come with her the next morning to the Hopgoods'. "Frances is expecting," she explained.

"Expecting us?"

"Well, yes, but expecting a young one. It'll be her sixth." Ellen explained that Bill Hopgood might have to deliver the baby himself. It was due any time, and even early in September snowfalls could suddenly block the roads up in the mountains.

"Why doesn't she go to a hospital?"

"And leave the five youngsters and Bill? She wouldn't do that. Hospital's eighty-five miles from here. With a sixth baby they'd never make it."

"Can't that all be done by appointment now?"

"Not with a sixth child. Or a fifth. You can't take the chance."

Ellen's needles clicked on, and the matter-of-fact way in which she explained all this struck Merry as more interesting than the explanation itself. The acceptance of what Merry would have thought barbaric and primitive necessities was what struck her, and the calmness.

"What are you going to do, then?"

"I'm bringing up a kit from the county medical office. Sterile scissors, and tapes, and all the things Bill will need. And a book. Not that he'll need it, I shouldn't think. It's no different from sheep and horses."

"What happened last time? With the fifth one?"

"That was the summertime. The roads were good. The doctor could get through."

"Oh."

"You'll come?"

"Yes. I'd like to."

There was nothing that Ellen had said, but Merry

had the feeling that the trip was not merely for her diversion, or in order for her to keep Ellen company on the drive. She understood, without anything having been spoken, that Ellen was trying to show her something of the life they all led there. And she was eager to see.

The next morning after breakfast they drove off, up into the mountains, along roads that twisted and turned through the valleys, often beside rushing streams. The mountains loomed about them in huge shapes of awesome power and yet with a wonderful freshness and serenity.

The Hopgood place was a large meadow between two mountains, in a widening of the valley. There was the house and the barn and the chicken house, and other odd buildings stood about in varying degrees of disrepair. The house needed painting, but it was clean and comfortable. There was an oil-burning stove in the kitchen, and the elder Hopgoods—the children were nowhere in sight—sat around the kitchen table with coffee from a big enamel pot, formally welcoming their visitors. Ellen gave them the book and the kit. They thanked her for coming all the way up with these things. Ellen said it was no trouble, and that she welcomed the excuse to show Merry the mountains.

"You don't know the country?" Mr. Hopgood asked.

"I'm a city girl," she said, adding, just a beat later, "I'm afraid."

"Pains my legs to walk on that concrete," Mr. Hopgood said. "But there are folks who like it."

They sat and drank coffee for a few minutes more, and then Mr. Hopgood rose from the table.

"You sit here and make yourselves to home with Frances. I have a mare foaling in the barn."

"You do?" Merry asked, her eyes widening.

"Sure. Want to come see? Is it all right, Mrs. Houseman? I mean, do you mind if she comes out to the barn?"

"May both of us come?"

"Surely."

He led the way out to the barn. Ellen stepped inside, and Merry kept close to her. They didn't go right close up to where the mare was, for fear of upsetting the animal. The mare lay on the ground, and Merry could hear it breathing even from twenty feet away. Every now and then a great shudder would seize the animal, as it produced one of its contractions.

"It may take her a while yet," Mr. Hopgood said, almost apologetic about their having to stand and wait.

"We'll go sit with Frances for a while, then," Ellen sad. "We'll be back."

"Fine."

They went back to the kitchen and waited for another hour. Then Ellen said that they had to go. She explained in the car that she hadn't wanted to stay any longer because if they did, the Hopgoods would have had to give them lunch, and she hadn't wanted to impose. Merry was sorry to have missed the foaling, and said so.

"Yes, it's real pretty," Ellen said.

The day before Merry left, Ellen drove her back to the Hopgood place. Frances had not yet had her baby, but the mare had foaled, and Merry went out to see the leggy little colt and watch it nurse. It was the most beautiful thing she had ever seen in her life.

"I wish I could have one," she said that night at supper.

"Have to settle down for a horse. You can't go off and leave them, you know. Have to ride them every day. They need exercise."

"I know, but I can wish."

"We can wish," Ellen said.

It was only on the bus, thinking back on it, that she understood what it might have been that Ellen was wishing for.

Skidmore was different. Or maybe Merry was different. Or both. But the life there was not at all what she had known at the Mather School. You didn't even have to go to class if you didn't feel like it. Nobody worried about where you were, except that you had to be in the dorm by eleven. And Merry's life was different, too. Maybe it was because the girls at college were a little more sophisticated, a little more polished than the girls at prep school had been, or perhaps it was because Merry arrived there with more of a sense of herself, knowing who she was and what she wanted, but the old tension was gone. It didn't matter what anyone thought, whether they revered or despised her father's fame and glamour or her resemblance to him. Or her own beauty. It just didn't matter any more.

She lived in Foley, which was a blessing because there were sophomores and juniors in Foley as well as freshmen. And it was with the juniors that she became friendly. It wasn't social climbing, any more than the way in which birds flock together can be said to be social climbing. It was just that these were the girls with whom there was something to share, with whom she felt comfortable. They had been around a little, and they knew a little and more than a little. They knew more than Merry did, some of them. Most of the freshmen were "a bunch of silly virgins," as Sarah Watson pointed out, and Merry was inclined to agree.

Sarah was a wonderful, crazy girl, brilliant but lazy—she admitted that herself. But she was bright enough so that she had worked out a rationale for her natural inclinations. "Robert Frost says that any student worth anything will ignore his assigned work to do other work of equal difficulty," she said. "And I'll go along with that." Sarah went along with at least the first part of it. She ignored most of her assignments. But in a perfectly practical, cynical way, she suggested to Merry that she do a little work at the beginning. "Once they decide that you're bright, it doesn't matter whether you do the work or not. They treat you as if you were some kind of a goddam natural resource. They won't flunk anyone they think is with it, even if their grade book tells them that the grade ought to be a flunk. Just make an impression, and then forget it. When you get to be a junior or a senior, you won't even have to do the work at the beginning of a term. The impression will already be made. They all talk about us all the time. God, it must be dull. But you get a reputation, and they just endorse what they've heard."

Not having much work to do, Sarah went out every night to a bar and grill, which was always called simply "The NoName," to drink. Merry often went there with her. Sometimes they went to D'Andreas to eat pizza and drink beer. The life was great, but Merry noticed that her clothes began to feel a little tight. She was gaining weight. She told Sarah, who introduced her to the Roman technique of banqueting and drinking and then retiring with a feather.

"A feather?"

"Sure. You tickle the back of your throat with it. And vomit."

"I hate to vomit."

"You get used to it. Besides, you have to choose. Give up eating, give up your figure, or give up your prejudice against vomiting."

Merry gave up her prejudice. Sarah hadn't mentioned that to give up eating and drinking would also probably mean that she would have to give up Sarah, but that played a part in it, certainly, and every night, after their excursions to The NoName, or to D'Andreas, or even just up to The Colonial snackbar for a bacon-lettuce-tomato-and-hamburger triple-decker and a couple of malted milks, she would retire to the bathroom with the feather she'd bought at the five-and-ten, tickle the back of her throat, and throw up. She stayed thin, and got used to the vomiting.

The weekends were dull, because Sarah went off to

New York to see some man. Merry couldn't stand the idea of going to the "mixers" at Dartmouth or Williams and didn't feel like going to New York, so she stayed at Skidmore and did in the two days the work she had put off during the five days before. And because she was bright and quick, she did well enough that way, and might have continued that way if Sarah had not failed to return from New York one Sunday night.

It was very abrupt. Sarah had quit Skidmore, had married a Polish count, and was going off to Rome. Bang. Just like that. Merry was not exactly filled with grief and dismay, but she was shaken a little. Sarah gone in the middle of junior year? She had assumed, somehow, that if Sarah could get through the four years, then she could, too, and somehow would manage to wait it out. There was no particular reason for her doing so, except that it was probably useful. Or not even that. If she really wanted to try her luck in the theater, she knew that the four years at Skidmore would be a waste of good time, and that by twenty-one, when she graduated, she would already be too old for certain parts, for certain breaks, for certain chances that would never come her way again. There were boys and girls her age who were already established household names, the earners of millions of dollars. And, if she was going to be absolutely honest with herself, the main reason for staying at Skidmore was to postpone the hazardous business as long as possible and delay the gamble and its risk of failure and defeat. She had tried to delude herself into thinking that she was there and would stay there because it was fun, but with Sarah gone it wasn't so much fun any more.

She tried to study, but it didn't do much for her. It wasn't the good old place to hide that it had been at the Mather School. Still, she had to do something. She remembered Sarah's advice about making a first impression. But she hadn't even done that. And she was flunking Art 273, not having had the time to sit down and just learn the hundreds and hundreds of slides of all those Egyptian frescoes, Greek columns and statues, and Roman bas-reliefs. She did the next best thing, and made an appointment to see Mr. Canfield, her section man, to plead that she'd had personal problems and to ask for special help. It was a standard maneuver, and Sarah had suggested it to her as one of the sure-fire ploys. It showed, anyway, a minimal interest in passing the course, which was more than the faculty got from a lot of the girls, who were interested only in boys or in their horses at the stables. Merry asked for an appointment for a conference with Mr. Canfield, and got it, and promptly forgot about it. It was hardly worth brooding about, anyway.

The appointed day and hour arrived, however, even without her having thought about it, and suddenly there it was, time for the conference, and she had only ten minutes to run to her room, change into a dress with a sufficiently low-cut scoop neck—Canfield was a notorious looker down low-cut dresses—and race back to the art building to his cubicle of an office. He was a young man, an instructor, and he asserted himself with a tawny little beard that he stroked all the time. Some of the girls thought he was attractive, but most of them, Merry included, thought he looked birdy. He was sort of fun, though, because he was very bright, very sarcastic, and even disdainful. He was only at Skidmore under necessity, needing someplace not too far from New York where he could live and teach until he had finished his dissertation—on Greuze or somebody like that. Merry couldn't remember. There were stories about him all around the campus, which was natural for any young, unmarried instructor. Well, she thought, she'd soon see for herself, and find out what kind of a guy he was outside the classroom, and away from the slides of Art 273.

"Come in, come in," he said. "Sit down, won't you?"

His door had been open, and he had heard her

footsteps approaching his office. She sat down in the wooden armchair next to his desk. "Thank you very much for seeing me this way," she said.

"It's my job," he said. It was hardly a promising beginning. "What's on your mind?"

"I . . . Well, I haven't been doing very well in art, I'm afraid."

"No, you haven't," he said. It looked as though it was going to be an absolute disaster.

"And I . . . I wanted to let you know that it wasn't for the lack of caring. It's been a difficult term for me. And . . . I wanted to know whether there might be some way for me to get back on the track, to catch up somehow. . . ."

"Sure there is. You could try doing a little work every now and then."

It looked to be hopeless. And yet, having gone this far, and having bothered to make the appointment and to keep it, she was not about to give up and to admit utter defeat. She leaned forward, so that the scoop neck of her dress fell forward just a little and the white valley between her breasts was partially exposed, and as she leaned, she talked, as earnestly as she could. "I try, but I suppose it depends on what you mean by work. I mean, in physics, if you push against a stone wall, there isn't any work being done, but only effort being expended. I expend the effort, but I don't get anything accomplished, so in that sense, I guess, I'm not doing much work. I either get interested in one of the slides, or I flip through them, trying to learn the details in each one that were talked about in class and that we're responsible for. And the one is too self-indulgent and takes too long because there are so many slides, but the other is so heartless and—well—dull that I forget it all as soon as I've put the box away."

"I see," he said. And whether he actually saw or not, at least he was looking, which put her for the first time at an advantage, or at least equalized somewhat the disadvantage she had labored under at the beginning of the conference. He could not devote all of his mind to the discussion if some of it, even just a small part of it, was concentrated on her cleavage, and on imagining the rest.

He ventured an answer about orderliness of mind and the unfortunate necessity to use works of art as "materials" for study, but the pauses between his words, and then the tumbling out of whole phrases as soon as they had occurred to him, as if he wanted to get rid of them and get on to something else, were more interesting than what he was saying. Or trying to say. Because he, too, was aware that he wasn't quite making sense. He paused, stopped, and she brought him back. She sat a little straighter and told him that there was one statue that she had looked at at least ten different times, before she realized that she knew the statue—not the slide of it in the box, but the statue itself. She had seen, in the museum in Basel, the statue itself, and she felt so stupid, but angry, too, because the statue was different, and it really did look tense and flexed, the way they had said in the lecture and then in the discussion group, but in the slide it didn't.

This was off the subject, relevant but just far enough off to open up a whole new range of subjects, and Merry knew that and had brought it up precisely for that reason. But he didn't try to bring her back. He talked for a while about the inadequacy of secondary materials, of reproductions, of slides, of the course itself, and as he talked she listened, and leaned forward to listen, and watched him lean forward to look at her leaning.

They talked for three-quarters of an hour, until Mr. Canfield said that he had a committee meeting to go to. And apologized, "I'm afraid I haven't helped you very much."

"I don't suppose there is much that anyone can do," she said.

"Oh, now let's not give up quite so easily," he countered. "Look, I'll be out of the meeting by five or five-thirty. Why don't we meet for a cup of coffee?"

"I'd like that," she said.

"Good," he said. "I'd like it, too."

"The snackbar in Fathers Hall?" she asked.

"How about The Colonial?"

"Fine," she said. "Five-thirty?"

"No later than that, I shouldn't think."

They left his office together and agreed again, in front of the art building, to meet at The Colonial at five-thirty. It was, Merry thought, a most successful meeting.

When the time came for her meeting with Mr. Canfield, he affected weariness with the college, with the committee meeting, with everything that smacked of Skidmore, and he asked her whether they might go downtown to an un-Skidmore-y place. It was as clear as the old line in the stories about "Would you like to come up and see my etchings?" but it was timid, too. The way he looked around to see if their going had been noticed was furtive and absurd. And then, at the little bar and grill down by the river that he took her to, he ordered beer for both of them, which was also indecisive and tentative. He could just as easily have ordered martinis. But beer was the drink of intellectuals, he said, and reminiscent of the old *Studentenleben* of European universities. Coffee was not for serious discussion. He did not mention, of course, that you also could get drunk on it, if your bladder held out. It was all so transparent that it was impossible for her to be frightened of it.

They talked about the course, about Merry's problems with the history of art, and then about Merry's problems, not the least of which was the question of what she was doing here at Skidmore. So they talked about that, too. Or rather, he talked while she listened, and she leaned while he looked. It was a way of not being bored, anyway. Somewhere between thoughts, he ordered dinner, and they continued to talk while they ate. She offered to pay, but he insisted. "You mustn't flash money at me that way," he said. "It's emasculating. Besides, it's after working hours."

"I guess it is," she said. "And that brings up something I've wanted to ask you for about an hour."

"Yes?"

"I haven't been able to address you. Do you want me to call you 'Mr. Canfield' still, it being after hours and all?"

"For God's sake, no. Charles, please."

"Yes, Charles," she said.

He stroked his beard, but it did not entirely hide the smile which his gesture had been intended to conceal. It was a cat-who-swallowed-the-canary smile. And it was funny to see it on the canary.

They left the seedy little bar and grill very soon afterward, and Merry was not at all surprised when Mr. Canfield—Charles—asked her if she'd like to come up to his place for a brandy. "I live just up the block there," he said. They were stopped for a red light, and he pointed off to the left. "You don't have to be back until eleven anyway, do you?"

"No," she said. "Not until eleven."

"A brandy, then?"

"Yes, I'd like that."

"Fine. I'd like that, too."

The pretenses were falling away at rather a faster clip than she was ready for. But there was no point in thinking about it too much now. She'd gone over it, or decided not to go over it, not to bother with it, hours before, after their conference in the art building and the invitation to "coffee." The light turned green, and the car turned left, and they went up a small hill to a group of garden apartments. He parked the car and led the way into one of the many identical doors, up a dreary steel staircase, and into a rather depressing living room in which the prints and lithographs on the wall seemed sadly pretentious among the tacky furniture, or contrariwise, the beat-up chairs and the sagging sofa seemed an annoying indignity to the pictures. There was a bricks-and-planks bookcase, of course, bulging with books, many of them the cheap white paperbacks of French publishers.

Merry sat down on the couch while Charles went to get the brandy. He surprised her when he came back by putting the two small brandy snifters down on the door that served as a coffee table, and taking her in his arms, even before she had had a sip of the brandy. It was sudden, but confident, and, she suspected, a practiced thing with him. It was, she had to admit, a good moment, not too soon—as it would have been, say, if he had kissed her as soon as he'd closed the door behind them—but not too late, either, so that the excitement and the feeling of adventure which had impelled her, and almost certainly all the others, to his apartment had not yet had a chance to dissipate. The kiss itself was not unpleasant, but she hardly responded to it as a kiss. Mainly she thought about the prickling of his beard. She had never been kissed before by anyone with a beard. Perhaps that was part of the program, too, deliberately thought out, so that, if only for the sake of curiosity, the first kiss was no trouble for him.

He followed up his advantage by releasing her, handing her one of the snifters of brandy, and asking her, even as she took her first sip of the amber liquid, "Are you a virgin?"

"No," she said. "Why? Do you like virgins especially?"

"No," he said. "I throw them out."

"Oh?"

"I teach enough during the daytime."

"I see," she said. "Well, not to worry."

"Good," he said. And he kissed her again, this time

more fully, more probingly, and with a hand on her breast. It bothered her a little that he had the routine so thoroughly worked out and, if only out of sheer perversity, she felt inclined to resist it.

"You have long lines of virgins, and nonvirgins, banging at your door every night?"

"Not at my door," he said and laughed. "And not every night. But it's not uncommon. I'm so wonderfully safe, you see."

"Safe?"

"Oh, yes. I'm outside of the world of most of these girls here. They wouldn't dream of going to bed with the nice boy from Cleveland or St. Louis or wherever, the one they hope to marry someday. But I'm not him. And I've got to keep my mouth closed, or I'm out of a job, or they think so, anyway. And I'm this poor, irrelevant, innocuous guy who hardly counts, so it hardly counts, somehow, that they've ever been here. I guess that's it."

"And you think that's what it is with me? That I have some nice boy in St. Louis?"

"No, not with you."

"Then what?"

"I have no idea," he said. "For all I know, you might be trying for a good grade in art."

"That's a miserable suggestion," she said.

"I only said, 'For all I know . . .' On the other hand, it could be because you like me. Or find me attractive."

"Oh?"

"But I don't think about it much. The important thing to me is that I find *you* attractive. Very attractive." And he kissed her again, this time with the hand on her thigh and working upward. She wondered about the crack about the grade. It was, she imagined, a kind of reverse blackmail. She had come to him thinking vaguely that he might trade one kind of pass for another. And he had accepted her offer, but changing the terms, so that she could choose which way she wanted to get plowed. It was kind of funny, actually.

"Come on," he said. "It's more comfortable in there."

It was abrupt, but deliberately so. She realized that if she declined to follow him through the door into the bedroom, he would usher her through the door to the stairwell and out of the house. He had made it clear that the supply was equal to the demand in the academic flesh market. It was up to her now to choose, to say yes or no, to go one way or another. And because she had already invested five or six hours in this project, and because of the not so very veiled threat about the grade in the course, and because there was no damned reason not to, she followed him into the bedroom.

His pace changed abruptly. She had already been wooed, after a fashion, and won. And now there was only the enjoyment of the fruits of victory, which he took much slower. They undressed and lay down on the bed together, and he propped himself up on an elbow and stroked her body, running his fingertips over her. And he put her hand on his penis, which she held while he stroked her. After a long while he kissed her again, and then climbed onto her and thrust into her, and then he asked her whether she had come prepared.

"Prepared?"

"Do you have a diaphragm?"

"No," she said.

"Jesus Christ," he said, and he withdrew. He reached over into the drawer of the night table and pulled out a package of condoms. "Here," he said, as he gave her one.

"But you're supposed to wear these things."

"I know that. But you can put it on for me."

He lay on his back and let her fumble with it, smiling bemusedly until she figured out how to roll it down his shaft. Then she lay back and let him mount her again, and screw her. She was pretty lucky, she decided. What had made her come to see him in the first place, and what had kept her interested in him between the conference and their meeting afterward, was the idea of whoring and the peculiar attraction that strange notion had held for her. And he had made her feel more like a whore than she had ever dreamed possible. Had he put a bill on the pillow afterward, she could not have felt more whorish. She was lucky, she thought, because that was what she had come for—luckier, anyway, than those long lines of other girls. Or maybe they all came to whore for him. And maybe he knew that, too.

She felt him come, and then go. He lit a cigarette, offered her a puff, and then said, "We'd better get back. You've only got twenty minutes before curfew."

"Yes, I guess we'd better."

They got dressed, and he drove her back to the campus. Not all the way to Foley, but to a spot nearby where she got out of the car unnoticed. He drove off with a great roar of the motor of his old Nash.

She hadn't liked it, after all. But because she hadn't like it, she worried about it. She wondered if anything was the matter with her. She hadn't come. She hadn't come with Denver James, either. And she had come with Melissa. And that was the frightening thing, because she wondered if she was a Lesbian. Her friendships with Helen Farnam and Sarah had not been sexual, or at least not overtly sexual, but they had been very close. And that worried her, too. And so, because she had disliked it, hated it really, and hated him and his smugness and his efficiency, she stayed after class when he asked her to a few days later, and when he asked her if she might like to have a beer with him that evening, running his fingers down her spine, she said that she would.

"About eight," he told her. "I'll pick you up. Across the street from Foley."

She said, "All right," and left to get to her next class.

And all day she hated herself for having agreed to see him again, and she told herself that she couldn't do it, not for any moral reasons but because she hadn't liked it last time and because she thought it was so unattractive. But there was the worry, and the knowledge that because of the worry she would go, and she did. But she was rather grumpy about it. Even after he picked her up and brought her back to his apartment, she maintained a kind of reserve, which was as far as she could get toward geniality from the sullenness that she felt.

There was no brandy this time, but beer, exactly as he had proposed. It was cheaper, she supposed. No dinner, and a beer for the sake of minimal manners. And off to the kip. But she didn't see why she should be any less blunt about things than he was being.

"Shall we go into the bedroom?" he asked her.

"I don't know. I don't know that I want to."

"Then what did you come for?"

"I don't know," she said. "I really don't."

"You want me to coax you? Go through the bit?"

"No, I don't want you to go through the bit. Not in here. But in there, it wasn't all that good."

"First time together, dear. It almost never works. People have to learn to get used to each other. It takes practice, like anything else."

So she went with him to the bedroom, and got laid again, and it was not better than it had been the first time with him. Or any time. With any man. And he told her, relax, baby. And she told him that she was relaxed. But that she had never made it, had never come. And that she was worried about it.

"Jesus Christ," he said. "Well, we'll give it another try."

But before he gave it another try, he made her get him ready, playing with him, and he played with her until she was very much aroused. He made her ask him for it.

"Now, what do you want?"

"I want to try it again," she said.

"Try what again?"

"Making love," she said.

"Don't give me any of that shit. Love's got nothing to do with it."

"I suppose not."

"What do you want then?"

"I want you to screw me."

"You mean fuck, dear, don't you?"

"I want you to fuck me."

"That's better," he said. And he rolled over and onto her and he entered her.

"You like to fuck?" he asked.

"Yes," she said.

"Then say it."

"I like to fuck."

"What do you like about it?"

"I like how it feels."

"How what feels."

"Your penis. Your cock."

"That's better. My cock. In your cunt. You like it?"

"Yes. I like it. I love it. I love your cock in my cunt. I love your fucking."

And he made her keep on saying all the words over and over, and eventually she began to feel them, and it was all cock and cunt and fucking, and she did, she could feel it growing in her, getting hotter and higher and louder and bigger until she couldn't imagine its getting any bigger, and it did, and it broke, and the shattering was it, was the coming, was the fuck. And she wasn't saying the words but just groaning, and then just breathing heavily afterward. She lay there, drenched with sweat, and watched and didn't even care but only thought it was funny as he took the condom off his cock and poured the silver-gray liquid onto her belly.

She took a shower, and he drove her back to the dark place across the street from Foley.

She saw him, slept with him, fucked with him three more times. Then the exam week came, and she had to study. And at the end of the exam week, when the marks were posted, and she saw that she had flunked Art 273, she left Skidmore. "The bastard," she said, when she saw the grades. "The fucking bastard."

It was easy to leave. She just called Jaggers, told him that she had flunked out, and that she was coming to New York. When you tell people you've failed, they never stop to ask whether you're lying.

CHAPTER

NINE

♥ "So you want to lead a band?"
"What?"

Jaggers leaned back in the large, upholstered chair behind his desk, laughed, and then stopped laughing with such abruptness that Merry was actually startled. He leaned forward, looked at her, and asked her why she wanted to be an actress. "Why? Why?"

"Because . . . because I can. I think I can, anyway. With Father's name, and your help, and reasonable talent, which I think I have . . ."

"That's not what I asked. I know you can do it. Because if you do it, I'll be the one who will be doing most of it for you. At first, anyway. I know what's possible. What I'm asking you is whether it is desirable. What the hell do you want to be an actress for?"

"I just want to. I don't know why."

"Well, think about it for a little bit. You know what

the life is like. It stinks, mostly. I don't have to tell you that."

"Then why are you telling it to me?"

"Because I like you," Jaggers answered. "Because you've been a guest in my house, have eaten at our table, have . . . Look! If I had a daughter, I'd tell her not to do it. And if you had a father who knew enough to do it, he'd tell you the same thing. If you want to, figure that I'm doing it for him. That I'm representing him. But I'm representing myself, too. You don't need the money. You haven't fought your way up from some slum. You're not stupid. I don't care what happened up at Skidmore. You're not an unintelligent girl. You can make any kind of a life for yourself that you want. And so, for the last time, I'm asking you—and I'm asking you to ask yourself—why you want to do this. Or whether you have to do it. If you don't have some good reason, or necessity, somehow or other, then forget it."

"You won't represent me?" Merry asked. The possibility had not even entered her mind. But suddenly all of her certainties had deserted her, leaving her alone and afraid in the office of Samuel Jaggers. But not the old Mr. Jaggers that she knew. No, it was the other Jaggers, the one whom every hopeful starlet had heard about, but no more expected to meet than the Maharaja of Jaipur or the Prince of Monaco. He was the top, one of the handful of men who could manipulate, bargain, coax, and bully the world of show business so that it seemed to revolve at his pleasure. If he refused, for whatever peculiar reason, to take her on, to help her, to make her a career, then where would she be? What would she do? How would she begin? Her palms were sweating, but she would not give him the satisfaction of seeing her wipe them on the wool of her skirt.

He waited a very long time before answering her question. He looked at her, then lifted the glasses off his nose to prop them on his forehead, massaged his eyes with his thumb and forefinger, and put his glasses back.

"Yes," he said. "Yes, I'll take you on. But do you know why?"

"No. Why?" Her voice sounded weaker, meeker than she would have liked.

"It's not because I like you. If I liked you enough, and if I had the right, I'd tie you up and never let you get near a stage or a camera. But I don't have that right, and I do like you, but not enough to throw away money. A lot of money. And I suppose it's better for you, too, if we do it right. I don't want you to turn out to be just another daughter of just another actor. You'd make a couple of Beach Party Fanny movies and then wind up in Rome doing cheap epics or horror movies. And that wouldn't do you any good. Or me. Or your father. We're going to be using his name a lot, at the beginning. And I can protect him by making sure that you do the right things, make the right choices, and don't embarrass yourself and him and me."

"I see," she said.

"Do you? I've never talked to you this way before. We've been friends until now. But there are no more friends. Not me, not anyone. It's not a nice business. When there are millions of dollars flying around like so many pieces of filth in a sewer, nobody is friends with anyone else. And the friendliest thing I can tell you is just that. That there are no friends. It's just one great big happy family of barracudas."

"Yes, sir," she said. She was both terrified and delighted. His bluntness was frightening, but, on the other hand, it was comforting to know that the incredible force of the man would now be exerted for her.

He took a piece of note paper from the leather box on his desk. She could see that the paper was engraved with a simple, massive monogram: SJ. He made a list of things he wanted her to do, telling her while he wrote the list, which he gave her afterward.

"First, I want you to get an apartment. In the east fifties or sixties. Not in the seventies. You don't want to waste your whole life in taxicabs. Go to Jean Cushing. She has more sublets than any of them. When you find the apartment, let me know. I'll tell you how to set up your phones."

"Phones?" she asked.

"Yes. You'll have two. One will be listed, but you'll never answer that one. You'll have an answering service on it. The other will be unlisted."

"But why do I need . . ." she started to ask.

"So you won't have crackpots calling you up at three o'clock in the morning to tell you they want to fuck you. All right?"

"Yes," she said. It was crazy. Who would have thought of a thing like that? But still, she felt stupid for not having thought of it.

"Until you find an apartment, you'll have to stay at . . . Or actually, if you want to, you can stay with us. Or in a hotel, as you wish. And I think you should go to school."

"I beg your pardon?"

"To study acting. I'll see what I can do about getting you into the Theater Workshop."

He handed her the piece of paper, asked her if she had any questions, and waited.

"Should I go to see this Jean Cushing right now?"

"That might be a good idea. Have you had lunch?"

"No," she said.

"Then eat. Go have a hamburger somewhere. Some coffee shop. Or a hot dog at Chock Full o' Nuts. In two months you won't be able to do that any more."

He sat back in his chair and smiled at her for the first time since she had come into the office.

"Thank you," she said.

"I haven't done anything yet," he said.

She got up to go. She was not all the way out of his office before he was busy placing calls with his secretary.

It was interesting to watch Jaggers work. She did not sit there in his office, looking at him while he talked on the telephone, dictated letters, or rocked in that huge chair of his, deep in thought. She did not have to. Everything she did from the time she got up in the morning was his doing. She was like a card in his poker hand, and he was playing her. Or for that matter, she was like a whole hand. Her name was the big ace. Her looks were the queen. His own business ability, his shrewdness in dealing with producers, was the jack. And the wild card, publicity, could be the ten. The only chance he was taking, but it was a big chance, was drawing for the king, and assuming that she had, somewhere, somehow, at least a little talent. "We can do it either way," he had told her not long after she had come to New York. "With talent or without. You don't need talent to make movies. You think Lassie has talent? Or Rin-Tin-Tin? Or Trigger? If they can lead an animal around in front of the camera, they can lead you around. You can understand simple commands. Acting in the movies is nothing. In fact, it gets in the way. You've seen them make films, haven't you?"

"No," she said.

"No? Well, it doesn't matter. It's all takes. Twenty seconds. Thirty seconds. A minute, maybe. And each take they do ten or twenty or thirty times. The odds are that one time out of thirty you'll do it right. It's just dumb luck, and believe me, a great many of the stars are pretty dumb. But if you do have some small ability, we ought to use it. We can start a little bigger. You can start at the top as easily as at the bottom. The only risk is that it's a lot farther to fall that way."

The shortest distance between two points being in show business a meandering S-curve, the way to stardom in Hollywood was in New York. There were the drama classes, of course, but the lessons were only a small part of the program that Jaggers made up for her. He set up modeling dates for her with fashion photographers. Homer Xenakis took her out to Jones Beach and spent four hours shooting her against expanses of sand and sea. With her hair combed. With her hair blown. With her shoes off. With a saluki. With a champagne glass. With an old brass telescope.

At the end of the session she was exhausted. Xenakis piled his equipment into his Jaguar and drove off. One of his assistants took Merry in the Ford, with the saluki in the back seat.

She called her answering service and, as usual, the girl told her that there had been a call from Jaggers' office. They called frequently, and Merry wondered whether Jaggers' main purpose in most of the calls wasn't to check up on her and make sure that she was doing what she was supposed to. Or maybe it was just to train her to check with the answering service, which was practically a reflex after only a week. But this time Jaggers took the call himself.

"Young lady, why haven't you written to your father?" he asked.

"I . . . I wanted to surprise him," she said haltingly.

"Well, he's surprised, all right. And he's pretty angry, too. I think it would be a good idea if you wrote to him tonight."

"What can I tell him? We really don't have very much to say to each other."

"I think you do. You might tell him that you're in New York, that you have begun work at the Theater Workshop."

"But—"

"No buts. I'm telling you to do this."

"Why?"

"Because your father is angry. My client is angry. I don't like my clients to be unhappy. So you do this."

"All right. I will. I promise."

"Good. And tell him that Mr. Kolodin said you're doing very well."

"Did he?"

"I talked to him this afternoon. He did. Oh, and tell your father you're taking voice lessons."

"Am I?"

"Starting tomorrow. You will be by the time he gets the letter."

"But why—"

"Kolodin's idea."

"Oh. Well, of course."

"Good."

"Oh, and Mr. Jaggers?"

"Yes?"

She hesitated, wondering whether she should presume to tell him what she was thinking, had half decided not to, and yet had already begun to blurt it out.

"I'm sorry if I've caused you any trouble. With Father."

"I half expected it," he said, cutting in and cutting short her discomfort. "It will be all right."

"I hope so."

"I'm sure it will. Anyway, don't get a swelled head over it."

"A swelled head?"

"I shouldn't have taken the risk, no matter how small I thought it was, if I hadn't thought that you would make it. And I'm sure you will. I was very pleased with Kolodin's report."

"I hadn't even thought of that," she said honestly.

"You'll learn," he said, laughed, and hung up.

She put on a saucepan of water for instant coffee, and sat down on the daybed with *The Three Sisters* to go over the scene she was preparing. For the fiftieth time.

It was, in a peculiar way, a very quiet life that she led. She was busy, busier than she had ever been at school, and tired at the end of a day. Bone tired, she would get into the tub with a script of a scene and lie there, intending to study the script, but able only to lie there in the hot water, feeling the fatigue drain out of her muscles and into the water. But she had no friends, no one to talk to, no one to have fun with. The people down at the Workshop resented her, as indeed she knew they had every right to do. They were working as hard as she was, but they knew that she would make it before any of them. Because of her name and its power and connections. They were polite enough, and perfectly pleasant to her, but she could feel the weight of their envy. Her only response to this was to work harder and to try to earn their respect as well.

That she had left a certain kind of easy companionship behind at Skidmore did not seem peculiar to her. Her friends were in school. Practically everyone her age was busy with assignments and classes and dates. She was working. And for all the glamour and fun that theater is supposed to offer, she felt rather subdued—when she had the time to allow herself to feel anything. There was even a challenge to it. One night, not very late—it couldn't have been much past ten-thirty—she was watching television, as she had been told to do. The volume was off, and she was watching the picture of the faces, studying the play of emotions and expressions as the actors projected not the lines but themselves. The point of the exercise was to try to follow the emotional lines of the drama without any reference whatever to the plot. Everything seemed very sad. They all seemed to be on the verge of tears. And Merry found that she was crying herself. She refused to take it seriously. She told herself she was tired, turned off the set, and went to bed. But deep in the back of her mind she knew that unless something happened soon, she would find herself alone in her room-and-a-half, crying herself to sleep again, and again.

But something did happen. It began in a small, silly way. She came back to the apartment one morning after her voice lesson to find a large envelope from

Jaggers. There was a tear sheet of a picture spread that was about to run in *Vogue* about spring coats. And there was Xenakis' picture of her on the beach. With the champagne glass. She called the answering service, and they told her to call Jaggers. She called him, and he took the call. It was time to begin, he told her. Nothing very strenuous at first, but small gestures to let the world know that she existed. He asked her if she had a pencil.

"Yes, right here."

"Good. You have an appointment at Elizabeth Arden's at three. And another at the St. Regis at four-thirty. Come in about four minutes late. Not the King Cole bar. That's for men. But there's a little cocktail lounge next to it. Do you know it?"

She didn't but she was sure she could find it.

"I'll be there with two other men. Bill Carr and James Waters."

"The playwright?"

"That's right. Now, tell me what you're supposed to do."

She repeated the schedule. Arden's at three. The St. Regis at four-thirty-four.

"Good," Jaggers said. "If you can, take a nap between now and three. You may be out late."

"Wonderful," she said.

"Your enthusiasm is infinitely depressing," Jaggers told her, and hung up.

He was not being quite fair. Merry was enthusiastic, but not just about the prospect of going nightclubbing. The fact that the wheels were beginning to turn was exciting. And the process itself was fascinating. She went to Arden's, and they already knew what was to be done to her. Jaggers had been in touch with them, and had specified how her hair was to be done, and how she was to be made up. And what time she was to be through. She arrived at the cocktail lounge at the St. Regis exactly at four thirty-four and found the three men drinking whiskeys. Jaggers did not ask her what she wanted, but ordered a dry sherry for her.

"A nice picture in *Vogue,*" Bill Carr said.

"But it isn't out yet," Merry answered.

"Mr. Carr sees advance copies," Jaggers explained.

"There's nothing deader than today's newspaper," Carr said.

Jaggers chuckled, Merry smiled, but Jim Waters' expression did not change at all. He sat there, looking slightly pained or perhaps bored. Anyway, indifferent. He hardly looked like the author of the brittle, high-style comedy that had been such a success the year before. She could hardly imagine him laughing.

Jaggers and Carr did most of the talking. And they talked apparently about nothing at all.

When the drinks were nearly finished, Carr pulled a typed sheet of paper from the inside pocket of his shiny silk suit and handed it to Waters.

"Have you any reason why the sentence should not be pronounced? No, your honor."

"Hardly flattering to Miss Houseman," Jaggers said. He was smiling, but he leaned forward a little.

"But neither is it unflattering. The sentence applies to both of us. If I'm insulting anyone, I suppose it's you two," Waters said, indicating Jaggers and Carr with glances. "And you don't care."

"No, we don't," Jaggers said.

"Very funny, very funny," Carr said.

But Waters was looking at the schedule. "Perfectly dreadful," he said. "Does she have a copy?"

"No, she'll be with you."

"Ah, yes. Of course."

"That is, after all, the point," Carr said.

"Quite," the playwright said. "Well, then, Miss Houseman, I shall have the honor of calling for you at ten o'clock this evening?"

"I suppose so."

"Thank you."

"Do you know where I—"

"It's right here. On the paper."

Carr called for the check, signed it, and left two dollars on the table for the waiter.

"Until ten o'clock then?"

"Yes," she said, and smiled at him. He was an odd fellow.

They left the lounge together and separated at the front door of the hotel.

Jaggers said nothing until they were fully half a block away from the hotel entrance. Then he asked, "What did you think of them?"

"I don't know. I didn't like Mr. Carr very much."

"He can be quite charming when it's necessary. Do you know what he does?"

"No."

"He's a planter."

"A planter?"

"Yes, of items. In columns. He gets people's names into columns. Winchell, Kilgallen, Lyons, Wilson, Sylvester, Sullivan. He sends them material and they print it. Jokes, funny sayings. Bits of gossip. And he gets his clients into the columns, too."

"Am I one of his clients?"

"Not exactly. But I am. And so I suppose you are, too."

"Is Mr. Waters?"

"Only in the way that you are. His press agents, the press agents for his new play, deal with Mr. Carr."

"He didn't seem very happy about it."

"No, he wasn't. You see it's different for him. With you the point is just to get your name into the papers. With him it's less simple. He and the leading man in the new play are—well—lovers. And the press agents don't want this generally known. So they've invented a romance for him. With you."

"With me?"

"It's all right. He's perfectly harmless. He couldn't care less about you."

"That's very good to know."

"It's just business. He'll take you around to various places. And most of them will have something going for them with the columns through Carr, for that matter. Either the place, or the singer, or the wine you'll be drinking, or . . . Well, it could be anything. It's very intricate."

"And it's all bought and paid for?"

"More or less, yes."

"Then why do we have to actually do it?"

"Now don't start asking philosophical questions. There's a fine line, I suppose. Carr can get the columnists to print things, but they don't like to look like liars. So he makes the things happen for them and keeps them honest. They all know that Waters is queer. But if they actually see you sitting with him at Elmer's, they have to choose between believing their own minds or their own eyes. And the eyes have it."

"Elmer's?"

"El Morocco."

"Oh, I see. I've never been there."

"You haven't missed a thing."

They had reached Jaggers' office. He stepped off the curb, hailed a cab, put Merry into it, and as he held the door, told her to have a good time.

"Thanks," she said, with a half laugh.

"That's the spirit," he said. And he closed the door.

The doorman called her a few minutes before ten to tell her that a Mr. Waters was there to see her. She said it was all right and to send him up. Then she ran to the bathroom, checked her face and her hair, and finding that she looked fine, she went back to the living room, where she sat down to wait for him to come up. The doorbell rang.

"Hello," he said, in a dull, glum voice, as she opened the door.

"Hello," she said. "Come on in."

"Thanks," he said. He put his coat on a chair and looked around the room. He went over to the bookcase and inspected the books.

"Most of my books are in storage," she said.

"Sure," he said.

"What do you mean by that?"

"Nothing. I'm sure that they are."

"I'm not so sure that you're sure. And anyway, what kind of a thing is that to do? To walk over and look at a bookshelf! It's . . . it's like looking in people's medicine chests."

"Is that what *you* do?"

"Look, Mr. Waters, I'm sorry if you're unhappy about this evening. But as long as we have to do this, wouldn't it be better if we acted as though it were fun?"

"Go ahead. You're the actress."

"You're a very sarcastic person."

"Yes, I am."

"Would you like a drink?"

"We'll be drinking enough this evening."

"You are a friendly one, aren't you?"

"Now who's being sarcastic?" he asked. "And yes, I was being friendly. There will be plenty of stuff to drink this evening, and all of it's free. You're a young girl who wants to be an actress. I have no idea whether your father is bankrolling you or not. If he isn't, a bottle of booze costs you a lot more money than it costs me."

"I'm sorry," she said. "I take it back."

"You ought to take all those dust jackets off. They make the books look gaudy."

"They protect them, don't they?"

"What have you got there that needs protecting? A

lot of first editions? If it's worth protecting a book, you have it boxed."

"I guess you're right."

"Of course I'm right. Do you want to get your coat? Shall we get it over with?"

Somehow the discussion of the dust jackets and the trace of cordiality in his voice as he asked her if she was ready to go, even though unmarked by any change whatever in the delicate features of his long, angular face, struck Merry as reassuring. And very sad. Of course he was bristly. What a dreadfully uncomfortable position for a man to be in!

He took her coat from her and held it while she slipped into it and then opened the door for her. He was an unpredictable sort of man, she thought. Brusque, even rude, but still, in certain ways, very polite.

In the elevator on the way down to the lobby, he pulled the list that Mr. Carr had given him out of his pocket. He sighed and put it back.

"Is it that bad?" she asked.

"I suppose it could be worse."

First they went to the Stork Club. They were shown into the Cub Room, and Sherman Billingsley came over with a bottle of Sortilege for Merry and a bottle of champagne for the two of them. He chatted for a moment and then went off to greet some other couple.

"That was nice of him," Merry said.

"Oh, sure. Winchell will drop by later and ask old Sherm if we were here. The item is already in the column. He'll just be checking up."

"But the perfume . . ."

"He distributes the stuff. I mean, he's the American distributor. It's all promotion. It's carnival barking, without the fun of a carnival."

"I've never been to a carnival."

"Wonderful!"

He drank a glass of champagne.

"What's your new play about?" Merry asked.

"What new play?"

"I thought you had a new play."

"There's a play. But it isn't mine, and it isn't new. It's Molnar, reworked a little."

"Oh," she said.

"I like a girl who knows when to shut up," he said. "Here, have another glass of wine."

They sat there, drinking the champagne and listening to the music. They didn't talk. But they'd put in their appearance, had fulfilled Carr's promise. After a while, Waters looked at his watch and announced, "Advance to St. Charles Place. Do not pass Go. Do not collect two hundred dollars."

"That's Monoploy. I've played that."

"You've really lived, haven't you?"

"All right, all right."

He left a tip for the waiter and they went on to the Metropole to hear Cozy Cole, and to the Harwyn, and finally to El Morocco. They were seated at one of the zebra-striped banquettes, and the waiter brought champagne.

"You hungry? Would you like a steak sandwich or something?" Waters asked.

"If you'll have one."

"All right. Two," he told the waiter. "Incredible, this place. That's Siberia, beyond the dance floor. And that's Miami over there, beyond that aisle where we came in. There are only eight good tables in the place. Those four over there, and these four. The banquettes. All that space in the middle is for debutantes and jerks who tip too much."

"Why do people come here?"

"To see celebrities, sweetie. To see the big, important, glamorous people. Like us."

The waiter brought their steak sandwiches. Merry was starving, and very grateful to Jim Waters for having thought of ordering food. They started to eat. Billy

Rose and Doris Lilly came in and sat down at the number-one banquette table. Merry saw him order coffee for two. Jim explained that he came in every night at around three in the morning, had a cup of coffee, and left. "Weird way to live, isn't it?"

She agreed it was.

"But don't say anything."

She was about to ask whom she could possibly say anything to, when a short man with a narrow face and very sharp features came up to their table. It was Leonard Lyons. Jim introduced him to Merry and Merry to him. They chatted about Jim's new play. He made no reference to Molnar at all, but said only that "One does one's best." Lyons wished him luck, and then went over to join Billy Rose.

"Good. Now we're done. We can go, as soon as we've finished the sandwiches."

It was hardly a great compliment. She knew, of course, that it had been a business evening, and that she should not have allowed herself to be misled by their surroundings and their itinerary. And she had not really done so, either. But this blunt statement of his, absolutely unadorned and entirely without pretense, was rather chilling.

"Would you mind if I had a cup of coffee?" she asked.

"Oh, not at all. Go ahead. Unless you'd rather go someplace else. Of all the places to sit and drink coffee, these crummy zebra couches are about my last choice."

"I wouldn't want to impose on you. It might be faster here."

"No imposition. You've been a lot more painless than I'd expected."

"I'll bet you say that to all the girls."

"No. As a matter of fact, I don't."

"Then thanks, I guess."

She finished her sandwich. He left half of his, but he said he didn't want any more. They left El Morocco and started to walk toward Merry's apartment, both of them assuming that they'd pass some place on the way where they could get some coffee. But nothing was open. They got to the corner near Merry's building.

"Do you want to come up for the coffee?"

"Sure. Thanks."

They walked on toward the entrance. It was quiet, noticeably quiet. The noises of traffic had died down to nothing. Only an occasional cab broke the quarter-to-four quiet. They went up to Merry's flat, and Jim sat down on the daybed while she put up the coffee. The apartment was so small that they could talk, easily, even while she was in the pullman kitchen. Now that the artificiality of their arranged evening was no longer oppressing him, Jim was able to relax, and he even asked her a little about herself. How long she had been living there, and what her father thought of her decision to go into the theater. She told him how it had been, and he nodded, tired but attentive, and observed that it was a tough, lonely life.

"But you're in it," she said.

"It's different for me. I have nothing to lose and everything to gain. I'm a kind of a cripple. The theater is a great place for oddballs. If you're successful, nobody cares what you are. And if you're not successful, nobody cares about you at all. But for a nice kid like you . . . But what do I know about you? You may be as screwed up as I am. In other ways, of course."

"You make it sound pretty grim."

"I am. But I guess I'm tired."

He picked up his coffee cup and drained it. He stood up, yawned, and begged her pardon. "Thanks for a tolerable evening. I don't know whether they'll make us do it again. But it wasn't so bad. And good luck, hey? And thanks for the coffee."

He threw her a salute with one finger and left. She put the cups in the sink and went to bed. It was a hell of a thing, but there it was. The glamour was damned near as dull as the work.

But it wasn't so dull, after all. Later that week, *Vogue* hit the stands, with her picture in it. And all that week the items kept breaking in the columns. It was ridiculous, but she very nearly believed them. Not that she thought that there was anything to the suggestion that there was a romance going on between her and Jim Waters, but the reports of their high life in all the bright spots was very convincing. She thought of those people who go places in the world laden with cameras and light meters, who visit cities only to pose for pictures and take pictures, so that, back home, they can look at themselves and relish the idea that they must have been there. It was not an album of photographs that she looked at, or a file of slides, but sentences and squibs in columns. She knew that it had all been a fake, but she enjoyed it, nevertheless, when Tony Bassoto, at the Theater Workshop, mentioned that he'd seen her name in Winchell. She was impressed with the way in which he seemed to be impressed.

Other people were impressed, too, apparently, or at least had noticed. Jaggers called and asked her to drop in at the office. When she got there he told her that he had turned down a television offer, because he didn't think it was the right way to start. And he was not sure whether she was ready for it. "It's a tough game, that. Only a week of rehearsals, and then the whole damned thing is live. If you blow it, it'll take us six months to overcome it. It isn't worth the risk."

She listened and agreed. She trusted his judgment.

But that was not the reason he had called her in. The television thing was only routine. There had also been an offer from Fox. For a five-year contract. His advice was to turn that down, too, but it was important enough, and attractive enough, for her to think about.

Either way, he explained, it would be a gamble. What she had to decide was whether she wanted to bet for herself or against herself. If she bet against herself, as one does with an insurance policy, she could count on a salary for the five years of the contract, even if she never made more than one movie. Even if she never made a movie at all. But the hitch was that if she made a movie that hit and got hot, she would be working for ridiculously small numbers. Or she could go the other way, turn the contract down, and hope that they'd come to her anyway, use her in a picture, that the picture would do well and that she'd do well in it, and then that there would be other offers. And if all that happened, she could come out very far ahead indeed.

"What do you think, Sam?"

"I'd be inclined to bet on you. And turn it down."

"All right. Let's do that."

"Good. Now, having decided that, what would you think about doing a play?"

"Sure. Off Broadway, you mean?"

"No. On."

"Wonderful! I'd love it."

"All right. I thought you might like the idea. Take this home and read it. Don't learn the part, but read it over and get comfortable with it."

"Which part?"

"Which part do you think? The lead! Clara."

"You're kidding."

"Agents never kid. Not about business."

It was not until she had got back to the apartment and had settled down in the overstuffed easy chair to read the script that she noticed that the author's name, on the page after the agency's white binder, was James Waters.

She had done her homework. She had not only read the play through several times, but had gone to the public library and found the Molnar play that Waters had used and adapted. He had been far too modest.

The plot was different, and there were new characters and new scenes. All that remained from the Molnar was the mordant, brittle humor, and that shone through all the more clearly for his changes.

She did not want to use the Waters play at the Workshop. She thought it unlikely that she would get the part, anyway. And to advertise that she was being considered for a lead in a Broadway show would be ruinous, she thought, if she didn't get the part. Absolutely humiliating. But she could use the Molnar, work up scenes from the Molnar play, and use whatever help Kolodin could give her when it came time to read for the producer and director. And author? Would Waters be there? She assumed so. She had no idea whether he had been instrumental in arranging for her to be invited to read. And it didn't bear thinking about very much. Either way, it was disappointing. If he hadn't had anything to do with it, then it was sad, because perhaps he should have. One helped one's friends, after all. But if he had helped her, then that was disappointing, too. How terribly trivial! How depressing to think that art could depend on absurd, chance encounters.

She decided not to think about it. The important thing was to do as well as she possibly could at the reading. She studied the role, trying for as much bitterness and meanness as she could manage without entirely losing her warmth and charm. It was very difficult. She found a scene in the Molnar, and did that at the Workshop.

"Vell, vhat to you t'ink?" Kolodin asked, after she had turned, put her finger to her lips, and, in an abrupt change, bit her thumbnail at the departing Gregory.

The response of the class was mixed. But then it was always mixed. Sarah Bernhardt herself could not have reduced that eager young group of novices to unanimous assent and praise. Merry took some degree of comfort and even pride in the contradictions. "Too bitchy." "Too sweet." "The moods alternate serially.

They ought to be simultaneous, but laminated."

"I t'ink," Kolodin said, "I t'ink she has got the right note"—he drew out the word, which he pronounced "nwoht"—"but the wrong class. Would the petite bourgeoise bite that way her thumbnail?"

They pounced upon that idea, like zoo animals pouncing upon a lump of flesh flung from the feeder. "There's no clear distinction between classes in emotional response." "No, that's the only significant difference in classes." "Americans don't bite their thumbnails, anyway." "But Molnar was Hungarian."

It was Tony Bassoto who came to Merry's defense with an idea of at least some novelty. "How do we know what the character's background really is? She is middle class now. Petite bourgeoise. But before she married the doctor, what had she been? A gesture like that, going outside the range of what is expected from her position, is all the more powerful, because it's also something of a self-betrayal. It reveals so much."

"Very goot. Very goot! Tell me, Merry," Kolodin asked, "how did you arrive at that singular solution to the problem? How did you think of biting the nail?"

"I hadn't been . . . I didn't plan it at all. But I found my hand at my face, at my mouth, and that was right. It felt right. But I was angry, too. And suddenly that seemed the natural thing to do."

"Goot! Goot!"

It was the most effusive praise he had lavished on anyone in weeks. Merry could hardly pay attention to the performance of the two students who followed her with a Beckett dialogue.

At the end of the three-hour session, on the way down the stairs, Tony Bassoto asked her if she wanted to have a beer with him.

She remembered what he had said about Clara's background, and how right that had been, and perhaps partly because of that, she said, "Sure, thanks," and smiled. Or was it because of his tousled black hair, his light-blue eyes—his mother, he told her later, was Irish—and his lithe figure? She had noticed him, of course. He burned with intensity, and was so very serious. And he always wore the same black turtleneck sweater and faded chino pants. And black canvas shoes. She had noticed that about him, too, and had even wondered whether it was affectation or mere poverty. Which was an appealing idea. She had, in the two weeks or so since he'd started coming to the Workshop, speculated about his poverty, and she had to admit that she had hoped he was poor. She had never known anyone before who had had to think about money. And the idea of this young man's coming to the classes out of the inexorable necessity of which Jaggers had spoken, because of raw ambition and ice-cold need, was most appealing.

Of course, Tony's jet-black hair and his light-blue eyes had something to do with it. She knew that. Her guilt and her charity, legitimate though they might have been, would probably not have been aroused that quickly and in just that way had Tony been less striking. She noticed, for instance, the way he settled himself into the booth in the bar he took her to. It was one of those old-fashioned neighborhood bars, with brown wood tables and brown wood double benches making booths along one wall. The smell of old draft beer permeated everything. Tony seemed perfectly at ease and at home, and yet not at all submerged by it. He settled into the booth like a cat folding itself onto a satin throw pillow, mixing animality and elegance like a cocktail.

He ordered a couple of beers and then turned to Merry and told her, "That was really good this afternoon." He said it as if he had been thinking about it, considering it carefully. "You surprised me."

"Oh?"

"It wasn't fair at all, but I just assumed, with your

name and all, that you had to be a fake. I mean, you don't need the Workshop. You don't even need to be able to act. You could go out and make it, easy. But I was wrong."

"Were you?"

"I hope I was. For my own sake as much as yours."

"For your sake?"

"Sure. What do you care what anybody thinks? What can any of us afford to care? For me, the main thing is not to go nuts. And if I let myself think about all the no-talent jerks who are pulling it in by the millions, I'd go off my head in a week."

"But isn't that what you want? To be pulling it in by the millions?"

"I used to think so. When I was a kid. But there are easier ways to make it than acting. Lots easier ways. The thing is to be good. To be the best. There'll be a point, I suppose, when they'll put it to me, and I'll have to turn down some fat offer. But I will. There's an old buddy of mine who made it in the linen racket. Tablecloths and towels to bars and restaurants. Crooked as hell, but safe. And rich? Jesus, yes. Well, I could have done that. I could have gone in with him."

"But it's crooked, you say."

He made sets of Ballantine rings with the moist bottom of his glass on the wood of the tabletop. "It's different for you. I guess in a way it's even worse. It'd be so easy for you to sell out. I mean, right away. And you've got something to lose. You've got the stuff."

"Thank you," she said.

"Don't thank me. I didn't give it to you."

"Still, I'm glad you think I have it. The stuff."

"Yeah. Big deal, what I think. You're already a budding something. Boozing it up with playwrights and getting your name in the columns."

"That's just publicity. It's all rigged."

"I figured. But you've got somebody rigging you." He chuckled, and she looked down at the table, not embarrassed by the dirty sound of it, but thinking that she ought to be. Then she laughed, too.

The mechanics of attraction are complicated and absurd, and if they could be duplicated in some external model, like those plastic models of molecules, they would seem to be elaborate Rube Goldberg devices. A chance comment not even intended to have any *double-entendre*, mutually recognized and enjoyed, worked like the peanuts that drop out of the hopper to make the squirrel start running on the treadmill which turns a gear which raises a razor that cuts the rope that drops the weight. . . .

He ordered another couple of beers, and they talked more, but distractedly, and in an odd way only half paying attention to what they were saying. Mainly they looked at each other, noticing small irregularities about each other that seemed, suddenly, urgently important and irresistible. She realized, for instance, that his ears were not quite level and that the left was perhaps a quarter of an inch higher than the right, and saw how that subtlety affected his whole face, giving his looks a kind of whimsical elusiveness. He was fascinated by the slenderness of her wrists and her neck, and the touching way in which they contrasted with her father's strong, definite face, softening it and giving her a fragility, a vulnerability that was wonderfully appealing. It was only because they could not admit to each other that they were gazing that way that they talked, inventing things to say, or falling back on their childhoods to fill up the silence.

Somewhere along the way, he invited her to have supper with him and she accepted, and at some time or other they actually moved from the booth in the bar to another booth, this one in leatherette, in a Chinese restaurant, but she could hardly remember having been outside, having crossed streets, having passed store windows and litter baskets and mailboxes. It was only when Tony left her for a moment to go to the men's room that Merry realized that she hadn't called her answering service all afternoon. She decided that she wouldn't and that nothing could be worth interrupting this best evening she'd had since she'd come to New York. But she felt uneasy. It was Jaggers' damned conditioning. She got up and went to the phone booth near the cashier's counter. There was no sense in allowing that tiny worry about the answering service to intrude itself, as she knew it would. It would be easier to call and forget about it. But there was a message. A Mr. Waters had called and had left his number.

She called him. The line was ringing when Tony returned from the men's room, saw the empty booth, and looked around for her. She opened the phone-booth door, waved at him, and he waved back. Then Jim Waters answered the phone.

"Hello?"

"Hello," she said. "It's Merry Houseman. You called?"

"Oh, yeah. Sure. I did. I've got these tickets for an opening tonight. Lousy play, I'm sure, but I've got to go. I thought you might want to come along. I mean, if you'd like to."

"Well . . . sure. Yes. I'd love it."

"No, you won't. It'll be a terrible play."

"That's all right," she said. "I've never been to an opening."

"That's what I'd figured. That's why I thought you might like it."

"That's very kind of you," she said. It was very strange to be standing there in the phone booth, talking to Jim Waters and looking out through the glass of the phone-booth door at Tony. But she had to go. She wanted the part, and whether Waters had made it possible for her to read for Clara or not, he would certainly be at the reading. And Tony, she was sure, would understand and would want her to go. But still, it didn't feel right. She didn't feel good about it.

"The Algonquin at seven-fifteen," she repeated. "I'll be there. And thank you."

"My pleasure," he said. "Really."

She hung up and went out to tell Tony that she had to leave. She had to run back to the apartment, bathe, dress, and get back to the Algonquin in a little less than an hour.

"Sure," he said. "I know how it is."

"Maybe tomorrow night?" she suggested.

"Yes," he said. And the smile reassured her that he did understand and that it was all right. But still, it wasn't the way she would have liked for it to be. And in the cab going up Third Avenue she kept thinking of him, sitting in that booth in the Chinese restaurant, with that pot of tea in front of him. And she felt like a monster that she had left him there, that she had been able to leave him.

It was not, after all, such a fantastic coincidence. Rather, it was a rather clumsy net of circumstances, with holes in it big enough for a whale to swim through. But Merry read everything as omen and augury, finding significance in the configuration of events as gypsies find meanings in the muck of tea leaves in the bottoms of cups. Jim had only called out of kindness. It meant nothing at all. If she had thought to ask the answering service, she could have found out that his call had come in at a little before four, which is a hell of a time to invite a girl to an opening with a seven-forty-five curtain. She had not been the first one he had called, but the last. After trying her, he had decided that it would be insulting to extend an invitation at such an hour.

But she had not checked with the answering service, had not even thought of it, because she was too busy thinking about Waters and his play, and the part in it for her, and how, clearly, he must have been the one who had made it possible for her to read for Clara. It was not true, and he knew nothing about it, but Merry didn't know that. Jaggers had not bothered her with the mechanics of his business, and she had no idea that she had the script in her apartment because of a comment Jaggers had made to Waters' producer in a steam bath.

Since it seemed to her not just an invitation but a command performance, she was puzzled when they got out of the play, which was as bad as Jim had expected it to be, because apparently that was all there was going to be. He offered to drop her off at her apartment!

"You'll come up for some coffee, won't you?" she asked. "I have some real coffee now. Not instant."

"Thank you," he said. "But I don't think so. I'm rather tired. And I can think of a thousand ways in which I'd rather spend an evening, if I were a girl like you, than with someone like me."

"That's not true."

"Don't lie. Not unless you can get away with it."

"But I wasn't . . ." she started to say and then stopped as the click of recognition sounded in her head. "That's a line from the play!"

"What play?"

"Your play. The doctor says that."

"How do you know? It is, but how have you seen it?"

"You didn't know?" she asked. "You don't know?"

"Know what? No!"

"That I'm reading for Clara. I thought you might have arranged it!"

"You? No, this is the first I heard about it."

"Really?"

"Yes, really," he snapped. "What an absurd idea."

"Thank you."

"No, not that you should read for it, but that I should have 'arranged' it. It isn't a game, you know, or a tea party!"

"I know that."

"And if I'd had any idea that you were reading for a part in a play of mine, I'd never have taken you to a play. It makes life so much more complicated this way. What if you're absolutely terrible? I shall have to say so, and you will feel betrayed. And angry. And with some justice. Unless you believe me when I tell you, as I do, that I had no idea whatever!"

"I believe you," she said. "And yes, you can drop me home."

"Oh, well, the damage is already done, isn't it? Why don't you come up and have a brandy at my place. It's all so deliciously corny!"

"Corny? What?"

"The neophyte actress and the older playwright. Can't you see it in a sort of thirties comedy with Katharine Hepburn and Spencer Tracy? Cute meet and everything."

"What's a cute meet?"

"Where they meet cute. The madame and the psychiatrist have each ordered a new couch from the same department store, and each one's couch is delivered to the other. And they meet at the complaint-department window. That kind of thing."

"I suppose so," she said. "I haven't seen many movies like that."

"I know. You're so depressingly young. But come have a brandy."

"Thanks, yes."

So even if he had invited her to the play just to have the seat beside him decoratively filled, it had worked out to what she had thought, wrongly, back in the phone booth of the Chinese restaurant. And as they went uptown to Jim's apartment, her thoughts wandered back downtown, back to that restaurant, where she had left Tony. And she thought of him, again and again, all the time that she was with Jim. She thought of him, not unreasonably, as she came into Jim's apartment and noticed the richness of the furnishings, the paintings on the walls, the evidence, everywhere, of the success for which Tony thirsted. And she thought of him as Jim told her what a tough life it was to be starting out in the theater, and how much he admired the courage of actors who lived on their smiles and their hope as they tramped from one casting office to another and sent out those expensive glossy photographs of themselves, and the mimeographed credit sheets.

It struck her that he might be letting her down easy, and preparing her for her rejection when the time came, by explaining his reasons. And they were good reasons, too. Of all the struggling young actors and actresses, she was probably the least struggling that he knew. But maybe he was just talking, rambling on about a pet subject. Or trying to instill in her some sense of obligation and responsibility for the easy time of it that he thought she would have.

He went off to the kitchen to get another bottle of brandy. The one on which they had started had been nearly empty. She took the opportunity to go to the bathroom.

"Through the bedroom!" he called.

The bedroom was a large baby-blue room, with a king-size double bed in it. She thought of Tony then, too, wondering what his room was like. She was sure it was nothing like this.

In the bathroom, washing her hands, she looked at her face in the mirror on the medicine-chest door. And she remembered the way Jim had looked at her books and that she had said it was like looking in people's medicine chests. She looked around the room, saw the tray with ten different kinds of cologne and after-shave lotion, and, partly as a joke, she opened the medicine cabinet.

She felt herself blush. On the inside of the door of the medicine chest there was an eleven-by-fourteen-inch glossy photograph—of Jim? or one of his lovers?—of an erect phallus. She closed the door quickly and fled from the room. It was only in the bedroom that she stopped, tried to make sure that she seemed perfectly calm. She did not want him to guess that she had looked in the cabinet and seen the picture. Or was he wondering now? Was he enjoying the idea? No, it was too complicated to deal with. The only thing, the only possible thing to do was to ignore it. To pretend that it had never happened and that she had not seen the photograph. Pretend to him, anyway. She would think about it later. When she was back in her own apartment, alone, with the door closed.

He handed her the snifter, in which there was a new splash of brandy from the new bottle. She could detect no curiosity, no questioning in his expression or his tone of voice. They talked a little about the play. His play. She told him that he had been far too modest, and that it was only tangentially related to the Molnar.

"A technical exercise only. But my technique has always been adequate. You've read the Molnar?"

She told him that she had been working up scenes for the Theater Workshop from the Molnar play.

"You're all right," he said. "You're doing your homework. Now all we have to see is whether you have any talent."

"Yes, that's all," she said. She finished her brandy and apologized to him for keeping him up. "I remember you said you were tired. You've been very kind, propping your eyelids open for me this way. But I'd better go."

"No, that's all right."

"You're sweet to say so," she said, and she thanked him again for taking her to the play.

"I'll see you at the audition then," he said. The implication, clearly, was that he would not see her again before that. Which was sensible. He helped her into her coat and took her downstairs.

Back in her apartment she tried to sort it out, to decide what she thought or felt about him. She kept asking herself how seeing that picture had changed anything. She had known that he was a homosexual. Jaggers had told her that the first day they had met at the St. Regis. And he had been kinder to her than it would have been reasonable to expect. But there was no getting around it, nor any possible evasion. That huge, obscene picture, those larger-than-life-size genitals, had changed things. She had seen too much. Not the genitals, but the psyche in which the need for such a display was hidden. It was imponderable, and a burden that was not her own. She felt the unfairness of it, that such a thing should be thrust upon her for her to have to deal with. And feeling that, she began to understand. He must have known when he put that picture there that there would be people who might see it. And he must have intended, then, that people should see it. That it was on the inside of the medicine chest was deliberate, too, must have been carefully thought out. Anyone peering in there, spying, could not blame him for anything so simple as indecent exposure. It made for a kind of complicity. Anyone who was subjected to that picture deserved to be, having opened the door and having taken that risk upon herself. Or himself. And then it was up to the snooper to accept or to reject what Jim Waters thought to be his essential self. To take up the invitation, if a man, or, if a woman, to accept his homosexuality, his weakness, his peculiarity. Whatever it was.

And thinking of it that way, she was saddened. If indeed her explanation was the right one, then what a poor thing it must be to be Jim Waters. To despise himself that way. To demand for himself such signs of approval or even just toleration from his guests, from people in his own apartment, in his own bathroom. And once more she thought, because of the contrast, of Tony Bassoto's self-confidence.

She thought about him in other ways, too. Lying in bed, in the dark, and drifting off toward sleep, she speculated about what would happen with him. With them. It had been a lonely time for her since she had come to New York. A damned lonely time. Once more she remembered the way he had looked, tolerant and amused, through the window of the phone booth. And that image blurred with the other one, from the inside of the medicine-chest door, as she drifted off.

When she woke in the morning, it was as if it had already happened. She looked forward to their meeting at the Workshop with the combined eagerness and certainty that would have been more appropriate, she thought, to already established lovers. She had decided. It had decided itself within her. And all there was now was the enjoyment of it. Of him. Of them. She was a little nervous, though, as she went downtown for her class, but she was worried about him more than herself. What if he was not so healthy and robust as she had supposed? One never really knew about people. But Tony? He had to be all right! If he wasn't, then she would not be able to rely on her feelings about anyone.

But her fears were allayed when he came into the room and she saw him. He waved at her and smiled. She smiled and nodded. And she could feel that he was there. All there. She felt curiously tranquil, seeing him and being in the same room with him. And, after the class was over, she thought she sensed that same kind of tranquillity in him, too. No apprehension, no nervousness, nothing but evident joy in being with her.

It was all very strange. She had been in the class for six weeks, and he had come into it three weeks after her. So they had been there, and had seen each other there for three weeks. She had noticed him, of course, had observed him, and had even decided that he was attractive, but it was an impersonal decision of the kind that she might have made about a painting or a dress or a fabric pattern. And the day before, when it had happened, when their notice of each other had moved from the impersonal to the very personal, nothing had really happened. They had had a couple of beers, and had almost had dinner. But today it was as if they had known each other for a long time. Or if not long, then well. On the stairs on the way out, he took her hand. He had never done that before, but it seemed so natural, so comfortable, so simply right, that it was impossible for her to believe that it was a first time.

"Shall we go up to my place?" she asked him when they were out on the street.

"No. My place," he said.

And that seemed right, too. There was no reason. It just did. She liked the protectiveness about it. She even liked the idea of being protected a little, which had always seemed to her to be contemptible.

They walked south, delightedly sauntering. "I've got to pick up a few things in here," Tony said, indicating a superette just ahead. "The apartment is across the street."

They went in to the superette and she followed him around as he picked groceries off the shelf. A jar of Tuscan peppers. A jar of pimiento. A jar of olive condite. A can of artichoke hearts. A package of Genoa salami. A can of anchovies. A can of tuna fish.

"What's all that going to be?" she asked.

"Can't you tell? Antipasto!"

"Oh, I see."

"You cook, don't you?"

"No. I mean, instant coffee and Campbell's soup. And I can make cheese sandwiches. But that's about it."

"How do you live, then?"

"On instant coffee and Campbell's soup—"

"And cheese sandwiches. Wonderful. I'll have to teach you to cook."

"How did you learn?"

"I had to. My mother worked, and I was home alone. I learned. And then I worked in a restaurant for a while. But I've always thought that those of us who have had the advantages in life ought to help others to help themselves. Right?"

"Right," she said, pleased not only with the joke but with the fact that he had been able to make a joke out of it.

He took the wagon up to the counter, paid for the groceries, and they left the store. He went next door, to the fruit-and-vegetable market, and got four enormous peaches. He let her carry them. And then they crossed the street, each with a brown paper bag, to go home to cook dinner. Not only was it something she had never done before, but something she had never even seen before. The idea of her mother and Novotny, or her father and Melissa crossing a street with bundles of groceries in their arms was ridiculous. She wondered whether her mother and her father had ever done it, had been able to do it, so beautifully and so simply. Jaggers and his wife, she was sure, had gone shopping together, had bought food and brought it home. She wondered why she was thinking of all these people, and decided that it was because she was happy. She was only checking to make sure that it wasn't playacting, that she wasn't pretending, or playing house by conforming to some pattern of living that she had learned somewhere. But then, what had she ever learned that was regular enough to be a pattern? She was making it all up for herself, freshly. They were.

He unlocked the downstairs door with his key and led the way through a dark but clean hallway to the stairs.

"It's two flights, I'm afraid."

"That's all right," she said.

"I tell myself that it's good exercise."

"It is."

They got to the third floor and Tony unlocked the door to his apartment. He opened the door and stood aside for her to go in. She did, and then he came in, took the lead, and led her to the kitchen. He started to put the groceries away.

"How would you like to cook tonight? I mean, I'll sit

in here and tell you what to do. But you can do it, if you want. It'd be good for you."

"Good for me? How do you mean?"

"I've been thinking about your lousy cheese sandwiches. That's no way to live!"

"I have other things, too. Pâté from the Caviarteria. Eggs. I can fry eggs."

"Can you broil steaks?"

"No."

"Well, you can tonight. And you can do it the best way. Which is leaving the broiler for somebody else to clean up later."

"You could do the steaks and I could do the broiler."

"You don't know what you're saying!"

"Did I say the wrong thing?"

"Yes, but it was sweet. Don't worry about it."

"I'm not," she said. "I'm not worried about a thing."

He turned to her, put down the can of artichoke hearts, and kissed her, lightly, on the lips. It wasn't much of a kiss, but that was the whole point of it. It wasn't even a kiss at all, but more of a remark, and as a remark it was wonderful, just suggestive enough, and yet graceful enough to be delightfully intriguing. He did not pursue it, nor did he have to. That would come later. And they both knew it. The thing was to take it nice and easy. When he had put the groceries away, he got two beers from the refrigerator and took them out to the other room. She wondered whether he liked beer, or just drank beer because it was cheaper. They drank out of the can. She remembered a girl in an English class at the Mather School—Mary Jane, Mary Lou, or something like that—whose idea of absolute depravity in a short story that she had written was to have a man come home at five-thirty in the afternoon to discover his wife, still in a negligee, lying on the sofa and drinking beer out of a can.

She told Tony this and they laughed. He offered her a cigarette and got an ashtray from the door slab he used as a desk. It and the chair that went with it were the only pieces of furniture in the room. There was a bed, too, of course. Or not a bed, really, but a mattress, an enormous king-size mattress on the floor, covered with a green corduroy throw.

The room was grubby looking, but neat enough. There was nothing on the walls but a couple of theatrical posters and a large picture of James Cagney.

"Why James Cagney?" she asked.

"I use it as a dart board," he said.

"But there aren't any holes in it."

"I don't have any darts yet."

She laughed. He only smiled. She liked that. She hated it when people laughed at their own jokes.

"Sit down," he suggested.

There was no place to sit but on the mattress. She sat down and tucked her legs under herself. He sat down beside her. They drank their beers.

Almost idly, he began stroking her leg, from her knee down to her ankle and back. His fingertips were so light on her nylons that she could barely feel his touch. It suddenly struck her that even though he was certainly older than she was, he was still the youngest man—or not even a man, but still a boy—with whom she had made love. Or actually the first one with whom she had made love. With the others it had been just screwing.

He smiled a tantalizingly lazy smile and drew her down beside him on the bed. She lay there, passive, while he held her. And for a long time he did nothing but hold her close to him. She even wondered, after a few moments, whether he didn't still intend for them to have dinner first. But in a way which was not so much idle now, and certainly not tentative, but still leisurely, still nice and easy, he began to kiss her face. Her cheek, her forehead, her chin, and then, very lightly, her lips.

He began stroking her earlobe, which she thought was a little odd. The whole experience was odd, so dreamlike, and so floaty that she was puzzled at first. But after a few minutes during which he had done nothing more than kiss her very lightly and touch her ears and the back of her neck, she realized that it was like dancing and that she should let him lead. She relaxed and lay back to enjoy his minute attentions. Only then did he kiss her seriously, deeply, searchingly, with his tongue darting into her mouth and then retreating in a half-playful but infinitely delicious way. Then he moved, rolling closer to her so that not the side but the whole length of his body was against her, and she realized the restraint which he had been exercising.

He touched her breast, but still gently, lightly, and she found herself still thinking. She wondered whether this was technique. But she dismissed the idea. No, it was—she was sure it was—a kind of reverence for her.

But was he not carrying it a bit too far? She reached with her hand around behind his neck and ran it down his back. Only then did he clutch her to him passionately. In his close embrace she felt a tremor of desire. More than a tremor. It seemed to course through her whole body, starting slowly down there and working upward and outward even to the very earlobes that he had been touching a few moments before. They could not hold each other tightly enough. Gradually, gently, but with ever greater insistence, they found that they were rocking against each other. But then, abruptly, suddenly, he stood up.

What had she done? What was wrong? But no; he smiled and helped her to her feet.

"Turn around," he said. It was quiet but commanding.

She did so. She felt the zipper move from her nape to the small of her back as he opened her dress. He undid the hook of her bra and put his hands inside the dress, through, around, and cupped her breasts with them. He released her again, kissed her neck, and pulled the dress free of her shoulders. It fell to a heap on the floor. She hunched forward and let her bra fall to follow it. She turned to face him. He kissed her. She could feel the nap of his turtleneck sweater against her bare breasts. It was ticklish, but not unpleasant. She could also feel the urgency of his need against her.

They finished undressing. She finished first. She curled up on the mattress on the floor. She lit a cigarette.

"What the hell did you do that for?" he asked.

"What?"

"Light a cigarette?"

"I was embarrassed, I guess," she said.

"Ridiculous," he said. "Put it out."

She did so, and then looked up at him. His body was even more beautiful without clothes on. She gazed at him because it was almost as if he had dared her to. There would be no more embarrassment, no more modesty, no more walls between them. She finally understood the beauty of all the statues she had studied in Art 273. His body was a study of planes, angles, and curves which she could appreciate all the more if she looked at him through half-closed eyes.

He turned around and came toward her. He began again, just holding her for a moment, and then kissing her, and then kissing her more deeply. And then his hands were running up and down her body, savoring the curve of her hip, the softness of her breast, the flatness of her belly, and the silken firmness of her thigh. She had stopped thinking and her body followed his. He sensed the intensity of her response and was upon her. At his approach her legs parted and he rolled on top of her, but although her whole body lay poised, waiting for him, yearning for him to enter her, it was not so easy.

"Relax," he said, looking down at her.

It was impossible for her to relax. What was wrong? she wondered. She thought of helping him, guiding him with her hand, but that seemed somehow terribly forward. He raised her knees to her chest and guided himself in. She locked her legs around his back. The hardness of his body in her and the hardness of his body on her roused her to a pitch of excitement which she had never known before. She was hungering for him, thirsting, burning, but he stopped. And began again.

Slowly, almost imperceptibly, he began to move, stretching out the pleasure. In the moment of respite she found herself able to think again, even though unwilling to do so. It struck her as curious that both Denver James and Canfield had been so crude with her. She felt that all those dreary hygiene teachers had been right: without love it was nothing. But then, as his movements became more and more vigorous, she no longer had any thoughts for Canfield, or James, or hygiene, or indeed anything, except the growing ecstasy that was possessing her entirely. Over and over she murmured his name, and then no longer his name but simply wordless delight in little, helpless animal cries as she felt him blossom wetly within her. The excitement of it drove her over the edge so that every cell of her body seemed to cry with the joy of her release. She could even feel the tingle of the flush across her breasts.

They lay together and realized that they were bathed in sweat. Still joined with her, he kissed her eyelids and blew gently over her moist face to cool her. He lay, still, within her, and then he started to move again. She protested feebly. He silenced her with a kiss.

The second time it was languorous and sure, perhaps not so sharp as the first, but closer, and more intimate. Now they knew each other's body. All she could do was murmur, "I love you. I love you."

"And I love you," he said. "I didn't want to tell you

before, because I was afraid you wouldn't believe me. But now I can."

"And I do believe you," she said.

Suddenly they were gay and young and hungry. Naked, they went into the kitchen.

"Now you are going to have a lesson in the art of the antipasto," he told her.

It struck them both as insanely funny. They laughed. He slapped her on the behind and handed her a can of artichoke hearts.

The next ten days were the happiest that she had ever known. After all, for all her wide experience, she had never before had a boy friend. She was with him virtually all the time. They went to the Central Park Zoo and to the Bronx Zoo. They even went to the Planetarium. And though, for the rest of the world, it was March and cold, for them it was springtime. They drank a lot of beer and made love very often. But the great thing was that when they weren't making love, they were touching each other and thinking about it.

Even aside from her own feelings for him, and aside from his extraordinary handsomeness, she thought frequently about the wonderful disinterestedness of his love for her. For the first time in her life she could be sure that she was loved in spite of, rather than because of the connection with her father, which had haunted her from her earliest memory—and even before that. Tony hated the movies, hated actors who acted in the movies, and felt nothing but contempt for Hollywood and all that it stood for. Broadway was a distressing but probably necessary compromise, and he saw in the growth of Off Broadway productions a new hope for the theater in America.

He did not come out with this all at once, but over the course of several conversations spread over many days she elicited his views, all of which he was cautious about expressing. He had, after all, no very clear idea of what her relationship with her father had been, and he was pleased to find that he was able to criticize Meredith Houseman without alienating Merry's feelings. In fact she subscribed to his criticisms, reveled in them, because these criticisms of her father meant that Tony was in love not with the Houseman name but with Merry herself.

Had she thought about it, as she did much later, she would have realized that it was a great relief for her to be able to express her resentments and her dissatisfactions about her father in such an intellectual and detached way. "Of course, he has been in plays," she told him one afternoon in Brooklyn Heights, on the promenade.

He had taken her there by subway to show her the New York City skyline. The wind blustered down the river and ruffled her hair. It was a cold, biting wind and seemed to have come straight from Canada.

"Those weren't plays," he said. "They were pieces of crap."

"What do you mean?"

"They were showcases," he said. "Frothy little comedies of no importance, produced only because there was a star, and with the star appearing in them only because they required nothing more of him than that he be a star."

She had not told Tony about the audition for the part of Clara in Waters' play. It was the only secret she had consciously kept to herself. At first she had wanted not to tell him about it because she had been afraid that she might not get the part. It had seemed to her that it would be a wonderful surprise, and she had anticipated their celebration of her success together. Then, after she had heard and endorsed his views about acting and the theater, she had wondered whether he might not be displeased. Indeed she wondered whether she would not herself be ashamed of the play and its purpose in Jaggers' plans for her career.

But in a strange way, it was really not so important after all, because when she was with him, he was all that she was thinking about, and even the play seemed to her unreal, remote and chimerical.

It was unendurably cold on the promenade, and they walked several blocks to a coffee shop for hot chocolate. The waitress brought it in heavy white mugs with a thin maroon line around the rims, and they sipped at the hot brown liquid. Tony leaned over to brush away the spot of whipped cream she had left on her upper lip. She took his hand and kissed his fingertips.

"I've got some wonderful news," he told her.

"Oh? What is it?"

"It's about a play. Or actually it's about four plays."

"Four?"

"Yes."

"What is it? You've got a part? Or four parts?"

"It's better than that," he said. "I think *we've* got parts." His eyes shone.

"Well? Well? Tell me about it," she urged.

The plays were four Yeats plays a friend of a friend of his was producing. Off Broadway, in a theater that had formerly been a bar mitzvah hall. It was not far from Ratner's.

"Where is the money coming from?" she asked.

"Noel—he's one of the partners—has an aunt who is putting up the money. There's not all that much, but the production costs will be very low."

"I don't know," she said. "I'll have to talk about it with my agent."

She felt it was phony to say that, and cruel, and she added, "But when he knows how much I want to do it, I'm sure he'll say yes."

Jaggers himself had nothing to do with it. It was what Jaggers stood for—all of the sensible, practical, necessary considerations which she had thus far managed to avoid. She would have to face these questions now, for herself, before she could talk to Jaggers, and that was what bothered her. She knew so little about Tony. She had no idea how he managed to live. Well, that was all right. But now that he had proposed a production, it was necessary for her to be more careful, which was an absurdity. If she was careless and even reckless in love, but cautious about her career, the clear implication was that her career was more important. Was it? She did not even want to consider the question.

Nor did she want to consider Tony too carefully. Not now, and not for the sake of the production. She told herself that she ought to have confidence in him, ought to trust him, even if it was foolish to do so, because she had already trusted him so far and could not stop now. There had been, for an instant, a suspicion in her mind that Noel's aunt was no aunt at all. Cynically, meanly, she had imagined, just for a fraction of an instant, an older woman who was being courted and used by Tony's friend. For her money.

But no, she would not permit this nastiness to fester in her mind. "Don't worry, Tony. I'm sure I can talk Jaggers into anything. Especially something good," she said. But she was talking about herself, unfortunately.

She squeezed Tony's hand. He returned the pressure and then, with his forefinger, started tracing letters on the back of her hand. She spelled them out: I,L,O,V,E,Y,O,U. Then he kissed the back of her hand.

They finished their hot chocolate. He paid the waitress and they walked back to the subway. They parted in the train. He got out at Astor Place to take a fencing lesson. She went on to Columbus Circle for a body-movement class.

After the class she called Jaggers to ask him to see her the next day. He suggested lunch.

"That would be fine," she said.

"Can you tell me what it's about?"

"I could, but I'd rather it waited until tomorrow. It's nothing all that important."

"Are you sure? Anything that you'd rather wait until tomorrow to tell me is probably important enough for you to tell me now. Do you want to come over now?"

"No," she said. "Tomorrow will be fine."

"All right. Suit yourself. I'll see you at a quarter of one. In my office?"

"Fine," she said.

"Good."

On the way back to Tony's apartment, she stopped at a liquor store to buy a bottle of champagne. Either Jaggers would allow her to be in the Yeats play with Tony, or he would not. But whatever happened, she felt somehow that this evening was an event, a watershed. She did not allow herself to formulate this consciously, though, or to face it head on. Indeed, she evaded the idea by telling herself that the fact that they were in love was reason enough to buy champagne. She took a cab downtown. She took subways with Tony, but when she was by herself she could relax and take taxicabs. Still, she had the cab stop at the corner and she walked the quarter of a block to the apartment house. She let herself in with the keys Tony had given her, and she put the champagne in the tiny half-refrigerator under the sink. She did not expect him for another hour, so she took a shower and put on one of his old shirts. She found a copy of the collected plays of W. B. Yeats, and sprawled out on the mattress to read them. She was still reading when Tony came home.

"What do you think of them?" he asked.

"They're marvelous."

She had read *Purgatory* and *The Resurrection* before. The others were new to her. She told him that.

"Which ones are your friends going to be doing?" she asked.

"They haven't decided yet," he told her, coming over and sitting down beside her. He started to stroke the back of her neck. "Beer?" he asked.

"You choose," she said.

"What do you mean?"

"Go look."

He went to the Kelvinator and saw the champagne. He turned and looked at her with amusement and love. "We'll have it later," he said, and opened two beers. He took off his clothes and went into the bathroom to shower. He had just come from his fencing class, and he was still overheated. When he returned from the bathroom, he threw her the towel and let her dry his back. After she had dried him, he lay down on the mattress and sipped his beer. He drained the beer with amazing speed and then crumpled the can and threw it across the room, just missing the plastic garbage pail. Almost in a continuation of that motion, he turned to her and drew her down to him.

"Come, wench," he said, and laughed as his mouth closed on hers.

He had entered her, and she was sitting astride him before he started to unbutton her shirt.

"I like it when you're on top of me. I like the way your breasts hang down in that pointy way."

She jounced on him, and it was a sufficient answer. As she moved, he reached up to hold her breasts. Then he reached down to hold her hips. He was trying to restrain her, but she misunderstood his signal and only continued her movements.

"Merry, Merry . . ." he started to say, but then his back arched and he came, taking them both by surprise. He sighed and said to her, "I've wanted you so much. All day."

She tried to move on him, to hold him inside her and achieve her own resolution. But it was impossible. She slid gracefully down beside him and laughed. It did not seem to be such a serious thing. One time had never been their limit anyway. He lit a cigarette and offered her occasional puffs from it.

She had been very much aroused by his orgasm because of the clarity with which she had been able to feel it. Usually they came together and the moment was too ecstatic to be distinct. Tony's body always responded to her quickly. Because she had been left at a plateau of excitement, she reached out to play with him. Whether it was because her advance was so importunate, or whether it was because of fatigue and the day he had had, or just because they had made love so frequently during the preceding ten days, he did not immediately respond to her hand.

"Kiss me there," he suggested. He seemed to be breathing carefully, waiting for her answer.

Without hesitation, she leaned over and traced the length of his penis with her lips. She could feel it tighten under her lips and she watched it as it grew hard, not steadily, but in a series of pulsations.

"Take me in your mouth," he said, stroking her hair with his hand.

She did. It was a curious sensation. She delighted in running her tongue along the length, while wondering at the strange combination of hardness and softness. She waited for him to pull her up and enter her again.

"I've never done that before," she said. "Did you like it?"

"How did *you* like it?"

"It was the sound of it. It sounded the way it does when we fuck. But it was so much clearer. It was the sound, but it was the idea of it, too."

She had liked it, and it had excited her. He began to move within her, and almost immediately she cried out and clutched his back. She had wanted it so much that it had been almost painful.

But this time he was not finished and was able to continue. Exuberantly, joyfully, they experimented, shifting from one position to another, finding what suited them best. They were a tangle of arms and legs and bodies, a sexual kaleidoscope in which each new design was more fascinating than the one that had gone before it. They were both bathed in sweat. They were so completely joined that it was impossible to say where one left off and the other began. She was surprised at her own excitement returning so quickly. She told him how close she was. They returned to their first position and he thrust at her with increasing sharpness. This time they came together, as she cried out his name over and over again.

She lay back exhausted and he sprawled on top of her. They were still joined together as they fell asleep. When she awoke he was standing above her with two glasses of the champagne. For the rest of the evening they read Yeats's plays together. Around midnight they went out for a pizza.

After the pizza, he put her in a cab to send her home. The cabby threw down the flag on the meter.

"Wait," she ordered.

She rolled down the window. "Tony!" she called.

He came back to the cab. She put her hand through the window and took his. He leaned in through the window.

"I'll call you tomorrow," she said, "after I've spoken with Jaggers."

"I'll be waiting."

He kissed her briefly, his tongue darting into her mouth for a second. Then he went back to the curb and watched the cab pull away.

Love made one feel beautiful, she reflected the following morning as she looked into her mirror, but she wasn't sure that it actually made one look one's best.

She wondered whether Jaggers would notice the slight puffiness of her face, the faint traces of the blue smudge beneath her eyes. She had not been getting enough sleep. She had been drinking too much beer. She had not been eating properly. Pizza and spaghetti were Italian and cheap, but they were not the steak and green salad and grapefruit halves that Jaggers had prescribed for her. She made herself up rather more carefully than usual and went off to his office.

She was admitted immediately. He was on the phone when she walked in. He waved her to a chair. After he had completed the call, he buzzed for Miss Bernstein. She came in from the outer office.

"Did you get it all?" he asked.

"Yes, sir."

"Be careful of those notes. He's a tricky customer. I may need them."

He swiveled and turned his chair to face Merry. He smiled and welcomed her. "How are you, honey? Let's go eat!"

In the elevator she felt his eyes carefully appraising her appearance. She felt chubby and blotchy under his gaze. The harsh neon light of the elevator cab didn't help, but she knew it was her own guilt at having neglected the discipline that made her feel so unattractive.

At the restaurant she declined his offer of a drink, and asked for a minute steak, a green salad, and black coffee. She would show him that if she had not been following the regime, at least she knew what it was.

"I had a letter yesterday from your father," he said.

"Oh?"

"He's finished shooting in Spain."

"That's nice."

Jaggers carved a piece of his lamb chop, put it into his mouth, chewed thoughtfully, and asked her, "What do you mean by that?"

"By what?"

"Your tone."

"Well, it's a money-changing operation," she said. "He told me about it. It isn't a movie, it's a piece of fancy banking."

"Actually," Jaggers said, "it isn't. The peseta was unblocked, you know. It all has to do with oil rights now."

"Oil rights?"

"The rights to export oil into Spain."

"Whatever it is," she said, waving her hand vaguely, "that's what I mean."

"What do you mean?" he asked. "Why this sudden contempt for large sums of money?"

"I don't know," she answered. "I've been thinking, I guess. About acting, and about the theater. And about my father."

"Oh," he said, and he let it go. "To change the subject, then, the Clara audition is the day after tomorrow. Do you think you're ready?"

"Yes, but that's what I wanted to talk to you about."

"I rather guessed that."

"Actually, I've met a boy."

"I guessed that, too."

"He's an actor. I met him at the Theater Workshop. He's real! He's wonderful!"

"Oh?"

"You'd like him," she said. "I know you would. He's going to be a great actor, someday. Not a star. An *actor!*"

"What's his name?" Jaggers asked quietly.

"Tony Bassoto." She took a deep breath and plunged into it. "Some of his friends are doing some Yeats plays. Do you know Yeats's plays?"

He looked at her for a moment, and said, "Yes. Actually, I met Yeats once, in London."

"You did?" she asked excitedly. "What was he like?"

"I thought he was crazy," Jaggers said.

She looked away, disappointed. She had hoped that there might be in Yeats a link between Tony and Jaggers.

"A great poet, mind you," Jaggers added. "But a nut."

He buttered a roll and changed his tack abruptly. "What are they using for money?"

"One of the partners has an aunt who is backing the production," Merry told him.

"What plays will they be doing?"

"They haven't decided that yet."

"I see."

She could not tell whether he was amused, annoyed, or merely inquisitive. She waited until the waitress had cleared their dishes away, and then she said, "I know it isn't Broadway, but it's good. It will be good."

"You don't think that Waters' play is any good?"

"No, it's good, I suppose. But it isn't serious. It doesn't have the kind of dedication that this does."

"I take it that this young man is as charming as he is talented," Jaggers said. He raised his eyebrows quizzically.

Merry blushed.

"And that it is from him that you have learned this contempt for Hollywood and the movies?"

She nodded.

"I see. Let me think about all this," he said.

"Of course." She smiled happily.

"You'll still read for the part of Clara, won't you?"

"If you want me to."

"It's always nice to have something to fall back on," he muttered.

As they left the restaurant, he asked her where she

would be that afternoon. "I may want to get in touch with you."

"I don't know. I have a voice lesson. I'll call the service every hour, though."

"Why don't you call me around four?"

"All right. I will."

She was puzzled by this, but she was more pleased by his lack of objection to the Yeats production than she was worried by his silence.

At four o'clock she called, and Jaggers' secretary asked her to drop by the office in half an hour. She had just left her voice coach. She grabbed a cab and went to Jaggers' office, practicing her breathing all the way across town.

"What do you know about Bassoto?" Jaggers asked her, as she came in.

"I love him," she said quietly.

"That's not what I asked you," Jaggers reminded her. "What do you know about him? How old is he?"

"I don't know," Merry said. "I should think twenty-one or twenty-two."

"He's twenty-eight."

"He's what?"

"Twenty-eight. He was married twice. He has one child."

"No," Merry said.

"Oh, yes. He has a general discharge from the Army."

"What's that?"

"Well, it's not quite a dishonorable discharge, but neither is it an honorable discharge. One conviction on a narcotics charge. Suspended sentence. No known means of support."

"What does that mean?"

"That he probably lives off women. Older women, I'd guess."

She sat there for a minute numbly. "I don't believe it. I don't believe any of it."

"Oh, yes. It's all true."

"But he's a talented actor. And I love him. And he loves me!"

"You think so?"

"I know so."

"All right," Jaggers said. "Pick up that earphone."

Jaggers had one of those European phones with the extra earpiece on which a third party could listen but not talk. He dialed a telephone number. The phone rang twice. Then Merry heard Tony's voice.

"Hello," Tony said.

"Hello, Mr. Bassoto?"

"Yes," he said.

"This is Samuel Jaggers. I've heard some very good things about your work at the Workshop from Mr. Kolodin."

"Oh?"

"And I have an interesting offer. It's small, but it's a start, and it could lead to bigger things. Tell me, do you have any commitments that would keep you in New York now?"

"Not a one," Tony said promptly.

Merry gasped.

Jaggers put a finger over his lips to signal to her to be quiet.

"Good," he said into the phone. "I have a friend who is a producer in Hollywood. He has a part open in *The Thing from Planet X*. The fellow he had for it broke his hip last week, surfing. It's five hundred a week. Who is your agent?"

"Well, I've been with George Wallenstein, but he hasn't found anything for me in a year and a half."

"Do you want me to send all this over to him?"

"Would you represent me, sir?" Tony asked.

"I would if I could, but our stable is full just now. If

you're not happy with Wallenstein, there's a friend of mine on the coast who would take you on, I'm sure."

"I'd be very grateful, sir," Tony said. "Do you think five hundred is the top that they'll go?"

"I'm afraid so. Of course, they'll pay your traveling expenses. And after this, you know, the sky's the limit."

"I don't think I can tell you how much this means to me," Tony said.

"Glad to be able to do you a favor. Look, shooting starts next Tuesday. I'm sending down your plane ticket by messenger. It'll be at your apartment in an hour. There's a flight out of Idlewild at eleven o'clock tonight. Is that all right?"

"I'll be on it," Tony said. "This is the break I've been waiting for."

"Good luck to you."

"Thank you, sir. Thank you very much."

Tony hung up. Jaggers hung up.

"Well?" he said to Merry.

"You bastard!" she said.

"Why?"

"You tempted him."

"He didn't have to go for it. And name-calling will not get us anywhere. You've been seventeen kinds of fool."

"But he said he didn't care about money. He hated Hollywood and he didn't care about money. He hated everything that my father stands for."

"When people who have it tell you that they hate money, they are liars. And when people who don't have it say so, then they are damned liars."

She began to weep.

"Don't take it so hard," he told her. "I'm not saying that it could have been worse, but you'll get over it. You'll be all right. As that nut Yeats said, 'Nothing can be sole or whole that has not been rent.' Come on, I'm going home now. I'll get you a cab. I want you to go home and go to bed."

The cab stopped at Merry's apartment house. She got out, paid, and went inside. From her apartment she made two telephone calls. The first was to the liquor store, to send up a bottle of 151-proof Demerara rum. The second was to Tony. He did not answer. The delivery boy from the liquor store arrived. She took the rum from him and paid him. She poured herself a stiff drink of rum and Coca-Cola. From five until ten she sat in her apartment, drinking the rum and the Coca-Cola, and calling Tony every ten minutes.

He was there; she knew he was there. He had to be packing, getting ready to go. Finally she realized that he was not answering the phone because he knew that it was she who was calling. At a quarter past ten, she gave up. He would have left by now. He would be in the cab on his way to Idlewild, to Hollywood, and to Planet X.

She poured the rest of the rum and the Coca-Cola down the drain and went to bed. Two days later she read for the part of Clara. Whether the affair with Tony had anything to do with it or not, she never knew. It didn't bear thinking about. But there was an edge, a mordant bite to her performance, a kind of wry bitterness that showed through and illuminated Waters' lines.

She got the part.

CHAPTER TEN

♥ Getting the part in Waters' play made rather less difference in Merry's life than she had expected. What it did, mainly, was to change the location of her activities, but they were the same activities. Instead of going down to the Theater Workshop or across town to her voice coach, she went to rehearsals. If there was any difference, it was in the intensity with which she worked. But she only welcomed the increased pace, which increased even more as time went on. Physically it was exhausting, but emotionally it was restful.

She discovered that the work, brutal though it was, long, arduous, and incredibly demanding, provided a refuge for her emotions. She did not trust it at first. She thought it was only the novelty and the pace. But as the novelty wore off and the pace built, she began to see a way of living—not through the character she was portraying, but through the activity. Her life had become a project, a career, a series of hurdles to jump and goals to attain. The best part of it was that she did not even have to decide herself what the goals were to be. There were people to tell her—the director, or Jim Waters, and above all, Jaggers. In a way, then, for all the hard work, there was a wonderful feeling of floating upon a current that took her through the rehearsals, up to New Haven for the tryouts, back to New York for the previews, and carried her through opening night.

The whole experience was blissfully anesthetic. She worried about that occasionally, especially at night as she was falling asleep. She wondered whether she was not some kind of emotional defective. She had snapped back so easily from the shock of the disaster with Tony. But if there were any doubts in her mind about the change in her threshold for emotional pain, they were resolved at the opening. Her father had flown in to see her. Or anyway, at least partly to see her. He was also doing some publicity for *Nero*. He had television interviews during the afternoon of the opening and could not come by to visit her, but that was just as well. She was taking a nap. He did send an enormous bunch of roses to her dressing room—there must have been four dozen, arranged in an elephant's-foot umbrella stand. There was a tag saying, "The roses for love, the elephant's foot for luck." It was signed, "Dad."

He came by, half an hour before curtain, to give her a kiss and pose for photographers with her. The publicity was good for both of them. It was only after the performance that she realized how she was merely incidental to his trip to New York. His main business was the promotion of the movie he had made, and his main interest was in Noni Green, the nineteen-year-old girl who played his daughter in the film. As one remembers the plot of a book one read as a child, she recalled how she had felt—at first, anyway—about Carlotta and about Melissa: irrelevant and excluded. And jealous. And resentful of them for the way in which they had made her feel outside of things. But tonight she was at the center, and he and that absurd little girl were at the fringes, at the edge somewhere. It was her night. Sitting at Sardi's, waiting for the newspapers, she was even able to feel fifteen seconds of genuine sympathy for the girl. Noni. She wondered what her real name was. But then the papers arrived with the reviews. They were good. They were great. She had done it. It had happened. Her exhilaration was such that she could not have cared if her father had been there with a whole harem of Nonis.

There was a further test the following day, when the three of them had lunch together at Le Pavillon, but she passed it with flying colors. She just felt too good to care. The next day her father and Noni flew back to Hollywood. After they left, Jaggers explained that he had kept her father away on the day of the opening for fear that a visit from him might upset Merry. Jaggers had been the one who had scheduled the television interviews.

"That was very thoughtful of you," she said. "But it didn't matter."

"Oh?"

"I could have stood it. That's the wonderful thing. I could have stood it."

"I thought so, but I didn't want to take the chance. I didn't want anything to upset you."

"It's a great thing," she said, "to feel strong. To feel tough. To be able to take it."

"Yes, it is, but don't push yourself. This is an erratic business. There are ups and downs in it enough. If you can take them in your stride, then you're strong."

"I suppose you're right."

She was sitting in his office. He had asked her to stop and see him there. She had not been in his office since that other time, that dreadful time, when he had talked to Tony on the telephone. She wondered whether Jaggers had deliberately maneuvered that, arranging things so that she would not have to come to this room, out of tact. She decided that he probably had. She would not put it past his shrewdness. Or his kindness. He could have thought of a thing like that.

"How are you feeling now?" he asked. "Strong?"

"Oh, yes, fine."

"Good, then I have something for you to deal with."

"Nothing too dreadful, I hope."

"No, this is good news. That takes strength, too, sometimes."

"Try me," she said.

It was a Harry Kleinsinger comedy.

"Do you know who Kleinsinger is?" Jaggers asked.

"He's a director. In Hollywood. He's . . . I can't name all the movies he's done, but he's been around forever."

"Yes, he has. And he's one of the great directors in the world for women. Which is what I'm going on. I haven't read the script. There isn't a finished script yet, but it doesn't matter. However the movie turns out, with Kleinsinger directing it you'll look good. Which is what we want."

He had been able to get a good deal for her. He explained it.

"It's a hundred thousand dollars against a participation of one percent of the net profits. Now, there probably won't be any net profits. There seldom are."

"What do you mean? How can there not be profits?"

"It's the way they work their bookkeeping. For every dollar they spend on the movie, they charge a dollar and a quarter against the picture. That way they pay their share of the office overhead. And then there's a twenty-seven-and-a-half percent fee the company charges itself for distributing its own films. Put it this way. If a movie costs a million to make, and it brings in a million four, then you'd think you'd have a four-hundred-thousand-dollar profit, wouldn't you?"

"Yes."

"But you don't. If the movie really cost a million, it gets charged as a million, two hundred and fifty thousand. Those quarters add up. The twenty-seven-and-a-half percent brings it to . . . Let's round it out to twenty-five percent. That'd make it . . ."

He jotted on a pad with his ballpoint pen and announced, "It's one million five hundred and sixty-two thousand five hundred dollars. So if your movie brought in a million four, you have a net loss of a hundred and sixty-two thousand five hundred. Or a little more than that."

"But that's crazy!"

"Not at all. What are the taxes, do you suppose, on a loss of a hundred and sixty-two thousand dollars?"

"I see," she said.

"Exactly."

"But then what is the point of my having a participation in the net profits?"

He drew a deep breath, leaned back in his chair, and explained it. "The point," he said, "is that we can say you had a participation in the film. It's very important to start out with a good price. Everyone in the business will know what your first price was. And your second price will be negotiated from that. It's a lot easier to work up from a hundred thousand against a participation than it is to work up from a hundred thousand dollars. And then, if the movie does make a profit, you get some more money out of it. And your next price will be that much higher."

"Fine," she said, "but what about the play?"

"What about it?" Jaggers asked. "You'll continue with the play through the summer and into the fall. If it's still running in October, Kleinsinger will buy you out. Cheerfully. Think how much more valuable you'll be by then."

"You make everything seem so simple."

"That's my job. To make it simple for you."

"Thank you," she said.

"I get my piece."

"I know, but thank you."

"Forget it. The contracts will be ready in a few days. I'll send them over for you to sign."

The euphoria from the play had not even worn off, and here was this new prospect, which was not so much elating as sustaining. The odd bastion she had found in busyness was even more secure. Her life, externally, continued unchanged. She walked through it, carefully, inventively, but formally, in the same way that she went through the pattern of speeches and gestures of her performance eight times a week in the theater. But even outside the theater she had the feeling that she was moving in a set. Having committed herself to go to Hollywood in October, she found that New York felt the way New Haven had felt. It was a way station, a base camp. The waiting, however, was strenuous enough to be endurable. Or orderly enough.

She slept until noon every day, and then read or walked in the park. Around four she had a light lunch, and by six-thirty she was in the theater. She was back home by midnight, and tired enough to enjoy her bath, her yogurt, and the Late Late Show, after which she went to bed. Life was so structured that it felt rather like that at the Mather School. Lonelier perhaps, but just as busy. And calmer.

She lived in this suspended way, taking note of the passing of time only in the park, where she watched the grass turn green, the trees come into leaf, and the flowers start to bloom. April gave way to May, and a hot spell announced the arrival of summer. It was at the end of May, when she went to the theater one day for a matinee, that she found a note from Helen Farnam.

"Dear Merry," it said. "Exams are over. I'm coming to New York for the summer. Let's have lunch or something. By the time you read this, I'll be in Darien. Call me. Love, Helen."

Merry was delighted. She didn't even wait until after

the performance, but called from the backstage pay phone. They agreed to have lunch the following day. Merry gave Helen her address and told her to come by as soon as she got to town. Then she apologized, told her that she had to go and make up, and would see her the next day. It was some time toward the end of the first act when Merry decided, on stage, that it would be a fine idea for Helen to move in with her. There was enough room in the apartment for both of them. She owed Helen that much, anyway, for the hospitality the Farnams had shown her during their years together at the Mather School. Not only did she like Helen, but she could stand her. It would be less lonely. It would be like old times again.

She awoke earlier than usual the next day, made the daybed herself, and then sat down to wait for Helen to arrive. She was surprised to discover that she was a little bit nervous about it. She was apprehensive about their reunion. Would they be able to pick up where they had left off? Would the differences in their lives form a gap too difficult to bridge? The more she thought about it the more anxious she became, for she realized how lonely she had been and how important it was to her to have a friend there with her, someone to talk to, someone with whom she could share her life.

But as it turned out, there was nothing she needed to have worried about. When Helen arrived, they hugged each other, sat down, and talked excitedly as if nothing had intervened but a longer than usual vacation. Helen brought Merry up to date about some of their classmates. Absurd girls had done absurd things.

"What about you?" Merry asked. "What are you doing?"

"Oh, nothing very much to report about me. I'm doing all right at Radcliffe. Working hard. Having fun."

Helen told Merry how her father had arranged for

her to get a job as a copyreader in a publishing house where he had some friends.

"Oh?" Merry asked. "And that's *all?"*

"Well, maybe not all. I have a man."

"Go on. Tell me!"

"His name is Tom McNeill, and he's at Harvard Law. And he'll be in New York this summer, too."

"Great. It looks as though you'll have a fine summer."

"A poor thing, but mine own."

"What do you mean by that?"

"Well, my God, you're the glamorous one. You're the one who's having the incredible time."

"Not really," Merry told her. "As a matter of fact, I've been thinking how much it's like the way it used to be back at school. The only difference is that I don't have to take geometry any more."

"You're kidding. I mean, you're putting me on!"

"No, I'm not. Do you know that you're the first person, besides the cleaning lady and me, I mean, who's been in this apartment in . . . well, months?"

"I'd never have guessed."

"Neither would I have."

The conversation stopped. Merry was wondering whether to offer to share the apartment with Helen now or to wait until after lunch to make the suggestion. Then she realized that Helen was trying to decide whether to ask now or wait until later. It seemed suddenly not unreasonable that Helen had had that in mind when she had written her.

"Look," she said. "With . . . What's his name?"

"Tom."

"With Tom in New York, you don't want to be running back and forth to Darien all the time. Why don't you move in here with me?"

"Are you sure?" Helen asked. "I wouldn't want to be in the way."

"I wouldn't ask you if I thought you would be in the way."

"Then great! Wonderful! I'd love to," Helen said. "What's the rent? I'll pay my half."

"Ridiculous," Merry said. "Don't think about it."

"No, I'd feel uncomfortable unless you let me pay my way."

"Well, if it'll make you feel better . . ."

She told Helen that the rent was a hundred a month. Helen said that she'd pay fifty. Really the rent was a hundred and eighty a month, but then, Merry was earning eleven hundred a week.

Instead of going out to a restaurant, they went out and bought some food, brought it back, and made lunch in the apartment. Then they went out to W. & J. Sloane to buy a daybed for Helen. They were both as pleased as they could be. Helen could look forward to a summer in which she could see Tom. Merry could look forward to three months of companionship. She would be able to get through the summer, and then it would be only a month before she would be leaving for the coast.

A few days later she met Tom and was happy to find that he was pleasant and presentable and that she could get on with him. Even though he was three years her senior, he was at first a little in awe of her, but she was able to get him over that soon enough. Very quickly they developed, the three of them, a workable arrangement in which Merry seemed to be rather in the position of an older sister or a young aunt. They included her in their plans whenever it was possible. She went with them up to Darien on occasional Sundays, or for drives out to Long Island. There was never any question of their getting in one another's hair. Merry's schedule at the theater and Helen's and Tom's with their jobs kept them apart most of the time. They were together only at rare, snatched moments. Often Helen and Tom would be waiting for Merry when she came home from the theater. They would cook omelets together and eat them.

What Merry did not know was that nearly every night when she was working in the play, Helen and Tom were in the apartment making love. She would not have cared, but if she had known, she might have been more helpful, sooner. As it was, the first she heard about it was in the second week of August. She woke up one morning and was surprised to find that Helen was still there.

"What's the matter? Why aren't you at work?" she said.

"I don't feel well."

"Is it anything serious? Shall I call a doctor?"

"I've seen a doctor. And it's damned serious."

"What? Go on, tell me."

"I'm pregnant," she said. "I—I'm . . ." But she could not go on. She broke down and wept.

"What do you want to do? Do you want to marry him?"

"Yes. No. I don't know."

"Well," said Merry, "those are the three choices. Pick one."

"I don't know. I don't want to marry him now. I want to finish school."

"How far gone are you?"

"I don't know. Six weeks, I think. Seven, maybe."

"Are you sure?"

"I told you. I've been to a doctor. I've had an A-Z test."

"Well, what do you want to do about it?"

"What can I do about it?"

"Well, you know what you can do about it."

"Do you think I should?"

"What difference does it make what I think? It's your life, isn't it?" Merry asked. "Do what you think you want to do."

"Can you help me?" Helen asked. "Can you help me find someone?"

"Can't he do that?"

"He could try, I suppose. But he'd screw it up. He doesn't know what he wants to do. He says we ought to get married, but I know he doesn't want to. He's just terrified."

"Well, he's young," Merry said.

"He's three years older than we are."

"Men are younger. Even when they're older than we are, they're younger."

"Look," Helen said. "I hate to ask you this. I feel like such a rat as it is. . . ."

"A rat? Why?"

"Using you the way I have been. Being here in the apartment and making love while you were at the theater. But last night I was thinking, after we went to bed, that with your being in the theater . . . I mean, Tom and I don't know people like that, but you would. You could find someone . . ."

"An abortionist?" Merry was not merely being helpful. She spat the word into Helen's miserable, condescending face.

"Yes, an abortionist," Helen said.

There was no point in Merry's rubbing her nose in it. She was in trouble enough as it was. Merry called Jaggers. He was out to lunch. She called again at three. When she got him on the phone, she asked him if Miss Bernstein was taking notes.

"No, she isn't," Jaggers said. "Should she be?"

"No. Listen, you won't believe me because it's such a corny thing. But I do need an abortionist, and it is for a friend."

"I believe you," Sam said.

"Can you help me?"

"Who is it for?"

"Helen, Helen Farnam. My roommate."

"How far along is she?"

"Six or seven weeks, she says."

"And how is she fixed for money?"

"All right, I suppose. How much is it?"

"The ones I know are expensive," Jaggers said. "They're good but they're expensive. It'll run about a thousand dollars, I'm sure."

"She can manage that."

"I'll get back to you in an hour or so."

"Thanks, Sam," she said, and hung up.

"How much?" Helen asked her. Her face was chalky white.

"A thousand."

"But I can't . . . We can't . . ."

"Your parents?" Merry asked.

"Oh, I couldn't . . ."

"Then what can you?"

"Three. Three-fifty, maybe."

"That's all right. The rest will be my treat."

Three days later Merry took Helen to the address on Park Avenue to which Jaggers had told them to go. Merry sat in the waiting room, looking at *Life* and *Look* and the *Saturday Evening Post,* while Helen was having the baby scraped out of her. The doctor came out after a while and sat down to wait with Merry for Helen to come out of the anesthesia.

"Is she all right?" Merry asked.

"Oh, she's fine. She'll be OK." He took a deep drag on his cigarette, blew the smoke toward the ceiling, and said, "The only thing I don't understand is why you damned stupid girls don't get yourselves fitted with plugs. She could have saved herself nine hundred and eighty-five bucks that way. And a lot of discomfort."

"Yes," Merry said.

"Or saved you nine hundred and eighty-five bucks. It was your money, wasn't it?"

"What makes you think that?" Merry asked.

"Just a guess."

Merry remembered how she had gone to the bank

with Helen's check and Tom's check, and had written her own check, and had folded the ten hundred-dollar bills carefully into her French purse, and dropped it inside her bag. The change in the weight of her bag was imperceptible.

"Well, some of it was," she admitted.

"Look, while we're waiting, do you want me to fit you? You ought to get something out of it, right?"

"All right," Merry said.

He led her through the reception room into a suite of examining rooms. She passed an open door through which she could see Helen lying on a bed. In the next cubicle she undressed while the doctor watched her. She got up on the obstetrical table and rested her legs in the stirrups. The metal of the doctor's instruments was cold down there. It was as cold as death.

Two days later Helen moved out of the apartment and back to Darien, leaving Merry alone. Merry went back to her regimen of reading, walking in the park, going to the theater, coming back, and watching the Late Late Show. It was not so bad, she decided. It was not so bad at all.

There was a limousine from the studio waiting for her at the Los Angeles International Airport. It was, she felt, another postponement. She could not have said what it was that she thought was being postponed, but something, some change, some shock. For seven months she had had the security of the play, with the same words to say in the same places on the same stage every night of the week but one. Now that was gone. She was out here in Hollywood to see what the movies were like and to test herself against them. To test herself, really, against her father. She had all but forgotten Tony. Indeed she had managed somehow to slough off all the men who had come roaring across, or shambling through, or sneaking into her life. But beyond them all, ineradicable and unreachable, there was the image of her father, as on a huge billboard in the hazy distance. This was his town. The movies were his game. And she had come here to play it.

But the impact had not yet come. The flight across the country had been luxurious and sterile. The PR man from the studio took care of getting her bags from the baggage-claim counter and getting them to the limousine. The huge car nosed forward like a black fish along the freeway, north into Los Angeles. It was as if she were still drifting along that current she had felt carrying her from the day she got the part in the play.

Everything was taken care of. Wemmick had found her an apartment in Coldwater Canyon. There was even a white MG in the breezeway. It had been rented for her. There were fresh-cut flowers on the mantel, bottles of liquor in the bar, and bottles of soft drinks and a pitcher of orange juice in the refrigerator. The PR man and the chauffeur carried the bags into the apartment.

"Mr. Kleinsinger is looking forward to seeing you," the PR man said. "He wanted me to welcome you back to Los Angeles."

"Thank you. Thank you very much."

"Your first call is for tomorrow morning at nine-thirty, for costume and make-up conferences. Would you rather drive yourself or shall we send the car for you?"

"I think I'd like it if you sent the car for me. For tomorrow, anyway. The first day."

"Be happy to. Is there anything else I can do for you?"

"No, I'm fine. I appreciate everything you've done already. You've been very kind."

"My pleasure," he said, and he left.

She wanted the car to pick her up the next morning because she wanted to continue her passive acceptance of everything that was happening for as long as she could do so. The womb of agreement seemed to be a safe place to be.

In a room on the fourth floor of the Merchants and Miners Bank Building on Wilshire Boulevard, a row of teletype machines clattered almost continually, speeding across the country answers to the questions which had been asked by the editors in the New York office. Facts, figures, names, dates, information, attitudes were translated first into words, then into holes on a punched tape, and then transmitted on the wires across the country. It was a complicatedly impressive room. For the benefit of visitors to the offices of the LA bureau of *Pulse*, there was a large plate-glass window through which people in the waiting room could look to see the machines typing away under the walnut panel in which six clocks showed the time in Los Angeles, Chicago, New York, London, Moscow, and Tokyo.

More complicated than the machines, however, and more interesting, though less immediately impressive, were the people—the stringers, the reporters, the editors whose words and thoughts fed into and out of the machines. And more delicate, too. Like the machines, they were scattered all over the world in a complicated network, but their maintenance was beyond the competence of any mere electrician or even systems engineer. There were three men in New York who understood the reason for the recent reshuffling of the correspondents, most of whom did not understand it themselves.

Joe Mylanos had been blown in Beirut. Mylanos, who was listed on the masthead as the bureau chief in Beirut and had in fact been the entire bureau there, had received his salary from the *Pulse* comptroller—but out of a special account. Deposits into that account had never been made by *Pulse* but by the Central Intelligence Agency. For as long as it had lasted, it had been a good arrangement. *Pulse* had got a bureau in Beirut out of it, and the CIA had got their man an unimpeachable cover. But after Mylanos had been blown it had been necessary to maintain the pretense of the cover, and Mylanos had been transferred to London. Ed Weeks, therefore, had been moved out of London and down to Nairobi to relieve Garret Holmes-Wallace. He was sent to Paris. From Paris, Jocelyn Strong went to Los Angeles, partly because Paris would have been overstaffed had she stayed and partly because George Mahr had been hitting the bottle more and more lately, and the feeling was that Mahr, the LA bureau chief, could do with some strong support—for which a clearer translation might have been "possible replacement."

It would have been improper to tell Strong why she was being sent to Los Angeles, and it was unnecessary for them to tell Mahr. He had been around long enough to be able to read between the letters, let alone between the lines. He knew that Jocelyn was a threat, but he also knew that she didn't know that, but considered her transfer to have been a kind of demotion. The day she arrived, he stuck his head in the door of her cubicle and said, "From the City of Light to Tinsel Town, eh? But welcome just the same."

The tone of her thanks, something between disgust and resignation, told him all he needed to know. It was just a matter now of giving her all the Mickey Mouse stories. One of three things would happen. She would make her play too soon and lose, or she would get disgusted and quit, or—and this was the most probable—she would disintegrate into another one of those zombies who made up the Hollywood press corps, a group which Mahr often described as a brigade of the undead who lived on press releases and hors d'oeuvres and who would all be grateful for a wooden stake driven through their hearts.

Jocelyn, unaware though she was of the reasons for her transfer, knew, nevertheless, what she had to do.

There are certain kinds of mathematical problems where too much information can be detrimental to the mathematician, confusing him more than helping him. And in the organization game, too, it is not necessarily disadvantageous to be in the dark. She knew that it was necessary for her to look good for a while. Whether she was in danger of losing her job or in a position now to move ahead was not clear, but either way, what she had to do was to excel, to take the Mickey Mouse stories and make something out of them. The editors in New York would notice, sooner or later, what she had been doing with the assignments she had been getting.

Still, she had not expected anything quite as preposterous as this. The mail girl had brought it in to her and had left it in the In box as if it were any other file, but she might as well have been leaving one of those plastic dog turds. Jocelyn knew the story. She had worked on it herself eight months before in Paris and had watched it die then. It had been dead from the first moment that the query had been sent out from New York. It was a tired, stupid, old idea. Old. Not news. Who was there who didn't know that American movie makers often made two versions of their pictures, one for domestic consumption and another for export? Or that the export versions were sexier, showed more cleavage, and occasionally had nude scenes? They were European movies for the Europeans. For that matter, who cared?

Jocelyn hardly thought about the story; what she thought about was Mahr's note, attached to the file. It was scrawled in the blue pencil he affected (it was an editor's blue pencil, but he was not an editor). "How about having a go at this?" the note said.

She was thinking not about the story, but about the fight with Mahr. Was it worth having? Was it worth having over this? Was it too soon? Should she go out and pretend to work on the story for a couple of days and tell him there was nothing? Or should she tell him now, having already worked on it in Paris? There were risks either way. She went to the water-cooler-cum-coffee-machine, made some instant coffee, and went back to her desk to read the *Hollywood Reporter* and *Daily Variety*.

She was drinking her coffee and reading the trade papers when her phone rang.

"Jocelyn Strong," she said.

"Jocelyn, it's Joe Barton, in New York. How are you?"

Barton was the entertainment editor in New York. "I called up to talk to Mahr," he said, "but I wanted to thank you for the Sputnik story. As long as I was on the wire, anyway, you know?"

The Sputnik story had been a piece about three low-budget productions by three different studios, all of them animal stories about a dog in space, inspired—if that was the right word—by the Russian orbiting of their Sputnik with Laika in it. All three were racing to be out first, and the likelihood was that they would all come out within a week of one another. And that they would all be terrible.

"Thanks," she said. "It was a great idea to begin with. All I had to do was to make the telephone calls."

"You're much too modest, Jocelyn."

"No, I'm not. I only seem that way. I can afford it because I've got you to blow my horn for me."

"Any time, baby. You got anything cooking this week?"

"I don't know," she began. And then she decided to take a flier. "What about the old foreign-version-of-American-movies story?"

"That dead thing?" he asked.

So it had been Mahr's idea, a wild-goose chase he had invented for her to waste time with.

"Yes, but there might be some way to freshen it. . . ."

"What way? You name it and you're a genius."

It was right there in front of her. All the time she had been drinking her coffee and talking on the telephone, it had been right there in front of her.

"Well, I was thinking of Harry Kleinsinger's *Three for the Money*. It has Merry Houseman in it."

"Well, what about it?"

"It's her first movie. She just might be young enough, innocent enough, to say something fresh about it. Kleinsinger shoots the two versions."

"I don't know," Barton said. "It might be worth a try. She might be worth a try anyway. Is she any good?"

"How the hell should I know? She's only been in one play in New York. I've been in Paris and Los Angeles."

"Well, come on now. You flew over New York, didn't you?"

"No, I took the polar route."

"I'll tell you. Why don't you go out, nose around some, and let me know what you find. If you've got something I'll schedule it."

"Wonderful," Jocelyn said. "Will do."

"Great. Now switch me to Kreiger, would you?"

"Sure."

"And thanks again for the Sputnik business."

"My pleasure."

She pushed the hold button, flashed the operator on the switchboard, and had Barton switched to Kreiger. Then she went in to see Mahr, to tell him she was going to work on the foreign-versions piece. Whatever happened now, she would come out smelling of roses. If it worked, Barton would remember that it was her idea. If it didn't work, she would have Merry Houseman to fall back on.

She called the studio, talked to a press agent, and arranged to visit the set that afternoon. All she had to do now was to deal with the story as deftly as she had been able to deal with the office politics involved. She sighed, and felt tired and old. She knew enough to avoid facing such absurdities as Merry Houseman's very existence offered her. It would have done no good to her to dwell on the fact that she was going out to interview a girl whose very birth she had helped to celebrate. It would have done her no good at all.

Harry Kleinsinger's bungalow was the only one left at the studio. All the others had been torn down years ago, and the stars and directors who merited such perquisites had been moved into a long, low, brick building that resembled a garden apartment. But Kleinsinger had refused to move, and it was a gauge of his importance, his prestige, and his earning power that he had been allowed to retain his private office-apartment in a separate building. The bungalow was in an inconvenient and remote part of the studio, a four- or five-minute drive from the sound stages where the shooting was done. It took at least that long to negotiate the winding road through the back lot—past the tropical jungle, the New England street, the block and a half of the Casbah, and the old Dodge City set. But it was large enough so that he could have his own cutting room and his own projection room there.

The real reason for his insistence on keeping the bungalow, though, was that it had once belonged to Harlow. It was, by Hollywood standards, a venerable landmark. What that meant to Kleinsinger no one in the executive offices knew. Whether it was his sense of history, or his admiration for Jean Harlow, or simply his orneriness and eccentricity, no one could have said. And he didn't volunteer, either. But he didn't have to. The consistent earnings of his motion pictures excused him from the necessity to explain. As Leo Kahn, the head of the studio, had once put it, "If Harry Kleinsinger wanted to burn down the studio, I'd be ready with a match."

Greg Overton drove his little Rambler along the blacktop road, saw the flashing red light that indicated shooting on the back lot, and stopped and cut the motor. It took four minutes to get to Kleinsinger's bungalow if there were no interruptions, if one didn't have to stop to wait for a take to be completed. With shooting going on and the lights flashing, it could take longer. Once it had taken Overton twenty minutes. It was a nuisance, but Overton's job was nuisances, dealing with nuisances. He wondered again whether it wouldn't have been better to have called Kleinsinger on the telephone, but decided again that it was better to see the man. To be there. This was nothing to discuss on the phone. It would be a matter of gauging the man's mood and putting it to him in the right way. This was the only way to do it.

The flashing red light stopped flashing. The studio guard waved him on. Overton continued on to the bungalow. He pulled his little car up to the parking area in front and sat there for a moment behind the wheel. He was not so much planning what his approach would be as he was gathering his energy for the encounter with Kleinsinger. He took a deep breath, got out of the car, and went inside.

In the anteroom Letty sat typing and talking on the telephone at the kidney-shaped desk. Making the shape of the words silently, with his lips, he asked, "Is he in?"

Letty nodded yes, and waved him in with one hand. She did not waste the gesture, but used it also to operate the carriage return on the typewriter. Her efficiency, Overton thought, was depressing. She was an example to the world of what Harry Kleinsinger expected from everybody. It was not exactly reassuring to watch her there, doing three things at once, all of them perfectly. He knocked lightly on the door.

"Come!"

He went inside. Kleinsinger was conferring with George Fuller, his assistant director, and also signing letters. "Three days ago I asked for him to do that," Kleinsinger was saying, "and he tells me it is impossible. I don't want explanations; I want done what I ask. Good morning, what can I do for you?"

There had been no break whatever in the flow of Kleinsinger's words, and it took Overton an instant to realize that Kleinsinger had shifted and was now addressing him.

"I came to ask you about the shooting for today," he said.

"You came to ask me what about the shooting? Whether we will have some? Yes."

"No, not whether you would have some—"

"Of course. Of course. I know that. You see how you waste my time."

"I'm sorry."

"Be sorry later. Now tell me what you came to ask about the shooting."

"Whether you might make an exception about the closed set."

"No."

"But we've had a request from *Pulse*."

"So. You didn't come to ask; you came to argue. Didn't you?"

"No, sir. To explain, really. They want to do a piece about the export cut. And Jocelyn Strong called me this morning—"

"Jocelyn Strong is a woman, I take it?"

"Yes, that's right."

"Well, I don't know. You might ask Miss Houseman. If it is agreeable to her, I shall consider it."

"That would be one way of doing it."

"Yes, that would be the honest way. Tell me, what is your way?"

"I thought that in order not to upset her, perhaps it might be better if Miss Strong could be there with a clipboard or something. She could appear to be a member of the production staff. . . ."

"That is very solicitous of you," Kleinsinger said with an insincere smile. The smile switched off like an electric light. "It is also dishonest and entirely characteristic. Not only dishonest with Miss Houseman, but dishonest with me. Telling me that you have concern for Miss Houseman's state of mind. Preposterous! You have concern for nothing but the inches of column space you get. Or are able to claim."

"Well, sir, it is for the good of the picture, after all."

"I know that. That is why I tolerate you here and do not have you thrown out of this office. As I should have done three minutes ago. You go and ask Miss Houseman. Or no, on second thought, perhaps you had better not. I think I had better do it myself. You see, *I* am concerned with Miss Houseman's feelings, and while I am not certain whether a reporter's presence would disturb her, I am certain that yours would."

Without pausing, Kleinsinger returned to the discussion upon which Overton had intruded. As usual, there was no transition. He continued, without change of inflection or any pause, saying, "I know there is such a thing as nonreflecting glass. You find it in museums all over the world. And that's what I want. And they must get it for me. The painting must have glass so that it can shatter later. And it has to be lit so that we can see it. And what I want to see is the painting. Not a reflection of a klieg light. Is there anything else?"

He had raised his heavy-lidded eyes in Overton's direction. Overton felt as if he were some kind of a mosquito that Kleinsinger had waved away but which had had the temerity to continue buzzing about his ears.

"No, sir."

"Well, then, do not let me keep you from what I am sure is a whole program of urgent business."

"You'll let me know what Miss Houseman says, so that I can let *Pulse* know?"

"I will not let you know, but you will receive word."

"Thank you, sir," Overton said.

He backed out of the office as one backs out of the presence of a king.

An hour later, Letty, Kleinsinger's secretary, called to tell him that it would be all right for Jocelyn Strong to visit the set that afternoon.

"Mr. Kleinsinger told me to say that there are to be no photographers. Miss Strong is to be alone. That is, he would rather that you did not accompany her. You are to bring her to the set and then to excuse yourself."

She did not wait for Overton's agreement to Kleinsinger's conditions. She did not have to.

In her dressing room at one end of the enormous sound stage, Merry prepared herself for the chase sequence. What Kleinsinger had told her had been true enough. Or it had seemed so when they had discussed the sequence.

"You must understand," he had said with that accent which was commanding and therefore, somehow, assuring, "that it will not be you up there on the screen. It will be Alexandra, the character. She will merely resemble you in certain superficial particulars. At all times, however, you will be clothed in the character and also in my own good taste, upon which I must ask you to rely."

Well, she was relying on it. She would have to rely on it. But as she looked at herself in the large dressing-table mirror, she felt naked, personally naked, even more naked than if she had been wearing nothing at all. The flesh-colored pasties—the bra cups which were held on by spirit gum—were more obscene than her bare breasts could have been. She shook herself to make sure that they were securely glued and would not fall off. They held all right. She put her brassiere on over the pasties and then her silk jersey over that.

The point of the scene was simple enough, and very clever. Alexandra was in the car in which Philip was making his getaway. They were being pursued by the detective. While Philip drove, Alexandra, in the back seat, was changing her clothes from the black slacks and black jersey she had worn during the theft to the cocktail dress she had worn at the party which they had just left and to which they were now returning. During the change she was spotted by the private detective, whose reaction was one of distraction by the glimpse of her *en déshabillé*. He gained on them in the chase, and in order to make good her getaway, Alexandra threw her brassiere out of the window. She then popped up and down, in the back seat, exposing herself to the private detective, who stared at her, went off the road, and crashed.

The entire sequence in the finished film would take perhaps two minutes. This was the fifth day of shooting, however, on that two-minute sequence.

Merry had not been involved herself in the four days of work that had gone before. Two days had been spent on the Los Angeles freeways, taking footage of traffic for the rear-projection screen in front of which the getaway car would be set up in the studio. Another day had been spent taking pictures of the getaway car on the freeways. Then a fourth day had been spent with the detective, sitting in cutaways of his car, reacting. What he was reacting to—Alexandra's strip—they would do today. And then the following week they would do the crash, wrecking two or three cars completely. Only in the cutting room would the sequence come together, as the editor cut back and forth under

Kleinsinger's eagle eye, from the pursuer to the pursued, from interior car shots that they had done in the studio to matching exterior shots they had taken out "on location" on the Santa Ana freeway. Merry remembered what Jaggers had said about acting in the movies, about how, if it was possible for Lassie and Trigger, it was possible for her. She had no choice then but to rely upon Kleinsinger and upon what he had called his good taste. Because she was relying upon him in this way—for her performance, for the rhythm of the acting, and for the quality of the film to which she was committing what talent she had—it seemed not unreasonable for her to rely upon him in other ways, too. If she had trusted to him the burden of her professional competence, it seemed absurd not to trust him also with such a trivial thing as her own modesty. There was a knock at her dressing-room door. A messenger called out to her that the shooting would begin in five minutes. She told him she would be there directly.

She wandered across the huge sound stage, past halves of offices, of living rooms, and of bedrooms, past a parking lot, a dock, and an area in which the workmen had just completed a section of racetrack grandstand, to the freeway area where the car was set up. The car had been sliced down the middle so that the director of cinematography could maneuver with his large Panavision camera and select from among a variety of angles and shots. At the front and rear fender a couple of grips were lounging, ready to rock the car to give the motion that would make for the illusion of driving. On a movie screen behind the car, which was now blank, the freeway would be projected by a machine that was synchronized with the Panavision camera.

They were still adjusting the lights. Merry sat down in her camp chair. Kleinsinger was conferring with the cinematographer and occasionally looking through the viewer on the camera.

"How are you, kid?"

She looked up. It was Hugh Gardner, her co-star—or, to be perfectly blunt about it, the star. Throughout the shooting, Gardner's manner had been avuncular but never condescending. He was able to carry it off because he was one of the miracles of Hollywood. He was, she knew, four years older than her own father, but he was still playing romantic leads, and playing them well. The lines around his eyes only exaggerated their twinkle. The sharpening of his chin only emphasized its cleft, which came across on the screen as a low dimple. He came across with a combination of boyishness and incredible sophistication. Or perhaps it had nothing to do with what he actually looked like and depended only on what the moviegoers of the world saw and had been conditioned to see. Over the course of thirty-five years they had learned to think of him as romantic and suave, and they found what they were looking for. In exchange they had given him tens of millions of dollars. Even without his shrewd investments in California real estate in the thirties and forties, his movie earnings would have made him a very wealthy man. As it was, he was one of the richest actors in Hollywood.

He limited himself to one film a year, and made that one only to prove to himself that he could still do it. Or no, perhaps that wasn't fair. Perhaps it was still for the money. To help pay his taxes.

"Hello," she said.

"Nervous?" he asked.

"A little."

"Good. It'll show on the screen."

"That glare is very annoying," Kleinsinger blared. "Must we put up with it?" He was shouting, as he sometimes did, complaining about an area of light on the roof of the automobile.

"It's established," the cinematographer said. "It's established in the scenes you'll have to cut to."

"No one will notice. Clouds come and clouds go. Do they not?"

"You'll limit yourself. You won't be able to get back to the board."

"Very well, then let us finesse it. Cut it by half."

One of the lighting men climbed up on a ladder to put a piece of screen mesh over the lamp that was causing the offensive glare.

"I am sorry to have been so long," Kleinsinger said, turning to Gardner and to Merry. "But . . . Are you ready? Would you go to your places, please?"

As they started toward the car, Kleinsinger stopped Merry and said, "I almost forgot. Let me introduce you to Jocelyn Strong, who has come today to watch the shooting. She is doing an article for . . . *Pulse* magazine, is it?"

"Yes, that's right," Jocelyn said. "How do you do, Miss Houseman?"

"How do you do?"

"Miss Strong, I think, believes that I am a dirty old man," Kleinsinger said, "because I am pandering to European depravity. Of course I am a dirty old man, but it is because I pander to the American puritanism."

"And what do you think, Miss Houseman?" Jocelyn asked.

"I do what Mr. Kleinsinger says," Merry answered. "He's the director."

"You see?" Kleinsinger beamed. "You will have trouble with her. Unlike so many of your victims out here, this one is intelligent. But you will talk later. Will that be all right?"

"Oh, certainly," Jocelyn said.

Kleinsinger inclined his head and extended his hand, offering Merry a chair—the back seat of the car.

Fortunately, the brightness of the lights was such that Merry could almost believe herself to be in an actual car. She could see only a blinding glare to the right, where the sound men, the script girl, the electricians, the grips, and the rest of the elaborate personnel clustered around the camera operator, the cinematographer, and the director, who rode on and flanked the huge mechanical eye that was the surrogate for those millions of eyes that would one day be watching this. But she could not see any of them, and when the sound man turned on the tape of the automobile motor and the grips began rocking the car gently to simulate the action of the springs on the road, it felt at least half real.

Fuller, the assistant director, called out, "Quiet, please. Quiet on the set. Camera!"

A man held the clap-board in front of the camera. "Scene 174-C, take one," he said.

"Action," Kleinsinger called.

Gardner pretended to drive, moving the wheel slightly to either side to compensate for the drift of driving, glanced into his rear-view mirror, and then stared into the mirror. "Isn't that Rogers behind us?" he asked.

"How could it be?"

"I don't know. But is it?"

She turned around, peered through the back window, reacted, and said her line. "I can't tell. I think so, but I'm not sure."

"Blasted luck!" Gardner said.

The chase was on. There were a few more moments of concentrated driving, of looking through the back window, and then she told Gardner that she had to change. He told her to go ahead, but to keep an eye on the detective while she was doing so. She slipped off her jersey. Somehow or other, her head got caught in the jersey and she was a beat or two slow in getting free of it.

"Cut!" Kleinsinger called. "Again, please."

They began it all over again. The second time her head came out of the jersey properly, but she had trouble getting the slacks off.

"Cut," Kleinsinger called. "I know it's awkward, and you must make it appear to be a little bit awkward, but not *very* awkward. There is a line. . . . I think if you try to keep your knees closer together."

She said she would try.

The third time she got out of the jersey and out of the slacks, but her tone of voice was wrong on her next line.

"Cut. You actually sound pleased that he is gaining on you. You must sound alarmed, worried. You will be sad when he kills himself, but try not to think ahead."

"Scene 174-C, take four."

"Action."

But that take had to be junked because the angle of her legs was bad again. And take five seemed to be going well, but Kleinsinger stopped it because he thought Gardner looked insufficiently worried. "No, you are bored. I am bored. Miss Houseman is bored. We are all bored. But let us not try to show it—or *they* will be bored, too."

Take six went all right, and by that time she felt almost relieved to be taking off the bra. She rolled down the window and threw the brassiere out onto the road. The wind machine blew it out of the frame, behind the car.

"Cut! Print!" Kleinsinger called.

A wardrobe mistress handed Merry a robe, which she put on.

"What do you think?" Kleinsinger asked the cinematographer.

"I can't tell," he said. "We'll have to see it in the rushes."

"The line of the pasty—you could see it, couldn't you?"

"Probably."

Merry had come over to listen to the discussion. Kleinsinger turned to her and asked her, "Tell me, dear, would you mind wearing the smaller pasties?"

"Well, they're sort of uncomfortable," she said. She had tried them at home the night before, and the application of the adhesive directly to her nipples had not been pleasant. It had hurt, taking them off. Merry hesitated for a moment. Then she decided to take the plunge. "Do I have to wear them at all?"

"To be perfectly honest, if you could get along without them I should be delighted."

"I don't mind," she said.

"Splendid! We'll try it once more then, without pasties."

"I'll go take these off," she said.

She went to her dressing room, took the large pasties off, scrubbed off the spirit gum, put on a new bra, and slipped into a new jersey and a new pair of slacks.

It seemed absurd to her that she had hesitated, and even more absurd was the point at which the hesitation had come. It was not the display of her breasts that had bothered her so much as the making of the offer to Kleinsinger. Not to have made it would have been ridiculously prudish, but having made it, she was afraid that she appeared to be brazen and forward. What had helped her finally to decide had been Gardner's comment before the shooting had begun about how her nervousness was good and might come across on the screen. Without the pasties on her breasts, the expression on her face might be a little better, a little truer. But she was not going to brood about it.

She went back to the car, got in, and did the scene again. Evidently she had decided correctly, because at the end of take seven, Kleinsinger said, "Cut. Print. Beautiful!"

Any comment at all from him was rare. "We'll go right on if you don't mind," he said. "We'll take the shot from the rear window."

There was a pause of about fifteen minutes, during which Merry put on her robe and they shifted the lights and moved the camera. Merry's stand-in was in the back of the car, popping up and down in the rear window as they studied her through viewers and held light meters up to her face and hair. Alice Beasely, the stand-in, looked nothing like Merry, but her flesh tones and her hair color were very close. She was wearing a bikini top. Merry watched her with a kind of detached interest and observed that Alice's figure was fuller than her own. She wondered if it made all that much difference.

To women, of course, it did. But men, she thought, were rather easily pleased and found all sorts of bosoms attractive. Women, she supposed, were more objective about it. She was sure that her own breasts were too small and too close together. Or most of the time they were too small. They got larger the week before she had her period and seemed to her then rather more acceptable. Passable. But still too close together. She remembered how Melissa's breasts had been so clearly defined, with the flatness of the sternum between them. Alice, she thought, was nice and full, but probably too low without the bra of the bikini top.

"That's fine," Kleinsinger said. "Now, Merry, if you please . . ."

She took her place in the back seat of the car.

"Everyone over to this side of the line, please," Kleinsinger ordered.

That was considerate of him, Merry thought. No one would be able to see her now except for the momentary appearances in the back window of the car. And with Kleinsinger there, it didn't seem to matter. He was like a doctor. Or, no, he was more concerned about her feelings, more protective than most doctors seemed to be. It was as if he was her own father, and . . .

"Camera," Kleinsinger called, interrupting her fleeting thought.

"Scene 175. Take one," called the man with the board.

"Action," Kleinsinger called.

The grip behind her, at the front door of the car, began rocking the bumper. Kneeling on the back seat, she raised herself up so that the detective could see her, ducked down, and raised herself up again. There was nothing to it. She remembered that Polaroid party and how licentious that had seemed at the time. It made her smile, because here she was repeating a part of that crazy evening, but now in such a professional, indeed clinical way. Or, no, not just clinical. It was for Art. For Kleinsinger and for Art. She gave the detective a better look than he had had before, and ducked down.

"Cut! Print! Thank you very much," Kleinsinger said.

The wardrobe mistress handed her the robe. She went back to her dressing room to dress. They were going to do a take now of Gardner's face as he watched her in his rearview mirror. The camera would be shooting the reflection of his eyes in the mirror. She didn't have to be there.

It was very strange. She had enjoyed it, really. She wondered whether she had not enjoyed it too much.

There was a knock at Merry's dressing-room door.

"Miss Houseman?" a voice called.

"Yes," she answered.

"Jocelyn Strong. May I come in?"

She opened the door. "Please do."

"Well, what did you think of it?" Jocelyn asked.

"I don't know. I'll have to see it in the rushes. It all depends on the way it's put together, doesn't it?" Merry suggested pleasantly.

"I expect so. But what did you feel when you were out there?"

"A little nervous, I guess."

"You took the pasties off. May I ask why?"

"They were uncomfortable and they got in the way

of the shot. But I suppose there was another reason, too. For the nervousness. To get the intensity, and to get the tone of it right."

"There will be some of our readers who would disapprove of what you've just done, and of what Mr. Kleinsinger has done. The practice of making a different version of the picture for Europe."

Jocelyn was sitting on the sofa that took up one wall of the dressing room. Merry, at her dressing table, thought for a moment and then commented. "You heard how Mr. Kleinsinger put it," she said. "You can take either position and disapprove of the other one."

"What does your father think of it?"

"Think of what? My being in movies, or my doing the scene?"

"Either one," Jocelyn said. "Both."

"I haven't discussed the scene with him. I'm a big girl now. Look, what are you trying to get me to say?"

"I'm not trying to get you to say anything. Only what you think."

"I'll tell you what I think. I don't think there is anything remarkable about the scene. It's clever. It has a dramatic function. But you saw it. There's nothing sensational about it. What is sensational, though, is the fact that you're here, that this is a story, that the magazine is going to run a piece about how I take off my brassiere."

Jocelyn tried to explain how that was only a part of it and how there was another side of it, too. "The movies," she said, "are the great art form of our time, the one with the mass audience. I suppose you could say that films are a sociological thermometer."

"I very probably agree with Mr. Kleinsinger," Merry answered. "We're sicker than the Europeans are."

"Do you think the MPAA, the Legion of Decency, and the various licensing and censoring boards of the different states and cities are all sick?"

"No. I dislike censorship. I don't think it accomplishes anything."

"What about the MPAA code?" Jocelyn asked.

"I think it's silly."

Jocelyn asked a series of questions about Merry's background, about her life before she had gone into the movies, and about her decision to follow in her father's footsteps. Merry answered them, but she did no more than that. Nothing that Jocelyn brought up seemed to start Merry talking in the way that all reporters hope their subjects will talk, rambling and pouring forth material from which they may pick and choose. Jocelyn tried silence, hoping that social convention would take over and that Merry would try to fill up the silence by making conversation, but Merry seemed perfectly content to sit quietly and wait. She succeeded in outwaiting Jocelyn, who resumed her questions, asking her the usual things and finding out very little. Merry did not yet know whether she preferred movies to the stage. She hadn't completed her first film. No, she was not romantically involved with anyone. Yes, the fact that her father was a prominent actor had been a great help to her, but only in getting started. She said she would succeed or fail because of her own merits or lack of them. It was all pretty obvious. Jocelyn was actually relieved when the messenger came to the door to call Merry for the next scene.

Jocelyn thanked Merry for receiving her and talking with her, closed her notebook, and went back to her car. It had not been a good interview. She knew that happened sometimes. Some subjects are better than others, or more responsive to one reporter than to another. There had been between them an unmistakable coolness, the reasons for which Jocelyn could not distinguish. She wondered about it, wondered whether it was the fact that she had come to see Merry do the nude scene. Perhaps the girl had been put off by that. But she didn't think so. She had seemed too self-possessed, too lucid, too calm about what she had been doing. Jocelyn wondered then whether it might not have been her own fault. But she did not brood about it. She was too busy. She had work to do.

It had occurred to her during the interview that the way of getting the spark of life into the piece would not be through Merry herself, but through her father. Meredith Houseman's reaction to the news of his daughter's making a nude scene would be good, no matter what it was. If he was shocked, it would be amusing; if he was amused, it would be shocking. Besides, she felt on surer ground with him.

She went back to the office, called the studio to find out where Meredith Houseman was, but was referred by them to Arthur Wemmick. He told her that Houseman was in Palm Springs. She picked up the phone to call the hotel in Palm Springs, but changed her mind. It would be better, she thought, if she just went out there and surprised him.

During the drive up over the mountains and out into the desert to Palm Springs, Jocelyn tried not to think of Meredith Houseman. She did not want to lock herself into any preconceived mental set about him; for the sake of the story she wanted to keep herself open. She wanted to play it by ear. But that was not all of it. She did not want to take any emotional position, either. She turned on the car radio and turned the volume up so that the cheap music would not fill just her ear but her whole head, blocking out anything else.

She was not happy about the story. That the interview with Merry had not gone especially well was no great cause for concern. The quotes were all right, she supposed. And the plan to visit Meredith was sensible. She was sure that his comments would help the piece a great deal. She could not guess at the words, but she could imagine the feeling that the editors in New York would be able to get into the kicker paragraph. Professionally, then, she was in reasonably good shape.

And personally? It was strange. She felt more grumpy than anything. Put upon. She had crossed the line that Kleinsinger had established. No one had called her back because it would have been embarrassing to have done so and because it would have called Merry's attention to the fact that people were looking at her. She had been able to get away with it because she was a woman anyway. There had been no particular reason for her to cross the line, except that as a reporter she thought of lines as challenges, as things to be crossed. And she had crossed it. She was not really depressed, but irked by the impertinence. It seemed presumptuous for Merry Houseman to have such firm, high breasts, for her to have breasts at all.

Gardner, of course, had been soothing. That was almost certainly his great value in the movies. The fact that he was as handsome and as young-looking as he had been thirty years before made every woman who saw him and remembered him from youth or even from childhood feel young still. In the darkness of movie theaters, every woman who looked up at him at the screen remembered how she had felt and how she had been the first time she had seen him. And his silken energy peeled the incrustation of the years.

Even with the music blaring out of the loudspeaker, filling the car and filling her, she could not help recognizing that it had been Gardner's presence and its soothing effect upon her that had suggested her visit to Meredith Houseman. She would not have considered it, she would not be making it now, if the only reason for it was the solace—which she did not want to admit to herself that she needed. Or, anyway, could use. It was a legitimate journalistic endeavor. She was, nevertheless, looking forward to seeing him and with more than ordinary journalistic interest. The comfort that other women took in the presence of such aging idols as

Gardner or Houseman was more intense for her because it was based on more than remembered fantasies. Jocelyn had learned not to be sentimental, to distrust sentiment, to avoid it, to flee it. But it was impossible for her, as a woman, entirely to ignore the fact—and it was a fact, a hard fact, even a journalistic fact—that she and Meredith Houseman had made love.

She adjusted the vent window so that the hot air of the desert blew directly into her face, and with the onslaught of the wind and the buffeting of the music, she was able at last to contain her thoughts in a vessel of sensation. She narrowed her eyes against the glare of the desert and stared out at the ribbon of road which perspective diminished to a vanishing point in the barrenness.

It was nearly six when she got to Palm Springs. She checked into a motel and called Houseman at the Palm Springs Biltmore. The switchboard operator there asked who was calling when Jocelyn told her that she wanted to speak to Mr. Houseman. Then she kept Jocelyn waiting while she called to report to Houseman that he had a call and to tell him who it was and find out if he wanted to take it or not. Jocelyn sat on the bed in the motel room, waiting, holding the dead phone to her ear. She wanted a cigarette but could not decide whether to risk putting the phone down while she ran across the room to get her bag from the dressing table where she had left it. It would only take a few seconds, she told herself. And she realized that she had already waited long enough to have made several trips to the dressing table and back. At each instant, however, she expected that Houseman would come onto the line. Finally there was a quiet click in her ear and the familiar voice said, "Hello, Jocelyn, how are you?"

"Fine, and how are you?"

"Good," he said. "What can I do for you?"

"I came out to talk to you."

"You came out? You're here in Palm Springs?"

"Yes, that's right." She told him the name of the motel at which she was staying.

"You're still with *Pulse*, are you?"

"Yes, I've just been switched from Paris to the Los Angeles bureau. I'm working on a piece, actually. About you and your daughter."

"I see," he said.

She did not think there was any edge to it. It was thoughtful, but no more than that.

"I suppose I could have called you from Los Angeles," she said, "but I haven't seen you for years. I thought I'd treat myself to a day away from the smog, a ride into the desert, and have dinner with you. Or drinks. Whatever's convenient."

"Sure, let's have dinner. Why don't you meet me here at the hotel? At eight or so."

"Fine, I'll see you then."

"Good."

She hung up, took her clothes off, and went into the bathroom to take a shower. Before she stepped into the shower stall, she glimpsed herself in the mirror. She turned and looked at herself. She raised her head so that her chin would sag less, took a deep breath and threw out her chest. Then she exhaled, looked down at herself, and stepped into the shower. She made the water as hot as she could stand it.

At eight o'clock, from one of the white house phones in the lobby of the Palm Springs Biltmore, Jocelyn called Meredith Houseman's room to let him know that she had arrived. He said that he would be right there. She had taken special care in dressing and making up, and she was not going to risk it all by sitting down. No woman looks as graceful sitting as she does standing. And Jocelyn knew herself well enough to realize that she was not one of those rare creatures who can look their best while rising from a seated position. So she stood and waited. Perhaps because she was standing, it seemed to her to be a very long time. It was long enough, anyway, so that she found herself making excuses for him. She told herself that, after all, she did not know the layout of the hotel. Perhaps it was like the Beverly Hills, with miles of carpeted corridors that he had to traverse.

As it turned out, there was an excuse, but not the one that she had expected. Meredith appeared in the company of a young lady. The smile on Jocelyn's face froze. She noticed her reflection in a mirrored column and saw that her expression looked fine. But it felt grotesque.

Gracefully, Meredith introduced his interviewer to his companion. Jocelyn studied Noni Green for a moment, decided that she really was as young as she looked, and of course wondered what the arrangement was. She did not, however, venture any guesses to herself. She had learned that guesses are often misleading, and almost invariably unnecessary anyway. The next half hour or so would make it all clear enough.

Meredith took them into the dining room and ordered a round of drinks. They made small talk. Nursing his champagne, Meredith told what it had been like in Spain; Jocelyn talked about the transition from Paris to Los Angeles; Noni asked if Jocelyn had been in Palm Springs before and whether she planned to stay for any length of time.

To Jocelyn's double no, she responded with a smile and the politely regretful thought that, "I could have shown you around. The shops, the best hairdresser . . . things that it would take half a day to discover on your own."

She carried it off well enough. Jocelyn wondered whether she had been coached or whether it was her own line. When they had finished the first round of drinks, Noni stood up. Meredith stood, too, while Noni thanked him for the drink and told Jocelyn how sorry she was that she had to run on to a dinner party.

"I look forward to seeing you in the picture," Jocelyn said. "Good luck, Noni."

"Thank you," she answered, with a sweet smile. "I hope to be meeting you again. Good-bye, Miss Strong."

With that, she turned, kissed Meredith on the cheek, and left the dining room. Jocelyn had not been able to decide whether the "Miss Strong" was merely prep-school manners or a deliberate coolness on the girl's part, but she didn't care. Clearly they were not together, for if they had been, Meredith either would have kept Noni out of sight for the entire evening or would have kept her with him all evening long.

He was no fool. He knew that, among other things, Jocelyn was a reporter. And to have introduced Noni that way seemed to Jocelyn clear enough evidence that they were together only for the purposes of the movie. Very likely the publicity department was engineering their whole trip.

"I believe I will have another drink, after all," she said. She had declined one upon Meredith's first offer, but she felt better now. He brightened too. It looked as though the evening would be successful after all.

In a perfectly natural and quite leisurely way she introduced the subject she had come to talk with him about. "It isn't that I want to get it out of the way," she said, "so that we can enjoy ourselves, but it's such a general thing. I can't even seriously ask, 'How are you?' without its being relevant, in a way. So I thought it might be better to start. We might as well deal with it so that there won't be all these forbidden areas—"

"Forbidden? Whatever do you mean?"

"Well, I don't want to talk about anything that the magazine is interested in without at least being sure that you know that it's relevant."

"That's very straightforward of you," Meredith said.

"Well, I think of myself as a friend."

"Good. So do I," he said. "Well, let's get at it, then."

He smiled at her, rather conspiratorially, and then asked, "Or would it be all right if we ordered first."

"Oh, by all means. I'm starving. It must be the desert air."

"That's one of the charms of Palm Springs," he said. "It makes you feel healthy even if you aren't."

They ordered steaks and a bottle of claret, and when the waiter left them, Jocelyn told him that she wanted to know what he thought of Merry's career in the movies.

"Yes, that's what you told me on the phone." He leaned back in his chair, smiled, shook his head slightly—it was a famous gesture of his, but entirely natural—and told her, "It's a difficult question. I mean, from any reporter, it would be a difficult question. But from you . . . My God! It's impossible."

"What do you mean?"

"To the reporter I can't say a thing. To the friend it should be obvious."

"What about a friendly reporter?" she asked.

"How friendly?"

"As friendly as you like. Very friendly."

"Well, I'll have to trust you," he said.

"Does it seem so very risky?"

"No. But you know what I'm talking about. I haven't been a very good father to Merry. I haven't been much of a father at all. Now, a girl can get along without a father, I suppose. Girls have. But without fathers, certainly they need mothers. And I haven't even let her have that. You remember how it was when I broke up with Elaine. You were there. I don't have to tell you. And you remember that other time, too. Carlotta . . ."

"Yes," Jocelyn said. "I remember."

"What can I say? What right do I have to say anything. I only wish that you weren't the one who is writing the story."

"I thought of that," she said. "I thought about that a

lot. But then I thought, if it wasn't me, it'd be somebody else."

"Yes, I suppose so."

"But what do you think? Asking you as a friend, I mean."

"All right," he said. "She's had a hell of a life. I suppose I've had a hell of a life, too. Who hasn't? But I feel responsible for hers. And the idea that she has gone into the movies . . . well, it both cheers me and saddens me."

"How do you mean?"

"For her to go into the movies is a sign, maybe, that there's something . . . something between us. And of course I'm glad of that. I don't know what it is. But any feeling she has for me at all I'm grateful for."

"But you said it saddened you, too."

"Oh, sure. Of course it does. I know the life. I know what it's like. And I know what the chances are for her to be happy in it. They're damned slim. I'm not sorry for myself, mind you. I think of it as a hard bargain I've driven with the devil. I got some things. I lost others. But when a man thinks of his daughter and the things he wants most for her . . . well, those are the things she's least likely to have. I know they're the things I haven't had."

"What things?" Jocelyn asked.

"Oh, I don't know. It's hard to make a list. I could say a family. And maybe you'd know what I mean. It isn't just a family, but the whole stability of life that goes with it. To grow up and to grow old, in one place. That's what I mean, too, I guess."

"It isn't just in the movies," Jocelyn said, "it's anywhere that people don't have families or stability. Or even roots. I know."

"I know you do. But the odds in the movies are worse than they would be in any other life that she chose."

"I suppose so," Jocelyn said.

"I remember what I hoped for her when she was born. And this isn't it. Of course I remember other things from that weekend, too. It wasn't your fault. It was mine. And Elaine's, too, partly. But it sure as hell wasn't Merry's."

"No, it wasn't."

"You know, now I'm glad that you came. That it's you who will be writing the story. I've avoided thinking about it, you know. I suppose the reason is that with Merry's being in the movies this way, I feel a little old. But with you here, talking with you, it's easier to face it and to think about the important things."

"I know what you mean. I felt positively ancient at the studio today, looking at Merry and remembering . . . us. It's lots better here, with you."

"How did she look?" Meredith asked.

"It's hard to tell. You know how it is. They do the thing in such little bits."

"I know."

"Oh, that reminds me. What she was doing was a seminude scene for the European version. I have to put on my reporter hat just for a moment and ask you about that. Any comment?"

"Something snappy, eh? Well, let me think. You might say that if she's a big enough girl for Mr. Kleinsinger to want her to do a scene like that, she's a big enough girl to make up her own mind about it. What the hell!" Meredith said. "Kleinsinger's the most harmless old coot in Hollywood."

"I know," Jocelyn said. "But I had to ask."

"Are we finished working now?"

"Yes, we're finished."

"Good. Have some more wine."

"Thank you."

She looked at him for a moment, studying him as he poured the wine first into her glass and then into his own. He was a handsome man. His features were less regular than Gardner's but the effect was even more pleasing. His age was not entirely concealed as Gardner's was, but gracefully worn. It enhanced him. There was more character in his face. There were lines in it that made it more interesting than the one he had had when he had started his career.

"I'm sorry," she said.

"About what?"

"Well, I know you don't blame me. You're too fair for that. But I hadn't thought about it before. Now that you've mentioned it . . . it was a horrible coincidence."

"What was?"

"What happened to us. The way what happened to us affected Merry."

"It doesn't bear thinking about," Meredith said. "We never intended to hurt her. What is it that Shakespeare said? 'The gods are just, and of our pleasant vices make instruments to plague us.' But it doesn't work that way. It's what we'd like to believe. In the same play he says it another way, the way it really is. 'As flies to wanton boys are we to the gods. They kill us for their sport.' "

"That's the more comforting line, I guess."

"No, it's the tougher one. I believe it, but it's the tougher one. You think about it for a while and you feel so damned alone."

"I don't feel alone. Not here. Not now. With you."

"Yes," Meredith said. "Even in this crazy life there are moments. Would you like some brandy with your coffee?"

She hesitated for a moment and then came out with it. "Yes, but how about coming over to my place for it?"

"I wish I could."

"Of course you can."

"No, I have to go on to that party, where Noni went."

"Oh, you can duck it, can't you?"

"No. I shouldn't tell you this," Meredith said, "but

I'm here with her. That business before . . . Well, it's an old poker player's trick. You show a high card to make them think you're bluffing. I let you see her because it was the best way to fool you. I'm sorry."

"Don't be," Jocelyn said. "Don't be sorry. But you don't have to be fanatic about her, either."

"I wish I didn't. You make me wish I didn't. But I do. She's nineteen years old. I'm fifty-two. She's about all I can handle right now. I don't suppose you'd take the thought for the deed?"

"If that's all I get, I guess I'll have to."

She got up. Meredith stood.

"Do you have to leave so soon?" Meredith asked.

"I might as well," she said.

She kissed him on the cheek, deliberately. It was a way of hiding her rage and disappointment. And then, walking slowly and with a studied nonchalance, she left the dining room, walked through the lobby and out to the parking lot. She drove back to the motel.

In the motel room she sat down on the foam-rubber easy chair, smoked a cigarette, and then decided that she could not stand that barren room in the middle of the barren desert, not alone. She got her things together, put them in the car, and drove back to Los Angeles.

Ten days later Merry got a call from Arthur Wemmick late in the afternoon. She had just got back from the studio. The phone was ringing when she opened the front door. She ran to answer it.

"Merry? Arthur."

"Yes?"

"Have you seen the current issue of *Pulse?* The new one, I mean. The one that came out today."

"No."

"I think you'd better. Shall I send it over to you?"

"No, I can go out for it," Merry said. "It'll be faster. There's no need for you to bother."

"All right. Call me when you've read it, will you? If I'm not here, I'll be at home."

"I will," she said. "And thank you. Is it . . . is it very bad?"

"It isn't good."

"OK. Thanks for letting me know."

She hung up and went back out to the car. She drove down to Schwab's on Sunset Strip, where she bought a copy of *Pulse*. She took it out to the car, and in the privacy of the automobile she opened it. Flipping the pages from the back, she found the entertainment section. As she read it she felt the prickle of the beads of sweat that broke out on her forehead and her upper lip.

It was a vicious article, and it was all the more vicious because it disguised itself, pretending to be sympathetic, understanding, and humane. The tack it took was to commiserate both with Merry and with her father. Merry came across as a brash, lost creature who had no idea what she was doing and who posed in the nude for Harry Kleinsinger because she desperately wanted his approval. It then proceeded to explain the need for such approval by quoting her father as saying "I haven't been very much of a father to Merry. I haven't been much of a father at all. For her to go into the movies is a sign that maybe there's something between us. And of course, I'm glad of that."

The next paragraph was worse. "Sipping a glass of Château Latour '47 in the dining room of a plush Palm Springs resort hotel, he said, 'I know the life. I know what it's like. And I know the chances for her to be happy in it. They're damned slim.' "

Merry read the piece a second time. The attack on her was much less serious, she thought. The magazine took a patronizing and condescending tone, while indulging her. " 'I'm a big girl now,' the nineteen-year-old starlet desperately proclaimed."

She had said the words, but she had neither proclaimed nor been desperate. It was all so brutally unfair.

She put the magazine down on the seat beside her and drove back to her apartment. She called Wemmick.

"What has my father said?" she asked him.

"He was worried about you."

"But that's silly," Merry said. "He was the one they were rough on."

"He knows that. But he knows why. What bothered him was that you were hurt by it."

"Do you have his phone number?"

Wemmick gave her the unlisted number, making no comment about her need to ask him. She was grateful for that. "It's out in Malibu," he added.

"Thank you," she said. "I'll call him."

"Good."

She hung up and dialed her father's number.

"Hello? Yes?"

"Daddy? It's Merry!"

"You've seen it?"

"Yes. Just a little while ago."

"I'm sorry about it," he said. "I haven't been much of a help to you. But I've never wanted to hurt you."

"Oh, Daddy, it doesn't matter," she told him. "I was sick about it because of the way it treated you. It was so unfair."

"I wasn't surprised. It's the reporter. She was out to get me."

"But why?"

"Hell hath no fury like a woman scorned," he said. "But it's too complicated to explain over the phone. Look, where are you?"

She told him where her apartment was.

"Why don't you come on out?"

"I'd love to."

"It'll be good to see you," he said.

"Oh, it'll be good to see you. I'll be there as soon as I can."

She hung up. She threw the magazine into the wastebasket. It didn't matter. It just didn't matter any more. She went out to the car.

Driving to Malibu, heading west, she could see the red sunset through the thin layer of clouds. The magazine article was of no importance. Or no, in a way it was. Talking to her father on the telephone had turned it from the nasty thing it was into a great, bright, beautiful Christmas card.

CHAPTER

ELEVEN

♥ "Happiness!" she said, raising her champagne glass.

She held the glass out toward her father and Noni—now Mrs. Meredith Houseman—who were standing across the room next to the fireplace.

"All the best to you," Judge Needleman said.

Arthur Wemmick nodded gravely and toasted the wedding couple with his upheld glass.

They drank the champagne. Noni, when she had finished, threw her glass into the fireplace, smashing it.

"What was that?" Meredith asked.

"I've always wanted to do that," Noni said. "It's . . . well, it's just like in the movies."

Meredith laughed and the others took up his laughter.

"I'd better go and get the car," Wemmick said. Wemmick was going to drive them to the Bakersfield airport, where a chartered plane would fly the Housemans to Acapulco.

"Well, Mrs. Houseman, how do you feel?" Meredith asked.

"Wonderful," Noni said. "It's the happiest day of my life."

"Good," the bridegroom answered.

"It's one of the happiest days of mine, too," Merry said.

Her father looked at her quizzically.

"I mean it," Merry said, and she did. She wished that there were some way she could tell her father how good it felt to be able to be friends with him. For the first time, she felt no resentment nor any sense of threat in the contemplation of one of her father's marriages. She did not see Noni as a threat to her own relationship with him. If anything, she felt rather sorry for the girl. Noni was simple, sweet, and utterly without guile. She seemed to be interested only in Meredith Houseman, horses, and going to the movies. It had never occurred to Noni to try to *deal* with Merry. She had accepted her as Meredith's daughter, and lately as her own friend. On Merry's part there was a compassion for the loneliness that a nineteen-year-old would necessarily find with a fifty-two-year-old man, and at the same time there was a kind of appreciation, too. It did not take overmuch subtlety to be able to figure out what function Noni played in her father's life, and why he needed her. Her father didn't look old, didn't sound old, didn't act at all old. And all the world thought of him as an ageless and ceaselessly vigorous man and lover. But the demands their very admiration placed upon him were such that he was haunted by the fear that one morning time would catch up with him. His life, his career, and the entire world would come crashing down around him. Noni was the visible proof that his movies were telling the truth. She was not only a prop for his own confidence, but his marriage to her was a sop that he could throw to the ravening public.

Merry did not expect that the marriage would last very long. But that did not bother her. She had already learned that happiness was a fleeting thing, a matter of luck, like the goldfish one buys in dime stores: ninety-nine die, and the hundredth gets fat, thrives, and lives for years.

She wondered whether they would have a child. It would be good for her father, she thought. But she was not so sure about the life that the child would have. She put her champagne glass down on the blotter of the judge's desk. It was not her decision to make. There was no point in her brooding about it.

"I think Arthur must have brought the car around now," Meredith said. "Thank you, Judge."

"My pleasure," the judge said. "Have a good trip."

Meredith offered an arm to Noni, and the other to Merry. The three of them left the judge's chambers together and went down to the car.

When Merry got back to her apartment she felt happy. She kept telling herself that she felt happy. But she did not entirely believe it. There was something wrong. There was something, somehow, incomplete. She walked aimlessly around the living room. She lit a cigarette and then realized that she had just lit one a moment before. There was something wrong.

She put out the cigarette that had been burning in the ashtray and sat down to think. Then it occurred to her. Elaine. Her mother.

She knew it was corny, but the miraculous improvement in her relationship with her father made her wonder whether another miracle might not be possible, too. Could she not perhaps reestablish some kind of closeness with her mother? At least a friendship?

She had avoided her mother during the months that she had been out on the coast. She had given herself the excuse of her work and the fatigue that came from it, but she knew that it was only an excuse. She had called her mother only twice, and her mother's response to both calls had been only lukewarm. Merry had felt extraordinarily lucky in having been able to avoid her mother, but she wondered now whether she had been so lucky after all.

She picked up the phone and dialed. Lyon answered the phone.

"Lyon? This is Merry."

"Hello, Merry," he said, in a flat, toneless way.

"I'd like to come over and see you and Mother this evening. I haven't seen you in ages."

"Mother's not here now. She won't be home for an hour or so."

"Do I need a ticket of admission?" Merry asked playfully.

"Our home is your home," Lyon said.

It was, Merry thought, an odd remark for a fourteen-year-old boy to make. Perhaps he was just joking, putting her on, trying to make light of their estrangement.

"I'll be over in an hour and a half then," she said, and hung up.

She parked her white MG in front of the familiar house and with a feeling of happy anticipation walked up to the porch and rang the bell. Lyon answered the door.

Merry's eyes widened in shock and disbelief. "What the hell is that?" she asked.

He was wearing saffron robes and rope sandals. His hair was cut in an incredible style. A bowl-like fringe encircled his head, and there was a bald, tonsured circle in the middle of his scalp.

"Would you leave your shoes on the porch, please?" he asked.

"What?" she asked. "What is this crap?"

"They're leather."

"Well, of course, they're leather!"

"I'll get you some rope sandals."

"What are you talking about?"

"Or perhaps you would prefer paper slippers."

"Come on, Lyon. What is this? Are you serious?"

"Oh, yes."

She was sure it was a joke. It had to be. But she was willing to play along with it for a while. She took off her shoes and started to go inside. But Lyon stopped her.

"Your handbag," he said.

"My what? I can't leave my handbag on the porch. Somebody will steal it! Besides, it has my cigarettes in it."

"You won't need them here. Mother and I don't hold with smoking now."

"What are you talking about?"

"Come in, won't you?" he invited.

She put her bag down on the porch, next to her shoes, and followed him into the house. There was an odd smell. She sniffed several times before she recognized it as sandalwood incense.

The room was dim, and it took her a moment to adjust to the light that came from the candles that flickered in front of the shrines. Placed at regular intervals around the walls of the living room were pictures of Jesus, Buddha, Moses, Muhammad, Confucius, Zeus, the Dalai Lama, and Ahura-Mazda. The odd thing was that in the center of the forehead of each of these likenesses there was a third eye from which rays emanated. They were like the eyes on the pyramids on the backs of dollar bills.

Her mother came out of the kitchen, smiled graciously, and said, "Peace!"

Elaine was wearing a long green gown and a circlet of myrtle about her head.

"It's good to see you again, Meredith," she said. She held out her arms and advanced toward Merry, who thought that she was going to kiss her on the cheek. Instead, her mother held her with a hand on each cheek and kissed her on the middle of her forehead. Merry was unsure how to return this greeting, so she did nothing.

"Sit down, child," Elaine said, and indicated a chair with a wave of her hand.

Merry did as she was told. Lyon sat down on a raffia mat on the floor.

"Mother, what is this?" Merry asked.

"We have been saved," her mother said. "We have been born again. We have joined the Church of the Transcendental Eye."

"Oh? But Lyon. Why is he dressed that way?"

"He is a monk," Elaine explained. "In seven years he will be ordained as a priest. In twenty years he will be a saint."

"And you?"

"I am only Sister Elaine, but I have come to the church after a long life of sin. Lyon is a fortunate boy. The church will be his whole life."

"But what church? I've never heard of it!"

Elaine gave her daughter a pained smile. "It's a wonderful faith," she said. "An ennobling faith. I was so lost after Harry passed over, but now I have found peace. The Church of the Transcendental Eye combines all of the great religions of the world into one transcendental religion. It is a faith unified as all the faiths must be unified in the sight of God's eye."

"Is it Christian?" Merry asked.

"Christian, Jewish, Buddhist, Islamic, Zoroastrian, Taoist . . . nothing is excluded. As our Leader says, 'It is all things to all men.' "

"But what about my purse and my shoes?" Merry asked. "I mean, my cigarettes are in my purse. This is a lot to take in, you know, all at once."

"We don't smoke," Elaine said. "And we don't use

leather or eat meat. We don't need to do those things."

"Well, could I have something to drink then, please?" Merry asked. She needed desperately to have something in her hands.

"Lyon, get your sister a glass of the elixir of love, please."

"Ths elixir of what? What's in it?"

"Don't worry, child. It's mainly celery juice."

"Celery juice!"

"You'll find it has a fresh, pure taste. It's the taste of contemplation."

Merry watched Lyon go out into the kitchen. He came back with a glass of a pale, green liquid. She took a sip and then put the glass down on the table beside her. It was awful. It was all awful.

"Mother, what have you done? What is this? Are you out of your mind?"

"No, my child. For the first time, I am *in* my mind, and my heart, and my soul . . . at peace with the world."

"Oh, come on," Merry said impatiently.

"You speak only from worldliness," Elaine said.

"No, I speak from common sense. Look, it's all right, I suppose, if you want to do this, and amuse yourself this way. But Lyon is just a kid. You're ruining him."

"I'm saving him. And I'll thank you to keep your impertinent and impious opinions to yourself. After all, who are you to come here and criticize me this way, to criticize us this way? I know what you do and how you pander to the lusts of the masses, exposing your flesh to the greedy eyes of sinful men, whoring after lucre—"

"Mother, what are you talking about?"

"I've seen that article."

"You mean the article in *Pulse?*"

"Yes, that article."

"But you can't believe that. That was written by a

woman who had some old score to settle with Father."

"You don't know what you're talking about," Elaine said. "I know what that old score was. It's a score I had to settle with her, not one that she had to settle with him. Do you know who broke up our marriage? The marriage between your father and me? Do you know?"

"No, who?"

"That Jocelyn Strong person from *Pulse*. She enticed your father, and weak, foolish man that he was, he succumbed to her wickedness."

Merry sat back, shocked. Her father had explained Jocelyn's animus, only casually mentioning that they once had had an inconsequential love affair, but he had not been at all specific about when this had been or about the results that had come of it.

Her mother rose, crossed the room, knelt down in front of the picture of Ahura-Mazda.

"Forgive me," she whispered. "I am guilty of the sin of anger."

She turned slightly and invited Lyon to join her in prayer. Then she asked, "Will you pray with us, Meredith? We will teach you how. There is nothing that would make me happier, or bring me the final measure of peace that I so yearn for, then to have you join with us in prayer, to have you join with us as a believer, as a member of the Church of the Transcendental Eye. Give up the wickedness of your life. Give up the movies. Devote yourself to God. And He will see you with His Eye, and you will bathe in the warm light of his vision."

"No, Mother, I can't. I . . . I . . ." But she could not say what revulsion, what horror, what disgust she felt.

She fled from the house, picking up her shoes and her bag from the porch, and running barefoot back out to her car. She lit a cigarette and then switched on the ignition.

It was too painful, too ridiculous, too preposterous to be real. She started to giggle. She took a great pleasure in the shifting of the gears and the response of the powerful motor under the hood of the MG. She was driving too fast, but she didn't care. She was laughing.

It wasn't until she approached a traffic light and saw how blurry it was that she realized that she was crying, too.

"As far as I am concerned, it certainly will not do the picture any harm," Kleinsinger said.

"But will it help the picture?"

"Indirectly, I suppose it will have a very slight effect that would be favorable. But it will have more of an effect on you, Miss Houseman."

"You think, then, that I ought to do it?"

"No, I did not say that. I neither recommend nor disapprove. It is as I say—it is your decision. But I would be misleading you if I led you to believe that I was unhappy about the idea."

Merry had come to Mr. Kleinsinger to ask him about the invitation she had had from the executive editor of *Lothario* magazine to pose for the gatefold photograph that was the trademark of the magazine. The girls in the gatefold were always naked and looked as provocative as they and the photographers could manage. The invitation had come in to her several days after the appearance of the article in *Pulse*. She had discarded it, but after the grotesque evening with her mother and Lyon and the Church of the Transcendental Eye, she had found herself thinking of it more and more frequently. There would be a wonderful satisfaction in the antipodal denial which such a gesture as her acceptance of their offer would imply.

"I appreciate, however, your coming to discuss the matter with me," Kleinsinger said. "Many actresses would be neither so scrupulous nor so thoughtful." He bestowed upon her one of his very rare smiles.

It occurred to Merry that, in his gruff, blustery way, he was a very shy man. She walked out of his office still undecided about what she would do. She thought probably that she wanted to pose for the picture. She knew she did. She decided to call the magazine and to accept their offer. There was no reason not to, and after all, it would be a found thousand dollars. There was no one and nothing to prevent her.

She rather surprised herself, however, when she got to the telephone. She did not call *Lothario,* as she intended to do, but Sam Jaggers in New York.

She was put through to him right away.

"Merry, how are you?" he asked.

"Just fine."

"What's the trouble?"

"No trouble. I just have a question. I wanted to discuss it with you."

"Oh?"

"I have an invitation from *Lothario*. They want me to pose for them."

"Forget it," he said.

"Why?"

"You don't need it," he said. "Besides, the image for you is talent."

"But I want to do it."

"Why?"

"I think it would be . . . fun."

"You're not in this business to have fun. The point is to make money. You want to pose for pictures, do it on your own time."

"Well, they've offered to pay me."

"Merry, I'm sure you won't get as much from them as it cost us to get the last set of pictures you posed for."

She was stunned. "That was a cruel thing to say," she said.

"What do you think this is, a game?" he asked. "You're a valuable property, and I've got to protect you, whether you want to protect yourself or not."

"Shit on the property!"

Jaggers said nothing. Merry knew that he was waiting for her to say something else, that he was putting the burden of her outburst on her—where it belonged—letting her listen to the reverberations of its echo.

"I'm going to do it," she said, after a long pause.

"Then you didn't call me up to discuss it but to announce it," Jaggers observed.

"All right, yes, I did."

"Merry, I can only advise you. I can't order you. And one piece of good advice is that you could make announcements of this kind a lot cheaper in an airmail letter."

"Thank you," she said. "Thanks a lot."

She hung up. She was angry enough now to call Drew Ebbet at *Lothario* to say yes and to set up the date for the pictures.

Leroy Lefrenier asked her to move her leg slightly to the left.

"No, no, not that much," he said. "A little less. No, more than that. No, that's too much. Wait a minute. Here."

He came over and put her leg where he wanted it. She was lying on a zebra rug, at an angle to the camera so that the fullness of her breasts were exaggerated by the arch of her back, which incidentally served to emphasize the swell of her behind. Her upper leg was crooked. As Lefrenier had perhaps inelegantly explained, "The only rule in this game is you can't show the woolly-woolly."

Physically it was less pleasant than she had expected.

The heat of the floodlights was no surprise, but the sticky cakiness of the body makeup and the greasy slick of the lipstick and the nipple rouge made her feel in desperate need of a shower. In spite of it all, Lefrenier's gross but engaging humor and his obvious workmanlike competence made it tolerable. He was rather inscrutable in the way in which he danced around her, with the cameras hanging from his neck, holding up one or another of his cameras or his light meter, and criticizing her facial expressions, which were, he told her, surprisingly important.

"The body is just a footnote. It's all in the face," he said. "You gotta be asking for it. Come on now, come on," he wheedled. "Think fuck."

She broke into nervous laughter, but the laughter subsided, and as the smile began to fade he clicked the 35-millimeter several times, then shouted, "Hold it!" He grabbed his reflex and took a shot with that.

It had been an arduous session. They had been at it now for more than two hours, during which he had shot her in a variety of postures and against a number of backdrops. There had been a shot of her in a pair of men's jeans, with the fly half unzipped, and a man's shirt, with all the buttons opened so that the curve of her breast was visible. There were shots with a peignoir and shots with a chiffon scarf.

"Scrunch down a little there, would you? No, that's too much. What I want is to line up the breast there with the zebra stripe."

The breast. Not hers. She felt, in a way, as though she were not there at all, but only a piece of flesh that was being used and manipulated by this man and his camera. Oddly, she rather enjoyed the curious selflessness that lay somewhere at the center of the experience. She was merely an object to be exploited for the editors of *Lothario* and the readers of the magazine for whom they were the surrogates. It was comforting, really.

"I guess that will do it," he said. "You're a good kid. The shower's in there."

"Thanks," she said. She got up and went into the shower. She washed the makeup off, then dried herself and went out to get the clothes she had left behind the screen in the studio. She was wrapped in a large white terrycloth towel. As she reached for her pants, the towel fell open, and she clutched it closed. It was crazy, but she had not felt so naked or exposed all afternoon. She finished dressing and came out from behind the screen.

Lefrenier offered her a beer. "You must be thirsty. It's hot under those lights."

"Yes, I am, thanks," she said. "An odd line of work, isn't it?" she asked.

"I enjoy it. Bodies are beautiful, some of them. The ones they send me mostly are."

"Doesn't it bother you?"

"It doesn't get in the way of the camera," he said.

She laughed at that and took another deep swallow of her beer. Lefrenier went around unplugging lights and putting his equipment away. Merry finished her beer and put the glass on the table at one end of the studio.

"I guess that's it then," she said.

It had not been the experience she had feared—or hoped for. It had not been complete. She was reluctant to go. Whether he sensed this or it was only a lucky coincidence, she never knew. She didn't even care much. The important thing was that he asked her, "How would you like to come to a party tonight?"

"I'd love to. Fine. Sure," she said. "All I do out here is work."

"You're lucky, then. Most people mainly spend their time looking for work. I'll be around to pick you up at nine-thirty, OK?"

She told him it was OK, and where she lived.

"Way the hell out there? Well, sure, all right," he said.

"What kind of a party is it going to be?"

"Oh, I don't know. You never know about these things. A bunch of swingers. Wear what you have on."

She was wearing a cable-knit sweater and a pair of slacks.

"OK, thanks," she said.

Merry was ready to go at a quarter after nine. She sat in her living room, every now and then looking out through the draperies at the street below, watching for Lefrenier's Porsche. She was embarrassed by her own eagerness for the party. But it was natural enough. After all, she had not been out on a date in all the time she had been in Los Angeles. She had just not wanted to get involved with anyone. Hollywood was a bad town for young actresses. Everybody was on the make, and not just for her, for bed, but for themselves, for profit and success. It had been easier to watch television and to read herself to sleep at night.

She was beginning to feel the depressurization, though. There was only a week and a half left of shooting and after that she would be on the loose again and at loose ends. She did not plan to stay in Hollywood, but neither had she any plans to go anywhere else. It was all open and free-floating. What she liked most about the party was the idea that there would not be movie people there, but that curious fringe world she had heard about in Los Angeles but had never found—because she had had neither the time nor the inclination to look for it.

She looked through the draperies again and saw a pair of headlights winding up the canyon. It would be only reasonable to spend as much time with Lefrenier dressed as she had spent undressed with him. The car pulled off the road and into the driveway that approached her apartment. She was waiting at the door when he rang the bell.

"Would you like a drink?" she asked. "Come on in."

"No, let's go on to the party. There'll be booze there."

"Let's go then," she said, and went out to the car.

Sitting beside him in the Porsche, she appraised him carefully. Curiously, she had not been able to study him with any degree of attention earlier in the day when she had been naked. Now that they were both dressed, there was a parity, an equality, so that she could notice such things as his barrel chest, which just missed stockiness, the sweep of his hair, which he brushed straight back to subdue its curliness, the bulge of his thighs in the white Levi's he wore to contrast with the black turtleneck sweater. His hands were surprising in their delicacy and in the long tapering of their fingers.

They descended from the Beverly Hills, swung around on Sunset strip, and then started climbing into the Hollywood Hills. He was an excellent driver, and she appreciated the way he maneuvered the hairpin turns of the road that snaked up into the mountains. The house at which he turned off was an ordinary structure for Los Angeles, rather larger than some, and perched on the mountainside on stilts. On clear days and nights the view out over the city would be breathtaking.

There must have been twenty cars parked along the road in front of the house and in the driveway, as well as a half-dozen motorcycles. There was the sound of music coming from one of the open windows of the house. He led the way up the front walk and opened the door. Several people greeted him. He led the way through the crush into the dining room, where there was a table that had been set up as a bar.

"What'll it be?"

"Scotch on the rocks, please."

"Coming up," he said, and he handed her half a tumbler of Scotch with a couple of ice cubes in it.

"Wonderful," she said.

"Yeah, but watch out for the ice cubes. A girl could get a black eye from those things. They've got sharp edges."

"Leroy, you old son of a bitch! How the hell are you?"

Leroy introduced the stranger to Merry. "Merry," he said, "this is Jocke Dunbar."

"Jocke?" Merry asked.

"Yes, with an *e*," he said. "J,O,C,K,E. My mother had a lousy sense of humor."

"Jocke, this is Merry Houseman," Lefrenier broke in.

"Houseman?" Dunbar asked. "You aren't related to the poet, are you?"

"No, I'm afraid not," she said. She was delighted.

"Are you a model, too?" he asked.

"I've modeled," she said. She looked around the room, and realized that most of the girls there either were models or could be models. It was an attractive group. The men were less homogenized-looking and came in all shapes, sizes, and ages, but they all had a kind of with-it look, she thought. Five or six feet away, there was a cluster of people engaged in some heated discussion. A tall, eagle-like man was gesturing excitedly with his left hand and talking about something. Merry was not close enough to hear what it was. What was curious, though, was the way he was talking and, with his right hand, holding the breast of the girl who was standing beside him. She didn't seem to notice and nobody else seemed to notice either.

There was George Shearing music on the record player. It was very relaxing. The best part of it was that she felt like just another girl at a party, looking around and thinking about nothing but having a good time.

Leroy wandered off to greet some newcomers he knew, and Jocke seemed to take her over. He led her across the room to join some friends. All that was demanded of her was that she make appropriate noises, agreeing or laughing, or nodding from time to time. When her glass was empty, she handed it to almost any man who was passing by, and it reappeared refilled.

After a while some of the couples began to dance, or not dance but sway, clinging to each other in corners. The George Shearing was gone, and now there was some quietly moaning saxophone with an insistent sensual beat. Jocke did not ask her to dance, but took her in his arms, held her, swaying with her, and moved only to dance her a little bit away from the group with whom they had been talking. It was very pleasant to be in a man's arms again. She closed her eyes and gave herself up to the music and the dancing. While her eyes were closed, she realized that she had not actually looked at Jocke, that she could not remember now what he looked like, anyway. She opened her eyes and peeked.

All she could see without moving her head were the whorls of his ear and the line of the haircut at the side of his neck. She could feel the way they fit together, though. The way everything fit together. In a strange, serene way, she realized that it was entirely possible that she might go to bed with him, that she wanted to go to bed with him, or with someone. At the party. She knew that she was a little drunk, or maybe more than a little, but that wasn't it. She had been drunk before and had not felt this way at all. And it wasn't even an irresistible feeling of physical desire. It was just a sense of the naturalness of it and the way it seemed to fit. Fit with what? Well, she wasn't sure. The posing that afternoon was a part of it. But the posing itself had not been particularly exciting. Nor did it connect very closely with the party. Except in a most indirect way. Without clearly making the connection to herself, she felt the results of the connection that had already been established, years before.

A woman, they say, never forgets her first lover. But Merry's lover had been a chance encounter at a party, or perhaps more precisely, the chance conjunction of a session of picture-taking and a party, so that what appealed to her was neither the one nor the other, but the coincidence of the two. It was like the vibration of a small cigarette lighter on a glass tabletop because of the striking of the right note on a piano across the room.

He held her close and then moved the hand that was at the small of her back up under her sweater. It felt nice on her bare skin. As they turned, in the dancing, she noticed Leroy, who was with some willowy blonde. He wasn't doing anything more than running his hand up and down her arm, but somehow there seemed to come from this a suggestion of established intimacy. She wondered whether she felt jealous and decided that if she had to ask herself, then she probably didn't. Then she wondered why Jocke hadn't been responding to her more in their dancing, why he hadn't been aroused, and then she noticed that he had been, he was. She just hadn't been aware of it. Or maybe she had been but the way one thing seemed to glide into another and the way everything was so charmingly indistinct, his erection had somehow not registered upon her consciousness.

They had been dancing in the direction of the hallway. Without saying anything, he released her from his embrace, took her hand, and led her down the hallway to one of the bedrooms.

"Wrong room," he said and closed the door, but not before she had glimpsed a couple entangled in each other's arms and legs on the bed.

He opened another door, across the hall from the

first one. That room was empty, but the bed there was piled high with coats. She thought he was going to dump all the coats on the floor, but he took only the one on top, a full-length Autumn Haze mink, spread it on the floor, and pulled her down beside him.

There were hardly any preliminaries. None were necessary. The liquor and the closeness and her long abstinence had inflamed her. He pulled her slacks and pants down and entered her immediately. She was afraid that she was going to giggle because of the wonderfully furry feeling of the coat under her bare ass. But it was not just funny; it was voluptuous, too.

It was brisk, fast, and efficient, and breathtakingly satisfying.

He fell away from her, and she got up to search for her pants and her slacks while he lay on the coat and smoked a cigarette, watching her.

"More later?" he asked.

"Maybe, if I'm still around," she said, and went out to find the bathroom. She felt great. She felt euphoric. She thought that she very well might take him up on the offer for another go-around. She had been missing a lot. She opened the bathroom door and walked in, still preoccupied with her own sensations.

She could not believe her eyes. She hadn't known the bathroom was occupied. She was as much puzzled as anything else. Why were four women sitting on the rim of the bathtub, stark naked? She walked two steps toward the tub and looked down to see Harry Kleinsinger lying in a pool of urine. He was stark naked, and with both hands he was holding his erect penis.

One of the girls giggled and wet him.

He was moaning. His eyes were closed. He lay there, stroking himself. Kleinsinger's eyes fluttered for a fraction of a second. She fled, hoping that he had not recognized her, had not seen her at all, or, if he had, that he would not remember it.

She went back to the bedroom where she had left Jocke.

"Take me home," she said in a tone that allowed no argument.

"Sure, baby, anything you say."

On the way home she asked him to stop the car. She got out, went behind the car, and vomited.

At her front door she dismissed him. "I'm sorry, but I'm not feeling well," she said. He shrugged his shoulders.

"Take it easy, baby," he said. And drove away.

The poor man, she thought, *the poor, poor man.* She thought of all the decisive strength, all the talent, all the brisk confidence of Harry Kleinsinger, and felt so sorry that it was all a mask for this pathetic weakness. The self-hatred. Whatever it was. She felt sorry for him, and sorry for herself, too. She had drawn confidence from his confidence in her, had relied upon him not only for direction but for other, vaguer things. Esteem. A sense of her own worth. It could not have been worse if she had discovered her own father in that tub.

In a slow, leaden way she got undressed and went to bed, curling up under the covers as if she were hiding from . . . from everything. From the whole world.

In the ten days of shooting that remained, Kleinsinger was very distant. Unless he could help it, he never spoke to her directly. She wanted to tell him how sorry she was, but of course that was impossible.

There was nine dollars' worth of orange juice on the table, which is to say, nine glasses. A glass of orange juice in the Polo Lounge of the Beverly Hills Hotel costs a dollar, but the men who come to breakfast there can afford it. For an hour or so, early in the morning, from seven until eight, the nerve center of the motion-picture industry is in that small dining room. When it is seven o'clock in Los Angeles, it is ten in New York.

The stock exchange is open. The men in the banquettes can talk to their brokers on the white phones that the waiters bring and plug into the wall jacks. If you are buying three thousand shares of Paramount or selling four thousand shares of Twentieth Century-Fox, you drink the glass of orange juice without noticing it and you pay the dollar without feeling it.

The best tables are the circular banquettes. Those are the ones with the phone jacks. But this morning something was going on. There were nine men sitting next to the plate-glass windows, through which there was a view of a subtropical garden. The other men, sitting in the banquettes, were curious, but only mildly so. Inevitably they would find out before the end of the day what it was that the men at the long table near the window were talking about. And knowing that, they could be patient.

The men at the table represented several hundred million dollars' worth of the entertainment business. There were five major studios represented there, and Isidore Shumsky from the MPAA, and there was a young man with a round face whom nobody recognized. That was Jason Podhoretz from the cultural affairs section of the Department of State.

Podhoretz was asking a question. "The Phoenix Nest? What's that?"

"A drive-in," Shumsky explained, "just outside of Phoenix. It's a crummy drive-in in the middle of the desert. Anybody ever been there?"

No, nobody had ever been there.

"Why is a drive-in like that so important then?" Podhoretz asked.

"Nobody knows. We've never been able to figure it out. But it's—what you say in politics—a key precinct. Whatever the patrons of the Phoenix Nest drive-in of Phoenix, Arizona, think of a movie, that is what the American public thinks of that movie."

"There are other theaters," Marty Golden continued. "We used to use theaters in Brentwood a lot. Sometimes we use the Loew's 86th Street because it's in New York, it's a middle-class theater in a New York situation. But the fastest, the most reliable way of finding out what you've got with a picture is to try it out at the Phoenix Nest."

"And they liked it?" Podhoretz asked.

"What are the numbers?" George Melnik asked.

"They liked it. They liked it," said Golden. He reached into his breast pocket and pulled out a wad of little slips of paper in varying stages of disintegration. It took a moment for him to find the right one. "Here," he said. "Two hundred and ten, excellent. Five hundred and forty, good. A hundred and eighteen, fair. And twenty-six, poor. And for all I know, the twenty-six, poor, is all Melnik here."

"What do you mean? What do you mean? I never been in Phoenix in my life."

"Do me a favor—go sometime. For twenty or thirty years. Phoenix, Albuquerque, Tucson . . ."

"Very funny, very funny," Melnik said. "Now, Mr. Poretz—"

"Podhoretz," he corrected.

"Yeah, like I said. Tell us again what you told Mr. Shumsky and Mr. Golden."

Podhoretz gave his report. Much of what he told them they already knew. They knew, for instance, that there was a good deal of resentment among the European motion-picture producers and even among some of the European governments because of the rather high-handed way in which America had manipulated the Cannes festival that had just concluded by threatening not to let them have another picture for five years unless one or another American picture received at least one prize. Cannes, which is a big, commercial festival, had been terrified at the prospect of an American pull-out. America was more important to Cannes than Cannes was to America. There had been twenty hours or so of frantic maneuvering, and suddenly the best-actor award, which rumor had already given to a brilliant young Czech comedian, was diverted to Edgar Sinclair. It had been done at the last minute, and it had been fairly messy.

All the men at the table knew that. What they did not know was the character of Ettore Sismondi, the new director of the Venice festival, the *Mostra Internazionale d'Arte Cinematografica di Venezia.*

"The best that we can figure it," Podhoretz said, "is that he's unpredictable."

"For that you came from Washington all the way three thousand miles to tell us?" Melnik asked.

"Shut up and listen to the boy," said Golden.

"He's a kind of maverick communist," Podhoretz continued.

"What does that mean?" Jack Farber asked.

"All the prizes will go to some Estonian nature picture," said Melnik.

"Please, George," Shumsky said.

"No," Podhoretz went on. "He's a maverick and he's interested in the movies as a popular art form and as a political tool. Now our view at State is that the picture with the best chance is *Addict*. That way he'd be giving the prize to an American picture, but to one which presents America in an unfavorable light. And then he could turn around and say that the reason he admires the picture is that it testifies to the freedom American film makers have to criticize."

"So let's send *Addict*," Melnik said.

"It makes me sick to my stomach," said Harvey Backert.

"You got a rotten stomach anyway," Melnik reminded him.

"Of course I'm only here to advise," Podhoretz went

on, "but we're not at all sure that *Addict* isn't a little too strong to send over. . . ."

"What do you mean, 'strong'?" Norman Epstein asked. "It's going to bomb. It's not a happy picture."

"With a budget of only three hundred thousand dollars they can be as miserable as they want and still smile," said Backert.

"From the point of view of the industry as a whole," Shumsky said from the head of the table, "I should think we might consider some pictures of more commercial importance. That is to say artistic pictures, of course, but with a financial weight to them."

"There was nothing on the list?" Melnik asked. "Nothing?"

"I was just getting to that," Podhoretz replied. "Now, it may be that we're being too intricate and tricky in our thinking, but then Sismondi is pretty intricate in his thinking, too. I should think that *Three for the Money* just might do it. It's Kleinsinger himself who might appeal to Sismondi, because of the tough time that HUAC gave him a couple of years ago. And the subject of the picture is corruption in business, if you want to think of it that way. The saving grace is that it's a comedy. So it doesn't matter."

"I don't know," Epstein said. "I think it's a good picture. I liked it. But if I liked it, what are they going to think in Europe? I mean, you know, it's not in black and white, it's not out of focus, the lighting is not incompetent. Those three things right there disqualify it, don't they? If he's a film nut, I mean."

"They would disqualify it for Cardini, but not for Sismondi."

"Sure, what about his retrospective?"

"What retrospective?" Melnik asked.

"You don't know?" Golden asked. "Go on, tell him."

Podhoretz told Golden about the retrospective

showing of American musical comedies of the thirties and forties—Busby Berkeley, Samuel Goldwin, Fred Astaire, Esther Williams . . .

"Some cockamamie idea he's got, no?" Golden interrupted.

"He's out of his mind," Melnik said. "This is art?"

"Yeah, sure. Why not?"

"You mean we've been right all these years?" Farber interjected. "I don't believe it."

"What else on the list struck you as being a possibility?" Shumsky asked Podhoretz.

"Well, it's difficult to say with any certainty," he answered. "We're only guessing. The way you are. But if *Nero* is ready in time—"

"No," Melnik said. "We couldn't take the chance. If it wins, it doesn't help us. And if it loses, it hurts us. What kind of a gamble is that?"

"Perhaps if you entered it out of competition?"

"What's the sense of that?" Melnik wanted to know.

"It'd mean that there's only one American picture up for a prize. So they'd have to give it something," Shumsky said, lighting a cigar.

"But what about *Nero?* What do we get out of it?"

"Come on, be a sport," Hector Stavrides said, speaking up for the first time.

"What are you talking about? We got fourteen million dollars tied up in that thing!" Melnik returned.

"You be a sport," Stavrides said, "and I'll be a sport. You can have the Criterion deal."

"Christmas week?"

"Open end?"

"The whole deal."

"OK, then," Melnik said. "I'll be a sport."

"Any objections?" Shumsky asked. "Any discussion?"

There was none.

"All right," he said. "It'll be *Three for the Money,* for the money, and *Nero,* out of competition."

A waiter was clearing the dirty ashtray in front of Shumsky's place and replacing it with a clean one.

The men at the table agreed. Only Melnik had any comment. Shaking his head, he said, "Esther Williams . . . for crying out loud!"

After the breakfast meeting had broken up, the waiter who had changed the ashtray went across the room to report to Lester Monaghan who had been sitting at one of the booths, lingering over his coffee and reading a newspaper. The waiter told him of the decision of the MPAA board. Monaghan tipped him fifty dollars.

Then he called his broker and bought a thousand shares of Celestial Pictures.

When he left the room there was still half of his orange juice in the glass, but the waiter was used to that. Still, it was a shame. It was the most expensive orange juice in the world.

Merry was having dinner with Jim Waters at the Hollywood Brown Derby. They had been seeing a good deal of each other, ever since Waters had come out to Hollywood to polish the dialogue of the movie on which Merry was now working. Each had been delighted to find that the other was working on the picture, and each had felt the special pleasure that comes of a reunion between old friends—for in the uncertain and erratic world of show business, their friendship had endured for a relatively long time, which is to say that it antedated the project on which they were now engaged and was not merely a byproduct of the packaging of agents, producers, and the gods.

They demanded nothing from each other, and expected nothing but the pleasure of good company, good will, and intelligence. True, Waters was giving Merry books to read and helping her to continue on her own the education which her abrupt departure from Skidmore had interrupted, but this was something that each found charming and delightful. His intellectual sophistication and her naïveté complemented each other nicely. In a practical way, too, it was good, because they never lacked for something to talk about.

It had been perfectly natural, then, for Merry to tell Waters—before anyone else, even before Wemmick—about Venice, that *Three for the Money* had been entered for the festival, and that the studio was sending her along. Their dinner at the Brown Derby was something of a celebration. It was Waters' gesture of congratulations. He also used it as an opportunity for another lesson, and had brought along a copy of Ruskin's *Stones of Venice* for her to read.

She had never been to Venice before and had never been to a film festival before. She was thrilled by the prospect of her trip.

"This will tell you about Venice," Waters said. "Nothing will tell you about the festival. Each one is different. A festival is like any other human gathering. It depends entirely upon the people who are there. And all of them are there for differing reasons. It's like a dinner party, I suppose. All dinner parties are the same and all are different. There'll be a lot of movies, and a lot of parties, and a lot of press people. But all that will be the furniture. You can't tell what will happen. My advice to you is to see as much as you can of the city."

"I will," she said. "What is the city like?"

"It's unbelievable. Literally. Even while you're there, you will hardly be able to believe it. It has about it the insistent unreality of a stage set. But it's very beautiful. I suppose the unreality comes from the fact that so many of its associations are secondary. I mean, there you are in Venice, really in Venice, yourself, and yet you keep seeing the city, the buildings, the canals through other eyes—Ruskin's, Byron's, Wagner's, Henry James's, Thomas Mann's, George Eliot's, Napoleon's. I have never been able to stand in the Piazza without thinking of Napoleon's remark that this is the grandest drawing room in Europe. Everything is indirect that way. And yet, through the indirection, or perhaps because of it, everything gets to you."

He took the Ruskin up from the table, riffled through the pages, and read to her a passage he especially liked:

> . . . *round the walls of the porches there are pillars of variegated stones, jasper and porphyry, and deep-green serpentine spotted with flakes of snow, and marbles, that half refuse and half yield to the sunshine, Cleopatra-like, "their bluest veins to kiss" —the shadow, as it steals back from them, revealing line after line of azure undulation, as a receding tide leaves the waved sand; their capitals rich with interwoven tracery, rooted knots of herbage, and drifting leaves of acanthus and vine, and mystical signs, all beginning and ending in the Cross; and above them, in the broad archivolts, a continuous chain of language and of life*. . . .

Merry had been leaning her elbow on the table and her chin in the cup of her hand, listening in rapt attention. "It sounds marvelous," she said.

"You'll like it," he told her. "I know you will."

Later that night when she got into bed, she picked up the Ruskin to start reading it. Written on the flyleaf of the book there was an inscription from Waters: "For Merry, With much love, Jim."

She sighed, stared at the flyleaf for a moment, then turned the page, and began to read: "Since first the dominion of men was asserted over the ocean, three thrones, of mark beyond all others, have been set upon its sands. . . ."

Waters' description of the film festival as a dinner party was not far wrong. The only difference between the two occasions is probably that of scale. In Montreux, where the telegram had arrived at the villa of Meredith Houseman, it was an offer of diversion and relief.

Noni was bored, bored to death, by the quiet and the seclusion of their life in the lakeside villa. They had been arguing for two days about another invitation which Meredith had not wanted to accept. That invitation was not important, was trivial in fact, as Meredith explained.

"I hardly know Ayscue. I've met him three or four times. No more than that. What he wants us for is not us, not our company, but my celebrity. He collects names, gets them all together on that damned yacht of his, and cruises all around the Greek islands. He does it every year."

"Well, it might be fun," she said.

"Look, if you want to go on a cruise of the Greek islands, we'll go. If you want to go on a yacht, I'll charter a yacht. But not Ayscue's yacht."

But that offer had not satisfied her. What she wanted was the glamour and the glitter of a party, which was precisely what Meredith did not want, had tired of years before, and would not now consider. Which changed the subject of the discussion from the invitation to the more general one of the kind of life they were to lead together. She thought it was not unreasonable for him to indulge her, to do these things because they would amuse her, and to let her see and experience a little of what he had known and grown tired of.

He could see the fairness of that, but he could also see that there was a spuriousness, too. Now that he was married to Noni, he wanted less than ever to do such things. He was even afraid of them.

The discussion turned to an argument—not a spat or a quarrel, but a long, simmering argument, in which the speeches were silence and the rhetoric that of averted eyes and formal politeness.

The telegram was a godsend. Meredith *had* to go to Venice, and Venice would be even more fun than Ayscue's yacht. The cloud of antagonism was blown away. At least for a while.

To Harry Kleinsinger, the news that *Three for the Money* was going to be the American entry at Venice came as a reprieve, too, but of a different kind. The picture was completed, edited, scored, had been previewed and reedited. Now he was done with it. He was sitting in the study in his house in Bel Air, and on top of his truly beautiful Regency desk there was a pile of books, outlines, treatments, and scripts.

It was a bad time for Kleinsinger; after he finished a movie, it was always a bad time. The pressure was suddenly relaxed, and he felt useless and discarded. Worse than that, he was convinced that he would never be able to do it again, that he was finished, that his career was finished, and that it had all been worthless. Opposite him on the desk, at the other end of the tooled Florentine leather blotter, between the little gold clock from Cartier's and the onyx pen stand, was a curious *objet d'art,* a bird's nest made of worked gold wire, in which there was a small green jade egg. From time to time Kleinsinger reached for the egg, held it in his hand, or rolled it in his fingers, then put it back and picked up the next property in the pile. He leafed through the book, read a page here and there, then discarded it and picked the egg up again. He was holding the egg when Jim Twan, his Chinese houseboy, entered. He had the telephone on a tray.

"Call for you, Mr. Kleinsinger," he said.

"I'm not taking calls. You know that."

"I know that, sir. But this important call. This call you might take, I think," Jim said. He smiled and urged, "Very important. Very good news."

"All right," Kleinsinger said. He indicated that Jim might plug the phone into the wall jack. He picked up the phone from the tray and listened while Marty Golden told him about *Three for the Money* and Venice and offered his congratulations.

"Thank you, Marty," Kleinsinger said. "I'm honored. I really am. And thanks for calling."

He hung up. Jim unplugged the phone and took it away. Kleinsinger waited until he was out of the room, then reached for the egg again. He twisted the egg open, looked at the single cyanide pill it contained, then screwed it closed again and put it back into its nest.

For Freddie Grindell, in Rome, the news had quite the opposite effect. It wasn't a reprieve, but the extension of a sentence. He had already written the note, had put it in the envelope, and had sealed it. He had not mailed it, however. And he carried the carbon copy around with him, looking at it, putting it back into his breast pocket, and then, ten minutes later, whipping it out again and looking at it again. This had been going on for two days.

He was sitting at his desk, looking at the carbon, when the office boy handed him the telegram. He put away the carbon, looked at the telegram, and then crumpled it up into a ball. He cocked his arm, was about to throw the crumpled page into the wastebasket, but he changed his mind, put it on the desk, and smoothed it out again.

Once more, he looked at the carbon copy of the letter.

Celestial Pictures
Rome, Italy
July 14, 1959

Mr. Martin B. Golden
Executive Offices
Celestial Pictures
Hollywood, California, USA

Dear Mr. Golden:

For seventeen years I have worked hard and faithfully for Celestial Pictures. This term of service does not entitle me to any special favors, I know, but it does, I believe, give me the right to speak out upon the occasion of my resignation.

During the recent tour of your son, Martin B. Golden, Jr., of the European offices and studios of Celestial Pictures, it fell to me to guide and entertain him here in Rome. I was happy to be able to do so.

His interest in our operations and in the business of making motion pictures seemed to me, let me be candid, quite negligible. His knowledge of the business seemed rather less impressive than his interest. But what the hell! As the son of the president and major stockholder, he is entitled to a certain allowance (no pun intended).

He is not entitled, however, to demand of me that I fix him up with girls, that I pimp for him, or that I supply him with marijuana. Nor is he entitled to be angry with me for declining to perform these services and arrange these imagined perquisites for him. Least of all, I think, is he entitled to speak about me to my associates here in Rome, as well as in Paris and London, calling me, variously, a ''priggish fag'' and a ''buggering shitface.'' You ought to tell him that with the kind of money he has, there comes a certain vulnerability. I could sue him for half a million dollars in each of three countries, and probably collect a sizable judgment in each one.

My distaste for the proceedings, however, and my sense of loyalty to the company preclude any such action. But I am disgusted and angry. And I hereby offer my resignation.

Very truly yours,
Frederick R. Grindell

He took the letter, and the carbon, tore them in strips, and put the strips in the wastebasket. He lit them with a match and watched them burn.

It was not such a final gesture, however, as it might have seemed. He had, by this time, practically memorized the letter. Still, he would not mail it. He knew he would not. If he waited until the middle of September it would be absurd. And he was going to wait until the middle of September. He was going to go to the Venice festival. He had to go. Not for Martin Golden, or Celestial Pictures, but for himself. For Merry Houseman, and for Carlotta. And for himself.

To Raul Carrera, in Paris, it was an absurdity, nothing more or less. It was an honor to be nominated for Venice, an honor which he had very much wanted. But the thing one longs for is seldom the thing one gets. Or worse than that, one gets exactly what one wants, and finds out only then how different it is from what it had seemed to be.

"You look very glum about it," said Aram Kayayan, Carrera's backer and distributor in France.

"Of course. What do you expect? I know why they've put my picture up. So do you. It doesn't have a chance. It's just to insult Fresney."

It was perfectly true. Sismondi had invited Fresney's *Rubber Boots,* a film about the paratroopers in Indochina with which the government of France was not at all happy. The minister of culture had countered by nominating Carrera's *Château d'Arly,* not because he admired it, but because he thought it was a slick, commercial job, and therefore insulting to the Venice festival. It also was a high-handed demonstration of his own power—to pick any film he wanted—and of France's power, too. In order to send a film to Venice, as a matter of right, a country must produce fifty feature-length films a year. France did that and qualified. The minister of culture was exercising his right of nomination and using it to slap Sismondi in the face, to return the insult he thought he saw in Sismondi's invitation to the Fresney film. And to send a film of Carrera, an Argentinian expatriate, that would be the ultimate insult.

Carrera would not have minded so much, except for the additional nuisance of Monique Fourichon, the leading lady of *Château d'Arly*, and now Carrera's ex-wife. It would be very fatiguing to have to see her there, to have to appear with her.

"But you know," Kayayan said, "I could not have refused. And even if I could have refused, I would not have wanted to do so. It translates into money. For both of us."

"I know," Carrera said. "But I don't care."

"You don't care about money?" Kayayan asked, raising his bushy eyebrows and wrinkling his olive-colored forehead.

"We cannot all be Armenians," Carrera joked. "There must be other people for you to prey upon."

"Always you have the levity."

"And always you have the money. It's a nice arrangement."

"Look," Kayayan said. "Who knows what could happen. Sismondi invited *Rubber Boots*. But perhaps he will not have the nerve to give it a prize. And if that happens, our *Château* might get something."

"If it gets anything, Monique will get it."

"It will help the picture."

"The picture is done," Carrera said. "It is beyond help. It is no longer even interesting to me."

"But your next picture is interesting. And I am going to back your next picture, and therefore I am interested. And for me you will perhaps do a small favor. Go to Venice. Look at the Tiepolos and the Canalettos. Eat at the Graspo de Ua. Bathe in the Adriatic. Is it so very much to ask?"

"No, I suppose not. But it is so ridiculous. So very ironic."

"You find everything ironic. But perhaps it will be to your taste. It would be the irony of ironies, would it not, if you were to have a fine time. Accomplish something. See something. Have some great success."

"Shit."

"In Armenia we have a saying, 'Shit makes the grass grow.' "

"In that case," said Carrera, "the grass will be waist high. But all right. You win. I'll go."

CHAPTER

TWELVE

"Freddie," Merry asked lazily, "put some more oil on my back, would you?"

He reached over with the Bain de Soleil, squeezed an inch-and-a-half-long orange worm of the suntan oil onto her back, and then spread it around with his hands.

"Thanks," Merry said. "You're a dear."

He patted her affectionately on the rump and wiped the excess suntan preparation off on his legs.

"Are you thirsty?" he asked. "How about a lemonade?"

"Love one," she said.

He signaled to the beach boy and ordered lemonades.

Merry lay on the white cot, looking out at the steely flatness of the Adriatic. There was almost no one in the water.

"Doesn't anyone ever go in?" she asked.

"Rarely," Freddie Grindell answered. "The children sometimes. It's rather warm. And there are those little crabs. The Mediterranean is more fun to swim in."

"Really? Have I been there?" she asked. "The Mediterranean, I mean."

Freddie Grindell had met her at the airport, had steered her through customs and the gaggle of *paparazzi,* and had taken her into the *motoscofo* he had had waiting, and across the lagoon, past Murāno and around the tip of Venice to the Lido Excelsior. He had come up to her, clutched both her hands, beamed, and said, "Merry . . . But you don't remember me, do you? I'm Freddie Grindell. We used to play croquet in Montreux. But that was a long time ago. You were eleven or twelve, maybe."

She had not remembered him at first. She had believed him perfectly well, but she had not been able to recall the features—either his or those of anyone or anything of that time in Montreux. She had blotted it all out. All she remembered of that summer to which he referred was that she had been sent away. Grindell's delight in seeing her, however, was so evident and so sincere as to be infectious, and anyway, whether through good manners or good sense, he did not presume too far upon their old acquaintance. He pointed out the sights along the way on the boat ride to the hotel, saw her to her room, and introduced her to his assistant, Aileen Keats.

"Mrs. Keats will be sharing your suite," he told her, "and she'll be around as much or as little as you want her to be. She can translate for you during the interviews, show you around, help you dress—all that kind of thing. Mainly she is our gesture toward the proprieties and your tender years."

"You mean a chaperon?" Merry asked playfully.

"Not exactly," Mrs. Keats said. "Have a martini?"

She went to the service bar to make the drinks and explained, as she mixed the drinks, "This is a Latin country, and it looks better if there's someone like me around."

"If we seem to value you more," Freddie said, "everyone else will, too."

"Exactly," said Mrs. Keats.

"Well, thank you very much," Merry said.

They filled her in on the schedule for the evening. *Three for the Money* was the opening film of the festival, and it was to be shown that evening in the grand arena.

"The program is supposed to begin at nine o'clock," Grindell told her, "but it won't start until ten after. And there's a short first that'll take thirty-five minutes. So at nine forty-five you'll be making your entrance. There are no interviews scheduled for today. I thought you might be tired from your flight, so the afternoon is entirely free. You can go sightseeing, or lie on the beach—whatever you like."

"I think I'll save the sightseeing until tomorrow," she said. "I'm too tired and jumpy."

"Good idea," he said.

"I've made an appointment for you with the hairdresser at five," Mrs. Keats said. "If that's all right."

"Oh, fine. Yes, that's very good. Thank you. Why don't we just go for a swim then?" Merry asked.

"I think I ought to stay here and tend to the unpacking. I have to call the maid and have your dresses pressed. And see that things get put away properly," Mrs. Keats suggested.

"Thank you," Merry said. And then, "Mr. Grindell? Freddie? I really don't know what to call you."

" 'Freddie,' by all means."

"Freddie, would you like to go swimming, then?"

"Your pleasure is my pleasure," he said, "and my business, too. I'll meet you down there. Just ask for your cabana. It's all arranged."

So she had come downstairs and out onto the

smooth, raked sand where the rows of cabanas tamed the beach so that it looked like a street of some improbable suburb.

It was restful on the beach. Even the very boringness of the serried rows of cabanas, the too tidy sand, and the too still sea was welcome for its restfulness. Merry was tired. She had completed her second film in Hollywood and then had flown to Paris to buy clothes for Venice. It was good to lie there on the cot and bake in the sunshine. Grindell chattered on, amusingly, affably, trivially. It was as if he understood how tired she was and, out of consideration for her, demanded as little as he could. She listened to what he was saying and made appropriate responses, answering, "Yes," or "No," but she could do this with only a small portion of her mind. Mostly, she just lay there and felt the warmth of the sun. And the warmth of his goodwill, too.

She felt quite comfortable with him, and secure. The fact that she had played croquet with him had nothing to do with it. His tact and charm had more to do with it, but they were not all. No, it was something else.

It was only when she asked him to help her with the suntan oil and she felt him smearing the yellow goo on her back that she realized what it was. They were quite different, he and Waters, altogether different in many ways. But in one respect they were the same. Of course. Grindell was queer. She sensed it, and at the same time she felt her own relief and gratitude. She knew they would get on well, that the friendship that he professed and indeed demonstrated was disinterested and generous, and that . . .

But it was too complicated to think about, at least for now. The sun beat down upon her. She could feel it soaking into her back and pouring onto her head. Her brain felt like an egg cooking in a pan of butter. She would think about it some other time.

She got up, went down to the water's edge, stood on the wet sand, and let the wavelets lap at her feet. Then, out of a kind of frugality—for it seemed sad to waste the sea—she waded out, plunged in, swam a few strokes, and treaded water. It was tepid, but the tang of the salt was nice. She came back out. Grindell held out a towel for her. She dried herself off. Then she went back to her room to shower and to begin the long routine of getting ready for her entrance that evening.

At eight o'clock there was a knock on the door. Mrs. Keats opened it and Freddie came in. He was wearing a dinner jacket now, and under it a dress vest covered with beautiful jet beading.

"I thought I'd bring these around for you to look at," he said.

Merry was sitting at the small round table that room service had wheeled in, eating a steak sandwich and a green salad. She took the large brown manila envelope from Grindell and opened it. Inside there was a program for the evening's showing, covered in red satin. There was also a large white envelope. She opened that and found an invitation to a party.

> *Il Presidente dell'Azienda Autonoma Soggiorno Tourismo di Venezia Avv. Leopoldo Nazzari si pregia invitare la S.V. al ricevimento offerto in occasione dell'inaugurazione della XXIa Mostra Internazionale d'Arte Cinematografica che avrà luogo Domenica 23 Agosto 1959 alle ore 24 in Palazzo Ducale.*
>
> *Strettamente personale.*

There was also a copy of *Cinemundus,* the Italian film daily, or as it said on the logo, *"Araldo dello Spettacolo . . . Quotidiano."* There was a large picture of her on the second page and an article in Italian.

"We're all meeting in the lobby downstairs at nine o'clock," Grindell said. "Actually, that's what I'm supposed to tell you. It will really be about a quarter after.

So just as long as you are downstairs by then, it'll be all right."

"Fine," she said. "I'll be down in plenty of time."

It was an evening of spun sugar and champagne foam, insubstantial, delicious but unsatisfying, beautiful but fleeting. It was like a good moment with a kaleidoscope, when there is a fine pattern. The pattern falls into something else and is impossible not only to retrieve but even to recall. The insubstantiality of Venice, the stage-set appearance of it that Waters had told her about, was even more remarkable over here on the Lido. The hotel, for all its size, seemed to be nothing more than a huge sand castle that an ambitious child had put up for the tides to wash away.

Merry emerged from the elevator and into the lobby at the appointed hour to find Kleinsinger and Hugh Gardner and the producer, Arnold Finkel, waiting for her, along with Grindell, who was to be her escort. But the room seemed to be waiting for her, too. For all its size—it looked big enough to play polo in, if one cleared out the sofas and easy chairs—it had a temporary look that came perhaps from the enormous photographs that lined the walls, photographs of Giulietta Masina, Sophia Loren, Anna Magnani, Marina Vlady, Ingrid Thulin, Monica Vitti, Vittorio Gassman, Edward G. Robinson, Simone Signoret. And her father. And herself. It seemed as though the walls had been erected merely as a backdrop for the pictures, and the building merely as a support for the walls.

There were appropriate greetings, inquiries about the comfort and convenience of one another's flights, and the suggestion, from Finkel, that they go on out to the cars. It was only a distance of two blocks from the Lido Excelsior to the festival building, but there were four limousines in front of the hotel to take them there.

They did not go in through the front, but went around to a rear entrance in order to avoid the crowds that had gathered in front of the police barriers outside the plate-glass doors of the main entrance. Sismondi welcomed them and invited them into his office for champagne.

When the time came, one of Sismondi's assistants came in and led them down a hall and into the arena. Onstage, another of his staff was announcing them, and the audience turned to stare at them and applaud as they came into the hall to take their reserved seats, first Finkel and his wife, then Merry and Hugh Gardner, and finally Harry Kleinsinger, for whom there was a great burst of applause. He sat down, but the applause continued. He stood again and, like the conductor of a symphony orchestra, invited the others to stand. They did so. Then, after they sat down, the lights dimmed and *Three for the Money* flashed onto the screen.

Merry had seen the movie three times before. Kleinsinger and Finkel had seen it dozens of times. She sat there waiting for it to be over so that she could have a cigarette. It was interesting at first to see whether the laughs would come at the right places, and they did. She watched Kleinsinger relax, lean back in his chair, and close his eyes, either to rest or to run his own mental film, for which the laughs of the audience were the cues. Through the remainder of the picture Merry amused herself by reading the French subtitles, which she thought were less good then they should have been, too formal and too stiff. She wondered why the subtitles were in French, anyway. This was Italy, wasn't it? She leaned over to ask Grindell.

"It's the international language," he whispered. "Besides, it doesn't matter. Most of the people here understand English, anyway."

When the chase sequence came on, and Merry watched herself on the screen taking off her bra, she was surprised to hear whistles from several members of the audience. And then an outburst of applause. Kleinsinger leaned across Grindell to reassure her.

"Don't worry about it," he said. "They approve of you, my dear."

She hoped he was right. She was glad, at any rate, that it was dark in the auditorium and that no one could see her blushing.

There were cheers and applause when the picture was over. They waited for the aisles to clear and were led out finally through a special door that opened into Sismondi's office. That way they could avoid the crush of the marble lobby downstairs. They waited in Sismondi's office and drank more champagne. Kleinsinger seemed very pleased. Finkel was delighted. It was hard to tell what Gardner was thinking, but it was always hard to tell what he was thinking. The mask of his sophistication never seemed to crack. Merry was surprised, therefore, when he held his glass up to her, toasted her, and said, "I don't think I've told you this but I should have. You were fine there. Just fine. I'm sure you'll do all right."

"Thank you," Merry said.

When the crowd had dissipated enough so that they could get through it, they went back down to the rear door and out to the canal, where a water taxi was waiting to take them across to the Doge's Palace.

The boat went down the canal, made a left turn a little bit past the festival hall, and then went out into the lagoon. Lights twinkled in the blackness of the water, and the boat danced over the choppiness of the water, which was caused by the wake and wash of the other boats. As they entered the basin of San Marco, they passed the gorgeous private yachts of Panamanian registry that seem always to be tied up there on the right, and on the left, the beautiful Palladian San Giorgio Maggiore. They pulled up at the landing at San Marco, and a sailor threw a thick hawser around the big iron cleat while the pilot gunned the engine to keep the boat pushed up close to the *pontile*. They got out and walked through the aisle that the police had kept clear in the Piazzetta.

At the entrance of the Doge's Palace there was a major-domo in old Venetian livery, carrying a tall staff with a golden ball at the top of it, and Venetian policemen in their gaudy dress uniforms, who saluted them as they ducked through the small portal in the large iron gate.

They walked the few feet through the vaulted passage and then suddenly, on their right, was the *cortile,* the large courtyard, full of people, and lit by oil lamps that twinkled in the arches above. Under the Arco Foscari there was a long bar set up, and Grindell went off to get drinks. Liveried servants passed through the crowd with large silver trays of canapes. Merry had never seen anything like it in her life. It was absolutely gorgeous.

The party itself was rather dull, but the setting was so extravagantly elegant that Merry was just as pleased not to be too much distracted by the people who milled around her, drinking and talking. Occasionally she was introduced to Signor Somebody, or Señor So-and-so, or M. Something, or Herr von Someplace. They all said the same kind of things about how much they had liked her performance in the film, and in return she told them all how kind they were to say so. Then they turned away from her to talk with Gardner or Kleinsinger.

One of them, she could not remember which—the Argentine?—had pointed out the Sansovino statues of Neptune and Mars as being particularly admirable. They had been talking about how beautiful the courtyard was.

"Sansovino?" she asked. She knew the name, but his accent had bent it a little and had made it sound odd and unfamiliar.

"San-so-vi-no," he repeated slowly. "If not for him

this building would have been torn down. Palladio wanted to tear it down. And build a new one . . ."

"Oh?"

He seemed to be about to continue, but just then Gardner joined them. The conversation went off in another direction, and then Grindell took her arm and steered her to some new person to whom she had to say hello.

They did not stay very long. After a while Finkel announced that he was tired. Kleinsinger said that he was, too. They all went back to the boat and across the lagoon to the hotel.

Mrs. Keats was asleep. Merry could hear her snoring through the half-opened door of her bedroom. She did not wake her but undressed by herself, slipped into the new silk-and-lace nightgown she had treated herself to in Paris, and went to bed. She promised herself that tomorrow she would see Venice.

In a way it was entirely appropriate that it should have happened the way it did, and where it did—in Venice. The streets of Venice are a maze of passageways, alleys, gates, and tunnels that twist and turn, lead one across bridges and through buildings, and suddenly, abruptly, open up into some startling prospect. One turns the last corner, expecting to find, finally, a *cul-de-sac,* a dead end, and instead is greeted with a view of a palazzo, a church, a canal, or simply an open *campo* in which two great gray cats are asleep in the sun on the pediment of an old wellhead.

Merry did not get to go sightseeing the following morning after all. There were interviews first, from eight-thirty until eleven. People from the trade press, from *The New York Times,* from *The Sunday Times* of London, and from *L'Express* all wanted to see her. After the last of them had left, she thought that she could go, but Mr. Finkel called to ask her to lunch, so the touring had to be put off a few hours more. To compound the disappointment, Freddie told her that he had to meet a plane that afternoon, so it would be Mrs. Keats who would be showing her around. But then, twisting back the way the streets do, the plans changed again. The man whom Freddie was supposed to meet had not made the plane after all. Freddie was free to go with her. He had left a note in her room to tell her this. She called him and they met in the lobby, and took the *vaporetto* to San Marco to begin their sightseeing.

Freddie Grindell was as pleasant company as he had been the day before. He was not particularly knowledgeable about the history and the art of Venice, but neither did he seem to be merely bored and patiently enduring their tour. Anyway, Merry had her *Guide Bleu.*

They went into San Marco and bathed in the gold light that washed down from the mosaics, stared at the Pala d'Oro, and then went outside for coffee at Florian's before addressing themselves to the Doge's Palace, of which they had seen only the courtyard the night before. Merry could not remember later which painting it had been, or even in which room they had been standing. Probably it was a Veronese. Anyway, there was in the painting one of those emblematic nudes: justice or peace or virtue was offering something to or praising or greeting Venice, but Merry made some comment to Grindell about how absurd she thought it was for there to have been whistles the night before at the screening of the picture. She remembered the comment, because that had been the random turning that their conversation had taken, the point at which a lost walker in Venice remembers where he last knew where he was. From that casual allusion, their talk turned, naturally enough, to that day months before when she had filmed the sequence, and the interview with Jocelyn Strong that had produced that horrid article. She mentioned this to Grindell because, after all, he was in the business, was a publicist, and more important, seemed to be a friend. She told him about the spite of the story and how it was a piece of personal revenge. She even mentioned Jocelyn Strong's old connection with her father.

"Yes, I know," Grindell said.

"You do?"

"I was there. I mean, not right, not actually *there*. But I was around at the time. A sad business."

"Yes," Merry said. "I mean, I sometimes wonder how different my life might have been if it hadn't happened."

"She was a wonderful person," Grindell said.

"Who? Mother? I didn't know you knew her."

"Oh, yes. Not well, unfortunately. I . . . I met her a couple of times. In Paris and in Switzerland."

"Where? Paris? But she's never been to Paris. And I know she's never been to Switzerland. She lives in Los Angeles."

"Lives in . . ." Grindell began. Then he stopped. "I'm sorry," he said. "I . . . I must be confused."

"But how strange," Merry said.

Grindell said nothing. He seemed to want to drop it, and Merry would have been willing to do so, too, but something kept nagging at her, bothering her. She was no longer looking at the paintings on the walls or the armor in the cases, but going over in her mind what he had said, trying to remember it sentence by sentence. Then she found the thing that had stuck, that hung on still, like a burr.

"What do you mean?" she asked. "What were you talking about? You said you were there."

"What did your father tell you?"

"Nothing," Merry said. "Or almost nothing. I heard about it from my mother."

"Heard about what from your mother?"

"The . . . well, I don't even know what to call it. It

wasn't an affair. Encounter, I guess. Between Jocelyn and my father. It happened just after I was born."

"I see," Grindell said.

"You see? I thought you said you knew about it."

"Apparently not. It was a long time ago. One gets confused. Things blur."

His explanation was not satisfactory, but the conversation might have ended there, might have gone no farther than that, except for the fact that Merry was no longer interested in inspecting the paintings and the architecture and the sculpture of the old Venetian dukes but wanted to sit down. She was tired. She asked Freddie if there wasn't some place they could go for a drink. He took her out and along the Riva degli Schiavoni to the Danieli, where they sat in the lounge in easy chairs and had gin and tonic. Perhaps it was because she was sitting down now, and was resting. Or possibly it was the feeling of incompleteness about their earlier conversation, the sense that there had been something amiss. Anyway she went back to it, even if only glancingly and obliquely.

"I sometimes try to imagine what my mother would have been like if she had stayed with my father. Better than she was, than she is now. And better for me. It's odd the way these things happen."

Grindell said nothing, and that in itself was peculiar, for he had been so responsive, so easy to talk to until now. But now he was thinking about something else. She went on, nevertheless, because she had started, and because it felt good to talk about it. If he was only half listening, she thought, then so much the better.

"What I don't understand," she went on, "is the vindictiveness of it. I mean, I don't know what happened between them, between Jocelyn and my father, or how it was. But to have kept a grudge that way for nearly twenty years . . . It's inhuman!"

"It wasn't twenty years," Grindell said, after a moment.

"What do you mean? It happened when I was born. I'll be twenty next week."

"It wasn't twenty years," he repeated. "I told you, I was there. In Switzerland. I may as well tell you. I wasn't thinking of your mother, but of Carlotta, your stepmother."

"What do you mean?"

"Your father has never said anything to you? Never told you anything about it?"

"No! About what?"

"They met again, your father and Jocelyn. In Montreux. About eight years ago. You had just been sent back to the States to school."

"I remember that. That's the only thing I do remember. That I was sent away."

"Well, it was a week or two after that. Jocelyn came down from Paris. To interview your father. I was there."

"You were there? But that . . . that was when Carlotta drowned."

"Yes."

Merry thought of it for a moment. Despite the heat of the afternoon and the mugginess of Venice in August, she suddenly felt cold. She had to put her icy glass down on the little table that separated them.

"Because of Jocelyn?" she asked. "Because of Jocelyn and my father?"

Grindell took a deep breath, licked his lips, looked at her for a moment, and then said, "Not entirely. That wasn't all of it. I suppose there's never just one reason. But that was part of it. Most of it."

"Oh. I see."

Merry finished her drink and then asked him to take her back to the Excelsior. They went out through the side door of the Danieli to the little pier where the water taxi that runs back and forth between the two hotels was waiting. On the way across the lagoon Merry stared out at the wake of the boat. Then she turned to

Grindell and asked him, "But why? It still doesn't make any sense. After so many years to hold a grudge like that."

"I don't think it was years," Grindell said. "I think it was three or four days."

"That's impossible. I . . . I don't understand."

"I think she went to see him. Mind you, I'm only guessing, but I've been in this business a long time, and this kind of nastiness from women reporters . . . well, it's happened before."

"What has? What are you talking about?"

"Your father was engaged then, wasn't he? To Noni?"

"Yes."

"Well, I think she went out to see him, and I think she probably made a pass. And I think he turned her down. And that's why the article was the way it was."

Merry didn't say anything. There was nothing to say. She only wished she did not have to have her hair combed out again in two hours, dress again, and go downstairs for Finkel's party at the Chez Vous.

Even worse than the dinner, however, was what followed it. Merry was able to get through the dinner perfectly well. She could have got through a hundred dinners. All that was required of her was that she apply herself to the business of being pleasant and lively. But that at least was something to do. After the dinner, the next day, and the day after that there was nothing for her to work at, no way in which she could apply herself, no possible technique for dealing with . . . nothing. She had not expected that the machinery of the festival, which had kept her so busy ever since she had arrived in the city, would suddenly release her, spew her out, now that she was processed, and leave her so abruptly to her own devices. But there it was. There were so many films to get through, and so many actors and actresses, directors, cinematographers, producers, and writers to be feted and interviewed, so many business deals to be made, that there was suddenly the prospect of days to go through and nights, too, in which nothing was demanded of her, or wanted. She had been caught up, as in the talons of a great bird, and now that she was put down she was, she told herself, relieved, but she was as much depressed as anything. Of all the things she needed or wanted, the last was leisure to digest and consider what Grindell had told her about her father and Jocelyn, and Carlotta.

So, to keep busy, she toured. She did not go to the starred attractions which her *Guide Bleu* recommended, but preferred to wander in the less frequented quarters of the city, where the moldering buildings seemed to be responsive to her own mood. A tenement or a warehouse in any other city in the world is, after all, necessary and functional, and one accepts that and passes it by without thinking at all of its aesthetic qualities. But in Venice, that absurd city built on the water with such a sublime disregard for function and necessity, there is no other criterion but the aesthetic, and all the great buildings proclaim it anyway, with their grace, or their extravagant grotesquerie, or their diffident charm. But because of the insistence of the glamorous ones, of the beautiful ones, of the haughty ones, the others—the merely necessary, the shabby, the ugly ones—are all the more sad. They are ugly women who are not merely on a bus or a subway or working in a field, but who have been brought by some whimsical cruelty to a ball, where they huddle in the darker corners of the room trying not to be noticed.

To these dark corners and to these assemblages of architectural wallflowers Merry repaired, finding in the melancholy they inspired a kind of relief. Here was an outlet into which the swamp of her depression could drain and through which her mood could flow out into the lagoon and the sea. She ate in workmen's *trattorias,* where the wine was served in little blue-and-white bowls, and where she could get a three-course *prezzi fisso* meal for six or seven hundred lire—or about a dollar. She walked, not caring particularly where she was going, and not bothering about the maps and the guidebooks except when she felt tired and wanted to find out where she was. Then she looked for a church, found the church on the little map she carried, and took her bearings from that. When she wanted to sit, she would either go into one of the churches or, if it was early afternoon when they were all closed, would go to the Grand Canal and get on one of the water buses, ride for a while, and watch the city floating by. No one bothered her. No one noticed her. The festival and the Lido seemed to be a thousand miles away.

The *vaporetto* stopped with a lurch as it hit the *pontile*. A knot of passengers got off, and others got on. The boat started off again. Merry was staring at the buildings and was almost entirely unaware of the people around her.

"Did you have a chance to look at the Sansovinos?" a voice asked.

She looked around, but did not see anyone she recognized, and assumed it must have been a fragment of conversation that the whimsy of wind and water had broken off and carried to her ear.

"Miss Houseman?" the same voice insisted.

She looked again.

"I beg your pardon," she said to the man beside her.

He smiled pleasantly. "Raul Carrera," he said, bowing his head slightly. "We met at the Palazzo Ducale."

She was not entirely pleased to have her solitude thus interrupted, but she returned his smile and admitted, "No, I never did get to see them very closely."

"A pity," he said. "But they have been there for a long time. There will be other chances."

He continued to make inconsequential conversation that demanded no answers. She remembered meeting him at the palace. He had been the only person she had noticed, was the only person she remembered at all. But then, it had not been a very lively party. She looked him over as he talked. He was wearing a beige sweater and beige slacks that matched. It could have been, on another man, an effeminate outfit, but he wore it well. He was not tall, or did not seem so as he sat beside her. He gave the impression of compactness, like a light heavyweight, powerful and wiry. His hair was cut very short, and the sun had bleached it while it had darkened his face. The effect was to emphasize the whiteness of his teeth, which called attention, in turn, to his mouth, his full lips and the rather contradictory tight lines at the corners.

But even as she recognized all this, noting it and taking it in, she thought, What the hell, who cares? Perhaps the final absurdity of the motion-picture business was that nearly every man one met in it was attractive, was an idol of some kind or other. Carrera, of course, was a director who had come to France to escape the restraints of Argentinian mores. As an expatriate he was more French than the French, and was the embodiment of the cult of French nonchalance that had grown up with the cynicism of postwar France.

He was still talking, as the *vaporetto* chugged through the water, now about the quality of the light in Canaletto's painting of the prospect which was at that moment before them. Quite without intending it, she said what she was thinking—not about Canaletto but about him, and Venice, and everything.

"But who cares?" she asked.

"I beg your pardon?"

"I'm sorry," she said, "but I'm sick of it. I really am sick of it. I fled from the Lido and the festival, and I'm fleeing now from Sansovino and Canaletto and Veronese and the whole pack of them. I've been walking in the slums all morning—"

"But why? Why the slums?"

"Because they are so sad here."

"Ah, but that is very romantic."

"Putting it in a category," she said, "does not make it go away."

"No, of course not, but it does qualify sometimes. It does shed light."

"That's very clever," she said. "But I'm sorry. I'm tired of cleverness, and I'm tired of Venice. It's no more real than I am."

He seemed to consider this for a moment. He looked away, then looked back at her. "You are as real as anyone," he said. "Do you think that the common people, those people whom you have been admiring, living in their picturesque slums, are any more real than you? Do you understand how they go to the movies and look at you, and through you exist? For them, you are real. Their lives are dull and dry and arid. And it is through you that they see some glimmer of hope, of joy, of being."

"No, no," she said. "You're talking about real art. The movies that I make and you make don't do that kind of thing—"

"But they do," he said. "That is the distressing part. They do. The quality—the intellectual or artistic quality—of the films is almost irrelevant. The crucial thing is only the degree to which they can identify, the degree to which they can project and see themselves as they would like to be. If they can do those things they can believe the picture, and if they can believe in it, then it is a good picture."

"How very depressing."

"Oh, yes, but I try not to think about it."

"Then why do you make movies?"

"To amuse myself," he said.

"An expensive hobby, isn't it?"

"No, not at all. I have backers. And I have been lucky. My films have been successful, but that has never been the point. I have never sought that. If they ceased to amuse me, I would cease to make them."

"I don't understand," she said. "Why do you do it? Why does it amuse you?"

"If you really must know, I do it because I am a kind of voyeur. All directors are voyeurs, as I think all actors and actresses are exhibitionists. I noticed the very interesting photographs that appeared of you in *Lothario* magazine recently. And it seemed to me that in those photographs you were the paradigmatic cinema actress. It was a great show of availability, which was only a show, and it is the showing itself that is interesting. What you object to, perhaps, about the art of the Venetians is the absence of any sexual content. Films, after all, are a living medium. We concern ourselves with style, but it would be hypocritical to deny the primary erotic element of the making of the movies and of their appeal to the audience."

"Perhaps," she said.

"You don't think so?"

"I don't know. I'm thinking about it."

And she was thinking about it, or not just about it but about him, too. "The mind," he said, intruding on and descanting upon her thoughts, "is the least commonly acknowledged erogenous zone."

It was true. She realized that in the space of their short conversation he had become immensely attractive to her. She wondered if she interested him at all, and the novelty of the challenge to her to interest a man and to do it in an intellectual way was almost as intriguing as he was himself. He was no corn-fed American boy to be seduced merely by the promise of her fair white body, nor was he a businessman who saw her as a commodity, nor a hungry young actor on the make, like Tony, who saw her as a passport to the great world. He was an Old World man, experienced, intelligent, and more of a celebrity than she was herself. She wondered whether she had what it took to capture his fancy as he had captured hers. For all her drifting around, she really knew so little of the world—and especially the world of the mind.

What she did not reckon on, however, was the vulnerability of Carrera, as a European intellectual, to the very shortcomings she felt so acutely. He saw them not at all as shortcomings but as American innocence. As far as he was concerned, she was naïve, she was a primitive, but there was enough about her of spirit and intelligence, enough originality and spontaneity, to appeal to him as the blank canvas appeals to an artist, as the block of marble, cold and inert, appealed to Pygmalion, as indeed, years before, Clothilde had appealed to him, calling out to him to educate her, to shape her, to create her.

The *vaporetto* was approaching the Accademia bridge.

"Excuse me," Carrera said, "but I must get off here. I'd invite you along except that your mood does not seem to be one in which to visit the paintings of the Accademia. Are you attending the film this evening?"

She had no idea whether he wanted her to say yes or no.

"I'm not sure," she said.

"In any case, will you dine with me? At seven. If you decide that you want to see the film afterward, there will be time enough."

She was delighted and surprised, and she said, "Yes. Yes, I'd like that."

He nodded again, the same nod with which he had introduced himself. "I am honored," he said. "I shall look forward to it. I'll ring you at the hotel."

The boat lurched to a stop. She watched him as he hopped across to the worn wood of the *pontile*. He did not look back.

Merry continued on the *vaporetto* to San Zaccaria,

where she changed for a boat to the Lido. Carrera spent forty minutes in the Accademia, but could not concentrate. He gave it up, then went out and took a water taxi to the Gritti, where he was staying because he preferred it to the barrenness of the Lido. He went up to his suite, poured himself a stiff brandy and soda, and sat down in a chair by the window to drink his drink and to look through the photographs in his album. It was a large, folio-size album, bound in lizard skin, and it locked with one of those luggage locks with wheels and a combination. He dialed the three numbers, took a sip of the brandy, and opened it, thinking, even as he did so, that he might have to get a new one for Merry. It was not an unpleasant idea.

Merry had forgotten that she had promised to have dinner that evening with Freddie. When she got to her room and told Mrs. Keats that she would be dining with Carrera that evening, Mrs. Keats reminded her of her other engagement and suggested quite tactfully that one of them ought to call Mr. Grindell.

"Oh, dear," Merry said. "I forgot all about it. I'll call him. Thank you."

She picked up the phone and asked for Grindell's room.

"Freddie? Merry."

"Well, hello," he said. "How was your afternoon?"

"Just fine," she said. "But I'm afraid I've done something dreadful."

"Oh?"

His tone was perfectly casual, but Merry knew that his mind had shifted gears and in that instant he had become the press agent again, waiting for whatever mess it was that she was about to drop in his lap for him to fix—bailing out, or buying off, cajoling, smoothing, soothing, hushing up . . .

"Well, actually, it's not *that* terrible."

"Yes?" he asked. "What can I do for you?"

"You can forgive me. I met Raul Carrera on the *vaporetto* and agreed to have dinner with him. It just slipped my mind that I had promised to have dinner with you. Could you be a dear and forgive me? Or a double dear and give me a rain check?"

"Well, we could have dinner tomorrow night, couldn't we?"

"Oh, fine. Yes. Thank you."

"But I'll tell you," he said. "I drive a hard bargain. Why don't we have a drink this afternoon?"

"Love to," Merry said. "But . . . I mean, do I have time? I have to be combed out again, and I have to dress."

"Just a quickie. Come on now. Having broken my heart, it's the least you can do."

"OK," she said. "Sure."

"I'll meet you in the bar then, in ten minutes."

"I'll be there," she said, and hung up.

Grindell held on to the disconnected phone for a moment before he hung up. He was not looking forward to this. He was not looking forward to it at all. It would not be easy. But if it was necessary it would have to be done. For her sake. He owed it, if not to Merry, then to Carlotta, or to the memory of Carlotta. He owed it to himself.

He met Merry in the bar and asked Merry what she wanted to have.

"I don't know," she said. "I just had a gin and tonic."

"Then have a vermouth and soda. By the time the vermouth catches up to the gin, you'll have a martini."

He ordered a vermouth and soda for her and a double Scotch for himself. He had had enough time between their telephone conversation and their meeting in the bar to be able to plan a little bit. And therefore, he did not ask her about her day or about her meeting with Carrera. He did not want to take the initiative until he had to. In all probability she would mention Carrera herself, without any prompting from him.

That far at least he was on sure ground. She repeated her apology and explained again how she could ask him to change their dinner date to another night because she knew him well enough to do so. She had only just met Carrera that afternoon on the *vaporetto*. "Or actually, I guess I met him before that. At the party. At the Doge's Palace. You introduced us. But I had forgotten about it."

"Well, that'll teach me," Grindell said. "If I go around introducing you to men that way, I guess I deserve to eat alone."

"Oh, don't be like that about it. I mean, really."

"I'm just joking," he said.

The waiter brought their drinks. He raised his glass to her and said, "Have a good time."

"Thank you," she said. And they drank to that.

"Have you ever seen any of Carrera's films?" Grindell asked after a moment.

"A couple."

"Weird, aren't they?"

"Yes," she said. "They are."

"And judging from what I hear, so is he."

"Oh, Freddie, don't be catty."

"I'm not," he said. "I'm honestly not. I'm thinking of you."

"I'm a big girl, Freddie. I've been allowed to cross the street by myself for years."

"He's not a street. He's a drag strip."

"Oh, Freddie!"

"Don't misunderstand me, Merry. Please. I'm not telling you not to have dinner with him or not to have a good time with him. I'm just suggesting that you ought to be careful. Please don't be angry with me."

"I couldn't be angry," she said. "I think it's very sweet of you to warn me this way. But it won't work.

There isn't anything that you could tell a girl to make her more interested in someone than that she ought to be careful. 'Beware of the dark stranger,' and all that. It's . . . so quaint."

"I know," Freddie said. "But I mean it. And how else can I say it? He's a strange, sick man. And I don't want you to get hurt."

"Don't worry, I'll be a good girl," she said.

"OK," he said.

He couldn't push it any more. If he insisted beyond the point where she was merely amused, he would risk losing all the lines of communication between them. He had not told her anything yet, really. But he had warned her, had at least suggested that she should watch herself, and while it was perfectly true that such a warning might appear to make Carrera all the more desirable, still he could not think that his words would fail to carry any weight at all.

She finished her drink and ran off to have her hair combed out. After she left him he sat down again and ordered another whiskey. He would be having dinner with her the following night. Perhaps she would tell him then what her evening with Carrera had been like. It still might come to nothing. There was still that hope. But if it didn't, what else could he do?

The waiter brought him his second Scotch, which he downed in one fast, searing gulp.

If it came to that, he could speak to Meredith. Maybe her father could tell her, could warn her, could stop her. To leave it to her father would not just be passing the buck, he thought. But in the next instant he challenged that, testing the thought, trying to decide whether he believed it or not. He was not at all sure that he did. Perhaps he should have been more direct with Merry. Maybe he shouldn't have contented himself with vague insinuations but should have come right out with the whole ugly truth of what he knew. And perhaps he should not have attributed his knowledge to mere rumor, but should have identified the source—Clothilde Chaumont, Carrera's first wife. Clothilde had not told Grindell himself, but he could have lied about that. There was no need to go into the provenance of the story too elaborately.

Or perhaps there was. Perhaps he should have done that. Possibly he should have told her how Clothilde had told Luis, and how Luis had told him, and how he believed Luis because he had lived with him for nearly a year.

But there was still time for that if it became necessary. He would see what she had to say when they finally did have dinner together.

But Merry was not able to have dinner with Grindell the following night either. Meredith and Noni had arrived a day before Grindell expected they would, had checked into the Danieli, and had invited Merry to have supper with them. The next night was that of the showing of *Nero*. Several times that day Grindell had had his hand on the phone and had been about to call Meredith Houseman to tell him what was bothering him and that Merry had been seeing Carrera, but he couldn't do it.

Besides, this was hardly the time to bother Houseman. He would be busy with his own interviews, and thinking about his own picture. Even if he was inclined to listen to Grindell and concern himself with what Grindell saw as a danger to Merry, he would not be able to do anything about it until the next day. So why not wait? And therefore Grindell waited.

He was right to have done so. For two reasons. The first was an invitation to a party at Barbara Ford's Palazzo Leporelli. Merry had been invited and she wanted Freddie to come along as her escort. Which was fine with him. He knew that Meredith Houseman would be there, too. It was the event of the festival.

Sismondi's ascetic notions about the way in which a festival should be conducted—it was even rumored that he wanted to get rid of black ties—had caused a predictable enough reaction in the opposite direction on the part of the *haut monde* of Venice, which would, if Sismondi was not willing to offer gewgaws and frippery, be perfectly willing and entirely able to supply its own. Therefore Mrs. Ford's anti-festival party at her palazzo.

For Grindell this promised to be an ideal opportunity for a conversation with Meredith. And a conversation was now in order, too. Grindell had noticed Merry's reaction the evening of the showing of *Nero* when they had passed Carrera in the lobby of the Excelsior. Carrera had been with a woman, and not just with her but in animated conversation, and evidently enjoying himself. The woman had been probably in her early forties, but marvelously chic, wonderfully elegant, beautifully turned out. Merry had recoiled from her glimpse of the two of them as if from a blow. It was more than she could have told Grindell had they had their scheduled supper and had she been in as talkative a mood as he had hoped for.

Grindell finished tying his tie, and was about to leave his room to call for Merry when he felt a sharp pain in his stomach. He went back to his bathroom, took a pill, drank a glass of water, and put three more pills in a little silver box. He tucked the pillbox in his pocket, and then went to the elevator to call for Merry. He was hoping that on the ride across the lagoon to the Danieli, where the Housemans were staying, she might say something to him, might confirm what he already pretty much knew. But she did not. She was very quiet. He could not even tell whether she was thinking or brooding or looking out at the lights of the city. Or for that matter, for all he knew she might be just looking forward to the party.

She was, but not in a way that Grindell could have imagined. She was thinking partly about Carrera and the splendid evening they had had together. They had gone first to Harry's Bar where he had ordered her a Roger, which was a decoction of gin, orange juice, lemon juice, and a blenderized peach. And then they had gone to the Graspo de Ua for a superb dinner, after which he had telephoned his own gondolier, who had met them at the Rialto Bridge and taken them around the canals in the moonlight. Carrera had been charming, witty, amiable, but, for all Grindell's absurd warnings, absolutely gentlemanly. Not only had he failed to live up to Grindell's characterization, he had even been less forward then Merry would have liked. She had wondered what in the world Freddie had been talking about. Carrera had been married twice. And anyway, she had felt when she had been with him that she was with a man. He had been like Freddie in some ways, charming and fun to be with, but there had been an added edge of excitement to it, too. Besides, had it been just that, had it been only queerness, Grindell would have been more pointed and less worried. She was thinking about their evening, and at the same time thinking of him with that woman in the hotel lobby, and how angry and hurt she had been.

It had been quite irrational, but her first association, the first thing that had popped into her head, had been her father—that was natural enough, for she had been with him and Noni at the time—and what Grindell had told her about Carlotta's death. If after only one evening with Carrera she could be so much affected by the sight of him sitting at a table in a bar and having a drink with a woman, then what could it have been like for Carlotta, married to her father and discovering him with Jocelyn.

It had been because of that peculiar connection that her mind had made that they were all going to the party. Barbara Ford was an American tin heiress, and one of her parties was hardly Meredith Houseman's idea of a pleasant way to spend an evening. But the invitation had come in, and Noni had been eager to go. They had argued about it, albeit in a restrained way, because Merry had been there. But it had been Merry who had decided the issue, urging her father to go, suggesting that they all go, and volunteering that she could take Freddie Grindell along as her escort. She had done this only to mention Grindell's name to her father, to throw Grindell up to her father, to see how he would react.

"Grindell?" he had asked. "Why him?"

"Why not? He's been very pleasant to me. Really very sweet. He told me that we played croquet once, in Montreux. And he was very kind and soothing about the *Pulse* story and told me not to worry about Jocelyn Strong. He said almost the same things you did."

The barbs had been sharp enough. Distracted, perhaps, by this allusion, Meredith had given up on the question of the invitation or had decided that, yes, he would go, in order to change the subject, setting Noni off on a bubbly monologue about what she would wear.

And therefore she was in the *motoscafo* with Grindell, disembarking at the Danieli, about to join her father and her—for God's sake—stepmother for an evening of gaiety and fun at the Palazzo Leporelli. Grindell called from the house phone and they went up to Meredith's suite for a drink. Meredith had a split of champagne for himself, but he had a well-stocked bar for guests and reporters, and Noni made drinks. Nobody said much.

"Well," Meredith said at last, as he drained his tulip glass, "I guess we might as well get it over and done with. Let's go, shall we?"

They went downstairs, and Meredith had the doorman engage a gondola for the short ride up the Grand Canal to the dock of the Ford palazzo.

It was a peculiar party. It was large, but it didn't seem so because of the way it was spread out through all the various rooms and apartments of the huge

Renaissance palace. Merry decided not two minutes after she had arrived that it would all be deadly dull and that she would leave early.

But that was such a depressing idea that she set about having a good time, or if not a good time, then at least a lively one. She would not admit to herself that Carrera had bothered her at all. No, she would have fun. She drank several martinis as fast as she could manage without being too conspicuous about it. And having been more or less picked up by two very svelte-looking Italians, Guido Something and Marco Something, she continued to drink, thinking that she might be able to find a bedroom with a mink coat in it. Not that she especially wanted to do this, really. But it would make her feel good to have put down her father, and Carrera, and the whole depressing bunch of them.

But she was not very far along in her program when she noticed that her father was drinking more champagne than usual. She did not know about his conversation with Grindell near the bar, when Meredith had asked Grindell why he had told Merry about Carlotta's suicide. Grindell had explained that he had thought Merry knew about it, had assumed so from what she had said about Jocelyn, but . . . "Well, I didn't know about Jocelyn and you and your first wife."

"I don't see what difference that makes. I don't have to report to you."

"I'm not saying that you do. It was a mistake, that's all. I'm sorry."

"That's not enough, Grindell. It's just not enough. I could break you. I could ruin you, do you know that? Your only hope is that I might decide it just isn't worth the bother."

"Thanks a lot."

"Don't mention it."

And Meredith had turned from the bar, taking another glass of champagne, and had gone back to watch

Noni twisting with some stranger in front of the bandstand, where a combo was blaring out the current crop of identical songs.

Merry was only half attending to the flattery of Guido, or was it Marco? With the rest of her mind she was wondering about her father, wondering why he was drinking, and whether it had anything to do with Noni. But then Grindell came up to her and said that he had to leave. He had violent stomach pains.

"I've taken my pills, but it still hurts. I think I'd better go back to the hotel and go to bed. I'm sorry."

"Shall I come with you?"

"No, I'll be all right," he said.

"Are you sure . . ."

"I'm fine. But will you be all right?"

"Guido and Marco here will take care of me. And after all, my father's right here. It's perfectly all right. Don't be silly."

He thanked her, blew her a kiss, and then went out to hail a water taxi. He did not ask to be taken to the hotel, but to a hospital. He lay in the bottom of the boat, curled up in a ball, around a burning center of pure pain.

And there was Merry free of Grindell and mildly curious about the unfamiliar sight of her father drunk. Well, not drunk, maybe, but on the way. A little unsteady and a little thick-tongued. She assumed it was Noni's doing, somehow, and didn't especially care. But it was interesting enough so that she stopped drinking herself. It would be more amusing to watch him instead. Besides, she had had nearly enough anyway.

Neither Guido nor Marco seemed to mind the fact that she was hardly paying any attention to them, and that made them even less interesting than they had been before. But her father, who laughed too loudly now and too high, was fascinating. It was curious, Merry thought, that she could watch him this way, clinically, coldly, and yet not so coldly, either. Because she was, after all, fascinated. She wondered what it could have been that Noni had done to knock him off the wagon this way.

And then it happened. There was no connection, no relevance, nothing at all but blunt, stupid coincidence. And yet a forest fire is not the random match thrown from the careless hand. Not just that. It is the result of the coincidence of the match and the dry weather, the tinder-dry woods and grass ready for burning, all but demanding that the match be thrown, waiting for it, tempting it.

Some stupid starlet, some young Italian hopeful, on a dare that had turned into a bet (albeit of 50,000 lire), suddenly started to take her clothes off. The musicians never missed a beat. But there was a lull in the conversation, and Barbara Ford, veteran hostess that she was, knew that it was a crucial moment in the progress of her party. Such an incident either makes or breaks an evening. And she was determined not to be broken by the antics of this desperate, deluded, and, as it turned out, very attractive girl. The trick was to make light of it somehow. And she turned the trick, with all the cleverness of all the decorated costume balls she had ever been to, with all the intricacy of all the carved ivory swizzle sticks she had ever twirled in her champagne glasses, with all the lightness of all the balloons she had ever popped with a deft, simple thrust of a lit cigarette.

"My dear," she said, "do put something on. Here, have one of these." And she offered to the naked starlet one of her *commedia dell'arte* masks. The collection was worth thousands of dollars, but what was that to the possibility of a ruined evening? She gave the girl one of the Columbine masks. Dutifully the girl put it on.

"What a delicious idea!"

"Divine!"

"How too, too cute!"

But it was not the comments such as these that gratified Barbara Ford. Compliments are easy to make, but hard to rely on. Like the currencies of various Latin American countries in which she had holdings. What pleased her was the reciprocity in kind. . . . Two other women took masks, smiled, and retired to undress. They returned to the *sala* entirely naked except for their beautiful masks. And it was hard to tell which of them was which.

The party continued. Various other volunteers presented themselves, materialized, took a mask off the wall or out of the case, and slipped off for a moment to turn up again as Pierrot, or Harlequin, or Pulcinella, or Pierrette, or Columbine. That some of the guests did not bother, were unwilling to display themselves, or were reluctant to leave even for a few minutes for fear they might miss something, only made it all the jollier. Nothing emphasizes nudity so much as the presence of a few people in dinner dress.

Still, there was a certain disadvantage in remaining clothed. The nudity was anonymous, or pseudonymous because of the masks. But to be dressed was to be known; one's face was exposed, mercilessly bare. For Guido and Marco it hardly made any difference. They hardly had faces. But for Merry it became increasingly uncomfortable to hold out, to remain where she was on a red-and-white candy-striped satin sofa in a lime-green cocktail dress. She excused herself, took a mask from the table where they had been put out, and went off to strip—to change from one set of clothes to another, for the mask was a kind of clothing.

The musicians, unshaken and unshakable, played on. With unerring instinct for the right thing at the right moment, Mrs. Ford required of them that they play a Mexican hat dance. *Tarump, tarump, tarump. Tariddledy-dum-te-dump.* And couples began to dance. It was a kind of mixed dance, with little physical contact, and all the funnier, all the more hilarious because of the jumping, which caused the most improbable jouncing and bouncing and bobbling of breasts and genitals. And without embarrassment, for they were not anybody's in particular.

The next step was obvious, even to the musicians, who, without having to be told, struck up a slow foxtrot. The dancers continued, but clinging now, rubbing against each other, taking every advantage of the pornographic liberation of their sexuality from their inhibiting identities. The masks, and Mrs. Ford's whispered suggestions to a few of the men that they cut in, double cut, and behave as one ought to behave at a dancing-school party, gave a certain structure and shape to the proceedings that was as useful as the anonymity.

It was not quite an orgy, or not yet anyway, but still a game, a marvelous game, in which a man with a Pulcinella mask and an impressive erection could tap a Pierrot on the shoulder and have him yield his tall, red-haired Columbine to his satyr embrace, all with a beautiful formality and grace. Merry danced with a stocky, rather swarthy fellow, with a lean middle-aged man (she could tell his age from the mat of gray hair on his chest), with another, younger man, and then with yet another. Occasionally, from one of the darker corners of the large *sala* there came a high giggle, or a middlish laugh. There were couples who wandered off to other, more private rooms. Merry was amused and in a curious way reassured, for here was a whole party behaving as she had once or twice behaved, and it was comforting to know that she was not alone in her depravity, that she was not so depraved after all. She had not worried about it, but had worried some about not worrying. But here in this lovely palazzo sixty or seventy people of some importance were endorsing her as, at least, relatively normal.

It was not the sharpest kind of sexual stimulation. The embraces she had known in private with, say, Tony had been more acute, more sweet, more personal.

But the odd, free-floating eroticism was like a great featherbed into which one could relax, almost drowsing, and where one was not quite sure of the demarcation between fantasy and reality, between daydream and actuality. Until someone suggested to her, having danced with her for perhaps five minutes, that they go off to a less public place.

"Shall we?" he asked and nodded toward a doorway through which a man and a woman were at that moment disappearing.

She didn't answer. It seemed too much trouble to form words, to articulate the phoneme of assent. He was holding her very close, stroking her buttocks with his hand, and rubbing against her and quite obviously reacting to her. He had been dancing in one place, swaying, really, to the slow beat of the music. Now he started to dance toward the door. She allowed herself to be led.

"That's right," he said. "You just come along with me."

She did so, until they were out of the room. Then, having recognized his voice, she broke from his embrace and ran as fast as she could toward the main hall. He ran after her.

"No!" she called back to him. "My God, no!"

He stopped. She didn't know whether he had been able to tell from her voice that she was his daughter, or whether it was just that any girl crying, and crying out, "My God, no!" was not worth the trouble. At any rate, and for whatever reason, he stopped running after her. She found the room where she had undressed. She was in too much of a hurry to dig through the piles of clothing that were all over the floor. She grabbed her dress and put it on without any underwear or stockings, and grabbed a pair of shoes. They didn't fit. She tried another pair. They didn't fit, either. The hell with it. She went barefoot. She looked for her mink jacket but couldn't find it. She grabbed another that looked like it, threw it over her shoulders, and fled.

She had the man at the *pontile* call a water taxi and went back to the Lido.

It had cooled off, and there was a breeze over the water. But she had the fur on, and she could not understand why she was shivering so. Her teeth were chattering. The taxi driver slowed the boat and threw her a blanket. It was not as clean as it might have been, but she wrapped herself in it just the same.

"The signorina is sick?" he asked.

"Yes, sick."

"I hurry then."

"Yes, thank you."

He opened the throttle wide and the boat skittered across the lagoon. In a few minutes they arrived at the landing of the Lido Excelsior. Merry had no money. She told the doorman to pay the taxi.

"I cannot," he said. "I'm sorry, but—"

"Look. Pay the damned taxi. I'm Merry Houseman."

"Yes, of course."

She half-walked, half-ran inside, and across the lobby toward the elevator. She pressed the button and waited. She was still shivering.

"Is there anything wrong?"

She turned. It was Carrera.

"No. Yes. I'm . . . I don't feel well."

"Allow me to see you to your room?" he asked. Or at least the intonation was that of a question. Actually it was a command. He took her arm and helped her into the elevator.

He asked her the number of her room and for her key. He unlocked the door and they walked in.

"Where is Mrs. Keats?"

"Who?"

"Mrs. Keats. She's my companion, sort of. She's supposed to be here."

Carrera found a note on the desk.

"Here," he said. "Here's Mrs. Keats."

Merry took the note.

"Freddie's in the hospital with a perforated stomach. I'm with him. Trust you'll be all right. If you need anything call Finkel or Kleinsinger or me at the hospital. Sorry. Aileen Keats." Underneath the note there was a telephone number, presumably that of the hospital.

She sat down on the chair near the desk and started to cry.

Carrera helped her rise and led her from the living room of the suite to her bedroom. She sat down on the bed. He unzipped her dress, and she took it off. If he was surprised to see that she was wearing nothing under it, he did not show what he thought. He opened cabinets and drawers of the wall of built-in closets and dressers and found a gown for her. He handed it to her. She put it on. He pulled back the covers. The bed had been turned down, but by pulling the covers down even further, he enabled her to ger into bed without having to get up. Then he tucked her in and turned out the light.

She thought he would go, but he didn't. He sat down in the armchair, lit a cigarette, and waited, watching her, making sure that she was all right.

It was very sweet of him, she thought. She closed her eyes. She opened them again and, yes, he was still there. She closed them again and tried to drift off to sleep. But she could not. Not right away. She thought of her father, and of the way he had rubbed against her, and shuddered again with revulsion. It was horrible and obscene, remembering it. And then, quite curiously, everything fell into place. Her father and Elaine, and her father and Jocelyn, and the business with Carlotta and her suicide, and with Noni . . . The whole thing was as clear as it could be. It made no difference that he was her father. He was just another driving, lusting, brutal man. Like Tony. Like Denver James. Like . . . But there was no point in listing them all. They were all the same, anyway. The nice ones, the ones who had been kind to her, considerate of her, and interested in her for herself, and not for her capacity to receive the battery of their pricks—they were the crippled ones, the sick ones. Waters and Kleinsinger, Grindell and now, perhaps, Raul Carrera. She half opened her eyes and through the slit of her lids saw the glow of his cigarette in the darkness. She remembered Grindell's warning that he was a tortured, sick man. But from torture and sickness he had learned a kind of gentleness, acquired a measure of understanding, found a portion of compassion.

She wished that she could stay there forever, under the covers, in the darkness of this anonymous hotel room, with Carrera sitting across the room from her, smoking his cigarette in silence and watching over her.

CHAPTER

THIRTEEN

♥ There were photographers at the airport, waiting to record whatever random conjunctions of celebrities the whims of the airline schedules might produce. It did not seem to be the photographers, however, but Venice itself that was calling out, "Just one more time, please," and because it was nearly over anyway, because it really was over, they posed, smiling, shaking hands, and pretending to talk. Merry was there with Carrera. They had been together nearly every moment of every day after that fateful night. She had wakened to the ringing of the telephone. It had been Carrera, inquiring how she was. He had taken her up. She had gone with him to the showing of his film, was going with him now to Paris, was going to be the star of his next picture.

Meredith and Noni were there, and inevitably Meredith and Merry were asked to pose together. She didn't mind. She could stand it if he could. And probably better than he could. Raul was only a few feet away, supporting her with his smile as he had supported her with his arms a few nights before. Merry noticed Noni, who looked drawn and tired. She had had, no doubt, a difficult time of it, weathering Meredith's drunk, nursing him back to sobriety, and dealing with the press agents who had required that she herself pretend to be sick—not for Meredith's sake, but for that of his career, and for the film. Merry did not envy Noni her burden, but on the other hand, neither did she feel extraordinarily sorry for her. She had found her berth and could lie in it.

One of the photographers asked Merry to pose between Carrera and Kleinsinger, and she obliged most willingly. Not only did it get her away from her father, but it was a palatable and more significant gesture to make. Between her old director and her new one, her old life and her new, she could stand with a certain measure of pride and happiness—for Kleinsinger, who had won the award for best director, and for Carrera and herself, because they were in love.

Kleinsinger was delighted to have won the prize, and Merry was pleased for his sake, even though Raul had explained to her something about the mechanics of the awards and how they were a compromise between artistic necessity and political expedience. "It's not sour grapes," he had said, "not at all. I can't imagine a better festival for myself. After all, I won you."

And it was true that the real results of the festival were not those which the press reported, listing the awards that the jury had made, but the personal satisfactions or disappointments that emerged from any concentration of such people, bubbling up out of the mysterious chemistry of vanity, pride, ambition, lust—and sometimes even generosity and kindness and love.

"I talked this morning with Grindell," Kleinsinger told her. "He seemed much better."

"Yes, I know," Merry said. "I saw him this morning."

"You went there? To the hospital? That was very thoughtful of you."

She had been to see Grindell three times and had sent him a hundred and fifty dollars' worth of flowers in the four days that had passed since his stomach attack.

"Carrera," Kleinsinger said, "you will take care of this girl."

"Yes, I will do my best."

"I think you will," Kleinsinger said. "And I am happy to think so."

Spontaneously, impulsively, Kleinsinger seized Carrera's hand and shook it. A photographer's camera flashed, but the gestures had not been for the camera. Neither was Merry posing for a picture when she kissed Kleinsinger on the cheek.

"Good luck," he said.

It was like the ritual moment in a wedding when the father gives the bride away to the groom.

Meredith Houseman was thirty feet away, at the flight bar. He had ordered a split of champagne. Noni had tried to stop him, but he had threatened to make a scene and there had been nothing that she could do. Houseman looked across the room, saw Kleinsinger shake hands with Carrera, saw Merry kiss Kleinsinger, said, "Shit!" and gulped down his champagne.

"Let's go," he said to Noni.

They went to board the plane for Geneva. Merry and Raul went to gate four to board the plane to Paris. Kleinsinger wandered over to the bar to order a cognac. He had half an hour to wait for the flight to Milan and New York.

Merry had not known what life with Carrera would be like. Going off with him had been an act of faith. To inquire about where he lived, how many rooms there were, what style of furnishings he preferred would have seemed to her irrelevant and as impious as for a believer to inquire of an angel about the details of the personal accommodations in heaven. Besides, speculation about these minor mysteries provided a kind of diversion from speculation about the major one—Carrera himself. In the small things as in the large one, she had assumed a passive receptivity. She would wait and see.

And what she saw was even better than anything she had been able to imagine. There was a duplex apartment in the *huitième,* with a grand balcony and its view of the river; there was a weekend house in Versailles; and there was a farm in Brittany. She had not yet seen the house or the farm, but had heard about them.

Even more important than the physical surroundings of their life, however, was its tempo, which was graceful and relaxed. Raul seemed to have little to do but to amuse himself and her. They went shopping, they went to the races, to the opera, to parties. They went to galleries and to the theater. And of course to movies. Raul liked to go to movies in theaters because even when the movies were boring, there was something to occupy his mind there.

"It is amusing to feel the audience and to recut the picture as I watch it."

He did work occasionally. There were conferences with screenwriters, meetings with Kayayan, and visits to screening rooms, where he looked at past performances of actors he was considering, but there was nothing of the frantic concentration of Hollywood in the pace of his preparations.

"I like to keep myself open," he explained. "I like to be able to improvise a little, and when everything is too carefully worked out in advance, that is impossible."

Whenever he could, he took her along to the screenings or on drives he took in his limousine to search for locations. Whether it was because he enjoyed her company, or out of a concern for her lest she feel lonely—which is to say a kind of politeness—she could not be certain, for at the center of their relationship there was still the great question which had yet to be answered. They had been living together for three weeks, and they had not yet made love.

More and more Merry found herself thinking about what Grindell had said, and going over it in her mind to try to wring from his vague hints some inkling of what Raul's trouble might be. But he had been so vague and had said so little. She thought once of calling him in Rome, but no, she couldn't do that. She had already made her decision, had cast her lot with Carrera, and now to call Grindell would be distasteful and disloyal. Besides, the knowledge that there was something—even if she had no idea about what it was precisely—had a reassuring effect. At the very least, it kept her from blaming herself for being insufficiently attractive and alluring, or it somewhat mitigated that blame.

Her curiosity alone would have been a considerable motive, but compounded with it was her love for him and her need to express that love. It was not an unreasonable idea, then, for her to entertain—that she should seduce him, that she go to the mountain if the mountain would not, or could not, come to her. And indeed it seemed as if that was what he wanted her to do. There was no other way to interpret the peculiar pattern she discerned of incredible restraint and, on the other side, a licentiousness that was nearly as incredible. His films were notoriously, magnificently sensual and erotic. And around the apartment there were the books and the prints, the rubbings and the paintings, which he did not try to hide, nor indeed could have hidden, so numerous were they. He was no mere dabbler, but a serious collector of pornography and erotica.

And Merry could hardly turn around in any room without having some image of sexual pleasure thrust upon her attention—ithyphallic primitive carvings, Beardsley prints, rubbings of Hindu bas-reliefs showing sexual combinations of mathematical intricacy. . . .

But there was no clue that she could find in her study of his collection as to the nature of his problem or the idiosyncrasy of his taste. There was a catholicity to the collection which pointed everywhere and therefore nowhere. The only consistency was that of artistic quality. There was no book or picture or figurine that was without technical merit or bibliographical or historical interest. He was, then, a connoisseur, which was, she supposed, flattering. But it was not helpful to her in her speculations about how she should proceed.

She thought about it for several days. And nights. And what she finally did was the simplest thing, the most direct thing. At least there could be no mistaking her intentions.

They slept, and had been sleeping from the start, in separate rooms. And what she did one night after they had come home from a dinner party at Kayayan's was to undress, put on a filmy peignoir she had bought that day, freshen her perfume, and go into him, to his room, to his bed.

"Is there anything wrong, my dear?" he asked.

"No, nothing's wrong."

"Ah, then you have come in to talk? How very pleasant!"

"To talk? No, not really. To be with you," she said. He was making it as difficult as he could, but she did not blame him. How difficult was it for him? But the point was to share the difficulty, to take up her share of his burden.

"To be with me. Well, here I am."

She was rather encouraged by that, for it was at least susceptible of some interpretation and could support, however precariously, a guess about his predilections.

What he wanted, she began to think, was to be passive. To exchange roles? To be the woman and let her be the man? If that was all, then her long hours of thought and worry would be almost ridiculous. Why, that was practically normal.

"May I join you, then?" she asked.

"Oh, by all means," he said, putting aside the book he had been holding in his lap. "Sit down."

"I had thought I might lie down. With you."

"Oh," he said. It was not a question. But neither was it an answer. There was almost no intonation at all of invitation or of rejection.

"Is it . . . is it all right?"

"Yes," he said. "It's all right."

But did he mean it? Was he only being polite, obliging her? But even as she wondered whether that was it, she was reassured by the thought that he could oblige, that he could welcome her for whatever reason. She would have preferred it not to be mere duty or good manners, but even that, and the ability to do that, had a healthiness and a soundness for which she could not help but be grateful.

She slid in under the covers, beside him.

"Oh, that's better, isn't it? I love you so much, and I love to be with you, to be close to you. Do you like it?"

"Yes," he said. "I like it."

He lit a cigarette, and Merry considered that action as a scientist would consider a new piece of evidence. It tended, she thought, to confirm her hypothesis—that he wanted to be, or had to be, passive. And yet even while recognizing intellectually the probability and what it demanded of her, she was unwilling to push too hard, to go too fast with him. She wanted to leave room for herself to retreat, for them to retreat together. She held out her hand, extending her two fingers in a Churchillian "V," in a request for a puff of the cigarette. He gave it to her. She took a drag and gave it back.

But as she did so, extending her arm toward him, she found her opportunity. She did not bring her arm all the way back, but let it fall, lightly, across his belly. He continued to smoke his cigarette, neither encouraging her nor discouraging her. She felt a physical tremor of nervousness, a shudder, which she hoped he did not notice. Or was *that* it? Was that what he wanted? Was it nervousness and fear that he needed to arouse, in order to be aroused himself?

But that did not seem to be it, either. There was another small tremor, which she did not try to suppress, but it evinced no response from him whatever. She was relieved by this, for while the idea that he might take his pleasure in inflicting pain had not horrified her, she had not been delighted with it. She started to move her hand, stroking his belly and his thigh, trying to appear as casual about it as she could, as if she were not thinking about it at all but doing it quite naturally and spontaneously. It was important to pretend that everything was natural and spontaneous.

She touched him, then moved her hand back to his thigh, then touched him again. He took her hand. For an instant she was afraid that he was going to tell her now that he would not, or could not . . . But no, to her surprise and relief he only held her hand for a moment and said, "I love you."

"I love you. Oh, so much. So very much," she said, and she kissed him.

After a very long time he touched her breasts, stroked her neck, and then, saying, "Oh, Merry. Oh, dear Merry. Poor, dear Merry," he held her to him, and then he kissed her and entered her.

Perhaps it was because she had been so worried, so mystified, so very much in the dark, or perhaps it was just because it was their first time together, but it was not the fireworks and moonlight she had hoped for—for his sake as much as for her own. For both their sakes. He was rather mechanical and too quick. And afterward, he withdrew immediately, not only from her body but from her company, rolling back to his side of the bed, lighting another cigarette, and thinking, but not telling her what he was thinking, or touching her, or in any way acknowledging her presence there in the bed with him. It was as if she had not come in at all, as if they had not made love.

"What are you thinking?" she asked.

"Nothing."

She did not believe him. But there was nothing she could do. She would not pry. Nor would she talk, make chat, or intrude herself upon him. Which was funny, she thought. It was all right, had been all right for her to come in and force her body upon him, but she would not force her words upon him afterward. The improbable distinctions one sets up for oneself!

She lay there in silence for a very long time. Finally, after she had begun to wonder what graceful way there was for her to leave and whether she would have to wait until he had fallen asleep and then sneak out of the room, she decided to try one last time to talk with him.

"I love you, Raul."

"And I love you, Merry."

"Good."

"But . . ."

"But?"

"But you must understand me. You must know, must already have noticed, during the weeks we have been together, and just now, too, that I am not . . . cannot be . . . that I am unable to perform as most lovers do."

"It takes time. We must get used to each other."

"No, it isn't that. If only it were that simple, how pleasant life would be. How much I should like to be able to agree with you. But I cannot. Out of fairness to you, I cannot."

"Give us a chance. Give yourself a chance."

"My wives said the very same thing, believe me," he said dryly. "I have been married to two of the most beautiful women in the world. Clothilde and Monique. And now I have you. It would be unreasonable of me to say to you or to myself that I have not given myself a chance. I have given myself more chances than most men have in a lifetime, or ten men in ten lifetimes."

"Is there nothing that you can do about it? Have you seen a doctor, or a psychiatrist?"

"No," he said, rather sharply. "I won't."

"You don't believe in it?"

"No, on the contrary. I do. But I am not convinced of the desirability of normality to the exclusion of everything else. Assuming that I could be 'cured'—which is by no means certain—what then? I should lose that special angle of vision, that cutting edge, which is my own. It would not be a fair exchange."

"You mean your creative vision?"

"That, of course. But not only that. My life is not confined to the films I have made or have yet to make. You see, I rather enjoy being the way I am. It has its uncomfortable moments—such as this one. For the normal people there are uncomfortable moments, too, I'm sure. But for me, being this way, I have a certain intensity of life, which I should hate to lose. They say that tubercular patients have that kind of intensity. Or perhaps it's another kind. But mine allows me to breathe and is not associated with any fatal disease."

"But what is it exactly? Your kind. Your 'disease.' "

"There is no term for it, no convenient name. I suppose for lack of anything more convenient one might simply say sexual weakness."

"And from weakness you get intensity?"

"Oh, yes. Indeed. Consider the fact that I am weak, but not dead. As you have seen. I appreciate you, I am able to desire you and to admire your physical attractiveness. But I am not able to satisfy your sexual appetites."

"How do you know that? How do you know what my appetites are?"

"You came to me this evening. Remember?"

"I remember."

"Yes, well I am not able, I will not be able to provide you with the full sexual life to which you are entitled, and which your great beauty so richly deserves. But I am not a cruel man, or an unfair or unjust one. So I shall expect you to find your partners elsewhere. I shall even require it of you. But not without some feeling on my own part. It is not suffering, which is just a romantic idea, anyway. But there will be a *frisson* of regret and, at the same time, a vicarious delight in what you do that I shall be able to take for myself. Because I do love you, and I am able to desire you at least enough to feel these pangs when I contemplate your adventures."

"You want me to . . . go with other men?"

"I do and I don't. But you will. And you have my consent. Intellectually. And emotionally, too, in part. In part."

"But . . ."

"Think about it. Please," he said. He turned to her, reached out to hold her neck with his hand, looked into her eyes, and repeated, "Please! Don't say anything tonight. Or even tomorrow. But think about it. You are free. Free to go, or to stay. Free to be 'faithful' or 'unfaithful'—and free of all responsibility, which is only mine—my psyche's and my glands'. Think about it and decide. And remember, and believe, that in my own poor way, in the only way in which I am capable, I do love you."

"I'll think about it," she said.

"Yes. Go and think. Go."

It was the most definite command he had given her since that night in the Excelsior when he had helped her to her room. She kissed him on the lips and went back to her room.

The sheets felt cold as she got into her bed. It had been a wet fall day, and the dampness had chilled all of Paris, but she did not think of the weather, or even the obvious enough fact that she had just left one warm bed to come to this cold one. She was sure that the chill was her own, that it came from her, and that she would have felt it anywhere.

Raul's confession and his proposal were frightening. It was not so bad; his peculiarity was not anywhere near so bad as what she had feared—and not even dared imagine. And his suggestion to her of how they should live, and of how she should live, was eminently reasonable and fair. But it was all the more frightening for that. Thrown back upon herself that way, without limits, without the fences people build for one another and for themselves, she had no idea what she would do, how she would behave, or what she would discover about herself. She thought she could understand what he had meant about the edge that his way of life gave to the world and the sharpness of his angle of vision. But she was not sure whether she wanted to see that clearly or that much. It was so very lonely.

And then she remembered his hand on her face and neck and the way he had asked her, "Please, think about it. Please."

She would. She promised herself that in the morning she would. She would make up her mind then. If it wasn't already made up.

She wondered whether he knew that, too.

The next morning she awoke, dressed, and went to join Raul for breakfast. Her first sight of him, sitting in his chair, wearing a maroon silk robe from Hermés, resolved whatever doubts there still were in her mind. He looked so vulnerable, so very appealing—even though he was obviously trying to hide whatever it was that he was thinking. Or no, he looked the same. But to her eyes, which were opened now by the knowledge of his pathetic disability, that sameness appeared now in a new light. She passed by his chair, stopped, and bent over to kiss him on the cheek. Then she took her seat opposite him, next to the large window overlooking the Seine. She drank her orange juice.

Without any special emphasis, as if he were merely remarking on the weather, he mentioned to her that René Blangis would be returning from Somaliland at the end of the week.

"Oh?"

"Yes. Your co-star," he said.

"Yes, of course."

She had forgotten about Blangis, if indeed Raul had ever mentioned him to her at all.

"What is he doing in Somaliland?" she asked.

"On safari, I expect. He does that between pictures. To relax."

"Oh," she said.

"Don't be put off. He is not so stupid as safaris would suggest. Rather clever, in fact. An odd-looking sort, but a fascinating face to photograph. No one before has ever succeeded in making him look appealing. Always he plays villains and thugs. But he is graceful in his brutal way. I'm looking forward to working with him."

"Then I'm looking forward to it, too."

"Good," he said. And then, abruptly, he changed the subject. "There is a very attractive necklace I saw at Cartier's last week. If you have nothing else to do, perhaps you might come with me to look at it this afternoon. You might find it beguiling."

"You don't have to do that, Raul."

"I want to," he said. He looked up at her a moment, smiled, and then returned his gaze to the crumbs on his plate.

Two weeks later Carrera and Merry joined Blangis and Kayayan in one of the small private dining rooms on the second floor of Lapérouse. It was a peculiar evening, because the three men spoke most of the time in rapid French, which Merry could only partly follow. What they were talking about, anyway, was mostly business, in which she was involved but not very much interested or very knowledgeable. Her contract had been sent to New York for Jaggers' approval, and there had been transatlantic telephone calls settling the details. She had forgotten how much money she was supposed to get, because it was all in francs, but she did remember that she had a twenty-five percent share of the net profits.

What they were talking about was Blangis's deal. Merry was able to devote her entire attention to the restaurant and to the food that Carrera ordered for her—*oeufs en gelée, gratiné de langoustines Georgette, pommes soufflés,* and *crêpes Mona.* She had been to Lapérouse with him once before, but he had ordered an entirely different meal then. Everything had been flawless and delicious, and she looked forward to seeing what miracles would come out of the ktichen this evening. The three men chatted on, while Merry examined the crystal, the silver, and admired, generally, the way in which the restaurant was planned, broken up into small rooms so that there was never the feeling of crowdedness or showiness. She was thinking about the theatricality of it, the showmanship of the understatement of the restaurant to underscore the excellence of the food, when Blangis shifted himself slightly in his chair, reached across the table for a cigarette, and in the same motion put a hand upon her thigh.

She had been putting down her wineglass, and it was perhaps two inches from the tablecloth when she felt the pressure of his hand. The glass froze in midair. She was unable either to set it down or pick it up again. She glanced quickly at Carrera, but he was not looking at her, and anyway, even if he had been, there would have been nothing that he would have told her, would have been able to tell her. Or would have wanted to tell her. She picked the glass up, took another sip, and then put it down on the table.

As she did so, Blangis, who was talking very rapidly —the word "percent" was frequently recurrent in his remarks—starting moving the hand in an ellipse up and down her thigh. She put her hand on his in order to restrain him and to stop the movement of his hand, but the effect was also that of keeping him from withdrawing it. She needed time to think. She had decided that she would try to adjust her desires to Carrera's and had been, for a week now, feeling a kind of glow of virtue. But now this dramatic gesture from this extremely attractive man had thrown her resolve into utter confusion. The waiter appeared to refill her wineglass, and the sloshing of the ice in the bucket seemed to her to be an appropriate external representation of her inward feelings. Her mind still clung to fidelity to Carrera, but fidelity how? To the man himself, or to what he had said? She was still thinking, trying to decide what she should do, when the waiter came to clear their places and to bring dessert. Blangis removed his hand.

"Ah, bon!" he said, and he addressed himself to his *crêpes.*

Merry was annoyed because she had not yet come to a decision about what she wanted, and there was no longer anything to decide. She did not like the idea of playing second fiddle to a plate of *crêpes Mona.*

But after the *crêpes* and during coffee, he lit a cigarette and dropped his lighter. He bent down to get it, flipped the hem of her dress over her knee, and while with one hand he flipped open the lid of the lighter and lit the cigarette that was dangling from his mouth, he insinuated the other under her skirt and between her thighs. By not having done anything more definite before, she had somehow abrogated the right to do anything now.

What was all the more extraordinary was that Blangis had addressed scarcely ten words to her during the course of the dinner.

"I am terribly sorry, my dear," Carrera said to Merry in English. "We have been boring you unforgivably. Come, come, gentlemen, our business is concluded. From now on we must speak English."

"Excellent," said Kayayan, whose English was heavily accented but quite correct.

"I will hardly try," Blangis said.

Carrera chuckled and said, "He means he will try very hard."

"Yes, that is what I meant. But try is a verb, no? And must take an adverb, isn't it? As 'hardly.' "

"Merry, explain it to him," Carrera said.

She explained that "hardly try" means "scarcely try," or "try not at all," and while she explained she looked at him appraisingly. He was tall but rather stocky, and he had a broken nose, a square jaw, and an irregular, jagged scar on his forehead. He looked kind of like an ugly Bogart. He had bleak gray eyes, with which he returned her appraising glance, even while his hand was still between her thighs under the tablecloth.

"I will try very hard," he said, obediently accepting her correction, even while giving the inside of her right thigh a squeeze. He had, she was forced to admit, colossal nerve.

Carrera invited the two men back to the apartment for a brandy. Kayayan declined, but Blangis accepted. Merry was not surprised. In the limousine on the way back to the apartment, she decided that it had all gone far enough. It had perhaps been tolerable at dinner, but Raul was the man she loved, and whatever sacrifices that love called for, she was willing to give. Merry was sitting between Carrera and Blangis, and having reached her decision, she took Raul's hand and squeezed it. He returned the pressure.

And having decided, she was able to be gay and vivacious. She felt relaxed and quite happy. They dropped Kayayan off at his flat, then went on to their own apartment, where Carrera offered cognac, but Blangis said that he would prefer a whiskey.

"Me, too," Merry said.

"Ah, then I will have one as well," Carrera said, and he fixed three Scotch and sodas.

They were having a good time, listening to Blangis describe his Somaliland safari in his absurd English, when the telephone rang. Carrera picked up the phone, said, *"Oui. Oui. Non. Oui,"* and then, covering the mouthpiece, announced, "I will take this in the other room. I'm sorry. I may be on the phone for some time. Would you hang up in here when I call?"

Merry said that she would. He went into the study, picked up the phone in there, called to her to hang up the living-room phone, and she did so. She heard the study door close.

Blangis went to the liquor cabinet, poured himself another drink, and held the bottle up to Merry questioningly.

"Yes, I think I will," she said.

He poured a generous amount of Scotch into her glass and sat down next to her on the sofa. She tensed for a moment, but then relaxed. It was ridiculous to worry about it. This "Is-he-or-isn't-he—only-his-hairdresser-knows" business was teen-ager-ish and stupid. She lived with Raul, and Blangis knew this.

"When we start shooting, I'm afraid that all of you will be laughing at my French more than we were laughing at your English this evening," she began.

He grunted and said, "They can dub. Besides, there is not so much of the dialogue in the films of Raul."

He took a deep pull of Scotch and then set his glass down, took hers, and set it down beside his own. Without pausing, he turned and pulled her to him. Before she could say anything, his mouth was upon hers. She was unable to move, but after a moment she recovered herself and pushed him away.

"What are you doing?" she asked. "Raul is in the next room. He will return at any moment."

"No, he won't. Have you not heard him say he would be on the phone a long time?"

"How can you be sure of that?" she asked. "And besides, this is impossible!"

"*Au contraire,* it is *absolument* possible. You are a beautiful woman and I want you much."

Without either delay or haste, but with an inevitable confidence, he reached for her again.

"No," she protested, "not here."

He kissed her.

She realized that she had in effect surrendered already in limiting her protest to the place and time, but either he had not heard that protest or was ignoring it. One hand cupped her breast. Her mouth opened under the insistent probing of his tongue. The sinewiness of his body aroused her even more than the hand or the mouth. She felt her body respond as it had not since Tony. She put her hand up to the back of his neck.

He took it and moved it from his neck to his loins, pushing her back against the pillows of the sofa. She strained against him, but eagerly now. Any will she had had to resist was gone. The present moment was all that counted.

He pulled her forward again, and she thought for a fraction of an instant that he was going to release her. But no, he merely ran a skillful hand down her back, pulling the zipper open. She leaned forward to make it easier for him to unhook her bra. As he did so, she opened two buttons of his shirt and put her hands and arms around his bare body.

He tried to pull the dress from her shoulders, but she said, "No, no, Raul . . ."

René kissed her neck and seized her nipple with his

thumb and forefinger. She could feel the pain of pleasure through her whole body.

He unzipped his fly. She took him in her hand, and heard a click. She froze.

"What was that?"

She thought it was the door. She reached to pull her dress back up, and as she did, she looked up and saw Raul. She had not heard him come back into the room because he had no shoes on, or anything else. He was absolutely naked except for the 35-millimeter camera with the long lens that he had hung on a strap around his neck. He was smoking a small, thin, black Italian cigar, and he was watching them through the range finder.

René pulled her dress all the way down. She hardly noticed what he was doing. She stared, horrified, at Carrera, who merely puffed on his cigar. She understood, finally, the whole horror of it, everything that Grindell had been trying to hint to her in the bar at the Excelsior. It was all clear. Carrera actually was enjoying himself. He was visibly excited, much more so than on that one night on which they had made love.

For a moment she thought of flight. She could run out of the apartment, out of Paris, out of France, and back to . . . But back to what? Back to where? She had no place left to run.

She relaxed the hand with which she had been holding Blangis's wrist and allowed him to continue to undress her. He made love to her, expertly and even with some elegance. Her body responded in spite of herself and in spite of the clicking of the shutter of the camera.

When it was over she left the room, forcing herself not to run, not to hurry from the living room to her bedroom. She went into her bathroom and filled the tub with water as hot as she could stand, and got into the tub. She took her bath brush and held it, unable to move, unable to do anything. But even the hot water cooled down. *Tiède,* she thought distractedly, was the French word for it. Tepid. She felt pity and contempt, but whether for Carrera or herself she was not sure. She remembered what he had said once about directors being voyeurs and actors being exhibitionists. But she had not enjoyed the performance she had been forced to give that night.

All these thoughts occurred to her in a random way, like the sloshes of water in the tub that she made when she moved her knees. Suddenly she was possessed by a thought that was definite enough for her to act upon. She would not permit them to think that she had been defeated by this. Deliberately, and yet still partly in a daze, she got out of the tub, dried herself, put on her quilted robe, and went back into the living room. René was sprawled on the sofa, smoking a cigarette. Raul was wearing a robe and holding a glass with whiskey in it. They stopped talking when she came in, and they watched her go to the liquor cabinet, pour herself a stiff Scotch, and take it with her back to her bedroom. She stopped before the door of her bedroom, turned, and said politely, "Good night."

Four days later she and Carrera were married at the *mairie* of the little town in Brittany where Raul had his farm.

Throughout the filming Carrera was unfailingly charming to her and unquestionably affectionate and loving. It made things both better and worse for her. In certain ways Raul was like Kleinsinger in his demeanor on the set—which was carefully courteous and unruffleable—but there was more of a personal involvement that was evident in the making of the film, perhaps because Raul's was partly an improvisational work. The subject was a version of *The Aspern Papers,* in which the scholar comes to Paris to meet the granddaughter of the mistress of the great poet and seduces her in order to get hold of the great man's letters and journals for his scholarly work. For much of the film Merry's attitude toward René, the scholar, was contemptuous and condescending, but after he seduced her she had to change to something like passive adoration, until finally she was obliterated and abandoned. The rhythm of the movie and rhythm of their lives displayed a certain congruity. The passivity in the film was easy enough for her to do; all that was required was that she project on the screen all that she felt during every waking moment.

Four times during the eight weeks, the tension of the movie-making reached such a point in Carrera that he required some kind of diversion. Or perhaps it was a way of freshening himself, of refreshing his eye and his mind. He found partners for Merry and took his pictures of her with the men he had brought home. Occasionally he would request a position or request a change of angle or attitude for the sake of composition—exactly as he did during the shooting of the film.

Merry, too, was caught up in the making of the film and in Carrera's biological rhythm, for during the making of the picture she was entirely his creature. Whether it was the physical release that she had found, although she had not sought it, or whether it was the abasement that was involved in these surrenders to strangers, it was certainly true that the odd passivity the picture required of her was easier for her to strike during the days that followed each of these episodes. By the fifth encounter she even took a kind of perverse pleasure in it. She could almost see herself through the camera's eye. She had never thought of the awkwardness of sex before, but now she wondered, with each movement on the bed or on the floor, how it looked, how they looked together. Was it attractive, was there animal grace or the balletic appeal that it ought to have? She knew Carrera had very high standards in erotica and she wanted to please him.

It was a strange kind of love but, after all, in her life she had known very little love, and if this was all there was for her, she would have to content herself with it. But at the end of the filming there was a party at Maxim's, after which Carrera took her home alone and, on a crest of gaiety and excitement, followed her into her bedroom, helped her out of her dress, and made love to her. It was very sweet and even childlike, but curiously satisfying, and she wondered why if he could do this he had to resort to the cameras. She felt a warmth and almost a hope that their relationship might improve, might approach some exurb of normality, might become the relationship of two people who loved each other and were contented with each other's bodies and with their own. . . .

Carrera was busy every day in the cutting rooms. She wandered around Paris, read a lot, and slept a great deal. She noticed that she had been sleeping more than usual, and still she was tired all the time. She mentioned this to Raul one night, and he suggested that she see his doctor. She had never been particularly fond of doctors, and Raul called himself to make an appointment for her with Dr. Dreyfuss for the following morning.

"Raul," she said, after they had finished dinner the following evening.

He looked up, politely and inquiringly, from the book of stills he had been going through.

"The A-Z test was positive," she said.

"Qu'est-ce que veut dire 'the A-Z test'?" he asked.

"I'm pregnant."

He put the photographs to one side and turned in his chair to face her.

"There is nothing to be concerned about," he said. He rose and walked over to her and put his hand on her shoulder. "We can take care of it. It's perfectly simple. I have a friend in Switzerland."

"Do you want me to do that?"

"I want you to do what you want to do. I always want you to do what you want to do."

"What would you say if I told you I wanted the child?"

"But . . . but why?" he asked.

"I don't know. Perhaps I want it. Perhaps I want my child?"

"Our child," he said.

She laughed. It was a short, bitter laugh. Who could say which of her partners was really the father?

"Actually," he said, walking back and forth now and considering it, "it's not such a bad idea. It's intriguing, you know. I've sometimes wondered what it would be like to raise a daughter . . ."

"A daughter? What makes you think it will be a daughter?"

"A son would not interest me," he said coldly, "but the rearing of a daughter . . . Now that," he said, with more animation, "would be interesting."

He paced and thought about it for another moment or two and then said, "Yes, by all means. Let us have a child."

He came over and kissed her on the forehead. "A daughter," he repeated, and he smiled.

Throughout his conversation Merry had felt an increasing disgust and nausea. What had happened to her she could stand, she could endure. She could endure anything. But her child! What kind of bizarre hobby would it be for Raul Carrera to raise a daughter? She—if it was a she—deserved a fresh start, far better than the one Merry had had herself.

She stayed with Raul for another ten days, until the rough cut was ready, saw it with him in the screening room at the studio, and shared his pleasure in its excellence. She had said little to him during that ten days. He had been especially solicitous of her, in a tender, protective way, and seemed really to like the idea of having a child and of playing the father to a little girl. In a way it seemed almost as if Merry herself no longer interested him except as the mother of the new being.

The day after the screening she called American Express and booked a jet seat from Paris to New York with connections to Chicago and Butte, Montana.

She did not call Sam Jaggers. She did not call anyone. She felt a kind of exhilaration from having decided the thing herself, and from having done it herself. Not since she had been nine years old and had managed to leave the Novotny household to join her father in New York had she felt that same glow of daring and accomplishment. She knew she could do it, could leave, as she had known it so many years before.

The night before the plane left they had a perfectly ordinary evening. She and Raul had dinner in a small restaurant on the Left Bank and then returned to the apartment. She said she was tired and went to bed soon after they got home. The following morning she slept late. He was not waking her these days, out of solicitousness for her condition, and when she awoke he had already left.

She went into his room. It was the first time she had been in that room since the night she had gone in there to seduce him. She sat down at his writing table to write him a note. She thought for a few minutes, but could think of nothing to say. At last she settled for "I'm sorry. I'm going. Merry."

She opened a drawer to look for an envelope in which to put her note. He would not like the servants to see it. In the drawer she found a thick, lizard-bound photo album. She tried to open it, but it was fastened by a combination lock. She held it up to her ear to listen for the clicks, but could not manage to open it the way they seemed to be able to do so easily in the movies. She took the letter opener from the top of his desk and forced it, breaking the lock as she did so.

The first few pages of pictures meant nothing to her.

They were, as she had expected they would be, pictures of people making love in a variety of positions. The woman was always the same. The men were different. But the second batch, beginning a third of the way through the book, showed Clothilde, his first wife. She flipped the pages, found Monique's section. And then there were others, strangers, women she did not recognize. A few pictures of each of them. And . . . But she stopped, turned back a page or two, looked again and laughed. It was Noni, her stepmother, in a picture that was almost laughable in its grotesqueness. Surely Raul had kept this picture because it was funny. It showed Noni and three men. Her face was blank and stupid with lust, but it looked about the way it always did. It was really very funny.

She was not surprised to see, at the end of the book, pictures of herself. She looked at them with detachment, admiring the composition of one, deploring the awkwardness in another. The intimacies which the pictures showed her were dead, mechanical, inert. She stared at them, trying to break through the indifference she felt. But she got no farther than sadness, not even for Raul or for herself, but for the pictures themselves, and how the little life that had been in them had gone out. That was why Raul had continually to take new ones, to try always to capture the moment, which eluded even the camera and the film, disintegrating as it does for anyone, everyone, always.

She could leave now. She wasn't running away, but just going. She closed the book, put it in the drawer, and closed the drawer. She knew she was closing more than a drawer.

EPILOGUE

"Push," said the Indian woman.

"I am," Merry said irritably.

"Harder."

Merry bit on the towel that the Indian woman had given her for the bad times. She strained. Then the pain subsided, leaving her sweaty and limp.

"Do you see him? Look out the window again and tell me if you see him."

The Indian woman went to the window to look out for the black Ford that Doc Gaines drove. He was the grandson of the old Doc Gaines, the veterinarian who had delivered Merry's father fifty-four years ago.

Merry was lying in Mother Houseman's big maple bed in the room that had been empty now for two years. Ellen, Merry's grandmother, was sitting in a chair across the room, crocheting.

"It hurts," Merry said. "When the pains come, they're so bad."

"Bear down with them," Ellen said.

"Pant. Like a puppy dog," the Indian woman ordered.

"The pain only seems bad," Ellen said. "Later on it will seem like there wasn't anything at all. The real pain is later," she said.

The crochet hook flashed in the late-afternoon sun that streamed in through the window. Ellen was thinking about the lives that had come out of that bed, and gone into it. She went over the list, thinking just for a moment of each of them, remembering each one, living and dead: Merry, lying there now in pain; Meredith, deprived even at birth of the comfort of that bed, out and away, more remote than a memory, fleeing from his own memory of his own father, her husband, Sam; Sam, and the torture he had known as Mother Houseman's bastard; Mother Houseman, dying there in that bed, never having regretted her brief love or her child; and finally old Amos Houseman, whom Ellen had once seen when she had been a little girl.

It all seemed so endless. And yet here it was, starting again.

There was a scream from Merry. Her head was tossing back and forth on the pillow.

"It's coming," said the Indian woman. "Push harder."

Merry gave a final, total exertion. The Indian woman pushed on her abdomen to help. Merry let out a piercing scream.

The baby was born.

The Indian woman caught the slippery child and held it up. She cut the cord and handed the purplish baby to Ellen, who hung it by its heels and slapped its buttocks to make it cry and clear its mouth and throat.

After several slaps the baby let out a thin, protesting wail. Ellen wrapped the baby in a shawl.

Merry sighed.

Ellen put the baby down beside its mother's face.
Merry gazed at her daughter and smiled.
"It's a girl," she said.
It was, she hoped, a new beginning.